HENNING MANKELL

The Fifth Woman

TRANSLATED FROM THE SWEDISH BY
Steven T. Murray

VINTAGE BOOKS
London

Published by Vintage 2009

2 4 6 8 10 9 7 5 3 1

First published in Great Britain in 2003 by The Harvill Press

Vintage
Random House, 20 Vauxhall Bridge Road,
London SW1V 2SA

www.vintage-books.co.uk

Addresses for companies within The Random House Group Limited can be found at: www.randomhouse.co.uk/offices.htm

The Random House Group Limited Reg. No. 954009

A CIP catalogue record for this book is available from the British Library

ISBN 9780099546368

The Random House Group Limited supports The Forest Stewardship Council (FSC), the leading international forest certification organisation. All our titles that are printed on Greenpeace approved FSC certified paper carry the FSC logo. Our paper procurement policy can be found at: www.rbooks.co.uk/environment

Printed and bound in Great Britain by
CPI Cox & Wyman, Reading RG1 8EX

"I saw God in a dream and He had two faces. One was soft and kind like a mother's face, and the other looked like the face of Satan."

From *The Fall of the Imam*, by Nawal El Saadawi

"With love and care the spiderweb weaves its spider."

African proverb

Africa – Sweden

May – August 1993

PROLOGUE

The letter arrived in Ystad on 19 August 1993. Since it had an African stamp and must be from her mother, she hadn't opened it immediately. She wanted to have peace and quiet when she read it. From the thickness of the envelope she could tell there were many pages. She hadn't heard from her mother in over three months and there must be plenty of news by now. She left the letter lying on the coffee table, deciding to wait until evening. But she felt vaguely uneasy. Why had her mother typed her name and address this time? No doubt the answer would be in the letter. It was close to midnight when she opened the door to the balcony and sat down among all her flowerpots. It was a lovely, warm August evening. Maybe one of the last of the year. Autumn was already at hand, hovering unseen. She opened the letter and started to read.

Only when she had read the letter to the end, did she start to cry. By then she knew that the letter was written by a woman. It wasn't just the handwriting, there was also something about the choice of words, how the woman had described as mercifully as possible the gruesome truth of what had occurred. There was no mercy involved. There was only the act itself. That was all.

The letter was signed by Françoise Bertrand, a police officer. Her position was not entirely clear, but she was employed as a criminal investigator for the country's central homicide commission. It was in this capacity that she had learned of the events that took place one night in May in a remote desert town in North Africa.

The facts of the case were clear, easy to grasp, and utterly terrifying. Four nuns, French citizens, had been slaughtered by unknown assailants, their throats slashed. The killers had left no traces, only blood; thick, congealed blood everywhere.

But there had also been a fifth woman, a Swedish tourist, who happened to be visiting the nuns on the night the assailants appeared with their knives. Her passport revealed that her name was Anna Ander, 66 years old, in the country on a tourist visa. With the passport was an open-return plane ticket. Since it was bad enough that four nuns had been murdered, and since Anna Ander seemed to have been travelling alone, under political pressure the police decided not to mention the fifth woman. She was simply not there on that fateful night. Her bed was empty. Instead, they reported her death in a traffic accident and then buried her in an unmarked grave. All traces of her were erased. And it was here that Françoise Bertrand entered the picture. *Early one morning I was called in by my boss*, she wrote in the long letter, *and told to drive out to the convent.* By this time the Swedish woman was already buried. Françoise Bertrand's job was to destroy her passport and belongings.

Anna Ander had supposedly never arrived or spent any time in the country. She had ceased to exist, erased from all official records. Françoise Bertrand found a travel bag that the investigators had overlooked, lying behind a wardrobe. Inside were letters that Anna Ander had begun to write, and they were addressed to her daughter in a town called Ystad in faraway Sweden. Françoise Bertrand apologised for reading these private letters. She had asked for help from an alcoholic Swedish artist she knew in the capital, and he had translated the letters for her. Françoise wrote down the translations as he read them to her, and a picture gradually began to take shape.

Even then she already had pangs of conscience about what had happened to this fifth woman. Not only about the fact that she was brutally murdered in the country that Françoise loved so much. In the letter, she tried to explain what was happening in her country, and she also told something about herself. Her father was born in France but came to North Africa with his parents as a child. There he grew up, and later married a local woman. Françoise, the oldest of their children, had always had the feeling of having one foot in France and the other in Africa. But now she no longer had any doubt. She was an African. And that was why she was tormented by the strife tearing her country apart. That was also why she didn't want to contribute to the wrongs against herself and her country by erasing this woman, by refusing even to take the responsibility for Anna Ander's presence. Françoise Bertrand had begun to suffer from insomnia. Finally she decided to write to the dead woman's daughter and tell her the truth. She forced herself to act in spite of the loyalty she felt to the police force, but she asked that her name be kept secret. *I'm telling you the truth*, she wrote at the end of her long letter. *Maybe I'm making a mistake by telling you what happened. But how could I do otherwise? I found a bag containing letters that a woman wrote to her daughter. Now I'm telling you how they came into my possession and forwarding them to you.*

Françoise Bertrand had enclosed the unfinished letters and Anna Ander's passport.

Her daughter didn't read the letters. She put them on the floor of the balcony and wept for a long time. Not until dawn did she get up. She went inside and sat motionless at the kitchen table, her head completely empty. But then suddenly everything seemed simple to her. She realised that she had done nothing but wait all these years. She hadn't understood that before: the fact that she had been waiting, or why. Now she knew. She had a mission, and she didn't need to wait any longer to carry it out. It was time. Her mother was gone. A door had been thrown wide open.

She stood up and went to get her box with the slips of paper she had cut up, and the big ledger she kept in a drawer under her bed. She spread the folded slips of paper on the table in front of her. She knew there were 43 of them. She started unfolding the slips, one by one.

The cross was on the 27th one. She opened the ledger and ran her finger down the column of names until she reached the right row. She stared at the name she had written there and slowly a face materialised before her. Then she closed the book and put the slips of paper back in the box.

Her mother was dead. She no longer had any doubt. And now there was no turning back. She would give herself a year to work through her grief, and to make all her preparations. She went back out onto the balcony, smoked a cigarette and gazed out over the waking city. A rain storm was moving in from the sea.

Just after 7 a.m. she went to bed. It was the morning of 20 August 1993.

Skåne

21 September – 11 October 1994

CHAPTER 1

Just after 10 p.m. he finally finished. The last stanzas had been difficult to write; they took him a long time. He had wanted to achieve a melancholy, yet beautiful expression. Several attempts were consigned to the waste-paper basket. Twice he'd been close to giving up altogether, but now the poem lay before him on the table – his lament for the middle spotted woodpecker, which had almost disappeared from Sweden. It hadn't been seen in the country since the early 1980s – one more species soon to be wiped out by humankind.

He got up from his desk and stretched. With every passing year, it was harder and harder to sit bent over his writings for hours on end.

An old man shouldn't be writing poems, he thought. When you're 78 years old, your thoughts are of little use to anyone. But at the same time, he knew this was wrong. It was only in the Western world that old people were viewed with indulgence or contemptuous sympathy. In other cultures, age was respected as the period of enlightened wisdom. He would go on writing poems as long as he could lift a pen and his mind was clear. He was not capable of much else. A long time ago he had been a car dealer, the most successful in the region. He was known as a tough negotiator. He had certainly sold a lot of cars. During the good years he had owned branches in Tomelilla and Sjöbo. He had made a fortune large enough to allow him to live in some style. But it was his poetry that really mattered to him. The verses lying on the table gave him a rare satisfaction.

He drew the curtains across the picture windows that faced the fields rolling down towards the sea, which lay out of sight. He went over to his bookshelf. He had published nine volumes of poetry. There they stood, in a row. None of them had sold more than a single, small printing. Not more than 300 copies. The unsold copies were in cardboard boxes in the basement. They were his pride and joy, although he had long ago decided to burn them one day. He would carry the cardboard boxes out to the courtyard and put a match to them. The day he received his death sentence, whether from a doctor or from a premonition that his life would soon be over, he would rid himself of the thin volumes that no-one wanted to buy. No-one would throw them onto a rubbish heap.

He looked at the books on the shelf. He had been reading poems his whole life, and he had memorised many. He had no illusions; his poems were not the best ever written, but they weren't the worst, either. In each of his volumes, published roughly every five years since the late 1940s, there were stanzas that could stand beside the best. But he had been a car dealer by profession, not a poet. His poems were not reviewed on the cultural pages. He hadn't received any literary awards. And his books had been printed at his own expense. He had sent his first collection to the big publishing houses in Stockholm. They came back with curt rejections on pre-printed forms. One editor had taken the trouble to make a personal comment. Nobody would want to read poems that were only about birds. *The spiritual life of the white wagtail is of no interest,* the editor had written.

After that, he wasted no more time on publishers. He paid for publication himself: simple covers, nothing lavish. The words between were what mattered. In spite of everything, many people had read his poems over the years, and many of them had expressed their appreciation to him. Now he had written a new one, about the middle spotted woodpecker, a lovely bird no longer seen in Sweden.

The bird poet, he thought. Almost everything I've written is about birds: the flapping of wings, the rushing in the night, a lone mating call somewhere in the distance. In the world of birds I have found a reflection of the innermost secrets of life.

He picked up the sheet of paper. The last stanza had worked. He put the paper back on the desk. He felt a sharp pain in his back as he crossed the large room. Was he getting sick? Every day he listened for signs that his body had begun to betray him. He had stayed in good shape throughout his life. He had never smoked, always eating and drinking in moderation. This regime had endowed him with good health. But soon he would be 80. The end of his allotted time was approaching. He went out to the kitchen and poured himself a cup of coffee from the coffee machine, which was always on.

The poem he had finished writing filled him with both sadness and joy. The autumn of my years, he thought. An apt name. Everything I write could be the last. And it's September. It's autumn. On the calendar and in my life.

He carried his coffee back to the living room. He sat down carefully in one of the brown leather armchairs that had kept him company for 40 years. He had bought them to celebrate his triumph when he was awarded the

Volkswagen franchise for southern Sweden. On the table next to his armrest stood the photograph of Werner, the Alsatian that he missed more than all the other dogs that had accompanied him through life. To grow old was to grow lonely. The people who filled your life died off. Even your dogs vanished into the shadows. Soon he would be alone. At a certain point in life, everyone was. Recently he had tried to write a poem about that idea, but he could never seem to finish it. Maybe he ought to try again. But birds were what he knew how to write about. Not people. Birds he could understand. People were unfathomable. Had he ever truly known himself? Writing poems about something he didn't understand would be like trespassing.

He closed his eyes and suddenly remembered "The 10,000-krona Question" TV programme of the late 1950s, or maybe it was the early 1960s. TV was still black-and-white back then. A cross-eyed young man with slicked-back hair had chosen the topic "Birds". He answered all the questions and received his cheque for 10,000 kronor, an incredible sum in those days.

He had not been sitting in the television studio, in the booth with headphones on. He had been sitting in this very same armchair. He too had known all the answers, and not once did he even need extra time to think. But he didn't win 10,000 kronor. Nobody knew of his vast knowledge of birds. He just went on writing his poems.

A noise woke him with a start from his daydream. He listened in the darkened room. Was there someone in the courtyard? He pushed away the thought. It was his imagination. Getting old meant suffering from anxiety. He had good locks on his doors. He kept a shotgun in his bedroom upstairs, and he had a revolver close at hand in a kitchen drawer. If any intruders came to this isolated farmhouse just north of Ystad, he could defend himself. And he wouldn't hesitate to do so.

He got up from his chair. There was another sharp twinge in his back. The pain came and went in waves. He set his coffee cup on the kitchen bench and looked at his watch. Almost 11 p.m. It was time to go. He squinted at the thermometer outside the kitchen window and saw it was 7°C. The barometer was rising. A slight breeze from the southwest was passing over Skåne. The conditions were ideal, he thought. Tonight the flight would be to the south. The migrating birds would pass overhead in their thousands, borne on invisible wings. He wouldn't be able to see them, but he'd feel them out there in the dark, high above. For more than 50 years he had spent countless autumn nights out in the fields, experiencing the sensation of the birds passing. Often it had seemed as though the whole sky was on the move.

Whole orchestras of silent songbirds would be leaving before the approaching winter, heading for warmer climes. The urge to move on was innate, and their ability to navigate by the stars and the earth's gravity kept them on course. They sought out the favourable winds, they had fattened themselves up over the summer, and they could stay aloft for hour after hour. A whole night sky, vibrating with wings, was beginning its annual pilgrimage towards Mecca.

What was a lonely, earthbound old man compared to a night flyer? He had often thought of this as the performance of a sacred act. His own autumnal high mass, as he stood there in the dark, sensing the departure of the migratory birds. And then, when spring came, he was there to welcome them back. Their migration was his religion.

He went out into the hall and stood with one hand on the coat hooks. Then he went back to the living room and pulled on the jumper lying on a stool by the desk. Along with all the other vexations, getting old meant that he got cold more quickly.

Once more he looked at the poem lying there finished on the desk. Maybe he would live long enough to put together enough poems for a tenth and final collection. He had already decided on the title: *High Mass in the Night*.

He went back to the hall, put on his jacket, and pulled a cap over his head. He opened the front door. Outside, the autumn air was redolent with the smell of wet clay. He closed the door behind him and let his eyes grow accustomed to the dark. The garden seemed desolate. In the distance he could see the glow of the lights of Ystad. He lived so far from his other neighbours that this was the only source of light. The sky was almost clear, and filled with stars. A few clouds were visible on the horizon. Tonight the migration was bound to pass over his property.

He set off. His farmhouse was old, with three wings. The fourth had burned down early in the century. He spent a lot of money renovating the building, although the work was still not completed. He would leave it all to the Cultural Association in Lund. He had never been married, never had any children. He sold cars and got rich. He had dogs. And then birds.

I have no regrets, he thought, as he followed the path down to the tower he had built himself. I regret nothing, since it is meaningless to regret.

It was a beautiful September night. Still, something was

making him uneasy. He stopped on the path and listened, but all he could hear was the soft sighing of the wind. He kept walking. Could it be the pain that was worrying him, those sudden sharp pains in his back? The worry was prompted by something inside him.

He stopped again and turned around. Nothing there. He was alone. The path sloped downwards, leading to a slight rise. Just before the rise there was a broad ditch over which he had placed a bridge. At the top of the rise stood his tower. He wondered how many times he had walked this path. He knew every bend, every hollow. And yet he walked slowly and cautiously. He didn't want to risk falling and breaking his leg. Old people's bones grew brittle, he knew that. If he wound up in the hospital with a broken hip he would die, unable to endure lying idle in a hospital bed. He would start worrying about his life. And then nothing could save him.

An owl hooted. Somewhere close by, a twig snapped. The sound had come from the grove just past the hillock on which his tower stood. He stood motionless, all his senses alert. The owl hooted again. Then all was silent once more. He grumbled under his breath, and continued.

Old and scared, he muttered. Afraid of ghosts and afraid of the dark. Now he could see the tower. A black silhouette against the night sky. In 20 metres he would be at the bridge crossing the deep ditch. He kept walking. The owl was gone. A tawny owl, he thought. No doubt about it, it was a tawny owl.

Suddenly he came to a halt. He had reached the bridge that led over the ditch.

There was something about the tower on the hill. Something was different. He squinted, trying to see the details in the dark. He couldn't make out what it was. But something had changed.

I'm imagining things, he thought. Everything's the same as always. The tower I built ten years ago hasn't changed. It's just my eyesight getting blurry, that's all. He took another step, out onto the bridge, and felt the planks beneath his feet. He kept staring at the tower.

There's something wrong, he thought. I'd swear it was a metre higher than it was last night. Or else it's all a dream, and I'm looking at myself standing up there in the tower.

The moment the thought occurred to him, he knew it was true. There was someone up in the tower. A silhouette, motionless. A twinge of fear passed through him, like a lone gust of wind. Then anger. Somebody was trespassing on his property, climbing his tower without asking him for permission. It was probably a poacher hunting the deer that grazed around the grove on the other side of the hill. It couldn't be another bird-watcher.

He called out to the figure in the tower. No reply, no movement. Again he grew uncertain. His eyes must be deceiving him; they were so blurry.

He called again. No answer. He started to walk across the bridge.

When the planks gave way he fell headlong. He pitched forwards and didn't even have time to stretch out his arms to break his fall. The ditch was more than two metres deep.

He felt a hideous pain. It came out of nowhere and cut right through him, like red-hot spears piercing his body. The pain was so intense he couldn't even scream. Just before he died he realised that he had never reached the bottom of the ditch. He remained suspended in his own pain.

His last thought was of the migrating birds, somewhere far above him. The sky moving towards the south.

One last time he tried to tear himself away from the pain. Then it was all over.

It was 11.20 p.m. on 21 September 1994. That night, huge flocks of thrushes and redwings were flying south.

They came from the north and set a southwest course over Falsterbo Point, heading for the warmth that awaited them, far away.

When all was quiet, she made her way carefully down the tower steps. She shone her torch into the ditch. Holger Eriksson was dead. She switched off the torch and stood still in the darkness. Then she walked quickly away.

CHAPTER 2

Just after 5 a.m. on Monday, 26 September, Kurt Wallander woke in his flat on Mariagatan in central Ystad.

The first thing he did when he opened his eyes was look at his hands. They were tanned. He leaned back on his pillow again and listened to the autumn rain drumming on the window. A feeling of satisfaction came over him at the memory of the trip that had ended two days earlier at Kastrup Airport in Copenhagen. He had spent an entire week with his father in Rome. It had been hot there. In the afternoons, when the heat was most intense, they had sought out a bench in the gardens of the Villa Borghese where his father could sit in the shade, while Kurt took off his shirt and turned his face to the sun. That had been the only area of conflict during their holiday. His father couldn't understand how he could be vain enough to waste time trying to get a tan.

That happy holiday, thought Wallander as he lay in bed. We took a trip to Rome, my father and I, and it went well. It went better than I could ever have hoped.

He looked at the clock. He had to go back on duty today. But he was in no hurry. He could stay in bed for a while yet. He reached for the stack of newspapers he had glanced through the night before, and started reading about the results of the parliamentary election. Because he had been in Rome on election day, he had sent in an absentee ballot. The Social Democrats had taken a good

45 per cent of the vote. But what did that mean? Would there be any changes?

He put the paper back on the floor, and thought again of Rome. They had stayed at an inexpensive hotel near the Campo dei Fiori. From the roof terrace directly above their two rooms they'd had a beautiful view over the city. There they drank their morning coffee and planned what they were going to do each day. Wallander's father knew what he wanted to see. Wallander had worried that his father wanted to do too much, that he wouldn't have the strength. He watched for signs that his father was confused or forgetful. Alzheimer's disease, the illness with the strange name, was lurking there and they both knew it. But for that entire, happy week, his father had been in terrific form. Wallander felt a lump in his throat at the realisation that the whole trip belonged to the past, could only be a memory. They would never return to Rome together.

There had been moments of great closeness, for the first time in nearly 40 years. Wallander pondered the discovery he had made, that they were alike, more so than he had been willing to admit. They were both definitely morning people. When Wallander told his father that the hotel didn't serve breakfast before 7 a.m., he had complained at once. He dragged Wallander down to the front desk and in a mixture of Skåne dialect, a few English words, and some German phrases, as well as a smattering of Italian words, he managed to explain that he wanted to have *breakfast presto*. Not *tardi*. Absolutely not *tardi*. For some reason he also said *passaggio a livello* several times as he was urging the hotel to start its breakfast service at least an hour earlier, or they would consider looking for another hotel. *Passaggio a livello*, said his father and the desk clerk had looked at him in shock but also with respect.

Naturally, they got their breakfast at 6 a.m. Later Wallander looked up *passaggio a livello* in his dictionary and found that it meant railway crossing. He assumed that his father had muddled it up with another phrase, but he was wise enough not to ask what that might be.

Wallander listened to the rain. Looking back, the trip to Rome, one brief week, seemed an endless and bewildering experience. When he took his morning coffee was not the only thing his father had fixed ideas about. He had guided his son through the city with complete confidence. Wallander could tell that his father had been planning this trip for a lifetime. It was a pilgrimage, which Wallander was allowed to share. He was a component in his father's journey, an ever-present servant. There was a secret significance to the journey that he hadn't quite understood. His father had travelled to Rome to see something he already seemed to have experienced within himself.

On the third day they had visited the Sistine Chapel. For almost an hour Wallander's father had stood staring at Michelangelo's ceiling. It was like watching a man send a wordless prayer to heaven. Wallander soon got a crick in his neck and had to give up. He knew that he was looking at something very beautiful, but his father saw much more. For a wicked moment, he'd wondered whether the old man was searching for a grouse or a sunset in the huge ceiling fresco. But he regretted this thought. There was no doubt that his father, commercial painter that he was, stood gazing at a master's work with reverence and insight.

Wallander opened his eyes and looked out at the rain.

It was on the same evening that he'd had the feeling that

his father was preparing something he wanted to keep secret. They had dined on the Via Veneto, which was far too expensive in Wallander's view, but his father insisted that they could afford it. After all, they were on their first and last trip together to Rome. Then they had strolled slowly back through the city. The evening was warm, they were surrounded by throngs of people, and Wallander's father had talked about the ceiling of the Sistine Chapel. They lost their way twice before they finally found their hotel. Wallander's father was treated with great respect after his initial outburst, and they had picked up their keys, received a polite bow from the desk clerk, and gone upstairs, said goodnight and gone to their rooms. Wallander lay listening to the sounds from the street. Maybe he thought about Baiba, maybe he was just falling asleep.

Suddenly he was wide awake again. Something had made him uneasy. He put on his dressing gown and went down to the lobby. Everything was quiet. The night clerk was sitting watching TV behind the front desk. Wallander bought a bottle of mineral water. The clerk was a young man. He'd told Wallander that he was working nights to finance his theological studies. He had dark, wavy hair and was born in Padua. His name was Mario and he spoke excellent English. Wallander stood there holding his bottle and found himself asking the clerk to wake him if his father appeared in the lobby during the night, or left the hotel. The young man looked at him. If he was surprised, he didn't show it. He simply nodded and said, certainly, if the senior Signor Wallander went out during the night, he would knock on the door of Room 32 at once.

It was on the sixth night that it happened. That day they had strolled around the Forum, and paid a visit to the Galleria Doria Pamphili. In the evening they went through the dark underground passages that led to the Spanish Steps from the Villa Borghese, and ate in a restaurant. Wallander was shocked when the bill arrived, but it was their last night, and this holiday, which couldn't be described as anything but happy, was coming to an end. Wallander's father showed the same boundless energy and curiosity that he'd had on the whole trip. They walked back to the hotel, stopping at a café for a cup of coffee on the way, and toasting each other with a glass of *grappa*. At the hotel they picked up their keys. Wallander fell asleep as soon as he got into bed.

The knock at the door came at 1.30 a.m. At first he had no idea where he was. He jumped up, half awake, and opened the door. The night clerk was standing there, and explained that Signor Wallander's father had just left the hotel. Wallander threw on his clothes. He caught up with his father easily, and followed him at a distance. His premonition had been right. When the streets began to narrow, he realised they were on their way to the Spanish Steps. Still he kept his distance. And then, in the warm Roman night, he watched his father climb the Spanish Steps to the church with two towers at the top and sit down, a black dot way up there. Wallander kept himself hidden in the shadows. His father stayed there for almost an hour. Then he stood and came slowly down the steps. Wallander continued to tail him – as if it were the strangest assignment he'd ever had to carry out – and soon they were at the Fontana di Trevi. His father did not toss a coin over his shoulder, but stood for a long time watching the water spraying out of the huge fountain. In the dim light Wallander could see the gleam in his eyes.

Eventually he followed his father back to the hotel.

The next day they flew back on an Alitalia plane to Copenhagen. Wallander's father had the window seat, as on the way there. Wallander waited until they were on the ferry heading back to Limhamn to ask whether his father was pleased with the trip. He nodded, mumbled something unintelligible, and Wallander knew that he couldn't demand more enthusiasm than that. Gertrud was waiting for them in Limhamn and drove them home. They'd dropped Wallander in Ystad, and later that night, when he called to ask if all was well, Gertrud told him that his father was back in his studio painting his trademark motif, the sun setting over a becalmed landscape.

Wallander got out of bed and went to the kitchen, and made some coffee. Why had his father sat there on the Spanish Steps? What had he been thinking at the fountain? He had no answers. But he knew he'd had a glimpse into his father's secret inner landscape. And he knew that he could never ask him about his solitary walk through Rome.

As the coffee was brewing, Wallander went into the bathroom. He noticed with pleasure that he looked healthy and energetic. The sun had bleached his hair. All that pasta must have added a few kilos, but he avoided the bathroom scales. He felt rested, that was the most important thing. He was glad they had made the journey.

The realisation that in just a few hours he would return to being a policeman again didn't bother him. Often he'd had trouble going back to work after a holiday. In recent years he'd been very reluctant. There were times when he'd seriously thought of finding another job, maybe as a security guard. But in the end he was a policeman. This knowledge had matured slowly but irrevocably. He could never be anything else.

As he showered, he thought of the hot summer and Sweden's triumph in the World Cup, recalling with anguish the desperate hunt for the serial killer who scalped his victims. During the week in Rome, he'd managed to banish it from his mind. Now the memories came flooding back. A week away had changed nothing.

He sat at his kitchen table until just after 7 a.m. The rain continued to lash the windows. The heat of Italy was already a distant memory. Autumn had come to Skåne.

At 7.30 a.m. he left his flat and drove to the police station. Martinsson arrived at the same time, parking next to him. They said a quick hello in the rain and hurried into the station.

"How was the trip?" Martinsson asked. "Welcome back, by the way."

"My father was very pleased," Wallander replied.

"What about you?"

"It was great. And hot."

Ebba, the station's receptionist for more than 30 years, greeted him with a big smile.

"Can you get so brown in Italy in September?" she asked in surprise.

"You can," Wallander answered, "if you stay in the sun."

They walked down the hall. Wallander realised he should have brought Ebba a little something. He was annoyed at his thoughtlessness.

"Everything's calm here," Martinsson said. "No serious cases. Almost nothing going on."

"Maybe we can hope for a calm autumn," Wallander said dubiously.

Martinsson went to get coffee. Wallander opened the door to his office. Everything was just as he'd left it. The desk top was empty. He hung up his jacket and opened the window a crack. In the in-tray was a stack of memos from the national police board. He picked up the top one, glanced at it and put it back. It was about the investigation into car smuggling from southern Sweden to the former Eastern bloc countries that he'd been working on for almost a year now. If nothing significant had happened while he'd been away, he'd have to go back to that investigation. He'd probably still be working on that case when he retired in 15 years.

At 8.30 a.m. all the officers gathered in the conference room to go over the work for the coming week. Wallander walked around the table, shaking hands with everyone. They all admired his tan. Then he sat down in his usual place. The mood was normal for a Monday morning in the autumn: grey and weary, everyone a little preoccupied. He wondered how many Monday mornings he had spent in this room. As Lisa Holgersson, their new chief, was in Stockholm, Hansson led the meeting. Martinsson was right. Not much had happened.

"I'll have to go back to my smugglers," Wallander said, with no attempt to conceal his reluctance.

"Unless you want to take on a burglary," Hansson said encouragingly. "At a florist's shop."

Wallander looked at him in surprise.

"A break-in at a florist's? What did they steal, tulip bulbs?"

"Nothing, as far as we can tell," Svedberg said, scratching his balding head.

At that moment the door opened and Ann-Britt Höglund hurried in. Since her husband seemed always to be overseas in a far-off country that no-one had heard of, she was mostly alone with their two children. Her mornings were chaotic, and she was frequently late to the meetings. She had been with the Ystad police for about a year now and was their youngest detective. At first, some of the older ones, among them Svedberg and Hansson, had done nothing to disguise their discomfort at having a female colleague. But Wallander, who quickly saw that she had real aptitude for police work, had come to her defence. Now no-one commented when she was late, at least not when he was there. She sat down and nodded cheerfully to Wallander.

"We're talking about the florist's," Hansson said. "We thought Kurt might be able to take a look at it."

"The break-in happened last Thursday night," she said. "The assistant discovered it when she came in on Friday morning. The burglar came in through a back window."

"And nothing was stolen?" asked Wallander.

"Not a thing."

Wallander frowned.

"What do you mean, not a thing?"

Höglund shrugged.

"Not a thing means not a thing."

"There were traces of blood on the floor," Svedberg said. "And the owner is away."

"Sounds very strange," Wallander said. "Is it really worth spending time on?"

"Strange, yes," Höglund answered. "Whether it's worth spending time on, I can't say."

Wallander thought fleetingly that at least he'd avoid getting back to the hopeless smuggling investigation. He'd give himself a day to get used to not being in Rome.

"I could take a look," he said.

"I've got all the information on it," said Höglund.

* * *

The meeting was over. Wallander went and got his jacket, and he and Höglund drove to the centre of town in his car. It was still raining.

"How was your trip?" she asked.

"I saw the Sistine Chapel," Wallander replied, as he stared out at the rain. "And I got to see my father in a good mood for a whole week."

"Sounds like a nice trip."

"So how are things here?" Wallander asked.

"Nothing changes in a week," she replied. "It's been quiet."

"And our new chief?"

"She's been in Stockholm discussing the proposed cutbacks. I think she'll be fine. At least as good as Björk."

Wallander shot her a quick look.

"I never thought you liked him."

"He did the best he could. What more can you expect?"

"Nothing," Wallander said. "Absolutely nothing."

They stopped at Västra Vallgatan, at the corner of Pottmakargränd. The shop was called *Cymbia*. Its sign was swinging in the blustery wind. They stayed in the car. Höglund gave Wallander some papers in a plastic folder. He looked at them as he listened.

"The owner is Gösta Runfeldt. His assistant arrived just before 9 a.m. on Friday. She found a broken window at the back of the shop. There were shards of glass both outside on the ground and inside. There was blood on the floor inside. Nothing seems to have been stolen. They never keep cash in the shop at night. She called the police immediately. I got here just after 10 a.m. It was just as she had described it. A broken window. Blood on the floor. Nothing stolen."

Wallander thought for a moment.

"Not a single flower?" he asked.

"That's what the assistant claimed."

"Could anyone really remember the exact number of flowers they have in each vase?"

He handed back the papers.

"We can always ask her," Höglund said. "The shop's open."

An old-fashioned bell jingled as Wallander opened the door. The scents inside the shop reminded him of the gardens in Rome. There were no customers. A woman came out from the back room. She nodded when she saw them.

"I've brought along my colleague," Höglund said.

Wallander shook hands and introduced himself.

"I've read about you in the newspapers," said the woman.

"Nothing derogatory, I hope." Wallander smiled.

"Oh no," the woman replied. "Only good things."

Wallander had seen in the file that the woman who worked in the shop was named Vanja Andersson and that she was 53 years old.

Wallander moved slowly around the shop. From old, ingrained habit he watched carefully where he stepped. The humid fragrance of flowers continued to fill his mind with memories. He went behind the counter and stopped at the back door, the top half of which was glass. The putty was new. This was where the burglar had entered. Wallander looked at the floor, which was covered with plastic mats.

"I presume the blood was found here," he said.

"No," said Höglund. "The traces of blood were in the storeroom at the back."

Wallander raised his eyebrows in surprise. Then he

followed her into the back among the flowers. Höglund stood in the middle of the room.

"Here," she said. "Right here."

"But none by the window?"

"No. Now do you understand why I think it's a little strange? Why is there blood in here, but not by the window? If we assume that whoever broke the window cut himself, that is."

"Who else would it be?" asked Wallander.

"That's just it. Who else would it be?"

Wallander went through the shop again, trying to picture what had happened. Someone had smashed the window and let himself into the shop. There was blood in the middle of the back room. Nothing had been stolen.

Every crime follows some kind of plan or reason, except those that are simply acts of insanity. He knew this from years of experience. But who would be so mad as to break into a florist's shop and not steal anything? It just didn't make sense.

"I presume it was drops of blood," he said.

To his surprise, Höglund shook her head.

"It was a little puddle," she said. "Not drops."

Wallander said nothing. He had nothing to say. Then he turned to the shop assistant, who was standing in the background, waiting.

"So nothing was stolen?"

"Nothing."

"Not even any flowers?"

"Not that I could see."

"Do you really know exactly how many flowers you have in the shop at any one time?"

"Yes, I do."

Her reply was immediate and firm. Wallander nodded.

"Do you have any explanation for this break-in?"

"No."

"You don't own the shop, is that right?"

"The owner is Gösta Runfeldt. I work for him."

"If I understand correctly, he's away. Have you been in contact with him?"

"That's not possible."

Wallander looked at her attentively.

"Why not?"

"He's on an orchid safari in Kenya."

Wallander considered what she had said.

"Can you tell me something more? An orchid safari?"

"Gösta is a passionate orchid lover," the woman answered. "He knows everything about them. He travels all over the world looking at all the types that exist. He's been writing a book on the history of orchids. Right now he's in Kenya. I don't know where, exactly. All I know is he'll be back next Wednesday."

Wallander nodded.

"We'll have to talk with him when he gets back," said Wallander. "Maybe you could ask him to call us at the police station?"

Vanja Andersson promised to pass on the message. A customer came into the shop. Höglund and Wallander went out into the rain and got into the car. Wallander waited to start the engine.

"Of course, it could be a burglar who made a mistake," he said. "A thief who smashed the wrong window. There's a computer shop right next door."

"But what about the pool of blood?"

Wallander shrugged.

"Maybe the thief didn't notice he cut himself. He stood

there with his arm hanging down and looked around. The blood dripped from his arm. Blood dripping in the same spot will eventually form a puddle."

She nodded. Wallander turned the ignition.

"This will be an insurance case," he said. "Nothing more."

They drove back to the police station in the rain.

It was 11 a.m. on Monday 26 September 1994.

In Wallander's mind the week in Rome was slipping away like a slowly dissolving mirage.

CHAPTER 3

On Tuesday, 27 September, rain was still falling in Skåne. The meteorologists had predicted that the hot summer would be followed by a wet autumn. Nothing had yet occurred to contradict their forecast.

Wallander had come home from his first day at work after his trip to Italy, put together a hasty meal and eaten it without pleasure. He made several attempts to reach his daughter, who lived in Stockholm. He propped open the door to the balcony when there was a brief lull in the rain, feeling annoyed that Linda hadn't called to ask him how the holiday had been. He tried, without much success, to convince himself that she was too busy to make contact. This autumn she was combining studies at a private theatre school with work as a waitress at a restaurant on Kungsholmen.

Late that evening he had called Baiba in Riga. He had thought about her a great deal while he'd been in Rome. They'd spent some time together in Denmark, just a few months earlier, when Wallander was worn out and depressed after the terrible manhunt. On one of their last days together, he had asked Baiba to marry him. She gave him an evasive answer, not a definite no, but she made no attempt to conceal the reasons for her reluctance. They were walking along the vast beach at Skagen, where the two seas meet. Wallander had walked the same stretch many years before with his wife Mona, and once alone at a time when he had seriously considered leaving the police force.

The evenings in Denmark had been almost tropically hot. The World Cup had people glued to their TV sets, and the beaches were deserted. They had strolled along, picking up pebbles and shells, and Baiba told him she didn't think she could ever live with a policeman again. Her first husband, the Latvian police major Karlis, had been murdered in 1992. That was when Wallander had met her, during that confused and unreal time in Riga.

In Rome, Wallander had asked himself whether deep down he really wanted to get married again. Was it even necessary to be married? To be tied by complicated, formal bonds which hardly had any meaning in this day and age?

He had been married to Linda's mother for a long time. Then one day, five years earlier, she had confronted him out of the blue and told him that she wanted a divorce. He had been dumbfounded. It was only now that he felt able to understand and begin to accept the reasons she had wanted to begin a new life without him. He could see now why things had turned out the way they had. He could even admit that he bore most of the blame, because of his frequent absences and his increasing lack of interest in what was important in Mona's life.

In Rome he had come to the conclusion that he did want to marry Baiba. He wanted her to leave Latvia and come to live in Ystad. And he had also decided to move, to sell his flat on Mariagatan and buy a house. Somewhere just outside town, with a flourishing garden. An inexpensive house, but in good enough shape that he could handle the necessary repairs himself. He had also thought about getting the dog he had been dreaming about for so long.

Now he talked about all of this with Baiba as the rain fell over Ystad. It was a continuation of the conversation he had been having in his head in Rome. On a few occasions he had started talking out loud to himself. His father, of course, hadn't let this go unnoticed, trudging along at his side in the heat. He'd asked which of them was the one getting old and senile.

Baiba sounded happy. Wallander told her about the trip and then repeated his question from the summer. For a moment the silence bounced back and forth between Riga and Ystad. Then she said that she had been thinking too. She still had doubts; they hadn't lessened, but they weren't growing.

"Why don't you come over here?" Wallander said. "We can't talk about this on the phone."

"You're right," she answered. "I'll come."

They didn't decide on a time. They would talk about that later. She had her job at the University of Riga, and her time away had to be planned far in advance. But when Wallander hung up he felt that he was now on his way to a new phase of his life. She would come. He would get married again.

That night it took a long time for him to fall asleep. Twice he got up and stood by the kitchen window, staring out at the rain. He would miss the streetlight swinging on its wire out there, lonesome in the wind.

Even though he didn't get much sleep, he was up early on Tuesday. A little after 7 a.m. he parked his car outside the police station and hurried through the rain and wind. He'd decided to start working through the pile of paperwork on the car thefts immediately. The longer he put it off, the more his lack of enthusiasm would weigh him down. He hung his jacket over the visitor's chair to dry. Then he lifted all the files, piled almost half a metre high, down from the shelf. He was just starting to organise the papers when there was a knock at the door. Wallander knew it would be Martinsson. He called to him to come in.

"When you're away I'm always the first one here in the morning," Martinsson said. "Now I have to settle for second place again."

"I've missed my cars," Wallander said, pointing at the files all over his desk.

Martinsson had a piece of paper in his hand.

"I forgot to give this to you yesterday," he said. "Chief Holgersson wanted you to have a look at it."

"What is it?"

"Read it for yourself. You know that people expect us policemen to make statements about all kinds of topics."

"Something political?"

"That sort of thing."

Wallander gave him an inquiring look. Martinsson didn't usually beat around the bush. Several years before, he had been active in the Liberal party and had probably dreamt of a political career. As far as Wallander knew, this hope had gradually faded as the party's popularity had dwindled. He decided not to mention their showing in the election the week before.

Martinsson left. Wallander sat down and read the paper. After reading it twice he was furious. He went out to the hall and strode into Svedberg's office.

"Have you seen this?" he asked, waving Martinsson's sheet of paper.

Svedberg shook his head.

"What is it?"

"It's from a new organisation that wants to know whether the police would have any objections to its name."

"Which is?"

"They were thinking of calling themselves 'Friends of the Axe'."

Svedberg gave Wallander a baffled look.

"Friends of the Axe?"

"That's right. And now they're wondering – in light of what happened here this summer – if the name might possibly be misconstrued. This organisation has no intention of going out and scalping people."

"What are they going to do?"

"If I understand correctly, it's some sort of home crafts association that wants to establish a museum for old-fashioned hand tools."

"That sounds all right, doesn't it? Why are you so worked up?"

"Because they think the police have time to make pronouncements about such things," Wallander said. "Personally, I think Friends of the Axe is a pretty strange name for a home crafts association. But I can't waste time on stuff like this."

"So tell the chief."

"I'm going to."

"Though she probably won't agree with you, since we're all supposed to become local police officers again."

Wallander knew that Svedberg was right. During the years he had been a policeman, the force had undergone endless and sweeping changes because of the complex relationship between the police and that vague and threatening entity known as "the public". This public, which hung like a nightmare over the national police board as well as over the individual officers, was characterised by one thing: fickleness. The latest attempt to satisfy the public was to change the entire Swedish police force to "local police". Just how this was supposed to be done, no-one knew. The national commissioner had proclaimed how important it was for the police to be seen. But since nobody had ever thought the police were invisible, they couldn't see how this strategy was to be implemented. They already had policemen walking the beat, officers were also riding bicycles around in small, swift mini-squads. The national commissioner seemed to be talking about some other kind of visibility, something less tangible. "Local police" sounded cosy, like a soft pillow under your head. But how it was actually going to be combined with the fact that crime in Sweden was growing more brutal and violent all the time, no-one could see. In all probability, this new regime would require them to spend time making decisions as to whether it was proper for a home crafts organisation to call itself "Friends of the Axe".

Wallander went back to his office with a cup of coffee, closing his door behind him. He tried again to make some headway with the huge amount of material. At first he found it hard to concentrate. His conversation with Baiba kept intruding. But he forced himself to act like a policeman again, and after a few hours he had reviewed the investigation and reached the point where he had left off before he went to Italy. He telephoned a detective in Göteborg with whom he was collaborating, and they discussed some of the issues. By the time he hung up it was midday, and Wallander was hungry. It was still raining. He went out to his car, drove to the centre of town, and ate lunch. He was back at the station within the hour. Just as he sat down, the telephone rang. It was Ebba in reception.

"You have a visitor," she said.

"Who is it?"

"A man named Tyrén. He wants to talk to you."

"What about?"

"Somebody who might be missing."

"Isn't there someone else who can handle it?"

"He says he absolutely has to speak with you."

Wallander took a look at the open folders on his desk. Nothing in them was so urgent that he couldn't take a report on a missing person.

"Send him in," he said and hung up.

He opened the door and began moving the folders off his desk. When he looked up, a man was standing at his door. Wallander had never seen him before. He was dressed in overalls bearing the logo of the O.K. oil company. As he entered, Wallander could smell oil and petrol.

He shook his hand and asked the man to take a seat. He was in his 50s, unshaven and with thin grey hair. He introduced himself as Sven Tyrén.

"You wanted to talk to me?" Wallander said.

"I've heard you're a good policeman," said Tyrén. His accent sounded like western Skåne, where Wallander himself had grown up.

"Most of us are good," Wallander answered.

Tyrén's reply surprised him.

"You know that's not true. I've been locked up for a thing or two in my day. And I've met a lot of policemen who were real arseholes, to put it mildly."

Wallander was startled by the force of his words.

"I doubt you came here to tell me that," he said,

changing the subject. "There was something about a missing person?"

Tyrén fidgeted with his O.K. cap.

"It's strange, actually," he said.

Wallander had taken out a notebook from a drawer and turned to a blank page.

"Let's start at the beginning," he said. "Who might have disappeared? And what's strange about it?"

"Holger Eriksson."

"Who's that?"

"One of my customers."

"I'm guessing that you own a petrol station."

Tyrén shook his head.

"I deliver heating oil," he said. "I take care of the district north of Ystad. Eriksson lives between Högestad and Lödinge. He called the office and said his tank was almost empty. We agreed on a delivery for Thursday morning. But, when I got there, nobody was home."

Wallander jotted this down.

"You're talking about last Thursday."

"Yes."

"And when did he call?"

"Last Monday."

Wallander thought for a moment.

"Could there have been some misunderstanding about the time?"

"I've delivered to Eriksson for more than ten years. There's never been a misunderstanding before."

"So what did you do when you discovered that he wasn't there."

"His oil tank is locked, so I left a message in his letter box."

"Then what?"

"I left."

Wallander put down his pen.

"When you deliver oil," Tyrén went on, "you tend to notice people's routines. I couldn't stop thinking about Holger Eriksson. It didn't make sense for him to be away. So I went out there again yesterday afternoon after work. My note was still in the letter box, underneath all the other post that had come since last Thursday. I rang the bell. Nobody was home. His car was still in the garage.

"Does he live alone?"

"He's not married. He made a lot of money selling cars. And he writes poems, too. He gave me a book once."

Wallander remembered seeing Eriksson's name on books on a shelf of literature by local writers at the Ystad Bookshop when he'd been looking for something to give Svedberg for his 40th birthday.

"There was something else that doesn't make sense," Tyrén said. "The door was unlocked. I thought maybe he was sick. He's almost 80. So I went inside. The house was empty, but the coffee maker in the kitchen was on. It smelled bad. The coffee had boiled dry and burned on the bottom. That's when I decided to come and see you."

Wallander could see that Tyrén's concern was genuine. From experience, however, he knew that most disappearances usually solved themselves. It was very seldom that anything serious happened.

"Doesn't he have any neighbours?" asked Wallander.

"The farmhouse is pretty isolated."

"What do you think might have happened?"

Tyrén's reply came at once, quite firmly.

"I think he's dead. I think somebody killed him."

Wallander said nothing. He was waiting for Tyrén to continue. But he didn't.

"Why do you think that?"

"He had ordered heating oil. He was always home when I came. He wouldn't have left the coffee machine on. He wouldn't have gone out without locking the door. Even if he was just taking a little walk around his property."

"Did you get the impression the house had been broken into?"

"No, everything seemed the same as usual. Except for that coffee machine."

"So you've been in his house before?"

"Every time I delivered oil. Usually he offered me some coffee and read me some of his poems. He was probably a pretty lonely man, and I think he looked forward to my visits."

Wallander paused to think about it.

"You said you think he's dead, but you also said you think someone killed him. Why would anyone do that? Did he have any enemies?"

"Not that I know of."

"But he was wealthy."

"Yes."

"How do you know that?"

"Everybody knows that."

Wallander let the question pass.

"We'll look into it," he said. "There's probably an ordinary explanation. There usually is."

Wallander wrote down the address. The name of the farm was "Seclusion".

Wallander walked out to reception with Tyrén.

"I'm sure something has happened," Tyrén said as he was leaving. "He'd never go out when I was coming with oil."

"I'll be in touch," Wallander said.

Just then Hansson came into reception.

"Who the hell is blocking the driveway with an oil truck?" he fumed.

"Me," Tyrén said calmly. "I'm leaving now."

"What was he doing here?" asked Hansson after Tyrén had gone.

"He wanted to report a missing person," said Wallander. "Have you ever heard of a writer named Holger Eriksson?"

"A writer?"

"Or a car dealer."

"Which?"

"He seems to have been both. And according to this truck driver, he's disappeared."

They went to get coffee.

"Seriously?" said Hansson.

"The man seems worried."

"I thought I recognised him," Hansson said.

Wallander had great respect for Hansson's memory. Whenever he forgot a name, it was to Hansson that he went for help.

"His name is Sven Tyrén," Wallander said. "He said he'd done time for a thing or two."

Hansson searched his memory.

"He might have been mixed up in some assault cases," he said after a while. "Quite a few years ago."

Wallander listened thoughtfully.

"I think I'll drive out to Eriksson's place," he said after a while. "I'll log him in as reported missing."

Wallander went into his office, grabbed his jacket, and stuffed the address of "Seclusion" in his pocket. He should have begun by filling out a missing-person form, but he skipped it for the time being. It was 2.30 p.m. when he left the police station. The heavy rain had eased to a steady drizzle. He shivered as he walked to his car.

Wallander drove north and had no problem finding the farmhouse. As the name implied, it lay quite isolated, high up on a hill. Brown fields sloped down towards the sea, but he couldn't see the water. A flock of rooks cawed in a tree. He raised the lid of the letter box. It was empty. Tyrén must have taken in the post. Wallander walked into the courtyard. Everything was well kept. He stood there and listened to the silence. The farmhouse consisted of three wings, and he could see that it had once formed a complete square. He admired the thatched roof. Tyrén was right. Anyone who could afford to maintain a roof like that was a wealthy man.

Wallander walked up to the door and rang the bell. Then he knocked. He opened the door and stepped inside, listening. The letters lay on a stool next to an umbrella stand. There were several binocular cases hanging on the wall. One was open and empty. Wallander moved slowly through the house. It still smelled of burnt coffee. The large living room was split-level with an exposed-beam ceiling. He stopped at the wooden desk and looked at a sheet of paper lying on it. Since the light was poor, he picked it up carefully and went over to a window.

It was a poem about a bird. At the bottom a date and time was written. *21 September 1994. 10.12 p.m.* On that evening Wallander and his father had eaten dinner at a restaurant near the Piazza del Popolo. As he stood in the silent house, Rome felt like a remote, surreal dream.

He put the paper back on the desk. On Wednesday night Eriksson had written a poem, even noting down the time. The next day Tyrén was supposed to deliver oil. By then he was gone, leaving the door unlocked. Wallander went outside and found the oil tank. The meter showed that it was almost empty. He went back inside the house. He sat down in an old Windsor chair and looked around. Instinct told him that Sven Tyrén was right. Holger Eriksson had truly disappeared. He wasn't just away from home.

After a while Wallander stood up and searched through several cupboards until he found a set of spare keys. He locked the house and left. The rain had picked up again. He was back in Ystad just before 5 p.m. He filled out the form on Holger Eriksson. Early the next morning they would start looking for him in earnest.

Wallander drove home. On the way he stopped and bought a pizza. He ate it while he watched TV. Linda still hadn't called. Just after 11 p.m. he went to bed and fell asleep almost at once.

At 4 a.m. Wallander sat up abruptly in bed feeling ill. He was going to throw up. He didn't make it to the bathroom. At the same time he realised he had diarrhoea. He didn't know whether it was the pizza or a stomach bug he had brought home from Italy. By 7 a.m. he was so exhausted that he called the police station to report in sick. He got hold of Martinsson.

"You heard what happened, I guess," Martinsson said.

"All I know is I'm puking and shitting," Wallander replied.

"A ferry boat sank last night," Martinsson went on. "Somewhere off the coast of Tallinn. Hundreds of people died, they think. And most of them were Swedes. There seem to have been quite a few police officers on board."

Wallander was about to throw up again. But he stayed on the line.

"Police from Ystad?" he asked.

"No. But it's terrible, what happened."

Wallander could hardly believe what Martinsson was saying. Several hundred people dead in a ferry accident? That just didn't happen. At least not around Sweden.

"I don't think I can talk," he said. "I'm going to be sick again. But there's a note on my desk about a man named Holger Eriksson. He's missing. One of you will have to look into it."

He put down the receiver and made it to the bathroom just in time. As he was on his way back to bed, the phone rang again. This time it was Mona, his ex-wife. He felt on edge at once. She never called unless something was wrong with Linda.

"I talked to Linda," she said. "She wasn't on the ferry."

It took a moment before Wallander grasped what she meant.

"You mean the ferry that sank?"

"What did you think I meant? When hundreds of people die in an accident, at least I call my daughter to see if she's all right."

"You're right, of course," Wallander said. "You'll have to excuse me if I'm a little slow today, but I'm sick. I'm throwing up. I've got a stomach bug. Maybe we can talk another time."

"I just didn't want you to worry," she said.

Wallander said goodbye and went back to bed. He was worried about Holger Eriksson, and about the ferry disaster that had occurred during the night, but he was feverish, and soon he was asleep.

CHAPTER 4

He began to gnaw on the rope again.

The feeling that he was about to go insane had been with him the whole time. He couldn't see; something was tied over his eyes and made the world dark. He couldn't hear either. Something had been forced into his ears, and was pressing on his eardrums. There were sounds, but they came from inside. An internal rushing that wanted to force its way out. But what bothered him most was that he couldn't move. That was what was driving him insane. Despite the fact that he was lying down, stretched out on his back, he had the constant feeling that he was falling. A dizzy plummeting, without end. Maybe it was just a hallucination, a manifestation of the fact that he was falling apart from within. Madness was about to shatter his mind into pieces.

He tried to cling to reality. He forced himself to think. Reason and the ability to remain calm might give him some possible explanation for what had happened. Why can't I move? Where am I? And why?

For the longest time he had fought against the panic and madness by forcing himself to keep track of time. He counted minutes and hours, trying to keep to an impossible, endless routine. The darkness never changed, and he had woken up where he lay, fettered on his back. He had no memory of being moved, so there was no beginning. He could have been born right where he lay. For the brief moments when he succeeded in keeping the panic at bay and thinking clearly, he tried to cling to anything that seemed related to reality.

What could he start from? What he was lying on. That wasn't his imagination. He was on his back and what he was lying on was hard. His shirt had ridden up just over his left hip and his skin lay against the hard, rough surface. He could feel that he had scraped his skin when he tried to move. He was lying on a cement floor.

He thought back to the last moment of normality before the darkness had fallen over him, but even that was beginning to seem vague. He knew what had happened, and yet he didn't. It was when he started to doubt what was his imagination, and what had actually happened, that panic would seize him. Then he would begin to sob. A brief outburst that stopped as quickly as it began, since no-one could hear him anyway. There are people who cry only when they're out of earshot of others, but he wasn't one of them.

Actually that was the one thing he was sure of. That no-one could hear him. Wherever he was, wherever this cement floor of terror had been poured, even if it was floating freely in a universe totally unknown to him, there was no-one close by. Nobody could hear him.

Beyond the growing madness, these were the only things he had left to hold on to. Everything else had been taken from him, not merely his identity but also his trousers.

It was the evening before he was supposed to leave for Nairobi. It was almost midnight, he had closed his suitcase and sat down at his desk to go over his travel plans one last time. He could see it all quite clearly. Without knowing it, he was waiting in death's anteroom, which some unknown person had prepared for him. His passport lay on the left side of his desk, and he held his plane tickets in his hand. The plastic pouch with the dollar notes, credit cards, and traveller's cheques was on his lap, waiting for him to check them too. Then the telephone rang. He put everything to one side, lifted the receiver, and answered.

Since that was the last living voice he had heard, he clung to it. It was his only link to the reality that held madness at bay. It was a lovely voice, soft and pleasant, and he knew at once that he was speaking to a stranger – a woman he had never met. She asked if she could buy some roses. She apologised for calling him at home and disturbing him so late, but she was in desperate need of those roses. She didn't say why. But he trusted her at once. Who would lie about needing roses? He couldn't remember whether he actually asked her or even wondered why she had discovered she didn't have the roses she needed so late at night, when there were no florists open. But he hadn't hesitated. He lived close to his shop, and he wasn't going to bed yet. It would take him no more than ten minutes to solve her problem.

Now as he lay in the dark and thought back, he realised that here was one thing he couldn't explain. He was convinced that the woman who called was somewhere close by. There was some reason, which wasn't clear to him, why she had called him instead of someone else. Who was she? What happened after that?

He had put on his coat and gone down to the street. He had the keys to the shop in his hand. There was no wind, and a cool scent wafted up towards him as he walked down the wet street. It had rained earlier that evening, a cloudburst that had passed as quickly as it began. He stopped outside the front door of the shop. He could remember that he unlocked the door and went inside. Then the world exploded.

He had walked down that street countless times in his mind, whenever the panic subsided for a moment. It was a fixed point in the constant, throbbing pain. There must have been someone there. I expected a woman to be standing outside the door. But there was no-one. I could have waited and then gone back home. I could have been angry because someone had played a joke on me, but I unlocked the shop because I knew she would come. She said that she really needed those roses. Nobody lies about roses.

The street had been deserted, he was sure of that. But one detail of the scene bothered him. There was a car parked, with its lights on. When he turned towards the door, searching for the keyhole to unlock it, the headlights were on him. And then the world ended in a sharp white glare.

The only possible explanation made him hysterical with fright. He must have been attacked. Behind him in the shadows was someone he hadn't seen. But a woman who telephones up at night, pleading for roses? He never got further than that. That's where everything rational ended. With a tremendous effort, he had managed to wrench his bound hands up to his mouth so he could gnaw on the rope. At first he ripped and tore at it like a beast of prey gorging on a kill. Almost at once he broke a tooth on the lower left side of his mouth. The pain was intense at first, but quickly subsided. When he began chewing on the rope again – he thought of himself as an animal in a trap who had to gnaw off its own leg to escape – he did it slowly.

Gnawing on the hard, dry rope was consoling. Even if he couldn't free himself, chewing on it kept him sane, and he could think relatively clearly. He had been attacked. He was being held captive, lying on a floor. Twice a day, or maybe it was twice a night, he could hear a scraping sound next to him. A gloved hand would prise open his mouth and pour water into it. Never anything else. The hand that gripped his jaw seemed more determined than brutal. Afterwards a straw was stuck into his mouth. He sucked up a little lukewarm soup and then he was again left alone in the dark and the silence.

He had been attacked and tied up. Beneath him was a cement floor. Someone was keeping him alive. He worked out that he had been lying here for a week. He had tried to understand why. It must be a mistake. But what kind of mistake? Why would a person be kept tied up in the dark? Somehow he sensed that the madness was based on an insight he didn't dare allow to surface. It was no mistake. This terrible thing had been planned specifically for him. But how would it end? Perhaps the nightmare would go on for ever, and he would never know why.

Twice each day or night he was given water and food. Twice he was also dragged along the floor by his feet until he came to a hole in the floor. He had no underpants on either, they had disappeared. There was only his shirt, and he was dragged back to his original position when he was finished. He had nothing to wipe himself with. Besides, his hands were tied. He noticed the smell around him.

Filth. But also perfume.

Was there someone near him? The woman who wanted to buy roses? Or just a pair of hands with gloves on? Hands that dragged him to the hole in the floor. And an almost imperceptible smell of perfume that lingered after the visits. The hands and perfume must come from somewhere.

Of course he had tried to speak to the hands. Somewhere

sledgehammer herself, and the whole house shook as the mortar crumbled. Then from the dust this gigantic room had grown, and the only thing she had left was the big baking oven that towered like a strange boulder in the middle. Everyone who came to see her back then, after the building work, was amazed at how beautiful it had become. It was the same old house, and yet completely different. Light flooded in from the new windows. If she wanted it dark, she could close the massive oak shutters on the outside of the house. She had exposed the roof beams and ripped up the old floors. Someone told her it looked like a church nave.

After that she had begun to regard the room as her sanctuary. When she was there alone she was in the centre of the world. She could feel completely calm, far from the dangers that threatened her.

There had been times when she rarely visited her cathedral. The routine of her life always fluctuated. On occasion she had asked herself whether she shouldn't get rid of the house. There were far too many memories that the sledgehammers could never demolish. But she couldn't leave the room with the huge, looming baking oven, the white boulder she had kept. It had become a part of her. Sometimes she saw it as the last bastion she had left to defend in her life.

Then the letter had arrived from Africa.

After that, everything changed.

She never again considered abandoning her house.

On Wednesday, 28 September, she arrived in Vollsjö just after 3 p.m. She had driven from Hässleholm, and before she drove to her house on the outskirts of town, she stopped and bought supplies. She knew what she needed. To be on the safe side, she had bought an extra package of straws. The shopkeeper nodded to her. She smiled back and they exchanged a few words about the weather, and about the terrible ferry accident. She paid and drove off.

Her closest neighbours weren't there. They were German, lived in Hamburg, and only came up to Skåne for the month of July. When they were there they greeted one another, but had no other contact.

She unlocked the front door, and stood quite still in the hall, listening. Then she went into the big room and stood motionless next to the baking oven. Everything was quiet. As quiet as she wanted the world to be.

The man lying down there inside the oven couldn't hear her. She knew he was alive, but she had no wish to be bothered by the sound of his breathing. Or sobbing.

She thought of the impulse that had led her to this unexpected conclusion. It began when she had decided to keep the house. And it was there when she decided to leave the oven untouched. Only later, when the letter from Africa came and she realised what she had to do, had the oven revealed its true purpose.

She was interrupted by the alarm on her watch. In an hour her guests would arrive. Before then she would have to give the man in the oven his food. He had been there for five days. Soon he would be so weak that he wouldn't be able to put up any resistance. She took her schedule from her handbag and saw that she had time off from next Sunday afternoon until Tuesday morning. That's when it would be. She would take him out and tell him what had happened.

She had not yet decided how she was going to kill him. There were several possibilities, but she still had plenty of time. She would think about what he had done and then resolve how he was supposed to die.

She went into the kitchen and heated the soup. Because she was careful about hygiene, she washed the plastic cup and lid that she used when she fed him. She poured water into another cup. Each day she reduced the amount she gave him. He would get no more than was necessary to keep him alive. When she finished preparing the meal, she pulled on a pair of latex gloves, splashed a few drops of perfume behind her ears, and went to the oven. At its back was a hole, hidden behind some loose stones. It was like a tunnel, almost a metre long, that she could carefully pull out. Before she'd put him in there, she had installed a powerful loudspeaker and then filled in the hole. When she played music at full volume, no sound seeped out.

She leaned forwards so she could see him. When she put her hand on one of his legs he didn't move. For a moment she was afraid that he was dead, but then she heard him gasping.

He's weak, she thought. Soon the waiting will be over.

After she had given him his food, and let him use the hole, she pulled him back to his place again, and filled in the hole. When she had washed the dishes and tidied up the kitchen, she sat down at the table and had a cup of coffee. From her handbag she took out her personnel newsletter and leafed through it. According to the new salary table, she would be getting 174 kronor more each month, backdated from the first of July. She looked at the clock again. She seldom went ten minutes without checking it. It was part of her identity. Her life and her work were held together by precise timetables. And nothing bothered her more than not being able to meet schedules.

Excuses were unacceptable. She always regarded it as a personal responsibility. She knew that many of her colleagues laughed at her behind her back. That hurt her, but she never said a word. The silence was a part of her too. But it hadn't always been that way.

I remember my voice when I was a child. It was strong, but not shrill. The muteness had come later. After I saw all the blood, and my mother when she almost died. I didn't scream that time. I hid in my own silence. There I could make myself invisible.

That's when it happened. When my mother lay on a table and, sobbing and bleeding, robbed me of the sister I had always waited for.

She looked at the clock. They would be here soon. It was Wednesday, time for their meeting. If she had her preference, it would always be on Wednesdays, that would create regularity. But her work schedule didn't permit it, and she had no control over that schedule.

She set out five chairs. She didn't want any more people than that to visit her at once. The intimacy might be lost. It was hard enough as it was to create sufficient trust that these silent women would dare to speak. She went into the bedroom and took off her uniform. For each article of clothing she removed, she muttered a prayer. And she remembered.

It was my mother who told me about Antonio. The man she had met in her youth, long before the Second World War, on a train between Cologne and Munich. They couldn't find seats, so they ended up squeezed close together in the smoky corridor. The lights from the boats on the Rhine had glimmered outside the dirty windows, and Antonio told her that he was going to be a

Catholic priest. He said that the mass started as soon as the priest changed his clothes. As a prelude to the holy ritual, the priests had to undergo a cleansing procedure. For each garment they took off or put on they had a prayer. Each garment brought them a step closer to their sacred task.

She had never forgotten her mother's recollection of the meeting with Antonio in the train. And since she had realised that she was a priestess, dedicated to the sacred task of proclaiming that justice was holy, she too had begun to view her change of clothes as something more than simply exchanging one set of garments for another. But the prayers she offered up were not part of a conversation with God. In a chaotic and absurd world, God was the ultimate absurdity. The mark of the world was an absent God. She directed her prayers to the child she had been, before everything fell apart. Before her mother robbed her of what she wanted most of all. Before the sinister men had towered up before her with eyes like writhing, menacing snakes.

She changed her clothes and prayed herself back to her childhood. She laid her uniform on the bed. Then she dressed in soft fabrics with gentle colours. Something happened inside her. It was as if her skin altered, as if it too was shifting back to its infant state. Last, she put on a wig and glasses. The final prayer faded inside her. *Ride, ride a cock-horse . . .*

She looked at her face in the big mirror. It wasn't Sleeping Beauty that awoke from her nightmare. It was Cinderella.

She heard the first car pull into the courtyard. She was ready, she was somebody else. She folded her uniform, smoothed out the bedspread, and left the room. Athough no-one would go in there, she locked the door and then tested the handle.

They gathered just before 6 p.m., but one of the women was missing. She had been taken to the hospital the night before with contractions. It was two weeks early, but the baby might already have been born.

She decided at once to visit her at the hospital the next day. She wanted to see her. She wanted to see her face after all she had gone through. Then she listened to their stories. Now and then she pretended to write something in her notebook, but she wrote only numbers. She was making timetables. Figures, times, distances. It was an obsessive game, a game that had increasingly become an incantation. She didn't need to write anything down to remember it. All the words spoken in those frightened voices, all the pain that they dared express, remained etched in her consciousness. She could see the way something loosened in each of them, if only for a moment. But what was life except a series of moments?

The timetable again. Times that coincide, one taking over from the other. Life is like a pendulum. It swings back and forth between pain and relief, endless, ceaseless.

She was sitting so that she could see the big oven behind the women. The light was turned down and muted. The room was bathed in a gentle light, which she imagined as being feminine. The oven was a boulder, immovable, mute, in the middle of an empty sea.

They talked for a couple of hours, and then drank tea in her kitchen. They all knew when they would meet next. No-one questioned the times she gave them.

It was 8.30 p.m. when she showed them out. She shook

their hands, accepted their gratitude. When the last car was gone she went back inside the house, changed her clothes and took off the wig and glasses. She took her uniform and left the room. She washed the teacups, then turned out all the lights and picked up her handbag.

For a moment she stood still in the dark beside the oven. Everything was very quiet.

Then she left the house. It was drizzling. She got into her car and drove towards Ystad. She was in her bed asleep before midnight.

CHAPTER 5

When Wallander woke on Thursday morning he felt better. He got up just after 6 a.m. and checked the thermometer outside the kitchen window. It was 5°C. Heavy clouds covered the sky, and the streets were wet, but the rain had stopped.

He arrived at the police station just after 7 a.m. As he walked down the hall to his office he wondered whether they had found Holger Eriksson. He hung up his jacket and sat down. There were a few telephone messages on his desk. Ebba reminded him that he had an appointment at the optician later in the day. He needed reading glasses. If he sat for too long leaning over his paperwork, he got a headache. He was going to be 47 soon. His age was catching up with him.

One message was from Per Åkeson. Wallander phoned him at the prosecutor's office, but was told that Åkeson would be in Malmö all day. He went to get a cup of coffee, then he leaned back in his chair and tried to devise a new strategy for the car-smuggling investigation. In almost all organised crime there was some weak point, a link that could be broken if leaned on hard enough.

His thoughts were interrupted by the telephone. It was Lisa Holgersson, their new chief, welcoming him home.

"How was the holiday?" she asked.

"Very successful."

"You rediscover your parents by doing these things," she said.

"And they might acquire a different view of their children," Wallander said.

She excused herself abruptly. Wallander heard someone come into her office and say something. Björk would never have asked him about his holiday. She came back on the line.

"I've been in Stockholm for a few days," she said. "It wasn't much fun."

"What are they up to now?"

"I'm thinking about the *Estonia*. All of our colleagues who died."

Wallander sat in silence. He should have thought about that himself.

"I think you can imagine the mood," she went on. "How could we just sit there, discussing organisational problems between the national police and the districts all over the country?"

"We're probably just as helpless in the face of death as everyone else," Wallander said. "Even though we shouldn't be, since we've seen so much of it. We think we're used to it, but we aren't."

"A ferry sinks one stormy night and suddenly death is visible in Sweden again," she said. "After it's been hidden away and ignored for so long."

"You're right, I suppose. Although I hadn't thought of it that way."

He heard her clearing her throat. After a pause she returned.

"We discussed organisational problems," she said, "and the eternal question of what should take priority."

"We ought to spend our time catching criminals,"

said Wallander. "Bringing them to justice and making sure we have enough evidence to get them convicted."

"If only it was that simple," she sighed.

"I'm glad I'm not the chief," Wallander said.

"I sometimes wonder myself," she said, and left the rest of her sentence unfinished. Wallander thought she was going to say goodbye, but she had more to say.

"I promised that you would come up to the police academy in early December," she said. "They want you to give a talk on the investigation of last summer. The trainee officers requested it."

Wallander was shocked.

"I can't do that," he said. "I just can't stand up in front of a group of people and pretend I'm teaching. Somebody else can do it. Martinsson's a good speaker. He ought to be a politician."

"I promised you'd come," she said, laughing. "It'll be fine, really."

"I'll call in sick," Wallander said.

"December is a long way off," she said. "We can talk more about this later. I really called to hear how your holiday was. Now I can tell it turned out fine."

"And everything's quiet here," Wallander said. "All we have is a missing person. But my colleagues are handling it."

"A missing person?"

Wallander recounted his conversation with Sven Tyrén.

"How often is it something serious when people go missing?" she asked. "What do the statistics say?"

"I don't know about the statistics," said Wallander. "But I do know that there's very seldom a crime or even an accident involved. When it comes to old or senile people, they may have simply wandered off. With young people there's usually a rebellion against their parents or a longing for adventure behind it. It's rare that anything serious is involved."

They said goodbye and hung up. Wallander was dead set against giving lectures at the police academy. It was flattering that they had asked for him, but his aversion was stronger. He would try to talk Martinsson into taking his place.

He went back to the smuggling operation. Just after 8 a.m. he went to get some more coffee. Since he felt hungry, he also helped himself to a few biscuits. His stomach no longer seemed upset. Martinsson knocked on the door and came in.

"Are you feeling better?"

"I feel fine," Wallander said. "How's it going with Holger Eriksson?"

Martinsson gave him a baffled look.

"Who?"

"Holger Eriksson. The man I wrote a report on, who might be missing? The one I talked to you about?"

Martinsson shook his head.

"When did you tell me? I can't have heard you. I was pretty upset about the ferry accident."

Wallander got up from his chair.

"Is Hansson here yet? We have to get started on this immediately."

"I saw him in the hall," Martinsson said. They went to Hansson's office. He was sitting staring at a lottery ticket. He tore it up and dropped the pieces in his waste-paper basket.

"Holger Eriksson," Wallander said. "The man who may have disappeared. Do you remember the oil truck blocking the driveway here? On Tuesday?"

Hansson nodded.

"The driver, Sven Tyrén," Wallander went on. "You remembered that he'd been mixed up in some assaults?"

"I remember," Hansson said.

Wallander was concealing his impatience with difficulty.

"He came here to report a missing person. I drove out to the farmhouse where Holger Eriksson lives. I wrote a report. Then I called here yesterday morning and asked the rest of you to take on the case. I considered it serious."

"It must be lying around here somewhere," said Martinsson. "I'll take care of it myself."

Wallander knew he couldn't be angry about it.

"Things like this shouldn't happen, you know," he said. "But we can blame it on bad timing. I'll go out to the farm one more time. If he's not there, we'll have to start looking for him. I hope we don't find him dead somewhere, considering we've wasted a whole day already."

"Should we call in a search party?" Martinsson asked.

"Not yet. I'll go there first. But I'll let you know what I find."

Wallander went to his office and looked up the number for O.K. Oil. A girl answered on the first ring. Wallander introduced himself and said he needed to speak to Sven Tyrén.

"He's out on a delivery," the girl said. "But he has a phone in the truck."

Wallander dialled his number. The connection was fuzzy.

"I think you may be right," Wallander said. "Holger Eriksson is missing."

"You're damn right I'm right," Tyrén shot back. "Did it take you this long to work that one out?"

"Is there anything else you wanted to tell me about?" Wallander asked.

"And what would that be?"

"You know better than I do. Does he have any relatives he visits? Does he ever travel? Who knows him best? Anything that might explain where he's gone."

"There isn't any reasonable explanation," Tyrén said. "I already told you that. That's why I went to the police."

Wallander thought for a moment. There was no reason for Sven Tyrén not to tell the truth.

"Where are you?" Wallander asked.

"I'm on the road from Malmö. I was at the terminal filling up."

"I'll drive up to Eriksson's place. Can you stop off there?"

"I'll be there within an hour," Tyrén said. "I have to deliver some oil to a nursing home first. We don't want the old folks to freeze, do we?"

Wallander left the station. It was drizzling again. He felt ill at ease as he drove out of Ystad. If he hadn't been sick, the misunderstanding wouldn't have happened. He was convinced that Tyrén's concern was warranted. He had already sensed it on Tuesday, and now it was Thursday.

By the time he reached the farmhouse the rain was coming down hard. He pulled on the gumboots he kept in the boot of his car. When he opened the letter box he found a newspaper and a few letters. He went into the courtyard and rang the bell, then used the spare keys to open the door. He tried to sense whether anyone else had been there. But everything was just as he had left it. The binocular case in the hall was still empty. The lone sheet of paper lay on the desk.

Wallander went out to the courtyard, and stood pondering an empty kennel. A flock of rooks cawed out in the fields. A dead hare, he thought absently. He got his torch out of the car and began a methodical search of the entire house. Eriksson had kept everything tidy. Wallander stood and admired an old, well-polished Harley-Davidson in part of one wing that served as a garage and workshop. Then he heard a truck coming down the road, and went out to greet Sven Tyrén.

"He's not here," he said.

Wallander took Tyrén to the kitchen and told him that he wanted to take a statement.

"I have nothing more to say," said Tyrén belligerently. "Wouldn't it be better if you started looking for him?"

"People generally know more than they think," said Wallander, not hiding his irritation at Tyrén's attitude.

"So what do you think I know?"

"Did you talk to him yourself when he ordered the oil?"

"He called the office. A girl there writes up the delivery slips. I talk to her several times a day."

"And he sounded normal when he called?"

"You'll have to ask her."

"I will. What's her name?"

"Ruth. Ruth Sturesson."

Wallander wrote this down.

"I stopped here one day in August," said Tyrén. "That was the last time I saw him. He was the same as always. He offered me coffee and read me some new poems. He was a good storyteller too. But in a crude kind of way."

"What do you mean, crude?"

"His stories made me blush is what I mean."

Wallander stared at him. He realised that he was thinking of his father, who liked telling crude stories too.

"You didn't have the feeling he was getting senile?"

"He was as clear-headed as you or I."

"Did Eriksson have any relatives?"

"He never married. He had no children, no girlfriend. Not that I know of, anyway."

"No relatives?"

"He didn't talk about any. He'd decided that an organisation in Lund would inherit all his property."

"What organisation?"

Tyrén shrugged.

"Some home crafts society or something. I don't know."

Wallander thought of Friends of the Axe, but then realised that Holger Eriksson must have decided to bequeath his farm to the Cultural Association in Lund.

"Do you know if he owned other property?"

"Like what?"

"Maybe another farmhouse? A house in town? Or a flat?"

Tyrén thought before he replied.

"No," he said. "There was just this farmhouse. The rest is in the bank. Handelsbanken."

"How do you know that?"

"He paid his bills through Handelsbanken."

Wallander nodded. He folded up his papers. He had no more questions. Now he was convinced that something terrible had happened to Eriksson.

"I'll be in touch," Wallander said, getting to his feet.

"What happens next?"

"The police have their procedures."

They went outside.

"I'd be happy to stay and help you search," Tyrén said.

"I'd rather you didn't," Wallander replied. "We prefer to do this our own way."

Sven Tyrén didn't object. Wallander watched the truck leave. Then he stood at the edge of the fields and gazed towards a grove of trees in the distance. The rooks were still cawing. Wallander pulled his phone from his pocket and called Martinsson at the station.

"How's it going?" Martinsson asked.

"We'll have to start with a complete search," said Wallander. "Hansson has the address. I want to get started as soon as possible. Send a couple of dog units out here."

Wallander was about to hang up when Martinsson stopped him.

"There's one more thing. I checked to see if we had anything on Holger Eriksson. And we do."

Wallander pressed the phone to his ear and moved under a tree to get out of the rain.

"About a year ago he reported that he had a break-in at his house. Is the farm called 'Seclusion'?"

"Yes," Wallander said. "Keep going."

"His report was filed on 19 October 1993. Svedberg took the message. But when I asked him about it, he'd forgotten."

"And?"

"The report was a little strange," said Martinsson hesitantly.

"What do you mean, strange?"

"Nothing was stolen, but he was certain that someone had broken into his house."

"What happened?"

"The whole thing was dismissed. But the report is here. And it was made by Holger Eriksson."

"That's odd," said Wallander. "We'll have to take a closer look at that later. Get those dog units out here as soon as possible."

"Isn't there anything that strikes you about Eriksson's report?" Martinsson asked.

"Such as?"

"It's the second time in a few days that we're discussing break-ins where nothing was stolen."

Martinsson was right. Nothing had been stolen from the florist's shop on Västra Vallgatan either.

"That's where the similarities end," said Wallander.

"The owner of the shop is missing too," said Martinsson.

"No, he isn't," said Wallander. "He's on a trip to Kenya. He hasn't disappeared. But it certainly looks like Holger Eriksson has."

Wallander hung up and pulled his jacket tighter around him, moving back to the garage. Nothing serious could be done until the dog units arrived and they could organise the search and start talking to the neighbours. After a while he went back to the house. In the kitchen he drank a glass of water. The pipes clunked when he turned on the tap, another sign that no-one had been in the house for several days. As he emptied the glass he watched the rooks in the distance. He put down the glass and went back outside.

It was raining steadily. The rooks were cawing. Suddenly Wallander halted. He thought of the empty binocular case hanging on the wall just inside the front door. He looked at the rooks. Just past them, on the hill, was a tower. He stood motionless, trying to think. Then he began walking slowly along the edge of the field. The clay stuck to his gumboots in clumps. He discovered a path leading straight through the field. He could see that it led to the hillock on which the tower stood, a few hundred metres away. He started to walk along the path. The rooks were diving down, vanishing, and then flying up again. There must be a hollow or a ditch there. The tower grew clearer. He guessed that it was used for hunting hares or deer. Below the hill on the opposite side was a patch of woods, probably also part of Eriksson's property. Then he saw the ditch in front of him. Some rough planks seemed to have fallen into it. As he came closer, the rooks got louder, then they rose up and flew off. Wallander looked down into the ditch.

He gave a start and took a step back. Instantly he felt sick. Later he would say that it was one of the worst things he had ever seen. And in his years as a policeman he'd encountered plenty of things he would have preferred not to see. As he stood there with the rain soaking him to the skin, he couldn't tell at first what he was looking at. Something alien and unreal lay in front of him. Something he could never have imagined. The only thing that was completely clear was that there was a dead body in the ditch.

He squatted down, forcing himself not to look away. The ditch was at least two metres deep. A number of sharp stakes were fixed in the bottom of it. On these stakes hung a man. The spearlike tips of the stakes had pierced the body in several places. The man lay prostrate, suspended on them. The rooks had attacked the back of his neck. Wallander stood up, his knees shaking. Somewhere in the distance he could hear cars approaching.

He looked down again. The stakes seemed to be made of bamboo, like thick fishing rods, with their tips sharpened to points. He looked at the planks that had fallen into the ditch. Since the path continued on the other side, they must have served as a bridge. Why did they break? They were thick boards that should withstand a heavy load, and the ditch was no more than two metres wide.

When he heard a dog barking he turned and walked back to the farmhouse. Now he really felt sick. And he was scared too. It was one thing to discover someone murdered. But the way this had been done . . .

Someone had planted sharpened bamboo stakes in the ditch. To impale a man. He stopped on the path to catch his breath. Images from the summer raced through his mind. Was it starting all over again? Were there no limits to what could happen in this country?

He kept walking. Two officers with dogs were waiting outside the house. He could see Höglund and Hansson there too. When he reached the end of the path and walked into the courtyard, they could see at once that something had happened.

Wallander wiped the rain off his face and told them. He knew that his voice was unsteady. He turned and pointed down towards the flock of rooks, which had returned as soon as he left the ditch.

"He's lying down there," he said. "He's dead. It's a murder. Get a full team out here."

They waited for him to say something else, but he didn't have anything to say.

CHAPTER 6

By nightfall on Thursday, 29 September, the police had put a canopy over the ditch where the body of Holger Eriksson hung impaled on nine solid bamboo poles. They had shovelled out the mud and blood at the bottom of the ditch. The macabre work and the relentless rain made the murder scene one of the most depressing and disgusting Wallander and his colleagues had ever witnessed. The clay stuck to their gumboots, they tripped over electrical cables winding through the mud, and the harsh light from the floodlights they had rigged up intensified the surreal impression. Sven Tyrén had come back and identified the man impaled on the stakes. It was Eriksson, all right, Tyrén told them. No doubt about it. The search for the missing man had ended even before it had begun. Tyrén remained unusually composed, as though not fully comprehending what he saw before him. He paced restlessly outside the cordon for several hours without saying a word, and then suddenly he was gone.

Down in the ditch Wallander felt like a rat drowning in a trap. His colleagues were having a hard time. Both Svedberg and Hansson had left the ditch several times because of acute nausea. But Höglund, the person he most wanted to send home early, appeared unperturbed.

Chief Holgersson had come out as soon as the discovery had been reported. She organised the murder scene so that people wouldn't slip and fall on top of each other, but a young police trainee stumbled in the clay and fell into the ditch, injuring his hand on one of the stakes. The wound was patched up by a doctor who was trying to work out how to remove the corpse. Wallander happened to see the trainee slip and got a glimpse of what must have happened when Eriksson fell.

Almost the first thing he had done with Nyberg, their forensic technician, was examine the rough planks. Tyrén had confirmed that they had formed a bridge. Eriksson had placed them there. He told them that he'd once been invited to the tower. Eriksson had been a passionate birdwatcher. It wasn't a hunting tower, but a viewing tower. The missing binoculars were hanging around Eriksson's neck. It took Nyberg only a few minutes to determine that the planks had been sawed through. After hearing this, Wallander climbed up out of the ditch and went off to think. He tried to assemble the sequence of events. When Nyberg discovered that the binoculars had night vision, he began to have some idea. At the same time he found it difficult to accept his interpretation. If he was right, then they were dealing with a murder that had been planned and prepared with such ghastly and cruel perfection as to be almost unbelievable.

Late in the evening they started removing Eriksson's corpse from the ditch. Along with the doctor and Chief Holgersson, they had to decide whether to dig out the bamboo poles, saw them off, or choose the gruesome option of hoisting the body free from the stakes. On Wallander's recommendation they chose the last option. They needed to see the murder scene exactly as it was before Eriksson stepped on the planks and fell to his death. Wallander felt compelled to take part in this grisly final act as Eriksson was lifted upwards and then taken away. It was past midnight when they finished; the rain had eased but showed no sign of stopping, and all that could be heard was a generator and the sound of gumboots squelching through the mud.

There was a momentary lull. Somebody had brought coffee. Weary faces glowed eerily in the white light. Wallander thought he ought to formulate an overview. What had actually happened? How were they going to proceed? Everyone was exhausted now, anxious, soaking wet, and hungry.

Martinsson stood with a phone pressed to his ear. Wallander wondered if he was talking to his wife, who often worried about him. But when he hung up he told them that a meteorologist had forecast that the rain would stop during the night. Wallander decided that the best thing to do was wait until dawn. They hadn't yet begun to hunt for the killer; they were still looking for leads to give them a starting point. The dog units hadn't picked up any scents. Wallander and Nyberg had been up in the tower but had found no clues. Wallander turned to Chief Holgersson.

"We're getting nowhere," he said. "I suggest we meet again at dawn. The best thing we can do now is rest."

No-one had any objection. They all wanted to go home. All except Sven Nyberg, of course. Wallander knew he'd want to stay. He'd keep at it through the night, and he'd be there when they returned. As the others started to head up towards the cars by the farmhouse, Wallander hung back.

"What do you think?" he asked.

"I don't think anything," Nyberg said. "Except that I've never in my life seen anything remotely like this."

They stood looking into the ditch. Plastic sheeting had been spread across it.

“What exactly are we looking at?” asked Wallander.

“A copy of an Asian trap for large predators,” Nyberg said, “which is also used in wars. They call them pungee stakes.”

Wallander nodded.

“Bamboo doesn’t grow this thick in Sweden,” Nyberg went on. “We import it to use for fishing rods and furniture.”

“Besides, there aren’t any large predators in Skåne,” Wallander said thoughtfully. “And we’re not at war. So what exactly are we looking at?”

“Something that doesn’t belong here,” Nyberg said. “Something that doesn’t fit. Something that gives me the creeps.”

Wallander watched him attentively. Nyberg was seldom this loquacious. His expression of both personal revulsion and fear was entirely out of character.

“Don’t work too late,” Wallander said as he left, but there was no answer.

Wallander climbed over the barricade, nodded to the officers who would be guarding the scene of the crime overnight, and continued up to the farmhouse. Lisa Holgersson had stopped halfway up the path to wait for him. She had a torch in her hand.

“We’ve got reporters up there,” she said. “What are we going to tell them?”

“Not much,” Wallander said.

“We can’t even give them Eriksson’s name?” she said.

Wallander pondered this before he replied.

“I think we can. I’ll assume that the oil-truck driver knows what he’s talking about. He told me Eriksson had no relatives. If we don’t have anyone to inform of his death, we might as well release his name. It might help us.”

They continued walking. Behind them the floodlights cast an eerie glow.

"Can we say anything else?" she asked.

"Tell them it's a murder," Wallander replied. "That's one thing we can say with certainty. But we have no motive and no leads to a suspect."

"Have you formed any opinion on that yet?"

Wallander could feel how tired he was. Every thought, every word he had to say, seemed to take huge effort.

"I didn't see any more than you did, but it was very well planned. Eriksson walked into a trap that slammed shut. That means there are at least three conclusions we can easily draw."

They stopped again.

"First, we can assume that whoever did it knew Eriksson and at least some of his habits," Wallander began. "Second, the killer intended him to die."

Wallander turned and was about to start walking again.

"You said three things."

He looked at her pale face in the light from the torch. He wondered vaguely how he looked himself. Had the rain washed away his Italian tan?

"The killer didn't just want to take Eriksson's life," he said. "He wanted him to suffer. Eriksson may have hung on those stakes for a long time before he died. No-one heard him but the crows. Maybe the doctors can tell us how long he stayed alive."

Chief Holgersson grimaced.

"Who would do something like this?"

"I don't know," said Wallander.

When they reached the edge of the field, two reporters and a photographer were waiting for them. Wallander knew them all from previous cases. He glanced at Chief

Holgersson, who shook her head. Wallander told them as briefly as he could what had happened. They wanted to ask questions, but he held up his hand in dismissal, and the reporters left.

"You're a detective with a good reputation," said the chief. "Last summer you demonstrated how talented you are. There isn't a police district in Sweden that wouldn't be glad to have you."

They had stopped by her car. Wallander could tell that she meant everything she said, but he was too tired to take it in.

"Set up this investigation as you see fit. Tell me what you need and I'll see that you get it."

Wallander nodded.

"We'll know more in a few hours. Right now we both need to get some sleep."

It was almost 2 a.m. when Wallander arrived home. He made a couple of sandwiches and ate them at the kitchen table. Then he set his alarm clock for just after 5 a.m. and lay down on top of his bed.

They gathered once more in the grey dawn. The rain had stopped, but the wind was blowing again, and it had turned colder. Nyberg and the officers who stayed at the scene overnight had been forced to rig up temporary fixtures to keep the plastic sheeting in place. Nyberg and the other forensic technicians were now working down in the ditch, exposed to the biting wind.

On his way there, Wallander had been turning over in his mind how best to run the investigation. They knew nothing about Eriksson. The fact that he was wealthy could be a motive, but this seemed unlikely. The stakes in the ditch spoke another language. He couldn't interpret it and didn't know in which direction it led.

As usual when he felt unsure, he thought of Rydberg, the old detective who had been his mentor and without whose wisdom, he suspected, he would have been a mediocre criminal investigator. Rydberg had died of cancer almost four years ago. Wallander shuddered when he thought how quickly time had passed. He asked himself what Rydberg would have done.

Patience, he thought. Rydberg would have told me that now the rule about being patient was more important than ever.

They set up temporary headquarters in Eriksson's house. Wallander listed the most important tasks and assigned them as efficiently as possible. Next he attempted the impossible task of summarising the situation, but found that he actually had only one thing to say: that they had nothing to go on.

"We know very little," he began. "An oil-truck driver named Sven Tyrén reported what he suspected was a disappearance on Tuesday. Based on what Tyrén has said, and taking into account the date on the poem, we can assume that the murder took place sometime after 10 p.m. last Wednesday night. Exactly when, we can't say. But it didn't happen any earlier. We'll have to wait to see what the pathologist can tell us."

Wallander paused. No-one had any questions. Svedberg sniffled. His eyes were glassy and feverish and he should be home in bed, but they both knew that right now they needed all available manpower.

"We don't know much about Holger Eriksson," Wallander went on. "A former car dealer. Wealthy, unmarried, no children. He was a poet and also clearly interested in birds."

"We do know a little more than that," Hansson interrupted. "Eriksson was quite well known in this area, particularly a decade or two ago. You might say he had a reputation for being a horse trader with cars. A tough negotiator. Didn't tolerate the unions. Made money hand over fist. He was mixed up in tax disputes and suspected of certain illegalities, but was never caught, if I remember correctly."

"So he may have had enemies," Wallander said.

"It's probably safe to assume so, but that doesn't mean they'd be prepared to commit murder. Especially not the way this one was done."

Wallander decided to wait to discuss the sharpened bamboo stakes and the bridge. He wanted to take things in order, to keep everything straight in his own mind. This was something else Rydberg had often reminded him of. A criminal investigation is like a construction site. Everything has to be done in the proper order or the building won't hold up.

"Mapping out Eriksson's life is the first thing we have to do," Wallander said. "But before we start I want to try and give you my impression of the chronology of the crime."

They were sitting at the big kitchen table. In the distance they could see the crime-scene tape and the white plastic canopy flapping in the wind. Nyberg stood like a yellow-clad scarecrow in the mud. Wallander could imagine his weary, irritated voice. But he knew that Nyberg was talented and meticulous. If he waved his arms about he had a reason for it.

Wallander felt his attention begin to sharpen. He had done this many times before, and he could sense that at this moment the investigative team was starting to track the murderer.

"I think it happened like this," Wallander began, speaking slowly. "Sometime after ten o'clock on Wednesday night, or maybe early Thursday morning, Holger Eriksson leaves his house. He doesn't lock the door because he intends to return soon. He takes a pair of night-vision binoculars with him. He walks down the path towards the ditch, over which he has laid a bridge. He's probably on his way to the tower. He's interested in birds. In September and October, the migratory birds head south. I don't know much about it, but I've heard that most of them take off and navigate at night. This would explain the late hour. He steps onto the bridge, which breaks in two because the planks have been sawed almost all the way through. He falls into the ditch and is impaled on the stakes. That's where he dies. If he called for help, there was no-one to hear him. The farm isn't named 'Seclusion' for nothing."

He poured some coffee from a thermos before he continued.

"That's how I think it happened," he said. "We end up with considerably more questions than answers. But it's where we have to start. We're dealing with a well-planned murder. Cruel and grisly. We have no obvious or even conceivable motive and no leads."

They were all silent. Wallander let his gaze travel around the table. Finally Höglund broke the silence.

"One more thing is important. Whoever did this had no intention of concealing his actions."

Wallander had planned to come to that very point.

"I think there's a chance it's even more than that," he said. "If we look at this ghastly trap we can interpret it as a kind of statement."

"Do you think we're searching for a madman?" Svedberg asked.

Everyone around the table knew what he meant. The events of the past summer were still raw in their memories.

"We can't rule out that possibility," Wallander said. "In fact, we can't rule out anything at all."

"It's like a bear trap," Hansson said. "Or something you'd see in an old war movie set in Asia. A peculiar combination: a bear trap and a bird-watcher."

"Or a car dealer," Martinsson added.

"Or a poet," Höglund said. "We have plenty of choices."

Wallander ended the meeting. They would use Eriksson's kitchen whenever they had to meet. Svedberg drove off to talk to Sven Tyrén and the girl at the oil company who'd taken Eriksson's order. Höglund would see to it that all the neighbours in the area were contacted and interviewed. Wallander remembered the letters and asked her to talk to the rural postman too. Hansson would go over the house with some of Nyberg's forensic technicians, while Chief Holgersson and Martinsson would work together to organise the other tasks.

The investigative wheel had started to turn.

Wallander put on his jacket and walked down to the ditch. Ragged clouds chased across the sky. He bent into the wind. Suddenly he heard the distinctive sound of geese. He stopped and looked up at the sky. It took a moment before he saw the birds, a small group high up, just below the clouds, heading southwest. He guessed that, like all other migratory birds crossing Skåne, they would leave Sweden over Falsterbo Point.

Wallander stood there, watching the geese, thinking of the poem lying on the desk. Then he walked on, his unease increasing steadily.

There was something in this brutal killing that shook

him to the core. It could be an act of blind hatred or insanity, but cold calculation lay behind the murder. He couldn't decide which scared him more.

Nyberg and his forensic technicians had begun lifting the bloody stakes from the clay. Each pole was wrapped in plastic and carried to a waiting car. Nyberg had spots of clay on his face and worked with abrupt, angry movements. Wallander felt as though he was looking down into a grave.

"How's it going?" he asked, trying to sound encouraging.

Nyberg muttered something unintelligible. Wallander decided to save his questions. Nyberg was irascible and moody and thought nothing of starting a quarrel with anyone. The general opinion at the station was that Nyberg wouldn't hesitate to yell at the national police commissioner at the slightest provocation.

The police had built a makeshift bridge across the ditch. Wallander walked up the hill on the other side, gusts of wind tearing at his jacket. He studied the tower, which stood about three metres high. It was built of the same wood that Eriksson had used for his bridge. A stepladder was leaning against the tower, and Wallander climbed up. The platform was no bigger than one square metre. The wind whipped at his face. From only three metres up, the appearance of the landscape was quite changed. He could see Nyberg in the ditch. In the distance he saw Eriksson's farmhouse. He squatted down and began studying the platform. Suddenly he regretted setting foot in the tower before Nyberg had finished his examinations. He climbed down again and tried to find a place out of the wind in the lee of the tower. He felt very tired, but something else was troubling him even more. He tried to pin down the feeling. Depression? His happiness had been so short-lived – the holiday, the decision to buy a house, and even get a dog. And Baiba's visit to look forward to.

But then an old man was discovered impaled in a ditch, and once again his world had started crumbling away beneath his feet. He wondered how long he could keep this up.

He forced himself to fend off these thoughts. They had to find whoever had set this macabre death trap for Eriksson as soon as possible. Wallander trudged back down the hill. In the distance he could see Martinsson coming along the path, in a hurry as usual. Wallander went to meet him. He still felt tentative and uncertain. How was he going to approach the investigation? He was searching for a way in.

Then he saw from Martinsson's face that something had happened.

"What is it?" he asked.

"You're to call someone named Vanja Andersson."

Wallander had to search his memory before he remembered. The florist's shop on Västra Vallgatan.

"Damn it, we don't have time for that now."

"I'm not so sure," Martinsson said.

"Why?"

"It seems that the owner, Gösta Runfeldt, never left for Nairobi."

Wallander didn't understand what Martinsson was saying.

"His assistant called the travel agency to find out the exact arrival time of his flight. That's when she found out."

"Found out what?"

"That Runfeldt never flew to Africa, even though he had picked up his ticket."

Wallander stared him.

"So another person seems to have disappeared," said Martinsson.

Wallander didn't answer.

CHAPTER 7

On the way in to Ystad, after he had decided to visit Vanja Andersson himself, Wallander remembered something someone had said earlier, that there was another similarity between the two cases. Eriksson had reported a break-in a year before, and nothing had been stolen. There had been a break-in at Gösta Runfeldt's shop in which nothing seemed to have been taken. Wallander drove with a growing sense of dread.

Eriksson's murder was enough for them to deal with. They didn't need another disappearance, especially not one that might have a connection to Eriksson's. They didn't need any more ditches with sharpened stakes in them. Wallander was driving much too fast, as if trying to leave behind him the realisation that once again he was plunging into a nightmare. Now and then he stamped hard on the brake, as if to give the car and not himself an order to take it easy and start thinking rationally. What evidence was there that Runfeldt was missing? There might be some reasonable explanation. What had happened to Eriksson was extraordinary, after all, and it certainly wouldn't happen twice. At least not in Skåne and definitely not in Ystad. There had to be an explanation, and Vanja Andersson would provide it.

Wallander never succeeded in convincing himself. Before he drove to Västra Vallgatan he stopped at the police station. He found Höglund in the hall and pulled her into the canteen, where some traffic officers were sitting half-asleep over their lunches. They got some coffee and sat down. Wallander told her Martinsson's news, and her reaction matched his own. It had to be coincidence. But Wallander asked Höglund to find a copy of the burglary report Eriksson had filed the year before. He also wanted her to check if there was any connection between Eriksson and Runfeldt. He knew she had plenty to do, but it was important that this be taken care of immediately. It was a matter of cleaning up before the guests arrived, he said, instantly regretting having used such a clumsy metaphor.

"We must hurry," he went on. "The less energy we have to spend on searching for a connection, the better."

He was about to get up from the table, but she stopped him with a question.

"Who could have done it?" she asked.

Wallander sank back into his chair. He could picture the bloody stakes, an unbearable sight.

"I can't imagine," he said. "It's so sadistic and macabre that I can't accept a normal motive – if there is such a thing for taking someone's life."

"There is," she replied firmly. "Both you and I have felt enough rage to imagine someone dead. For some people, the usual barriers don't exist, so they kill."

"What scares me is that it was so well planned. Whoever did this took his time. He also knew Eriksson's habits in detail. He probably stalked him."

"Maybe that gives us an opening right there," she said. "Eriksson didn't seem to have any close friends, but the person who killed him must have had some proximity to him. He sawed through the planks. In any case, he must have come there and he must have left. Somebody might have seen him, or maybe a car that didn't belong out there. People keep an eye on what happens around them. People in villages are like deer in the forest. They watch us, but we don't notice them."

Wallander nodded distractedly. He wasn't listening with as much concentration as usual.

"We'll have to talk more about this later," he said. "I'm going to the florist's shop now."

As Wallander left the station, Ebba called out to him that his father had rung.

"Later," Wallander said, "not now."

"It's terrible what happened," Ebba said. Wallander thought she sounded as if she felt personally sorry for some sorrow he had suffered.

"I bought a car from him once," she said. "A second-hand Volvo."

It took Wallander a moment before he realised that she was talking about Holger Eriksson.

"Do you drive?" he asked, surprised. "I didn't even know you had a licence."

"I've had a flawless record for 39 years," Ebba replied. "And I still have that Volvo."

Wallander recalled occasionally seeing a well-kept black Volvo in the police car park over the years, without ever wondering whose it was.

"I hope you got a good deal," he said.

"Eriksson got a good deal,"' she replied firmly. "I paid far too much for that car, but I've taken care of it for all this time, and I'm the one who's come out ahead. It's a collector's item now."

"I've got to go," Wallander said. "But sometime you'll have to take me for a ride in it."

"Don't forget to call your father."

Wallander stopped in his tracks and thought a moment. Then he decided.

"You call him, would you? Do me a favour. Call him and explain what I'm involved with. Tell him I'll call as soon as I can. I presume it wasn't anything urgent, right?"

"He wanted to talk about Italy," she said.

"We'll talk about Italy, but right now I can't. Tell him that."

Wallander parked hastily, half up on the narrow footpath outside the florist's. There were a few customers inside. He gestured to Vanja Andersson that he would wait. Ten minutes later the shop emptied out, and Vanja Andersson printed a note, taped it to the inside of the door, and locked up. They went into the tiny office at the back. The scent of flowers made Wallander queasy. As usual, he had nothing to write on, so he picked up a stack of gift cards and started making notes on the back.

"Let's take it from the beginning," Wallander said. "You called the travel agency. Why did you do that?"

He could see that she was upset. A copy of the local newspaper, *Ystad's Allehanda*, was lying on the table, with a big headline about the murder of Holger Eriksson. At least she doesn't know why I'm here, Wallander thought. That I'm hoping there won't be a connection between Eriksson and Gösta Runfeldt.

"Gösta wrote me a note saying when he would be coming back," she began. "I couldn't find it anywhere. So I called the travel agency. They told me he hadn't shown up at Kastrup Airport."

"What's the name of the travel agency?"

"Special Tours in Malmö."

"Who did you talk to there?"

"Anita Lagergren."

Wallander made a note.

"When did you call?"

She told him.

"And what else did she say?"

"Gösta never left. He didn't check in at Kastrup. They called the phone number he'd given them, but nobody answered. The plane had to leave without him."

"And they didn't do anything else after that?"

"Anita Lagergren said that they sent a letter explaining that Gösta could not expect a refund for any of the travel costs."

Wallander could tell she was about to say something else, but she stopped herself.

"You were thinking of something," he coaxed.

"The trip was extremely expensive," she said. "Anita Lagergren told me the price."

"How much was it?"

"Almost 30,000 kronor. For two weeks."

Wallander agreed. The trip really was quite expensive. Never in his life would he consider taking such an expensive trip. He and his father together had spent about a third of that amount for their week in Rome.

"I don't get it," she said. "Gösta just wouldn't do anything like this."

"How long have you worked for him?"

"Nearly eleven years."

"And things have gone well?"

"Gösta is a very nice man. He truly loves flowers. Not just orchids."

"We'll come back to that later. How would you describe him?"

She thought for a moment.

"Considerate and friendly," she said. "A little eccentric.

A recluse." Wallander thought uneasily that this description might also fit Holger Eriksson. Although it had been suggested that Eriksson wasn't a very considerate person.

"He wasn't married?"

"He was a widower."

"Did he have children?"

"Two. Both of them are married and have their own children. Neither of them lives in Skåne."

"How old is he?"

"He is 49."

Wallander looked at his notes.

"A widower," he said. "So his wife must have been quite young when she died. Was it an accident?"

"I'm not sure. He never talked about it. But I think she drowned."

Wallander dropped the line of questioning. They would go over it all in detail soon enough, if it proved necessary. He put his pen down on the table. The scent of flowers was overwhelming.

"You must have thought about this," he said. "You must have wondered about two things in the past few hours. First, why he didn't get on the plane to Africa. Second, where he is now instead of in Nairobi."

She nodded. Wallander saw that she had tears in her eyes.

"Something must have happened," she said. "As soon as I talked to the travel agency I went over to his flat. It's right down the street, and I have a key. I was supposed to water his flowers. After I thought he'd left on his trip I was there twice, and put his post on the table. Now I went back. He wasn't there, and he hasn't been there, either."

"How do you know?"

"I can tell."

"So what do you think happened?"

"I have no idea. He was looking forward to this trip so much. He was planning to finish writing his book about orchids this winter."

Wallander could feel his own anxiety increasing. A warning bell had started ringing inside him. He recognised the silent alarm. He gathered up the cards he had used for his notes.

"I'll have to take a look at his flat," he said. "And you need to open the shop again. I'm sure all of this has a reasonable explanation."

She sought assurance in his eyes that he really meant what he said. But Wallander knew she wouldn't find it. He took the keys to the flat. It was on the same street, one block closer to the centre of town.

"I'll drop the keys off when I'm done," he said.

When he came out onto the narrow street, an elderly couple was trying with difficulty to squeeze past his parked car. They gave him an imploring look. But he ignored them and walked away.

The flat was on the third floor of a building that dated from around the turn of the century. There was a lift, but Wallander took the stairs. Several years ago he had considered exchanging his own flat for one in a building like this. Now he couldn't imagine what he had been thinking of. If he sold the flat on Mariagatan, it would have to be for a house with a garden. Where Baiba could live. And maybe a dog too.

He unlocked the door and entered Runfeldt's flat. He wondered how many times in his life he had walked into a stranger's home. He stopped just inside the door. Every flat had its own character. Over the years Wallander had perfected his habit of listening for traces of the occupants. He walked slowly through the rooms. Often it was the first impression that he would return to later. Gösta Runfeldt lived here, a man who had failed to show up where he was expected one morning. Wallander thought about what Vanja Andersson had said. About Runfeldt's eager excitement at his expedition.

After going through all four rooms and the kitchen, Wallander stopped in the middle of the living room. It was a large, bright flat. He had a vague feeling that it was furnished with some indifference. The only room that had any personality was the study. A comfortable chaos prevailed there. Books, papers, lithographs of flowers, maps. A desk piled with clutter. A computer. A few photographs of children and grandchildren on a windowsill. A photograph of Runfeldt somewhere in an Asian landscape, surrounded by giant orchids. On the back someone had written that it was taken in Burma in 1972. Runfeldt was smiling at the unknown photographer, a friendly smile from a sun-tanned man. The colours had faded, but not Runfeldt's smile. Wallander put it back and looked at a map of the world hanging on the wall. With a little effort he located Burma. Then he sat down at the desk. Runfeldt was supposed to leave on a trip, but he hadn't left. At least not for Nairobi on the Special Travels charter flight.

Wallander got up and went into the bedroom. The bed was made, a narrow, single bed. There was a stack of books next to the bed. Wallander looked at the titles. Books about flowers. The only one that stood out was a book about the international currency market. Wallander bent down and looked under the bed. Nothing. He opened the doors to the wardrobe. On a shelf at the top of the wardrobe lay two suitcases. He stood on tiptoe and lifted them down. Both were empty. Then he went to the kitchen and got a chair. He looked at the top shelf. Now he found what he was looking for. A single man's flat is seldom completely free of dust. Runfeldt's was no exception. The outline in the dust was quite clear. A third suitcase had been there. Because the other two he had taken down were old, and one of them even had a broken lock, Wallander imagined that Runfeldt would have used the third suitcase. If he had gone on the trip. If it wasn't somewhere else in the flat. He hung his jacket over the back of a chair and opened all the cupboards and storage spaces. He found nothing. Then he returned to the study.

If Runfeldt had left on the trip, he would have had to take his passport with him. Wallander searched through the desk drawers, which weren't locked. In one of them was an old herbarium. He opened it. *Gösta Runfeldt 1955.* Even during his school days he had pressed flowers. Wallander looked at a 40-year-old cornflower. The blue colour was still present, or a pale memory of it. He had pressed flowers himself once. He kept on searching. He couldn't find a passport. He frowned. A suitcase was gone, and the passport too. He hadn't found the tickets, either. He left the study and sat down in an armchair in the living room. Sometimes changing places helped him to think. There were plenty of signs that Runfeldt had actually left his flat with his passport, tickets, and a packed suitcase.

He let his mind wander. Could something have happened on the way to Copenhagen? Could he have fallen into the sea from one of the ferries? If that had happened then his suitcase would have been found. He pulled out one of the gift cards he had in his pocket. He had written the phone number of the shop on it. He went to the kitchen to make the call. Through the window he could see the tall grain lift in Ystad harbour. One of the ferries to Poland was on its way out past the stone jetty. Vanja Andersson answered the phone.

"I'm still at the flat," he said. "I've got a couple of questions. Did he tell you how he was travelling to Copenhagen?"

Her reply was precise.

"He always went via Limhamn and Dragør."

So now he knew that much.

"Do you know how many suitcases he owned?"

"No. How should I know that?"

Wallander saw that he must ask the question in a different way.

"What did his suitcase look like?"

"He didn't usually take a lot of luggage," she replied. "He knew how to travel light. He had a shoulder bag and a larger suitcase with wheels."

"What colour was it?"

"It was black."

"Are you sure about that?"

"Yes, I am. I'm sure. I picked him up a few times after his trips. At the train station or at Sturup Airport. Gösta never threw anything away. If he'd had to buy a new suitcase I would have known about it, because he would have complained about how expensive it was. He could be stingy sometimes."

But the trip to Nairobi cost 30,000 kronor, Wallander thought. And that money was just thrown away. I'm sure it wasn't voluntarily. He told her he'd drop off the keys within half an hour.

After he hung up he thought about what she had said. A black suitcase. The two he had found in the wardrobe were grey. He hadn't seen a shoulder bag either. Besides, now he knew that Runfeldt travelled out into the world via Limhamn. He stood by the window and looked over the rooftops. The Poland ferry was gone.

It doesn't make sense, he thought. There may have been an accident. But even that wasn't certain. To follow up on one of the most important questions, he called information and asked for the number of the ferry line between Limhamn and Dragør. He was lucky and got the person who was responsible for lost property on the ferries. The man was Danish. Wallander told him who he was and asked about a black suitcase. He told him the date. Then he waited. It took a few minutes before the Dane, who had introduced himself as Mogensen, came back.

"Nothing," he said.

Wallander tried to think. Then he asked his question.

"Do people ever disappear from your boats? Fall overboard?"

"Hardly ever," Mogensen replied. Wallander thought he sounded convincing.

"But it does happen?"

"It happens in all boat traffic," said Mogensen. "People commit suicide. People get drunk. Some are mad and try to balance on the railing. But it doesn't happen often."

"Are people who fall overboard usually recovered? Either drowned or alive?"

"Most of them float ashore, dead," Mogensen answered. "Some get caught in fishing nets. Only a few disappear completely."

Wallander had no more questions. He thanked the man for his help and said goodbye.

He had nothing tangible to go on, and yet now he was convinced that Runfeldt had never gone to Copenhagen.

He had packed his bag, taken his passport and ticket, and left his flat. Then he had disappeared.

Wallander thought about the puddle of blood inside the florist's shop. What did that mean? Maybe they had it all wrong. It might well be that the break-in was no mistake.

He paced around the flat, trying to understand. The telephone in the kitchen rang, making him jump. He hurried over to answer it. It was Hansson, calling from Eriksson's.

"I heard from Martinsson that Runfeldt has disappeared," he said.

"He's not here, at any rate," Wallander answered.

"You have any ideas?"

"No. I think he did intend to take his trip, but something prevented him."

"You think there's a connection?"

Wallander thought about it. What did he actually believe? He didn't know.

"We can't rule out the possibility," was all he said.

He asked what had happened out at the farm, but Hansson had nothing new to report. After he hung up, Wallander walked through the flat once more. He had a feeling that there was something he should be noticing. Finally he gave up. He looked through the post out in the hall. There was the letter from the travel agency. An electricity bill. There was also a receipt for a parcel from a mail-order company in Borås. It had to be paid for at the post office. Wallander stuck the slip in his pocket.

Vanja Andersson was waiting for him when he arrived with the keys. He asked her to get in touch with him if she thought of anything else that might be important. Then he drove to the station. He left the slip with Ebba and asked her to have someone pick up the parcel. At 1 p.m. he closed the door to his office. He was hungry. But he was more anxious than hungry. He recognised the feeling. He knew what it meant.

He doubted that they would find Gösta Runfeldt alive.

CHAPTER 8

At midnight, Ylva Brink finally sat down to have a cup of coffee. She was one of two midwives working the night of 30 September in the maternity ward of Ystad's hospital. Her colleague, Lena Söderström, was with a woman who had just started to have contractions. It had been a busy night – without drama, but with a steady stream of tasks that had to be carried out.

They were understaffed. Two midwives and two nurses had to handle all the work. There was an obstetrician they could call if there was serious haemorrhaging or any other complication, but otherwise they were on their own. It used to be worse, thought Ylva Brink as she sat down on the sofa with her coffee. A few years ago she had been the only midwife on duty all night long, and sometimes this had resulted in difficulties. They had finally managed to talk some sense into the hospital administration and push through their demand to have at least two midwives on every night.

Her office was in the middle of a large ward. The glass walls allowed her to see what was going on outside. In the daytime there was constant activity, but at night, everything was different. She liked working nights. A lot of her colleagues preferred other shifts. They had families, and they couldn't get enough sleep during the day. But Ylva Brink's children were grown up, and her husband was chief engineer on an oil tanker that sailed between ports in the Middle East and Asia. For her it was peaceful to work while everyone else was asleep.

She drank her coffee with pleasure and took a piece of sugar cake from a tray on her desk. One of the nurses came in and sat down, and then the other one joined them. A radio was playing softly in the corner. They talked about autumn and the persistent rain. One of the nurses had heard from her mother, who could predict the weather, that it was going to be a long, cold winter.

Ylva Brink thought back on the times when Skåne had been snowed in. It didn't happen often, but when it did, it was terrible for women who were in labour but couldn't get to the hospital. She remembered sitting freezing in a tractor as it crept along through the blizzard and snowdrifts to an isolated farm north of town. The woman was haemorrhaging. It was the only time in her years as a midwife that she had been seriously afraid of losing a patient. And that couldn't be allowed to happen. Women simply did not die giving birth in Sweden.

But still, it was autumn now. Ylva came from the far north of Sweden, and sometimes missed the melancholy Norrland forests. She had never got used to the open landscape of Skåne where the wind reigned supreme. But her husband had been born in Trelleborg and couldn't imagine living anywhere but in Skåne. When he had time at home, that is.

Her musings were interrupted when Lena Söderström came into the room. She was about 30. She could be my daughter, Ylva thought. I'm twice her age.

"She probably won't deliver before early morning," Lena said. "We'll get to go home."

"It'll be quiet tonight," said Ylva. "Take a nap if you're tired."

A nurse hurried by in the hall. Lena Söderström was drinking her tea. The other two nurses sat bent over a crossword puzzle.

Already October, Ylva thought. The middle of autumn already. Soon winter will be here. In December Harry has a holiday, a month off, and we'll remodel the kitchen. Not because it needs it, but so he can have something to do. Harry's not wild about holidays. He gets restless.

Someone had pressed a call button. A nurse got up and left. A few minutes later she came back.

"Maria in Room 3 has a headache," she said, sitting back down to her crossword puzzle. Ylva sipped her coffee. Suddenly she realised that she was sitting wondering about something, without knowing exactly what it was. Then it came to her. The nurse who had walked past in the hall. Hadn't all the women working in the ward been here in the office? And no call bells had rung from intensive care. She must have been imagining things.

But at the same time she knew she hadn't been.

"Who just walked by?" she asked softly.

The two nurses gave her curious looks.

"What's that?" Lena Söderström asked.

"A nurse walked down the hall a few minutes ago. While we were sitting here."

They still couldn't understand what she was talking about. She didn't understand it herself. Another bell rang. Ylva quickly set down her cup.

"I'll get it."

The woman in Room 2 was feeling bad. She was about to have her third child. Ylva suspected that the child hadn't exactly been planned. After she had given the woman something to drink she went out into the hall. She looked around. All the doors were closed. But a nurse had walked past. She hadn't imagined it, and suddenly she felt uneasy. Something wasn't quite right. She stood still in the hall and listened. The muted radio could be heard in the office. She went back and picked up her coffee cup.

"It was nothing," she said.

At that instant the nurse she had seen earlier went by in the other direction. This time Lena saw her too. They both gave a start as they heard the door to the main hall close.

"Who was that?" asked Lena.

Ylva shook her head. The nurses looked up from their puzzle.

"Who are you talking about?" one of them asked.

"The nurse who just walked past."

The one sitting with a pen in her hand, filling in the crossword, started to laugh.

"But we're right here, both of us."

Ylva got up quickly. When she pulled open the door to the outer hall, which connected the maternity ward to the rest of the hospital, it was empty. She listened, and far off she heard a door close. She went back to the nurses' station, shaking her head.

"What's a nurse from another ward doing here?" Lena asked. "Without even saying hello?"

Ylva didn't know, but she knew it hadn't been her imagination.

"Let's take a look in all the rooms," she said, "and see if everything's all right."

Lena gave her a searching look.

"What could be wrong?"

"Just for safety's sake, that's all."

They went into all the rooms. Everything seemed normal. At 1 a.m. a woman started bleeding. The rest of the night was taken up with work.

At 7 a.m., after briefing the day shift, Ylva Brink went home. She lived in a house right near the hospital. When she got home she started thinking again about the strange nurse she had seen in the hall. Suddenly she was sure it hadn't been a nurse at all. Even if she did have a uniform on. A nurse wouldn't have come into the maternity ward at night without saying hello and telling them what she was doing there.

Ylva kept thinking about it. She grew more and more anxious. The woman must have had some purpose. She stayed for ten minutes, then she vanished. Ten minutes. She must have been in a room visiting someone. Who? And why?

Ylva lay there trying to sleep, but it was no use. The strange woman kept appearing in her thoughts. At 11 a.m. she gave up, and got out of bed and made some coffee. She thought she'd better talk to somebody.

I've got a cousin who's a policeman. I'm sure he could tell me if I'm worrying about this for nothing.

She picked up the phone and dialled his home number. The message on his answering machine said that he was on duty. Since it wasn't far to the police station, she decided to walk over. Maybe the police didn't take visitors on Saturdays. She had read about the terrible thing that happened outside Lödinge – a car dealer had been murdered and tossed in a ditch. Maybe the police wouldn't have time for her. Not even her cousin. At the front desk she asked if Inspector Svedberg was in. He was, but he was very busy.

"Tell him it's Ylva," she said. "I'm his cousin."

Svedberg came out to meet her. He was fond of her, and couldn't resist giving her a few minutes of his time. He got coffee for both of them and they went to his office.

She told him what had happened the night before. Svedberg said that it was odd, of course, but hardly anything to worry about. She let herself be reassured. She had three days off and soon forgot about the nurse who had walked through the maternity ward.

Late on Friday evening Wallander called his weary colleagues together for a meeting of the investigative team at the police station. They closed the doors at 10 p.m., and the meeting dragged on until past midnight. He began by telling them about the second missing person inquiry that they now had on their hands. Martinsson and Höglund had finished their preliminary check of the records, but had found nothing to indicate a connection between Eriksson and Runfeldt. Vanja Andersson didn't recall Runfeldt ever mentioning Eriksson. Wallander made it clear that all they could do was keep on working without making any assumptions. Runfeldt might show up at any time with a perfectly reasonable explanation for his disappearance. But they couldn't ignore the ominous signs.

Wallander asked Höglund to take responsibility for the Runfeldt investigation, but that didn't mean she was released from the Eriksson case. In the past Wallander had been opposed to asking Stockholm for reinforcements, but this time he had a feeling that maybe they should do so right from the start. He'd mentioned this to Hansson, and they'd agreed to wait until early next week.

They sat around the conference table and went over what they had learned so far. Wallander asked if anyone had anything important to report. His gaze wandered around the table. They all shook their heads. Nyberg sat sniffling quietly at the end of the table in his usual place, by himself. Wallander let him have the first word.

"Nothing at all so far. You've all seen exactly what we've seen. The planks were sawed through. He fell and was impaled. We didn't find anything in the ditch. We don't know yet where the bamboo stakes came from."

"And the tower?" Wallander asked.

"We didn't find anything there either," said Nyberg. "But of course we're nowhere near finished yet. It would be a big help if you could tell us what we should be looking for."

"I don't know, but whoever did this must have come from somewhere. We have the path leading from Eriksson's house. There are fields all around it. And a patch of woods behind the hill."

"There's a tractor path up to the woods," said Höglund, "with tracks from car tyres, but none of the neighbours noticed anything unusual."

"Apparently Eriksson owned a lot of land," Svedberg said. "I talked a farmer named Lundberg. He sold off more than 50 hectares to Eriksson ten years ago. Since it was Eriksson's property, there was no reason for anyone else to be on it. Which means no-one ever paid much attention to it."

"We still have a lot of people to talk to," Martinsson said as he shuffled through his papers. "By the way, I got in touch with the forensics laboratory in Lund. They think they'll probably have something to tell us by Monday morning."

Wallander made a note. Then he turned to Nyberg again.

"How's it going with Eriksson's house?"

"We can't do everything at once," Nyberg grumbled. "We've been out in the mud because it might start raining again soon. I think we can start on the house in the morning."

"That sounds good," said Wallander soothingly. He didn't want to annoy Nyberg. That could create a bad atmosphere that would affect the whole meeting. At the same time he couldn't get over his irritation at Nyberg's continual grouchiness. He also saw that Lisa Holgersson had noted Nyberg's surly reply.

They continued the review of the case, still very much in its introductory phase. The interviews with Ruth Sturesson and Sven Tyrén hadn't taken them any further. Eriksson had placed his order for oil, four cubic metres. There was nothing unusual in that. The mysterious break-in that he had reported the year before was unexplained. Their exploration of Eriksson's life and character had barely begun. They were still at the most basic stage of a criminal investigation. The search had not yet begun to take on a life of its own.

When no-one had anything to add, Wallander tried to sum up. During the whole meeting he'd had a feeling that he'd seen something at the murder scene that should have prompted discussion. Something he couldn't explain.

The *modus operandi*, he thought. There's something about those bamboo stakes. A killer uses a language that he deliberately chooses. Why would he impale a person? Why would he go to such trouble? For the time being he kept these thoughts to himself. They were still too vague to present to the team.

He poured himself a glass of mineral water and shoved aside the papers in front of him.

"We're still searching for a way in," he began. "What we have is a murder unlike anything we've ever seen. This may mean that the motive and the killer too are unlike anything we've ever encountered. In a way, it reminds me of the situation we were in last summer. We solved that case by refusing to get hung up on any one thing. And we can't afford to do that now, either."

He turned to face the chief.

"We'll have to work hard. It's already Saturday morning, but it can't be helped. Everyone will continue working on the tasks at hand over the weekend. We can't wait until Monday."

Holgersson nodded.

The meeting was adjourned. They were all exhausted. The chief and Höglund stayed. Soon they were alone in the conference room. Wallander thought that here, for once, women were in the majority in his world.

"Per Åkeson needs to talk to you," said Holgersson.

Wallander shook his head in resignation.

"I'll call him tomorrow."

Holgersson had put on her coat, but Wallander could tell that she wasn't finished with him.

"Isn't it possible that this murder might have been committed by an insane person?" she asked. "Impaling someone on stakes! It sounds like the Middle Ages to me."

"Not necessarily," Wallander said. "Stake pits were used during the Second World War. Atrocity and insanity don't always go hand in hand."

Holgersson didn't seem satisfied with his answer. She leant against the doorframe and looked at him.

"I'm still not convinced. Maybe we could call in that criminal psychologist who was here last summer. Wasn't he a big help to you?"

Wallander couldn't deny that Mats Ekholm had been

important to the success of the investigation. He had helped them draw up a profile of the killer. But Wallander didn't think it was time to call him in yet – in fact, he was afraid to draw parallels.

"Maybe," he said. "But I think we should wait a while."

She studied him.

"You aren't afraid it'll happen again, are you? A new pit with sharpened stakes in it?"

"No."

"What about Runfeldt?"

Wallander was suddenly unsure whether he might be speaking against his better judgement. But he shook his head, he didn't think it would be repeated. Or was that just what he hoped? He didn't know.

"Eriksson's murder must have required a lot of preparation," he said. "Something you do only once. Something that depends on a special set of circumstances. Like a ditch that's deep enough. And a bridge. And a victim who goes out at night or at dawn to look at migrating birds. I'm the one who linked Runfeldt's disappearance with what happened in Lödinge. But that's for reasons of caution."

"I understand," she said. "But think about calling in Ekholm."

"I will," Wallander said. "You may be right, I just think it's too early. Timing often determines the success of certain efforts."

Holgersson buttoned her coat.

"You need sleep too. Don't stay here all night," she said as she left.

Wallander began gathering up his papers.

"I have some things to work out," he told Höglund. "Do you remember when you first came here? You said you thought I had a lot I could teach you. Now maybe you can see how wrong you were."

She was sitting on the table, looking at her nails. Wallander thought she looked pale and tired and definitely not beautiful. But she was talented. And that rarity: a dedicated police officer. In that they were alike.

He dropped the stack of papers on the table and sank back into his chair.

"Tell me what you see," he said.

"Something that scares me."

"Why?"

"The savagery. The calculation. And no motive."

"Eriksson was rich. Everyone says he was a tough businessman. He may have made enemies."

"That doesn't explain why he would be impaled on bamboo stakes."

"Hate can blind people in the same way envy can. Or jealousy."

She shook her head.

"When I saw Eriksson's body on the stakes I felt instinctively that we were dealing with much more than the murder of an old man," she said. "I can't explain it better than that, but the feeling was there. And it was strong."

Wallander snapped out of his weariness. She had said something important. Something that vaguely touched on thoughts that had crossed his own mind.

"Keep going," he said. "Think harder!"

"There isn't that much more. The man was dead. Nobody who saw the scene will ever forget it. It was a murder. But there was more."

"Every murderer has his own language," Wallander said. "Is that what you mean?"

"More or less."

"He was making a statement?"

"Possibly."

In a code, Wallander thought. A code we haven't cracked.

"You may be right," he said.

They sat in silence. Wallander got up and went back to gathering his papers. He discovered something that didn't belong to him.

"Is this yours?"

She glanced at the paper.

"That looks like Svedberg's writing."

Wallander tried to make out what had been scrawled in pencil. It was something about a maternity ward. About a woman he didn't know.

"What the hell is this?" he said. "Is Svedberg having a baby? He isn't even married. Is he even dating anyone?"

She took the note out of his hand and read it.

"Evidently somebody reported a woman wandering around the maternity ward dressed like a nurse," she said, handing back the paper.

"We'll have to check it out when we have time," Wallander replied sarcastically. He considered tossing the note in the waste-paper basket, but changed his mind. He'd give it to Svedberg the next day.

They parted in the hall.

"Who's taking care of your children?" he asked. "Is your husband home?"

"He's in Mali."

Wallander didn't know where Mali was, but he didn't ask.

Höglund left the deserted station. Wallander put Svedberg's piece of paper on his desk and picked up his jacket. On the way out to the front desk he stopped at the dispatch office, where a lone officer sat reading a newspaper.

"Anybody call about Lödinge?" he asked.

"Not a peep."

Wallander went outside to his car. It was windy. Ann-Britt hadn't really answered his question about her children. He searched through all his pockets before he found his car keys. Then he drove home. Even though he was tired, he sat on his sofa and thought through everything that had happened during the day. Most of all he worried about what Höglund had said just before she left. That the murder of Holger Eriksson was something more. But how could a murder be more than a murder?

It was almost 3 a.m. when he went to bed. Before he fell asleep he remembered that he had to call his father and Linda the next day.

He woke up with a start at 6 a.m. He had been dreaming. Eriksson was alive. He was standing on the wooden bridge across the ditch. Just as it collapsed, Wallander woke up. He forced himself to get out of bed. It had started raining again. In the kitchen he discovered he was out of coffee, so he made do with two aspirin, and then sat for a long time at the table with his head propped on one hand.

At 6.45 a.m. he arrived at the station. When he opened the door of his office he noticed something he hadn't seen the night before. There was a parcel on the chair by the window. Ebba had arranged for Gösta Runfeldt's mail-order to be picked up. He hung up this jacket, wondering for a second whether he actually had the right to open it. Then he pulled off the paper and opened the box inside.

He was frowning at the contents when Martinsson walked past his door.

"Come here," Wallander called to him. "Come and take a look at this."

CHAPTER 9

They peered at Gösta Runfeldt's parcel. To Wallander it seemed like junk: wires and tiny black boxes whose purpose he couldn't guess. But it was clear to Martinsson what Runfeldt had ordered and the police had paid for.

"This is highly sophisticated bugging equipment," he said, picking up one of the boxes.

Wallander shot him a sceptical look.

"Can you really buy bugging equipment from a mail-order company in Borås?" he asked.

"You can buy anything you want by mail order," replied Martinsson. "This is the real thing. Whether it's legal is another question. The importation of this type of equipment is strictly regulated."

They unpacked the parcel onto Wallander's desk. There was more than bugging equipment inside. To their amazement they also found a box containing a magnetic brush and iron filings. That could only mean one thing. Runfeldt intended to test for fingerprints.

"What do you make of this?" Wallander said.

Martinsson shook his head. "It seems pretty strange."

"What's a florist doing with bugging equipment? Is he going to spy on his competitors in the tulip business?"

"The fingerprint stuff is even weirder."

Wallander frowned. The equipment was expensive. The company that had sold it was called Secure, with an address on Getängsvägen in Borås.

"Let's call and find out if Runfeldt bought anything else," Wallander said.

"I suspect they won't be too willing to give out information on their customers," Martinsson replied. "Besides, it's Saturday morning."

"They have a 24-hour order line," Wallander said, pointing to the brochure.

"That will just be an answering machine," Martinsson said. "I've bought gardening tools through a mail-order company in Borås. They don't have operators sitting there around the clock, if that's what you think."

Wallander stared at one of the tiny microphones.

"Can this stuff really be legal?"

"I think I can tell you now," Martinsson said. "I've got some material in my office that deals with this sort of thing."

He returned in a few minutes with some booklets.

"From the information unit of the national police board," he said. "The materials they publish are pretty good."

"I read them whenever I get a chance," Wallander said. "But sometimes I wonder if they aren't publishing too much."

"Take a look at this: 'Bugging as a coercive method in criminal interrogations,'" Martinsson said, placing one of the booklets on the desk. "But maybe that's not quite what we're looking for. How about this one: 'Memorandum on bugging equipment.'"

Martinsson leafed through it, then stopped and read aloud. "'According to Swedish law it is illegal to possess, sell, or install bugging equipment.' Which probably means that it's also forbidden to manufacture it."

"Then we ought to ask our colleagues in Borås to clamp

down on that mail-order business," Wallander said. "It means they're making illegal sales. And importing illegal goods."

"Mail-order businesses are generally legitimate in this country," Martinsson said. "I suspect this is a rotten apple that the industry itself would like to be rid of."

"Get hold of Borås," Wallander said. "Do it as soon as possible."

He thought back on his visit to Runfeldt's flat. He hadn't discovered technical equipment of this kind.

"I think we should ask Nyberg to take a look at this stuff. That should be enough for now. But it does seem strange."

Martinsson agreed.

"I'm going out to Lödinge," Wallander told him as he put everything back into the box.

"I managed to track down a salesman who sold cars for Holger Eriksson for more than 20 years," Martinsson said. "I'm seeing him in Svarte in half an hour. He should be able to give us an idea of the sort of man Eriksson was, if anyone can."

They parted out in reception. Wallander was carrying Runfeldt's box of equipment under one arm. He stopped at Ebba's desk.

"What did my father say?" he asked.

"Just asked to tell you to call if you had time."

Wallander was instantly suspicious.

"Did he sound sarcastic?"

Ebba gave him a stern look.

"Your father is a very nice man. He has great respect for your work."

Wallander, knowing the truth, just shook his head. Ebba pointed at the box.

"I had to pay for that myself. There isn't any petty cash at the moment."

"Give me the receipt," said Wallander. "Is it all right if I get you the money by Monday?"

Ebba agreed, and Wallander left the station. It had stopped raining and the sky was clearing. It was going to be a beautiful autumn day. Wallander put the box on the back seat and drove out of Ystad. The countryside seemed less oppressive in the sunshine, and for a moment his mood lifted. Then Eriksson's impaled body rose up before him like a nightmare. The fact that Runfeldt was also missing didn't mean that a similar fate had befallen him, he tried to tell himself. The fact that Runfeldt had ordered bugging equipment could be taken as an indication, paradoxically, that he was still alive. Wallander had wondered whether Runfeldt might have taken his own life – but the equipment made him doubt that this was the case. As Wallander drove through the bright autumn countryside he thought that sometimes he gave in to his inner demons much too easily.

He turned into the courtyard of Eriksson's farmhouse and parked. A man Wallander recognised as a reporter from *Arbetet* was walking towards him. Wallander was carrying Runfeldt's box under his arm. They said hello, and the reporter nodded at the box.

"Are you carrying the solution in there?"

"No, nothing like that."

"But honestly, how's it going?"

"There'll be a press conference on Monday. Until then we don't have anything to tell you."

"But he was impaled on sharpened steel pipes?"

Wallander gave him an astonished look.

"Who on earth said that?"

"One of your colleagues."

"There must be a misunderstanding. There weren't any steel pipes."

"But he was impaled?"

"That's correct."

"It sounds like some sort of torture chamber dug into a field in Skåne."

"Your words, not mine."

"What are your words, then?"

"That there will be a press conference on Monday."

The reporter shook his head.

"You've got to give me something."

"We're still in the preliminary stage of this investigation. We can confirm that a murder has been committed. But we don't have any leads."

"Nothing?"

"I have no further comment."

The reporter gave up. Wallander knew he would quote him accurately. He was one of the few reporters who didn't misquote him.

In the distance the abandoned plastic canopy fluttered down by the ditch. The crime-scene tape was still there. An officer appeared near the tower. They could probably stop guarding the site now. Just as he got to the house the door opened. Nyberg stood there with plastic covers on his shoes.

"I saw you from the window," he said.

Nyberg was in a cheerful mood. That was a good omen for the day's work.

"I've got a something for you," Wallander said as he entered. "Take a look at this."

"Does it have anything to do with Eriksson?"

"No, Runfeldt. The florist."

Wallander set the box down on the desk. Nyberg moved the poem aside to make room to unpack it. His reaction was the same as Martinsson's. It was definitely bugging equipment. And it was highly sophisticated. Nyberg put on his glasses and searched for the manufacturer's stamp.

"It says Singapore. But it was probably made somewhere else."

"Where?"

"The US, or Israel."

"So why does it say Singapore?"

"Some of these manufacturers try to maintain as low a profile as possible. They're involved in one way or another with the international arms trade, and they don't reveal secrets to each other unless they have to. The parts are manufactured in various countries. Assembly is done somewhere else. And another country altogether provides the stamp of origin."

"What could you use this for?" Wallander asked him.

"You could bug a flat. Or a car."

Wallander shook his head.

"Runfeldt is a florist. What would he need this for?"

"Find him and ask him yourself," Nyberg said.

They put everything back in the box. Nyberg sniffled. He had a bad cold.

"Try and take it a little easier," Wallander said. "Get some sleep."

"It's that bloody mud. I get sick from standing out in the rain. I don't understand why it should be so damned difficult to design a shelter that would hold up under the weather conditions of Skåne."

"Write an article about it for *Swedish Police*," Wallander suggested.

"When am I going to have time for that?"

The question went unanswered. They moved through the house.

"I haven't found anything out of the ordinary," said Nyberg. "At least not yet. But the house has a lot of nooks and crannies."

"I'll hang around for a while," Wallander said. "I want to think."

Nyberg went to join his forensic technicians. Wallander sat down by the window in the sun.

His gaze took in the large room. What kind of man writes poems about a woodpecker? He read again what Holger Eriksson had written. There were some beautiful turns of phrase. Wallander had written verse in the autograph books of his female friends at school when he was young, but he had never really read poetry. Linda had complained that there were too few books in the house when she was growing up, and Wallander couldn't argue with her.

A wealthy car dealer, almost 80 years old, who writes poems, and is interested in birds. So interested that he goes out late at night or in the early dawn and stares at the migrating night birds.

The sunshine was still warming him as he looked around the room. He remembered something from the report of the break-in. According to Eriksson, the front door was forced open with a crowbar. But nothing seemed to have been stolen.

There was something else. Wallander searched his memory. Then he remembered. Yes, the safe was untouched. He stood up and went to find Nyberg. He was in one of the bedrooms.

"Did you find a safe?"

"No."

"We have to find it," Wallander said. "Let's start looking."

Nyberg was on his knees next to the bed.

"Are you sure?" Nyberg asked. "I would have found it."

"Yes, I am. Somewhere there's a safe."

They searched the house methodically. It took them half an hour before they found the safe. One of Nyberg's assistants discovered it behind a false oven door in a serving area of the kitchen. The door could be swung open laterally. The safe was built into the wall and had a combination lock.

"I think I know where the combination is," Nyberg said. "Eriksson was probably afraid his memory might fail him in his old age."

Wallander followed Nyberg back to the desk. In one of the drawers Nyberg had found a little box containing a slip of paper with a row of numbers on it. They tried it on the safe, and the lock clicked into place. Nyberg stepped aside to allow Wallander to open it.

Wallander peered inside. Then he gave a start. He took a step back and trod on Nyberg's toes.

"What is it?" Nyberg asked.

Wallander nodded for him to look. Nyberg leaned forwards. He recoiled, but less violently than Wallander.

"It looks like a human head," Nyberg said.

He turned to one of his assistants, who had blanched when he'd heard Nyberg's words, and asked him to get a torch. They stood there waiting uneasily. Wallander felt dizzy. He took a few deep breaths. Nyberg gave him a curious look. The torch arrived. Nyberg shone it into the safe. There really was a head in there, cut off at the neck. Its eyes were open. But it was shrunken and dried.

They couldn't tell whether it was an ape or a human. Only a few pocket diaries and a notebook were in there with it.

At that moment Höglund came in. From the tense atmosphere she knew that something had happened. She didn't ask what, but stood quietly in the background.

"Should we call in the photographer?" asked Nyberg.

"No, just take a few pictures yourself," replied Wallander. "The most important thing is to get it out of the safe."

He turned to Höglund.

"There's a head in there," he said. "A shrunken human head. Or maybe it's an ape."

She leaned forwards and looked. Wallander noticed that she didn't flinch. They left the serving area to give Nyberg and his assistants room to work. Wallander could feel himself sweating.

"A safe with a head in it," she said. "Possibly shrunken, possibly an ape. How do we interpret that?"

"Eriksson must have been a more complex man than we imagined," Wallander said.

They waited for Nyberg and his team to empty the safe. It was 9 a.m. Wallander told Höglund about the parcel from the mail-order company in Borås. They decided that someone should go through Runfeldt's flat more methodically than Wallander had had time to do. It would be best if Nyberg could spare some of his technicians. Höglund called the station and was told that the Danish police had confirmed that no bodies had drifted ashore recently. The Malmö police and the sea rescue service hadn't found any either.

At 9.30 a.m. Nyberg appeared carrying the head and the other things he had found in the safe. Wallander moved the poem about the woodpecker aside, and Nyberg set down the head. In the safe with the diaries and notebook, there had been a box with a medal in it. But it was the shrunken head that captured their full attention. In the daylight there was no longer any doubt. It was a human head. A black head. Maybe a child. Or at least a young person. When Nyberg looked at it with a magnifying glass he could see that moths had been at the skin. Wallander grimaced with disgust when Nyberg leaned close to the head and sniffed it.

"Who do we know that might know about shrunken heads?" Wallander asked.

"The Ethnographic Museum," Nyberg said. "These days it's called the Museum of World Peoples. The national police board have issued a little booklet that's excellent. It lists where you can find information on the most peculiar phenomena."

"Then we'll get in touch with them," Wallander said.

Nyberg laid the head gently on a plastic bag. Wallander and Höglund sat down at the desk and started examining the other items. The medal, which rested on a little silk pillow, was foreign. It had an inscription in French. None of them could read it. They started going through the books. The diaries were from the early 1960s. On the half-title page they could make out a name: *Harald Berggren*. Wallander shot Höglund a questioning glance. She shook her head. That name hadn't come up in the investigation so far. There were very few entries in the diaries. A few times of day noted with initials. In one place were the initials *H.E.* It was dated February 1960 – more than 30 years earlier.

Wallander began to leaf through the notebook. It was a diary, crammed with entries. The first entry had been made in November of 1960, the last in July of 1961. The handwriting was cramped and hard to read. He realised that he had forgotten to keep his appointment with the optician. He borrowed the magnifying glass from Nyberg and read a line here and there.

"It's about the Belgian Congo," he said. "Somebody who was there during the war. As a soldier."

"Holger Eriksson or Harald Berggren?"

"Harald Berggren. Whoever that is."

He put down the notebook. It might be important and he'd have to read it carefully. They looked at each other. Wallander knew they were thinking the same thing.

"A shrunken human head," he said. "And a diary about a war in Africa."

"A pungee pit," Höglund said. "A reminder of the war. In my mind shrunken heads and impaled people go together."

"Mine too," Wallander said. "The question is whether we've found a lead or not."

"Who is Harald Berggren?"

"That's one of the first things we have to find out."

Wallander remembered that Martinsson was visiting a former employee of Eriksson in Svarte. He asked Höglund to call him. Starting right now, the name Harald Berggren would be mentioned and examined in all conceivable connections. She punched in the number. Waited. Then she shook her head.

"His phone isn't switched on," she said.

Wallander was irritated. "How are we supposed to conduct an investigation if we aren't all contactable?"

He knew he often broke the rule himself – he was probably the hardest to reach of all. At least sometimes. But Höglund didn't say a word.

"I'll find him," she said, getting to her feet.

"Harald Berggren," said Wallander. "That name is important."

"I'll see that word gets out," she replied.

When Wallander was alone in the room, he turned on the desk lamp. He was just about to open the diary when he noticed that something was stuck inside the leather cover. Carefully he coaxed out a photograph. It was black-and-white, well-thumbed and stained. One corner was torn off. The photograph showed three men in uniform, laughing towards the camera. Wallander remembered the photograph of Runfeldt surrounded by giant orchids. The landscape in this picture wasn't Sweden either. He studied the photograph with the magnifying glass. The men were very tanned. Their shirts were unbuttoned and their sleeves rolled up. There were rifles at their feet. They were leaning against an oddly shaped boulder and behind it was open countryside with no distinguishable features. The ground was crushed gravel or sand.

The men looked like they were in their early 20s. He turned the picture over. It was probably taken at about the same time the diary entries were made. The early 1960s. Their age meant that he could eliminate Holger Eriksson. In 1960 he would have been between 40 and 50 years old.

Wallander opened one of the desk drawers. He had seen some loose passport photographs in an envelope earlier. He placed one of the photographs of Eriksson on the desk. It was dated 1989. Holger Eriksson, aged 73. Wallander stared at his face. The pointed nose, the thin lips. He tried to imagine away the wrinkles and see a younger face. He went back to the photograph with the three men posing. He studied their faces one by one. The man on the left had some features that resembled Holger Eriksson. Wallander leaned back in his chair and closed his eyes.

Holger Eriksson lies dead in a ditch. In his safe we find a shrunken head, a diary, and a photograph.

Suddenly Wallander sat up straight in the chair, his eyes wide. He was thinking about the break-in. The safe was untouched. Let's assume, thought Wallander, that whoever broke in also had a hard time finding the safe. And assume the contents were the same then as they are now. That's precisely what the thief was looking for. He failed and apparently didn't repeat the attempt. And Eriksson died a year later.

But there was something that presented a serious contradiction to this attempt to find a link between the two events. After Eriksson's death, his safe would be found – by the executors of the estate if no-one else. The intruder must have been aware of this.

Still, this was something. A lead.

He looked at the photograph one more time. The men were smiling. They had been smiling in this picture for 30 years. Could the photographer have been Eriksson? But Eriksson had been selling cars in Ystad, Tomelilla, and Sjöbo. He hadn't taken part in some far-off African war. Or had he?

Wallander regarded the diary lying in front of him pensively. He slipped the photograph into his jacket pocket, picked up the book, and went in to Nyberg, who was busy with a technical examination of the bathroom.

"I'm taking this diary. I'll leave the pocket calendars."

"You think there's something there?" asked Nyberg.

"I think so," said Wallander. "If anyone wants me I'll be at home."

When he came out into the courtyard he could see that

some officers were busy taking down the crime-scene tape by the ditch. The rain canopy was already gone.

An hour later he was sitting at his kitchen table. He opened the diary.

The first entry was made on 20 November 1960.

CHAPTER 10

It took Wallander almost six hours to read Harald Berggren's diary from cover to cover. With interruptions, of course. The telephone rang again and again. Wallander tried to keep the interruptions brief.

The diary was one of the most fascinating yet frightening things he had ever encountered. It was a record of several years in the man's life. For Wallander it was like stepping into an alien world. Although Harald Berggren, whoever he was, couldn't be described as a master of language – he often expressed himself sentimentally or with an uncertainty that gave way to helplessness – the descriptions of his experiences had a force that shone through the prose. Wallander sensed that they must decipher the diary in order to understand what had happened to Eriksson. And yet he could hear a voice inside warning him that this could lead them in completely the wrong direction. Wallander knew that most truths were both expected and unexpected at the same time. It was simply a matter of knowing how to interpret the connection. Besides, no criminal investigation ever resembled another, not deep down, not once they went past the superficial similarities.

The diary was a war journal. As Wallander read it, he learned the names of the other two men in the photograph. But when he had read to the end, he still couldn't tell which man was which. The photograph was of Harald

Berggren flanked by an Irishman, Terry O'Banion, and a Frenchman, Simon Marchand. It was taken by a man named Raul. They had been mercenaries in a war in Africa for more than a year. Early on, Berggren described how in Stockholm he had heard about a café in Brussels where contacts could be made with the secret world of mercenaries. He'd first heard of it around New Year, 1958. He didn't explain what drove him to go there a few years later. Berggren stepped into his own diary out of nowhere: no parents, no background. The only sure things were that he was 23 years old and desperate at Hitler's defeat in the war that had ended 15 years earlier.

Wallander stopped at this point. That was Berggren's exact word: *desperate*. Wallander read the passage again: *the desperate defeat that Hitler was subjected to by his treacherous generals*. The word *desperate* said something crucial about Berggren. Was he expressing a political conviction? Or were these the writings of a madman? Wallander found no clues to indicate whether either of these things were correct. Nor did Berggren mention Hitler again.

In June 1960 he had left Sweden by train and stayed a day in Copenhagen so he could go to Tivoli. There he danced in the warm summer night with a girl named Irene. He wrote that she was *sweet but much too tall*. The next day he was in Hamburg. The day after that – 12 June 1960 – he arrived in Brussels. After about a month he achieved his goal: a contract as a mercenary. He noted proudly that now he was drawing a salary and would be going off to war. He wrote all this down much later, under the date 20 November 1960. By now he was in Africa. In this first entry in the diary, which was also the longest, he summarised the events that had led him to the place where he now found himself. Wallander dug out his old school atlas and looked up the place Berggren described, Omerutu. It wasn't on the map, but he left it open on the kitchen table as he continued reading the diary.

Together with Terry O'Banion and Simon Marchand, Berggren joined a fighting company that consisted solely of mercenaries. Their leader, about whom Berggren was quite reticent, was a Canadian only referred to as Sam. Berggren didn't seem to concern himself with what the war was over. Wallander was extremely hazy himself about the conflict in what was then the Belgian Congo. Berggren didn't try to justify his presence as a hired soldier. He merely noted that they were fighting for freedom. Whose was never made clear. In more than one entry he wrote that he would not hesitate to use his gun if he found himself in a combat situation with Swedish UN soldiers.

Berggren also made a careful note of each time he received his pay. He did a simple accounting on the last day of each month: how much he was paid, how much he spent, and how much he saved. He also listed every item of booty that he took. In a particularly unpleasant passage, he described how the mercenaries arrived at an abandoned, burnt-out plantation, and found the rotting corpses of the Belgian plantation owner and his wife, swarming with flies. They lay in their beds with their arms and legs hacked off. The stench was unbelievable, but the mercenaries had still searched the house and found diamonds and gold jewellery, which a Lebanese jeweller later valued at more than 20,000 Swedish kronor.

Berggren wrote that the war was justified because the profits were good. In a more personal reflection not repeated elsewhere in the diary, he'd asked himself whether he could have achieved the same wealth if he had stayed in Sweden working as a car mechanic. His conclusion was that he couldn't. Living that sort of life, he never would have advanced his prospects. With great zeal he continued to participate in his war.

Apart from his obsession with keeping accounts, Berggren was also meticulous in his other entries. He killed people. He wrote down the dates and the body count. He noted whether they were men or women or children, and if he'd managed to examine their bodies, he coolly recorded where the shots he'd fired had struck. Wallander read these passages with growing distaste and anger. Berggren had nothing to do with this war. He was paid to kill, by whom was unclear. The people he killed were seldom in uniform. The mercenaries raided villages that were thought to oppose the freedom they were fighting to preserve. They murdered and plundered and then withdrew. They were a death squad, all Europeans, and they didn't regard the people they killed as equals. Berggren didn't hide his contempt for the blacks. He wrote that they *ran like bewildered goats when we approached. But bullets fly faster than people can jump or run.*

Wallander almost threw the book across the room at those lines. But he forced himself to read on, after taking a break and washing his tired eyes. More than ever he regretted having missed his appointment with the optician.

Berggren killed roughly ten people a month, assuming he wasn't exaggerating. After seven months of war he fell ill and was transported by plane to a hospital in Léopoldville. He had contracted amoebic dysentery and was sick for several weeks. The diary entries stopped during this period. By then he had killed more than 50 people in this war he was fighting instead of becoming a mechanic in Sweden.

When Berggren recovered, he returned to his company.

A month later they were back in Omerutu. They posed in front of a big boulder, which was not a rock but a termite mound, and the unknown Raul took a picture of Berggren, O'Banion and Marchand. Wallander went over to the kitchen window with the photograph. He had never seen a termite mound before, but he could tell that the diary described that very picture.

Three weeks later they got caught in an ambush and O'Banion was killed. They were forced to retreat, and it turned into a panicked rout. Wallander tried to sense the fear in Berggren. He was convinced it was there, but Berggren concealed it. He wrote only that they had buried their dead in the bush and marked their graves with wooden crosses. The war went on. On one occasion they used a group of apes for target practice. Another time they gathered crocodile eggs on the bank of a river. Berggren's savings were now close to 30,000 kronor.

But then, in the summer of 1961, everything was over. The diary ended suddenly. Wallander thought it must have been as abrupt for Harald Berggren. He must have imagined that this peculiar jungle war would go on forever. In his last entries he described how they fled the country at night, in a cargo plane with no lights. One of its engines started shuddering as they lifted off from the runway they had made by clearing the jungle. The diary ended there, as though Berggren had grown tired of it, or else no longer had anything to say. Wallander didn't even discover where the plane was headed. Berggren was flying through the African night, the engine noise died away, and he no longer existed.

Wallander stretched and went out onto the balcony. It was now 5 p.m. A cloud front was on its way in from the sea. Why was the diary kept in Eriksson's safe along with a shrunken head? If Berggren was still alive, he would be at least 50. Wallander felt cold standing out on the balcony. He went inside and sat down on the sofa. His eyes hurt. Who was Berggren writing the diary for? Himself or someone else?

A young man keeps a diary of a war in Africa. Often what he describes is rich in detail, but it is also constrained in some way. Something was missing, something that Wallander couldn't read even between the lines.

Not until Höglund rang the bell did it dawn on him what it was. He saw her in the door and suddenly he knew. The diary described a world dominated by men. The women Berggren wrote about were either dead or fleeing in panic. Except for Irene, who'd been sweet but too tall. Otherwise he didn't mention women. He wrote about furloughs in various cities in the Congo, about how he got drunk and got into fights. But there were no women. Wallander couldn't help thinking that this was significant. Berggren was a young man when he went off to Africa. The war was an adventure. In a young man's world, women are an important part of the adventure. He was starting to wonder. But for the time being he kept his thoughts to himself.

Höglund had come to tell him that she had gone through Runfeldt's flat with one of Nyberg's forensic technicians. The result was negative. They had found nothing that would explain why he had bought bugging equipment.

"Gösta Runfeldt's world consists of orchids," she said. "I get the impression of a kindly and intense widower."

"His wife seems to have drowned," Wallander said.

"She was quite beautiful," Höglund said. "I saw their wedding picture."

"Maybe we ought to find out what happened to her," Wallander said. "Sooner or later."

"Martinsson and Svedberg are getting in touch with his children."

Wallander had already talked to Martinsson on the phone. He had been in touch with Runfeldt's daughter. She was utterly astonished at the idea that her father might have deliberately disappeared. She was extremely worried. She knew he was supposed to fly to Nairobi and had assumed that's where he was.

"There's too much that doesn't add up," he said. "Svedberg was supposed to call when he'd spoken to the son. He was out at a farm somewhere in Hälsingland where there wasn't a phone."

They decided to hold a meeting of the investigative team early on Sunday afternoon. Höglund would make the arrangements. Then Wallander recounted to her the contents of the diary. He took his time and tried to be thorough. Telling her about it was like reviewing it in his own mind.

"Berggren," she said when he was through. "Could he be the one?"

"I don't know, but at any rate as a young man he committed atrocities on a regular basis and for money," Wallander said. "The diary makes horrifying reading. Maybe these days he's living his life in fear that the contents might be divulged."

"We'll have to find him," Höglund said. "The question is where to start looking."

"The diary was in Eriksson's safe," Wallander said. "For the moment that's the clearest lead we have. But we must continue to work with an open mind."

"You know that's impossible," she said, surprised. "When we find a clue it shapes the search."

"I'm just reminding you," he replied evasively, "that

we can be wrong in spite of everything."

She was about to leave when the telephone rang. It was Svedberg, who had reached Runfeldt's son.

"He was pretty upset," Svedberg said. "He wanted to jump on a plane and come here right away."

"When was the last time he heard from his father?"

"A few days before he was due to leave for Nairobi. Everything was normal. According to the son, his father always looked forward to his trips."

Wallander handed the phone to Höglund, who set a time for the meeting of the investigative team. Wallander didn't remember until she hung up that he had a note that was written by Svedberg. A report of a woman acting strangely in the Ystad hospital maternity ward.

Höglund went home to her children. When Wallander was alone he called his father. They decided that he would go out on Sunday morning. The pictures that his father had taken with his ancient camera had been developed.

Wallander devoted the rest of Saturday evening to writing up a summary of Eriksson's murder. As he worked he mulled over Runfeldt's disappearance. He was uneasy and restless and found it difficult to concentrate. The feeling that they were skirting something very big was growing stronger. The feeling of anxiety wouldn't let up. By 9 p.m. he was so tired that he couldn't think any longer. He shoved his notebook aside and called his daughter Linda. The phone rang into a void. She wasn't home. He put on a heavy jacket and walked to a Chinese restaurant on the square. The place was unusually packed, even for a Saturday night. He indulged in a carafe of wine. After he'd eaten, he walked home in the rain, his head aching.

That night he dreamed that he was in a huge dark place,

it was very hot, and somewhere in the dense night Berggren was pointing a gun at him.

He woke early. It was clear again. He got into his car at 7.15 a.m. and drove out to Löderup to see his father. In the morning light, the curves of the countryside were sharp and clear. Wallander thought he would try to tempt his father and Gertrud to come with him down to the beach. Soon it would be too cold to go.

He thought with displeasure about the dream he'd had. As he drove he also decided that at the investigative team's meeting that afternoon they would have to make a schedule of the order in which various questions were to be answered. Locating Berggren was important. Especially if it turned out that that trail led to a dead end.

His father was standing on the steps waiting for him. They went into the kitchen, where Gertrud had set out some breakfast. They looked through the photographs. Some of them were blurred, and in some the subject was only partly inside the frame, but since his father was obviously pleased and proud of them, Wallander nodded appreciatively.

One picture stood out from the rest. It was taken by a waiter on their last night in Rome. They had just finished their dinner. Wallander and his father were squeezed close together. A bottle of red wine stood on the white tablecloth. Both of them were smiling straight at the camera.

For an instant the faded photograph from Eriksson's diary flashed into Wallander's mind, but he pushed it away. Right now he wanted to look at himself and his father. He realised that the picture confirmed once and for all what he had discovered on the trip. They were a lot alike. They even looked alike.

"I'd like to have a copy of this picture," Wallander said.

"I've already taken care of it," his father replied contentedly, handing him an envelope.

After breakfast they went to his father's studio. He had nearly finished a landscape with a grouse in it. The bird was always the last thing he painted.

"How many pictures have you painted in your life?" Wallander asked.

"You ask me that every time you come here," his father said. "How am I supposed to keep track? What would be the point? The main thing is that they're all the same."

Long ago Wallander had realised that there was only one explanation for his father painting the same subject over and over. It was his way of keeping at bay all the things that were changing around him. In his paintings he even controlled the path of the sun. It was motionless, locked in time, always at the same height above the forested ridges.

"It was a great holiday," Wallander said as he looked at his father, who was busy mixing colours.

"I told you it would be," said his father. "If it wasn't for me you would have gone to your grave without ever seeing the Sistine Chapel."

Wallander wondered briefly whether to ask about the solitary walk he'd taken on that night in Rome, but decided not to. It was nobody's business but his father's.

Wallander suggested that they drive down to the sea. To his surprise his father agreed at once. Gertrud preferred to stay home. They got into Wallander's car and drove down to Sandhammaren. There was almost no breeze. They headed for the beach. His father took him by the arm when they passed the last cliff. The sea spread itself out before them. The beach was almost deserted. In the distance they could see some people playing with a dog. That was all.

"It's beautiful," his father said.

Wallander sneaked a look at him. Rome seemed to have made a fundamental change in his mood. Maybe it would also have a positive effect on the insidious disease the doctors had diagnosed. But he would never fully understand what the holiday had meant to his father. It had been the journey of a lifetime, and Wallander had been given the honour of accompanying him.

Rome was his father's Mecca.

They took a long walk on the beach. Wallander wondered whether to bring up the old days. But there was no hurry, they had time. Suddenly his father stopped short.

"What is it?" Wallander asked.

"I've been feeling bad for a few days," he said. "But it'll pass."

"Do you want to go home?"

"I said it'll pass."

They were on the beach more than two hours before his father thought they had walked enough. Wallander, who had forgotten the time, knew that he'd have to hurry so he wouldn't be late for the meeting at the police station.

After he dropped off his father in Löderup he returned to Ystad with a feeling of relief. Maybe now they could regain the contact they had lost when Wallander had decided to become a policeman. His father had never accepted his choice of profession, but he'd never explained what he had against it. Wallander wondered whether he might finally get an answer to the question he had spent far too much of his life worrying about.

* * *

At 2.30 p.m. they closed the door to the conference room. Even Chief Holgersson showed up. Seeing her there reminded Wallander that he still hadn't called Per Åkeson. He wrote a note to himself in his notebook.

He reported on finding the shrunken head and Harald Berggren's diary. There was general agreement that this really did look like a lead. After they divided up the various tasks, Wallander shifted the discussion to Gösta Runfeldt.

"We have to assume that something has happened to Runfeldt," he said. "We can't rule out either an accident or foul play. Naturally there's always the possibility that it's a voluntary disappearance. On the other hand, I think we can discount the likelihood of any sort of connection between Eriksson and Runfeldt. There's nothing to suggest that this is the case."

Wallander wanted the meeting to be as short as possible. After all, it was Sunday. He knew that his colleagues were putting a lot of effort into completing their assignments, but he also knew that sometimes the best way to work meant taking a break. The hours he had spent with his father that morning had given him renewed energy. When he left the police station just after 4 p.m., he felt more rested than he had in days. His anxiety seemed to have abated a little.

If they did find Harald Berggren, there was a good chance they would find the solution. The murder was too well planned not to have been carried out by someone extremely unusual. Berggren might be just that killer.

On his way home Wallander stopped and bought groceries. He couldn't resist the impulse to take out a video. It was a classic, *Waterloo Bridge*. He had seen it in Malmö with Mona in the early years of their marriage, but he had only a vague recollection of what it was about.

He was in the middle of the movie when Linda called. When he heard it was her he said he'd call her right back. He turned off the video and sat down in the kitchen. They talked for almost half an hour. She didn't apologise for not having called in such a long time. He didn't mention it either. He knew they were a lot alike. They could both be absentminded, but they knew how to concentrate if there was a task to be done. She told him that everything was fine, both the job in the restaurant and her drama classes. He didn't press her on that subject. He had a strong impression that she still doubted her talent.

Just before they finished their conversation, he told her about his morning on the beach.

"It sounds like you had a wonderful day together," she said.

"We did. It feels as if something has changed."

When they hung up, Wallander went out on the balcony. There was almost no wind, a rare thing in Skåne. For a moment all his worries were gone. Now he had to get some sleep. Tomorrow he'd get down to work again. When he turned out the light in the kitchen, the diary was in his mind again. He wondered where Harald Berggren was at that very moment.

CHAPTER 11

When Wallander woke up on the morning of Monday, 3 October, the first thing he thought was that he needed to speak to Sven Tyrén again. Whether he had dreamed this he couldn't tell, but he was sure that he needed to. As he waited for his coffee to brew, he called information and got Tyrén's home number. Tyrén's wife answered the phone, and told him that her husband had already left. Wallander called him on his mobile. In the background Wallander could hear the muffled sound of his truck's engine.

Tyrén told him he was on the road outside Högestad. He had two deliveries to make before he went back to the terminal in Malmö. Wallander asked him to come to the station as soon as he could. When Tyrén asked whether they had caught the person who killed Eriksson, Wallander explained that was just a routine conversation. They were still in the early stages of the investigation. They were bound to catch the murderer. It might happen soon, but it could also take time. Tyrén promised to be at the station by 9 a.m.

"Please don't park in front of the driveway," Wallander added.

Tyrén muttered something inaudible in reply.

At 7.15 a.m. Wallander arrived at the station. Walking towards the glass doors, he changed his mind and turned left, to the prosecutor's office, which had its own entrance.

Per Åkeson was sitting behind his desk, which was piled high with work as always. The entire office was a chaotic jumble of papers and files, but appearances were deceptive. Åkeson was an extraordinarily efficient and methodical prosecutor, and Wallander enjoyed working with him. They had known each other for a long time, and over the years they had developed a relationship that went beyond the purely professional. Sometimes they would share confidences and seek each other's advice or help. Still, there was a boundary that they never overstepped. They would never really be close friends; they were not enough alike for that.

Åkeson nodded amiably when Wallander stepped into the room. He got up and moved a box of documents, making room on a chair. Wallander sat down, and Åkeson told the switchboard to hold his calls.

"I've been waiting to hear from you," he said. "Thanks for the card, by the way."

Wallander had forgotten about the postcard he had sent Åkeson from Rome, a view of the Forum Romanum.

"It was a great holiday for both of us."

"I've never been to Rome. How does that proverb go? See Rome and then die? Or is it Naples?"

Wallander didn't know. "I'd been hoping for a peaceful autumn. So I come home and find an old man impaled in a ditch."

Åkeson grimaced. "I've seen some of the photographs. And Chief Holgersson told me about it. Have you got anything to go on?"

"Maybe," Wallander said, and gave him a brief summary of what they had found in Eriksson's safe. Wallander knew that Åkeson respected his ability to lead an investigation. He seldom disagreed with his conclusions or the way he handled a case.

"Of course it sounds like pure insanity to set out sharpened bamboo stakes in a ditch," Åkeson said. "On the other hand, these days it's getting harder and harder to distinguish between what's insane and what's normal."

"How's it going with Uganda?" Wallander asked.

"You mean the Sudan," said Åkeson.

Åkeson had applied for a position with the UN High Commission on Refugees. He wanted to get away from Ystad for a while, to see something else before it was too late. Åkeson was several years older than Wallander. He was over 50.

"Of course, the Sudan," Wallander said. "Have you talked about it with your wife yet?"

Åkeson nodded.

"I got up the courage last week. She was considerably more understanding than I could have hoped. I got the distinct feeling she wouldn't mind getting me out of the house for a while. I'm still waiting for official notification, but I'd be surprised if I didn't get the post. As you know, I have my connections."

Åkeson had a highly developed knack for acquiring inside information. Wallander had no idea how he did it. He was always well informed, for instance, as to what was being discussed in the various committees in Parliament, or in the most elite and confidential circles of the national police board.

"If all goes well, I'll be leaving in the new year," he said. "I'll be gone for at least two years."

"Let's hope we solve the Eriksson case before then. Do you have any directives you want to give me?"

"You should be telling me what you want."

Wallander thought for a moment before replying.

"Chief Holgersson thinks that we ought to call in

Mats Ekholm. You remember him from this summer, the man who does psychological profiles? He hunts insane people by trying to classify them. He's pretty talented."

Åkeson remembered him, of course.

"But I think we should wait," Wallander said, "until we are sure that we're dealing with an insane person."

"If you think we should wait, then so be it," Åkeson said, getting to his feet. He pointed at the box.

"I have a particularly complicated case today," he excused himself. "I have to prepare."

Wallander got up.

"What is it you're actually going to do in the Sudan?" he asked. "Do refugees really need Swedish legal advice?"

"Refugees need all the help they can get," Åkeson replied as he accompanied Wallander to reception. "Not just in Sweden."

Suddenly he said, "I was in Stockholm for a few days while you were in Rome. I ran into Anette Brolin. She asked me to say hello to everyone down here. But especially to you."

Wallander gave him a wary look, but didn't reply. A few years earlier, Anette Brolin had filled in for Åkeson. Despite the fact that she was married, Wallander and she had spent a night together. It was something he preferred to forget.

He walked out of the prosecutor's wing. There was a gusty wind blowing and the sky was grey. Wallander guessed that it was no more than 8°C. He ran into Svedberg in reception, and remembered the note.

"I took one of your notes with me by mistake the other day," he said.

Svedberg looked surprised. "I didn't notice anything missing."

"Something about a woman in the maternity ward at the hospital."

"Oh, you can bin that," Svedberg answered. "It was just someone who saw a ghost."

"You bin it if you want to," Wallander said. "I'll put it on your desk."

"We're still talking to people in the area around Eriksson's farm," Svedberg said. "I'm going to see the postman."

Wallander nodded. They went their separate ways.

By the time Wallander entered his office he had already forgotten about Svedberg's note. He took Berggren's diary from his inside jacket pocket and put it in a desk drawer. He left the photograph of the three men posing by the termite mound lying on his desk. As he waited for Tyrén he read quickly through a stack of papers the other investigators had left for him. At 8.45 a.m. he went to get some coffee. Höglund passed him in the hall and told him that Runfeldt's disappearance had been formally recorded and was being given priority.

"I spoke to one of his neighbours," she said. "A teacher who seemed reliable. He claimed he had heard Runfeldt in his flat on Tuesday night. But not after that."

"Which suggests that he left that night," said Wallander, "although not for Nairobi."

"I asked the neighbour whether he had noticed anything unusual about Runfeldt. But he seems to have been a reserved man with regular, discreet habits. Polite but no more than that. And he seldom had visitors. The only thing out of the ordinary was that Runfeldt sometimes came home very late. The teacher lives in the flat below his, and the building is not well insulated."

Wallander stood there with his cup in his hand, thinking about what she had said.

"We have to find out what the stuff in that box means," he said. "Could someone call the mail-order company today? And have our colleagues in Borås been informed? What was the name of that company? 'Secure'? Nyberg knows. We need to discover whether Runfeldt bought other things from them. He must have placed the order because he was going to use it for something."

"Bugging equipment," she said. "Fingerprints. Who uses things like that?"

"We do."

"But who else?"

Wallander saw that she was thinking of something in particular.

"Of course a bugging device could be used for unauthorised purposes."

"I was thinking more of the fingerprints."

Wallander nodded. Now he got it.

"A private investigator," he said. "A private eye. The thought crossed my mind too. But Runfeldt is a florist whose only passion is orchids."

"It was just an idea," she said. "I'll call the mail-order company myself."

Wallander went back to his office. The telephone rang. It was Ebba. Tyrén was waiting in reception.

"He didn't park his truck across the driveway, did he?" Wallander asked. "Hansson will have a fit."

"I don't see a truck," Ebba said. "Are you coming to get him? And Martinsson wants to talk to you."

"Where is he?"

"In his office, I should think."

"Ask Tyrén to wait a few minutes while I talk to Martinsson."

Martinsson was on the phone when Wallander walked in. He ended the conversation. Wallander assumed he'd been speaking to his wife. They talked several times a day, nobody knew what about.

"I got in touch with the forensic medicine division in Lund," Martinsson told him. "They have some preliminary results. The problem is, they're having trouble determining the thing that we most want to know."

"Time of death?"

Martinsson nodded.

"None of the stakes went through his heart. And none of the main arteries was perforated. That means he could have hung there for quite a while before he died. The immediate cause of death can be given as drowning."

"What's that supposed to mean?" Wallander asked in surprise. "He was hanging in a ditch, wasn't he? He couldn't have drowned there."

"The doctor I talked to was full of gruesome details," Martinsson said. "He told me that Eriksson's lungs were so full of blood that finally he couldn't breathe. Technically, he drowned."

"We have to find out when he died," Wallander said. "Contact them again."

"I'll see to it you get the report as soon as it comes in."

"I'll believe that when I see it. Considering how stuff keeps disappearing around here."

He hadn't meant to criticise Martinsson. When he was out in the hall he realised that his words could have been misconstrued. But by then it was too late to do anything about it. He went out to reception and greeted Tyrén, who was sitting on a vinyl sofa, staring at the floor. He was unshaven and had bloodshot eyes. The smell of oil and petrol was strong. They went to Wallander's office.

"Why haven't you arrested whoever killed Holger?" Tyrén asked.

"If you can tell me who did it, I'll drive out and arrest him right now," Wallander answered, trying to hide his irritation.

"I'm not a policeman."

"You don't have to tell me that. If you were, you wouldn't have asked such a stupid question."

When Tyrén opened his mouth to protest, Wallander held up his hand. "I'm the one asking the questions."

"Am I under suspicion for something?"

"Not a thing. But I'll ask the questions. And you have to answer them. That's all."

Tyrén shrugged his shoulders. Wallander sensed that he was on his guard. He could feel his instincts sharpening. His first question was the only one he had prepared.

"Harald Berggren," he said. "Does that name mean anything to you?"

Tyrén looked at him.

"I don't know any Harald Berggren. Should I?"

"Are you sure?"

"Yes, I am."

"Think!"

"I don't have to think. If I'm sure, I'm sure."

Wallander pushed the photograph across the desk and pointed. Tyrén leaned forwards.

"See if you recognise any of these men. Look closely. Take your time."

Tyrén picked up the photograph in his grubby fingers. He looked at it for a long time. Wallander was beginning to feel vaguely hopeful when Tyrén put it back on the table.

"No."

"You looked at it for a long time. Did you think you recognised one of them?"

"You told me to take my time. Who are they? Where was it taken?"

"Are you sure?"

"I've never seen them before."

Instinct told him that Tyrén was telling the truth.

"They're mercenaries," he said. "It was taken in Africa more than 30 years ago."

"The Foreign Legion?"

"Not exactly, but almost. Soldiers who fight for whoever pays the most."

"Got to make a living somehow."

Wallander gave him a puzzled look, but he didn't ask Tyrén to explain himself.

"Did you ever hear that Eriksson had contact with mercenaries?"

"Holger Eriksson sold cars. I thought you knew that."

"He also wrote poems and watched birds," Wallander said, not hiding his irritation. "Did you or did you not ever hear Eriksson talk about mercenaries? Or about a war in Africa?"

Tyrén stared at him. "Why do policemen have to be so unpleasant?"

"Because we deal with unpleasant things," Wallander replied. "And please just answer my questions. That's all. Don't make comments that have nothing to do with the case."

"What happens if I do?"

Wallander was on the verge of losing control. But he didn't care. There was something about this man across the desk that he just couldn't stand.

"Then I'll have to call you in for a talk every single day

for the foreseeable future. And I'll have to request a warrant from the prosecutor to search your home."

"What do you think you'd find there?"

"That's beside the point. Do you understand what's at stake now?"

Wallander knew he was taking a risk, but Tyrén backed down.

"Eriksson was a peaceful man, even though he could be tough when it came to business. But he never talked about any mercenaries. Although he certainly could have."

"What do you mean?"

"Mercenaries fight against revolutionaries and communists, don't they? And Holger was a conservative, I'd say. To put it mildly."

"In what way?"

"He thought society was going to hell. He thought we should bring back flogging and we should hang murderers. If it were up to him, his killer would wind up with a rope around his neck."

"And he spoke to you about this?"

"He stood up for his beliefs."

"Was he in contact with any right-wing organisation?"

"How should I know?"

"If you know one thing, you might know something else. Answer the question!"

"I don't know."

"No neo-Nazis?"

"No idea."

"Was he one himself?"

"I don't know anything about them. All I know is that he didn't see any difference between Social Democrats and communists. The People's Party was probably the most radical one he would accept."

Wallander considered the picture of Eriksson that Tyrén had created. Poet and ultra-conservative, bird-watcher and advocate of capital punishment.

"Did he tell you that he had any enemies?"

"You've asked me that already."

"I know. I'm asking you again."

"He never came right out and said so. But he did lock his doors at night."

"Why?"

"Maybe he had enemies."

"But you don't know of any?"

"No."

"Did he say why he might have enemies?"

"He never said he had any. How many times do I have to tell you that?"

Wallander raised a hand in admonition.

"If I feel like it I can ask you the same question every day for the next five years. No enemies? But he locked his doors at night?"

"Right."

"How do you know?"

"He told me. How else would I know? I didn't drive out there and try his door at night! In Sweden today you can't trust anybody. That's what he said."

Wallander decided to end the interview for now. He'd get back to him soon enough. He had a feeling that Tyrén knew more than he was telling him, but he wanted to proceed cautiously. He didn't want to scare Tyrén off completely.

"That'll be all for now," Wallander said.

"For now? Does that mean I have to come back here again? When am I going to have time to do my job?"

"We'll be in touch. Thanks for coming," Wallander said, getting to his feet. He extended his hand.

The courtesy surprised Tyrén. He had a powerful handshake, Wallander thought.

"I think you can find your way out."

After Tyrén left, Wallander called Hansson. He answered him immediately.

"Sven Tyrén," he said. "The truck driver. The one you thought had been mixed up in an assault case. Remember?"

"I remember."

"See what you can find out about him."

"Is it urgent?"

"No more than anything else, but no less either."

Hansson said that he'd take care of it.

It was 10 a.m. Wallander got some coffee, and wrote a report of his conversation with Tyrén. The next time the investigative team met, they would discuss it in detail. Wallander was convinced it was important.

When he closed his notebook, he discovered the note that he kept forgetting to return to Svedberg. He'd do so now, before he got involved in anything else. He took the sheet of paper and left the office, but once he was out in the hall he heard his telephone ring. He hesitated for a second, then went back and picked it up.

It was Gertrud. She was crying.

"You have to come right away," she said.

Wallander felt a cold chill.

"What's happened?" he asked.

"Your father is dead. He's lying in his studio in the middle of his paintings."

CHAPTER 12

Kurt Wallander's father was buried in the churchyard in Ystad on 11 October. It was a day of heavy downpours and blustery wind, with the sun showing through the clouds from time to time. Wallander felt unable to come to terms with what had happened. A sense of denial had been with him from the moment he had hung up the phone. It was unthinkable that his father could die. Not now, just after their trip to Rome. Not when they had recaptured the closeness they had lost so many years before.

Wallander had left the police station without speaking to anyone, convinced that Gertrud was mistaken. He arrived in Löderup and ran to the studio. His father lay prone across the painting he had been working on. He had shut his eyes and held on tight to the paintbrush he had used to add tiny dabs of white to the grouse's plumage. His father had been finishing the painting he was working on the day before, when they'd walked along the beach at Sandhammaren. Death had come suddenly.

Later, after Gertrud had calmed down enough to talk coherently, she told him that his father had eaten his breakfast as usual. Everything was normal. At 6.30 a.m. he went out to his studio. When he didn't come back to the kitchen at 10 a.m. for coffee, she'd gone out to remind him. By then he was already dead. It occurred to Wallander that no matter when death comes, it disrupts everything. Death always arrives at the wrong time – something is left undone.

They waited for the ambulance. Gertrud stood and held his arm tight. Wallander felt completely empty inside. He didn't feel anything at all, other than a vague sense that it was unfair. He couldn't feel sorry for his father.

Wallander knew the ambulance driver. His name was Prytz and he understood at once that it was Wallander's father they were collecting.

"He wasn't sick," Wallander said. "Yesterday we were out walking on the beach. He complained about feeling bad, that's all."

"It was probably a stroke," Prytz said, with compassion in his voice. "That's what it looks like."

That was also what the doctor told Wallander later. It had happened very quickly. His father would have had no idea he was dying. A blood vessel had burst in his brain. For Gertrud the sorrow and the shock were mixed with relief that it had happened so quickly; that he was spared a slow decline into a no-man's-land of confusion.

Wallander was thinking completely different thoughts. His father had been alone when he died. No-one should be alone in their final moments. He felt guilty that he hadn't responded to his father's complaint. It was something that might indicate an impending heart attack or stroke. But even worse was that it had happened now. Even though his father had been 80, it was too soon. It should have happened later. Not now. Not like this. Wallander had tried to shake life back into his father. But there was nothing he could do. The grouse would never be finished.

In the midst of the chaos that death always creates, Wallander retained his ability to act calmly and rationally. Gertrud went in the ambulance. Wallander stood there in the studio, engulfed in the silence and the smell of turpentine, and wept to think how his father would have hated to leave the grouse unfinished. As a gesture towards the invisible border between life and death, Wallander took the paintbrush and filled in the two white points that were still missing in the grouse's plumage. It was the first time in his life that he had touched any of his father's paintings with a brush. Then he cleaned the brush and put it with the others in an old jam jar.

He went back to the house and called Ebba. She was upset and sad, and Wallander found that he could hardly speak. With difficulty, he asked her to tell the others what had happened. They should go on without him. All they had to do was keep him informed if anything important happened in the investigation. He wouldn't be coming back to work that day. He didn't know what he was going to do tomorrow.

Next he called his sister Kristina and told her the news. They talked for a long time. It seemed as though she had prepared already herself for the possibility that their father might die suddenly. She said she would help him get hold of Linda, since he didn't have the number of the restaurant where she worked.

Finally he called Mona at the beauty shop in Malmö where she worked. She was surprised to hear from him, at first thinking that something had happened to Linda. When Wallander told her that it was his father who had died, he could hear that she was slightly relieved. That made him angry, but he didn't say anything. He knew that Mona and his father had got along well. It was only natural that she would be worried about Linda. He remembered the morning that the *Estonia* had sunk.

"I know what you're going through," she said. "You've been afraid of this moment your whole life."

"We had so much to talk about," he replied. "We were finally seeing eye to eye. And now it's too late."

"It's always too late," she said.

She promised to come to the funeral and help out if he needed her. After they hung up he felt a lingering emptiness. He dialled Baiba's number in Riga, but she didn't answer. He called back again and again, but she wasn't home.

He went back out to the studio, and sat down on the old rickety toboggan where his father had sat, a coffee cup always in his hand. It was raining again. Wallander felt that he was holding his own fear of death in his hands. The studio had become a crypt. He got up quickly and went back to the kitchen. The phone rang. It was Linda, and she was crying. Wallander started crying too. She wanted to come as soon as possible. Wallander asked if he should call her employer and talk to him, but Linda had already arranged to take time off. She would take a bus to Arlanda and try to get on a plane that afternoon. He offered to pick her up from the airport, but she told him to stay with Gertrud. She would get to Ystad and out to Löderup on her own.

That evening they gathered in the house in Löderup. Gertrud was very calm. They began to discuss the funeral arrangements. Wallander doubted that his father would have wanted a religious ceremony, but he let Gertrud decide. She was his widow, after all.

"He never talked about death," she said. "I can't tell you if he was afraid of it or not. He didn't talk about where he wanted to be buried. But I want to have a vicar."

They agreed that it would be at the churchyard in Ystad. A simple funeral. His father hadn't had a lot of friends. Linda said she would read a poem, Wallander agreed that he wouldn't give a eulogy, and they chose "Wondrous Is the Earth" as the hymn they would sing.

Kristina arrived the next day. She stayed with Gertrud, and Linda stayed with Wallander. It was a time in which death brought them together. Kristina said that now that their father had passed on, the two of them were next in line. Wallander noticed the whole time that his fear of death was growing, but he didn't talk about it. Not to anyone. Not to Linda, not even to his sister. Maybe he could with Baiba sometime. She had reacted with deep feeling when he finally managed to get hold of her and tell her what had happened. They talked for almost an hour. She told him about her feelings when her own father had passed away ten years before, and she also talked about how she had felt when her husband Karlis was murdered. Afterwards Wallander felt comforted. She was there and she wasn't going away.

The day the obituary was printed in *Ystad's Allehanda*, Sten Widén called from his farm outside Skurup. It had been a few years since Wallander last talked to him. Once they had been close friends. They had shared an interest in opera and had high hopes for the future together. Widén had a beautiful voice, and Wallander would be his impresario. But everything changed when Widén's father died suddenly and he was forced to take over the farm, where they trained racehorses. Wallander became a policeman, and gradually they had drifted apart. After their conversation, Wallander wondered whether Widén had ever even met his father. But he was grateful that he had called. Someone outside the immediate family hadn't forgotten him.

In the midst of all this, Wallander had to force himself to continue to be a policeman. The day after his father died,

Tuesday, 4 October, he had returned to the police station, after spending a sleepless night in the flat. Linda slept in her old room. Mona had also come to visit the night before with supper, trying to take their minds off the old man's death for a while. For the first time since their devastating divorce, Wallander felt that his marriage was finally over. Somehow his father's death had shown him that the life he had led with Mona was over for good.

Despite sleeping badly the whole week before the funeral, he gave his colleagues the impression that he was in command of the situation. They had expressed their condolences and he had thanked them. When Chief Holgersson took him aside in the hall and suggested that he take some time off, he turned down her offer: his grief eased while he was working.

The investigation moved slowly during that week before the funeral. The other case they were concentrating on, always overshadowed by the murder of Eriksson, was Runfeldt's disappearance. He had vanished without trace. None of the detectives believed that there was a normal explanation. On the other hand, they hadn't been able to find any connection between Eriksson and Runfeldt. The only thing that seemed perfectly clear about Runfeldt was that his great passion in life was orchids.

"We ought to take a look at his wife's death," Wallander said at one of the investigative team's meetings. Höglund said she would take care of it.

"How about the mail-order company in Borås?" Wallander asked later. "What's happening with that? What do our colleagues there say?"

"They got onto it right away," Svedberg said. "It obviously wasn't the first time the company was involved in illegal importing of bugging devices. According to the

Borås police, the company would pop up and then vanish, only to reappear with a new name and address. Sometimes even with different owners. They've already made some progress there. We're waiting for a written report."

"The most important thing is to find out if Runfeldt had ever bought anything else from them," Wallander said. "The rest is not our immediate concern."

"Their list of customers is incomplete, to say the least. But the Borås police have found prohibited and highly sophisticated equipment at their offices. It sounds as though Runfeldt could practically be a spy."

Wallander pondered this for a moment.

"Why not?" he said finally. "We can't rule anything out. He must have had some reason for buying the stuff."

They had searched for Harald Berggren but hadn't found the slightest trace of him. The museum in Stockholm confirmed that the shrunken head was definitely human, and probably came from the Congo. So far so good. But who was this Berggren? They had already spoken with people who had known Eriksson during different periods of his life, but none had ever heard him speak of Berggren. No-one had heard that he'd had contact with the underworld in which mercenaries moved like wary rats and wrote their contracts with messengers of the Devil, either. It was Wallander who came up with the idea that got the investigation moving again.

"There's a lot of mystery surrounding Eriksson," he said. "Particularly the fact that there isn't a woman in his life. Not anywhere, not ever. That made me start to wonder whether there was a homosexual relationship between Eriksson and this Harald Berggren. There are almost no women in Berggren's diary either."

There was silence in the conference room. No-one seemed to have considered this possibility.

"It sounds a little strange that homosexual men would choose such a macho occupation as being soldiers," Höglund said.

"Not at all," Wallander replied. "It's not unusual for gay men to become soldiers. They do it to hide their preference. Or just to be around other men."

Martinsson studied the photograph of the three men.

"I get a feeling you might be right," he said. "These men have something feminine about them."

"Like what?" Höglund asked.

"I don't know," Martinsson said. "Maybe the way they're leaning against the termite mound. Or is their hair?"

"It doesn't do us any good to sit here guessing," Wallander interrupted. "I'm only pointing out one more possibility. We should keep it in mind, just like everything else."

"In other words, we're looking for a gay mercenary," Martinsson said dourly. "Where would we find one of those?"

"That's not exactly what we're doing," Wallander said. "But we have to weigh this possibility alongside the rest of the material."

"Nobody I spoke to so much as intimated that Eriksson might have been gay," said Hansson, who had been sitting in silence.

"It's not something people talk about openly," Wallander said. "At least not the older generation. If Eriksson was gay, then he can remember the time when blackmail was used against people of that persuasion in this country."

"So you mean we have to start asking people if

Eriksson may have been homosexual?" Svedberg asked.

"You have to decide how you want to proceed," Wallander said. "I don't even know if this is the right track, but we shouldn't ignore the possibility."

It was as if they all suddenly understood that there wasn't anything simple or easily understandable about the murder of Holger Eriksson. They were dealing with one – or maybe more – cunning killers, and it was possible that the motive for the murder lay hidden in a past well shielded from view.

They continued with the painstaking work. They recorded everything they knew about Eriksson's life. Svedberg spent long evenings reading carefully through the books of poetry Eriksson had published. In the end he thought he would go mad if he read any more about the spiritual complexities that existed in the world of birds, but he'd gained no insight into Eriksson.

Martinsson took his daughter Terese to Falsterbo Point one windy afternoon and walked around talking to bird-watchers standing straining their necks and staring up at the grey clouds. The only thing he gained – apart from time well-spent with his daughter, who wanted to become a field biologist – was that on the night Eriksson was murdered huge flocks of red-winged blackbirds had left Sweden. Martinsson conferred with Svedberg, who claimed that there were no poems about red-winged blackbirds in any of the books.

"On the other hand, there are three long poems about the single snipe," said Svedberg hesitantly. "Is there such a thing as a double snipe?"

Martinsson didn't know. The investigation continued.

The day of the funeral arrived. They were all meeting at the cemetery. A few days before, Wallander had learned to his surprise that a certain female vicar would officiate. He had met her on a memorable occasion in the summer. Afterwards he was glad that she was the one; her words were simple, and never sentimental. The day before, she had called to ask whether his father had been religious. Wallander said no. Instead, he told her about his paintings, and their week in Rome. The funeral was not as unbearable as Wallander had feared. The casket was made of dark wood with a simple decoration of roses. Linda was the one who showed her emotions most openly. No-one doubted that her sorrow was genuine. She was probably the one who would miss him the most.

After the ceremony they drove to Löderup. Wallander felt relieved that it was over. How he would react later he had no idea. He belonged to a generation that was particularly ill-prepared to accept that death was always nearby, he thought. This was intensified for him by the fact that he had to deal with dead people so often in his work.

On the night of the funeral he and Linda stayed up talking for hours. She was going back to Stockholm early the next morning. Wallander asked tentatively whether she would visit him less frequently now that her grandfather was gone, but she promised that she would come more often. In turn, Wallander promised that he wouldn't neglect Gertrud.

When he went to bed that night he felt that it was time to get back to work at full speed. For a week he had been distracted. Only when he had put some distance between himself and his father's sudden death could he begin to come to terms with it. To get that distance he had to work. There was no other way.

I never did find out why he didn't want me to be a

policeman, he thought before he went to sleep. Now I'll never know. If there is a spirit world, which I doubt, then my father and Rydberg can keep each other company. Even though they met very seldom when they were alive, they would find a lot to talk about.

She had made an exact and detailed timetable for Runfeldt's last hours. He was so weak now that he wouldn't be able to put up any resistance. She had broken him down. *The worm hidden in the flower portends the flower's death*, she thought as she unlocked the door to the house in Vollsjö. According to her timetable, she was to arrive at 4 p.m. She was three minutes ahead of schedule. She had to wait until dark. Then she would pull him out of the oven. For safety's sake she'd put handcuffs on him. And a gag. But nothing over his eyes. Even though he'd have trouble with the light after so many days spent in utter darkness, after a few hours he would see again. She wanted him to really see her. And then she would show him the photographs. The pictures that would make him understand.

There were some elements she couldn't completely ignore which might affect her planning. One was the risk that he might be so weak that he couldn't stand up, so she had borrowed a small baggage cart from the Central Station in Malmö. No-one had seen her taking it. She could use it to roll him out to the car if necessary.

The rest of the timetable was quite simple. Just before 9 p.m. she would drive him to the woods. She would tie him to the tree she had already picked out. And show him the photographs.

Then she would strangle him. Leave him where he was. She would be home in bed no later than midnight. Her alarm clock would go off at 5.15 a.m., and by 7.15 she'd be at work.

Her timetable was perfect. Nothing could go wrong. She sat down in a chair and looked at the oven towering like a sacrificial altar in the middle of the room. My mother would have understood, she thought. If no-one does it, it won't happen. Evil must be driven out with evil. Where there is no justice, it must be created.

She took her timetable out of her pocket and looked at the clock. In three hours and 15 minutes, Gösta Runfeldt would die.

Lars Olsson didn't really feel much like training on the evening of 11 October. He had been wondering whether he should go out on his run or forget about it. It wasn't just that he felt tired, there was a film on TV that he wanted to see. In the end he decided to go for his run after the movie, even though it would be late.

Olsson lived on a farm near Svarte. He had been born there, and still lived with his parents although he was over 30. He was the part owner of a digger and was the one who knew best how to operate it. This week he was busy digging a ditch for a new drainage system on a farm in Skårby. He was also a devoted orienteer. He lived for the joy of running in the Swedish woods. He ran for a team in Malmö that was preparing for a national night-orienteering run. He had often asked himself why he devoted so much time to it. What was the point of running around in the woods, often cold and wet, his body aching, with a map and compass? Was this really something to spend his life doing? But he knew he was a good orienteer. He had a feeling for the terrain, as well as both speed and endurance.

He watched the film on TV, but it wasn't as good as he expected. Just after 11 p.m. he started out on his run, headed for the woods just north of the farm, on the boundary of Marsvinsholm's huge fields. He could choose to run either five or eight kilometres, depending on which path he took. Tonight he chose the shorter route. He strapped his running light to his head and started off. It had rained that day, heavy showers followed by sunshine. He could smell the wet earth. He ran along the path into the woods. The tree trunks glistened in the light from his headlamp. In the densest part of the forest there was a little creek. If he kept close to it, it made a good shortcut. He decided to do that. He turned off the path and ran up a small hill.

Suddenly he stopped short. He had seen someone in the light of his lamp. At first he couldn't work out what he was looking at. Then he realised that a half-naked man was tied to a tree in front of him. Olsson stood quite still. He was breathing hard and felt very frightened. He took a quick look around. The lamp cast its glow over trees and bushes, but he was alone. Cautiously he took a few steps forward. The man was hanging over the ropes tied around his body.

He didn't have to go any closer. He could see that the man was dead. Without really knowing why, he glanced at his watch. It was 11.19 p.m.

He turned around and ran home. He had never run so fast in his life. Without even taking the time to remove his headlamp he called the police in Ystad. The officer who took the call listened attentively, then without hesitating, he called up Kurt Wallander's name on his computer screen and punched in his home number.

Skåne

12 – 17 October 1994

CHAPTER 13

Wallander was awake thinking about his father and Rydberg lying in the same cemetery when the telephone next to his bed rang. He grabbed it before the ringing woke Linda. With a feeling of mounting helplessness he listened to what the officer on duty had to say. Information was still sparse. Officers hadn't yet reached the woods south of Marsvinsholm. It was possible that the runner had been mistaken, but that was unlikely. The officer thought he sounded unusually lucid even though he was breathless and frightened. Wallander said he'd come at once. He dressed as quietly as he could, but Linda came out in her nightgown as he sat in the kitchen writing her a note.

"What's happened?" she asked.

"They found a man dead in the woods," he replied. "That means they call me."

She shook her head.

"Don't you get scared?"

"Why should I be scared?"

"About all the people who are dying."

He sensed rather than understood what she was trying to say.

"I can't. It's my job. Somebody has to deal with it."

He promised to be back in plenty of time to drive her to the airport in the morning.

It wasn't until he was on his way out to Marsvinsholm that it occurred to him that it might be Gösta Runfeldt who had been found in the woods. He had just left the town behind him when his phone rang. Police officers had confirmed the report.

"Any identification on him?" asked Wallander.

"No. Sounds like he barely had any clothes on. It looks pretty bad."

Wallander felt his stomach tying itself in knots, but he didn't say anything.

"They'll meet you at the crossroads. Take the first exit towards Marsvinsholm."

Wallander hung up and accelerated. He was dreading the sight that awaited him.

He saw the squad car at a distance and slowed to a stop. An officer was standing outside the car. He recognised Peters. Wallander rolled down his window and gave him an inquiring look.

"It's not a pretty sight," said Peters.

Wallander knew what that meant. Peters had plenty of experience. He wouldn't use those words casually.

"Has he been identified?"

"He barely has a stitch on. Go see for yourself."

"And the man who found him?"

"He's there too."

Peters went back to his car. Wallander drove behind him. They reached a clearing. The road ended near the remains of a logging operation.

"We'll have to walk the last stretch," Peters said.

Wallander got his gumboots out of the boot of his car. Peters and his partner, a young officer named Bergman who Wallander didn't really know, had brought powerful torches. They followed a path that led uphill to a little creek. There was a strong smell of autumn in the air. Wallander realised he should have worn a heavier jumper.

If he had to stay out in the woods all night he was going to get cold.

"We're almost there," Peters said.

Wallander knew he said it to warn him to brace himself. Even so, the sight that greeted him took him by surprise. The two torches shone with macabre precision on a man who hung, half-naked, tied to a tree. The beams of light quivered. Wallander stood quite still. Close by a night bird cried. He advanced cautiously. Peters shone his light so Wallander could see where he was putting his feet. The man's head and torso had fallen forward. Wallander got down on his knees to look at his face, and confirmed what he had suspected. Even though the photographs he had seen in Runfeldt's flat were several years old, there was no doubt that it was him. Now they knew what had happened.

Wallander got to his feet and took a step back. There was no longer any doubt in his mind about another thing. There was a connection between Eriksson and Runfeldt. The killer's language was the same, even if the choice of words was different this time. A pungee pit and a tree. It simply couldn't be a coincidence.

He turned towards Peters. "Get the team," he said.

Peters nodded. Wallander discovered he had left his telephone in the car. He asked Bergman to get it for him, and to bring the torch from the glove compartment.

"Where's the man who found him?" he asked.

Peters shone his torch to one side. On a rock sat a man in a tracksuit, his face buried in his hands.

"His name is Lars Olsson," Peters said. "He lives on a farm near here."

"What was he doing out in the woods in the middle of the night?"

"He's an orienteer," said Peters, handing him his torch.

Wallander went up to the man, who looked up quickly when the beam struck his face. He was very pale. Wallander introduced himself and sat down on a rock next to him, shivering involuntarily.

"So you're the one who found him."

Olsson told Wallander his story. About the bad movie on TV and his training run; how he'd decided to take a shortcut, and how he'd caught sight of the man in the beam of his headlamp.

"You've given a very exact time," Wallander said, remembering what the officer on duty had told him.

"I looked at my watch," Olsson replied. "It's a habit of mine – or rather a bad habit. When something important happens I look at my watch. If I could have, I would have looked at my watch when I was born."

Wallander smiled at him.

"So you take a run out here almost every night."

"I ran here last night, but earlier in the evening. I ran two routes. The long one first, followed by the short one. Then I took a shortcut."

"What time was that?"

"Between 9.30 and 10.00 p.m."

"And you didn't see anything then?"

"No."

"Could he have been here by the tree without you seeing him?"

Olsson thought for a moment and then shook his head.

"I always pass close to that tree. I would have seen him."

Wallander got up from the rock. There were torches approaching through the woods.

"Who would do something like this?" Olsson asked.

"That's what I'm wondering too," Wallander replied.

As Bergman took down Olsson's name and phone

number, Peters talked to the station. Wallander took a deep breath and approached the man hanging in the ropes. It astonished him for a moment that he wasn't thinking about his father at all, now that he was in the presence of death. But deep inside he knew why. He had been through it so many times before. Dead people weren't just dead, they had nothing human left in them. After the first wave of disgust passed, it was like approaching any other lifeless object.

Wallander felt the back of Runfeldt's neck cautiously. All body heat was gone. He hadn't really expected there to be any. Trying to determine the time of death outdoors was difficult. Wallander looked at the man's bare chest. The colour of the skin told him nothing about how long he had been hanging there either. Wallander shone his torch at Rundfeldt's throat and saw bruising. That could mean that he had been hanged. Next he inspected the ropes. They were wound round his body from his thighs up to his ribs. The knots were simple, and the ropes weren't tied very tightly. It surprised him.

He took a step backwards and shone his light on the whole body. Then he walked around the tree, watching carefully where he put his feet. He made only one circuit. He assumed that Peters had told Bergman not to tramp around unnecessarily. Peters was still talking on the phone. Wallander needed another jumper. He knew he should keep a spare in his car. It was going to be a long night.

He tried to imagine the sequence of events. The loosely tied ropes made him nervous. He thought about Eriksson. Runfeldt's murder might provide the solution. When they resumed the investigative work they would have to develop double vision. The clues would keep pointing in two directions at the same time. This could increase their confusion, and make the landscape of the investigation more and more difficult to define.

For a moment Wallander turned off his torch and thought in the dark. Peters was still talking on the phone. Bergman stood motionless nearby. Gösta Runfeldt hung dead in his loosely tied ropes. Is this a beginning, a middle, or an end? Wallander wondered. Do we have another serial killer on our hands? An even more difficult chain of events to unravel than we had in the summer? He had no answers. It was too early, far too early.

He heard engines in the distance. Peters went to meet the emergency vehicles that were approaching. Wallander thought of Linda and hoped she was asleep. Whatever happened, he would drive her to the airport in the morning. Suddenly a great wave of grief for his father surged through him. He longed for Baiba. And he was exhausted. He felt burnt out. All the energy he had felt on his return from Rome was gone. There was nothing left.

He forced himself to push away these dismal thoughts. Martinsson and Hansson came tramping through the trees, followed by Höglund and Nyberg. After them came the ambulance men and forensic technicians. Then Svedberg. Finally a doctor. They gave the impression of a poorly organised caravan that had wound up in the wrong place. Wallander started by gathering his closest colleagues round him in a circle. A floodlight hooked up to a portable generator was already aiming its eerie light on the man tied to the tree. Wallander couldn't help but be reminded of the macabre experience they had had by the ditch on Eriksson's property. It was being repeated. The framework was different and yet the same. The killer's designs were related.

"It's Gösta Runfeldt," said Wallander. "We'll have to wake up Vanja Andersson and bring her out here to give us a positive identification as soon as possible. We can wait until we've taken him down from the tree. She doesn't need to see that."

He described how Runfeldt had been found.

"He's been missing for almost three weeks," he went on. "But if I'm not mistaken, and if Lars Olsson is right, he's been dead for less than 24 hours. At least he hasn't been tied to this tree any longer than that. So where has he been all this time?"

"I don't believe that this is a coincidence. It has to be the same killer. We must find out what these two men have in common. So there are three investigations: Eriksson, Runfeldt, and the two of them together."

"What happens if we can't find a connection?" Svedberg asked.

"We will," replied Wallander firmly. "Sooner or later. The planning of both of these murders seems to exclude the possibility that the victims were chosen at random. Both men were killed with a specific aim in mind, for specific reasons."

"Gösta Runfeldt couldn't have been homosexual," Martinsson said. "He was married with two children."

"He could have been bisexual," Wallander said. "But it's too soon for those questions. We have things to do that are more urgent."

The circle broke up. It hadn't taken long to organise their work. Wallander went to speak to Nyberg, who was waiting for the doctor to finish.

"So it's happened again," Nyberg said in a weary voice.

"Yes," Wallander said, "and we have to get through it one more time."

"Just yesterday I decided to take a couple of weeks' holiday," Nyberg said. "As soon as we find out who killed

Eriksson. I thought I'd go to the Canary Islands. Not particularly imaginative, maybe – but warmer."

Nyberg seldom talked about personal matters. Wallander could see that he was exhausted. His workload was unreasonable. Wallander decided to take it up with Chief Holgersson. They didn't have the right to go on exploiting Nyberg's dedication. Just then he saw that the chief had arrived, and stood talking to Hansson and Höglund. She too had a lot on her plate, Wallander thought. With this second murder the media would have a field day. Her predecessor, Björk, could never handle pressure. Now they'd see if she could.

Wallander knew that Holgersson was married to a man who worked for a company that exported computers overseas. They had two grown children, and had bought a house in Hedeskoga, north of Ystad. Wallander hoped her husband gave her plenty of support. She'd need it.

The doctor got to his feet. Wallander had met him before, but he couldn't remember his name.

"It looks like he was strangled," the doctor said.

"Not hanged?"

The doctor held out his hands.

"Strangled with bare hands," he said. "It causes different types of pressure wounds than a rope. You can see the marks from the thumbs quite clearly."

A strong man, Wallander thought instantly. A person in good shape, who has no qualms about killing with his bare hands.

"How long ago?" he asked.

"It's impossible to say for sure. Within the last 24 hours, not longer. You'll have to wait for the pathologist's report."

"Can we take him down?"

"I've finished," said the doctor.

"Then I can get started," muttered Nyberg.

Höglund came up beside them. "Vanja Andersson is here. She's waiting in a car down there."

"How did she take the news?" asked Wallander.

"It's a hell of a way to be woken up, of course, but I got the feeling she wasn't surprised."

Nyberg had unwound the ropes. Runfeldt's body lay on a stretcher.

"Bring her up here," Wallander said. "Then she can go straight home."

Vanja Andersson was very pale. Wallander noticed she was dressed in black. She looked at the dead man's face, took a deep breath, and nodded.

"You can identify him as Gösta Runfeldt?" Wallander asked. He groaned inwardly at how clumsy this sounded.

"He's so thin," she murmured.

Wallander pricked up his ears. "What do you mean, thin?"

"His face is all sunken in. He didn't look like this three weeks ago."

Wallander knew that death could alter a person's face dramatically, but he guessed that Vanja Andersson was talking about something else.

"You mean he's lost weight since the last time you saw him?"

"Yes. He's grown terribly thin."

Wallander sensed that what she was saying was important.

"You don't have to stay here any longer," he said. "We'll drive you home."

She gave him a forlorn look.

"What am I supposed to do with the shop?" she asked. "And all the flowers?"

"Tomorrow you can leave it closed, I'm sure," Wallander answered. "Start with that. Don't think any further ahead."

She nodded mutely and allowed Höglund to lead her away. Wallander thought about what she had said. For almost three weeks Runfeldt had been missing without a trace. When he reappeared, tied to a tree and possibly strangled, he was inexplicably thin. Wallander knew what that meant: imprisonment.

He stood still. Imprisonment could be related to a wartime situation. Soldiers take prisoners.

He was interrupted when Chief Holgersson stumbled and almost fell as she walked over to him.

"You're freezing," she said.

"I forgot to bring a warmer jumper," Wallander replied. "Some things you never learn."

She nodded at the stretcher. It was being carried off towards the ambulance.

"What do you think of all this?" she asked.

"Same killer. It wouldn't make sense to think otherwise."

"The doctor says he was strangled."

"I try not to draw conclusions too soon," Wallander said. "But I think I can imagine how it all happened. He was alive when he was tied to the tree. Maybe unconscious, but he was strangled here. And he didn't put up any resistance."

"How can you be sure of that?"

"The ropes were tied loosely. If he'd wanted to, he could have struggled free."

"Couldn't the loose ropes indicate that he did try to free himself?"

Good question, thought Wallander. Lisa Holgersson is a detective, all right.

"That could be," he replied. "But I don't think so, because of something Vanja Andersson said. That he had grown terribly thin."

"I don't get the connection."

"He would have been very weak."

She understood.

"He was left hanging on the ropes," Wallander went on. "The killer didn't try to hide the body. It is very like what happened with Eriksson."

"Why here?" she asked. "Why tie a person to a tree? Why this brutality?"

"When we understand that, maybe we'll know why this happened in the first place," Wallander said.

"Have you any ideas?"

"I have plenty of ideas, but I think the best thing we can do now is let Nyberg and his people work in peace. It's more important to have a meeting in Ystad than to wander around out here wearing ourselves out. There's nothing left to see, anyway."

She didn't object. By 2 a.m. Nyberg and his forensic technicians were alone in the woods. It had started to drizzle and the wind came up. Wallander was the last to leave the scene.

What do we do now? he asked himself. How do we proceed? We don't have a motive or a suspect. All we have is a diary that belonged to a man named Harald Berggren. A bird-watcher and a passionate orchid lover have been killed with consummate savagery.

He tried to remember what Höglund had said. It was important. Something about the masculine world of Berggren. This made him think of a killer with a military background. Harald Berggren had been a mercenary. A person who defended neither his country, nor a cause. A man who killed people for a monthly wage, paid in cold cash.

At least we have a starting point, he thought. We have to stick with it until it collapses. He went over to say goodbye to Nyberg.

"Is there anything special you want us to look for?" he asked.

"No, but look for anything that reminds you of what happened to Eriksson."

"I think everything does," Nyberg said. "Only the bamboo stakes are missing."

"I want dogs up here early tomorrow," Wallander said.

"I'll probably still be here," said Nyberg dismally.

"I'm going to bring up your work situation with Lisa," Wallander said, hoping it would at least offer him a modicum of encouragement.

"It probably won't do any good."

"Well, it won't do any good not to try," Wallander said, putting an end to the conversation.

By 3 a.m. they were all gathered in the conference room. Wallander looked at the tired, sallow faces round the table, and realised that his main task was to infuse the investigative team with renewed energy. From experience he knew that there were moments in any investigation when it seemed as though all their self-confidence was gone. That moment had arrived unusually early this time.

We could have used a calm autumn, Wallander thought. The summer wore us out. He sat down and Hansson brought him a cup of coffee.

"This isn't going to be easy," he began. "What we feared most has happened. Gösta Runfeldt has been murdered.

Apparently by the same person who killed Holger Eriksson. We don't know what this means, and we don't know whether we're going to have more unpleasant surprises. We don't know if this will be similar to what we went through this summer. We shouldn't draw any parallels beyond the fact that the same man has been at work. There are a lot of differences between these two crimes. More differences than similarities."

He paused for comments. No-one had anything to say.

"We'll have to continue working on a wide front. We have to track down Harald Berggren. We have to find out why Runfeldt wasn't on that plane to Nairobi. We have to find out why he ordered sophisticated bugging equipment just before he died. We have to find a connection between these two men, who seem to have lived their lives with no contact with one another. Since the victims were obviously not chosen at random, there has to be some kind of link."

Still nobody had any comments. Wallander decided to adjourn the meeting. What they needed more than anything was a few hours' sleep. They would meet again in the morning.

Outside, the wind and rain had got worse. As Wallander hurried across the wet car park to his car, he thought about Nyberg and his forensic technicians. He also thought about Vanja Andersson having said that Runfeldt had become emaciated in the three weeks that he was missing. This had to mean imprisonment. But where had he been held captive? Why? And by whom?

CHAPTER 14

Wallander slept fitfully under a blanket on the sofa in his living room, since he had to get up in a few hours. It had been quiet in Linda's room when he'd come in. He had dozed off, then woken abruptly, drenched in sweat, after a nightmare he could only vaguely recall. He had dreamed about his father; they were in Rome again, and something frightening happened. What it was vanished into the darkness. Maybe in the dream, death had already been with them, like a warning. He sat up on the sofa with the blanket wrapped around him. It was 5 a.m. The alarm clock would ring any minute now. He sat there heavy and unmoving, exhaustion like a dull ache through his whole body. It seemed to take all his strength to get up and go to the bathroom. After a shower he felt a little better. He made breakfast and woke Linda at 5.45 a.m. By 6.30 a.m. they were on their way out to the airport. She was groggy and didn't say much during the ride. She didn't seem to wake up until they turned off the E65 for the last few kilometres to Sturup.

"What happened last night?" she asked.

"Someone found a dead man in the woods."

"Can't you tell me any more than that?"

"The body was found by an orienteer who was out running. He practically tripped over it."

"Who was it?"

"The orienteer or the dead man?"

"The dead man."

"A florist."

"Did he commit suicide?"

"No, unfortunately."

"Unfortunately?"

"He was murdered, and that means a lot of work for us."

She was silent for a while.

"I don't see how you stand it," she said.

"I don't either. But I have to. Somebody has to."

The question she asked next astonished him.

"Do you think I would make a good policewoman?"

"I thought you had other plans."

"I do, but answer the question."

"I don't know," he said. "You might."

They didn't say any more. Wallander pulled into the car park. She had only a backpack, which he lifted out of the boot. When he went to follow her in, she shook her head.

"Go home now," she said. "You're so tired you can hardly stand up."

"I have to work," he replied. "But you're right, I am tired."

Then there was a moment of sadness. They talked about his father, her grandfather. They said goodbye, and he watched her vanish through the glass doors that slid open and closed behind her.

He sat in the car and thought about something she had said. Was what made death so terrifying the fact that you had to be dead for such a long time?

He drove off. The grey landscape seemed just as dismal as the entire investigation. Wallander thought through what had happened. A man is impaled in a ditch. Another man is tied to a tree and strangled. Could deaths be any more repellent than those? It hadn't been any better seeing his father lying among his paintings. He needed to see Baiba again soon. He was going to call her. He couldn't stand the loneliness any more. It had been going on long enough. He had been divorced for five years. He was on the way to becoming an old, shaggy dog, scared of people. And that's not what he wanted to be.

He arrived at the police station, getting himself some coffee straight away. Then he called Gertrud. Her voice was cheerful. His sister was still there. Since Wallander was so busy with the investigation, they had agreed that the two of them would go through his father's meagre estate. His assets consisted mainly of the house in Löderup, but there were almost no debts. Gertrud asked if there was anything special that Wallander wanted to have. At first he said no. Then he changed his mind and said he'd like a painting, with a grouse, from the stacks of finished canvases leaning against the walls of the studio. Not the one his father had almost finished when he'd died.

He turned into a policeman again, starting by quickly reading a report on Höglund's conversation with the woman who delivered the post to Eriksson. Höglund wrote well, without awkward sentences or irrelevant details, but there was nothing that seemed to have direct significance for the investigation. The last time Eriksson had hung out the little sign on his letter box that meant he needed to talk to the postwoman was several months ago. As far as she could remember, it had had something to do with money orders. She hadn't noticed anything unusual at Eriksson's farm recently, or seen any strange cars or people in the area.

Wallander put the report aside, pulled over his notebook, and wrote some notes on the investigation. Someone had to interview Anita Lagergren at the travel agency in Malmö. When had Runfeldt reserved his trip? What was this orchid safari all about? They had to chart his life, just as they had to for Eriksson. It was especially important that they talked to his children. Wallander also wanted to know more about the equipment Runfeldt had bought. What exactly was it for? Why would a florist have these things? He was convinced that it was crucial to an understanding of what had happened. Wallander pushed the notebook away and sat hesitantly with his hand on the telephone. It was 8.15 a.m., and it was possible that Nyberg was asleep. But it couldn't be helped. He dialled his mobile phone. Nyberg answered at once, still out in the woods. Wallander asked him how it was going.

"We've got dogs here," Nyberg said. "They've picked up the scent from the rope at the logging site. But that's not so strange, since it's the only way up here. I think we can assume that Runfeldt didn't walk. There must have been a car."

"Any tyre tracks?"

"Quite a few. But I can't tell you which is which yet."

"Anything else?"

"The rope is from a factory in Denmark."

"Denmark?"

"I should think it could be bought just about anywhere that sells rope. Anyway, it seems new. Bought for the occasion," said Nyberg, to Wallander's disgust.

"Have you been able to find any sign that he resisted being tied to the tree? Or that he tried to work his way loose?"

"No. I haven't found any traces of a struggle nearby, the ground wasn't disturbed. And there are no marks on the rope or the tree trunk. He was tied up there, and he stood still."

"How do you interpret that?"

"There are two possibilities," Nyberg replied. "Either he was already dead, or at least unconscious, when he was tied up, or else he chose not to resist. But that's hard to believe."

Wallander thought about it.

"There's a third possibility," he said finally. "Runfeldt simply didn't have the strength to put up any resistance."

That was also a possibility, and maybe the most likely, Nyberg agreed.

"Let me ask one more thing," Wallander said. "I know you can't be certain, but we always imagine how something might have happened. Nobody guesses more often than policemen do, even though we might deny that we do. Was there more than one person there, do you think?"

"There are plenty of reasons why there should have been more than one person. Dragging a man into the woods and tying him up isn't that easy. But I doubt that there was."

"Why?"

"I don't know, to be honest."

"Go back to the ditch in Lödinge. What sort of feeling did you have there?"

"The same. There should have been more than one. But I'm not sure.

"I have that feeling too," Wallander said. "And it bothers me."

"At any rate, I think we're dealing with a person of great physical strength," Nyberg said. "There are plenty of indicators."

Wallander had no more questions.

"Otherwise nothing else at the scene?"

"A couple of beer cans and a false nail. That's it."

"A false nail?"

"The kind that women use. But it could have been here quite a while."

"Try to get some sleep," Wallander said.

"And when would I have time for that?" Nyberg answered. Wallander could hear him suddenly getting annoyed. He hung up, and the phone rang instantly. It was Martinsson.

"Can I come and see you?" he asked. "When are we supposed to have another meeting?"

"Nine o'clock. We've got time."

Wallander hung up. Martinsson must have come up with something. He could feel the tension. What they needed most of all right now was a breakthrough.

Martinsson came in and sat down. He got straight to the point.

"I've been thinking about all that mercenary stuff. And Berggren's diary. This morning when I woke up it struck me that I've actually met a person who was in the Congo at the same time as Harald Berggren."

"As a mercenary?" asked Wallander in surprise.

"No. As a member of the Swedish UN contingent that was supposed to disarm the Belgian forces in Katanga province."

Wallander shook his head. "I was 12 or 13 when all that happened. I don't remember much about it. Actually, nothing except that Dag Hammarskjöld was in a plane crash."

"I wasn't even born," Martinsson said. "But I remember something about it from school."

"Who was it you met?"

"Several years ago I was going to meetings of the People's Party," Martinsson continued. "There was often coffee afterwards. I got an ulcer from all the coffee I drank in those days."

Wallander drummed his fingers impatiently on the desk.

"At one of the meetings I wound up sitting next to a man of about 60. How we got to talking about it I don't know, but he told me he'd been a captain and adjutant to General von Horn, who was commander of the Swedish UN force in the Congo. I remember him mentioning that there were mercenaries involved."

Wallander listened with growing interest.

"I made a few calls this morning. One of my fellow party members knew who that captain was. His name is Olof Hanzell, and he's retired. He lives in Nybrostrand."

"Great," Wallander said. "Let's pay him a visit as soon as possible."

"I've already called him. He said he'd gladly talk to the police if we thought he could help. He sounded lucid and claimed he has an excellent memory."

Martinsson placed a slip of paper with a phone number on Wallander's desk.

"We have to try everything," Wallander said. "This morning's meeting will be short."

Martinsson stood up to go. He stopped in the door.

"Did you see the papers?" he asked.

"When would I have time for that?"

"People in Lödinge and other areas have been talking to the press. After what happened to Eriksson they've started talking about the need for a citizen militia."

"They've always done that," Wallander replied. "That's nothing to worry about."

"I'm not so sure," Martinsson said. "There's something different about these stories."

"What's that?"

"People aren't speaking anonymously any more. They're giving their names. That's never happened before. The idea of a citizen militia is acceptable all of a sudden."

Wallander knew that Martinsson was right, but he still doubted that it was more than the usual manifestation of fear when a brutal crime had been committed.

"There'll be more tomorrow once the news about Runfeldt gets out. It would probably be a good idea for us to prepare Chief Holgersson for what's coming."

"What's your impression?" Martinsson asked.

"Of Lisa Holgersson? I think she seems first-rate."

Martinsson stepped back into the room. Wallander saw how tired he was. He had aged rapidly during his years as a policeman.

"I thought what happened this summer was the exception," he said. "Now I realise it wasn't."

"There aren't many similarities," Wallander said. "We shouldn't draw parallels that aren't there."

"That's not what I was thinking about. It's all this violence. As if nowadays it's not enough to kill, you have to torture your victims as well."

"I know. But I can't tell you how we're supposed to deal with it."

Martinsson left the room. Wallander thought about what he had heard. He decided to talk to Captain Olof Hanzell himself that very day.

As Wallander had predicted, the meeting was brief. Even though no-one had had much sleep, they all seemed determined and energised. Per Åkeson had shown up to listen to Wallander's summary. Afterwards he had very few questions.

They divided up the assignments and discussed what should be given priority. The question of calling in extra manpower was left for the time being. Chief Holgersson had released more officers from other assignments so they could take part in the murder investigations, which would now involve twice as much work. When the meeting neared its conclusion after about an hour, they all had far too much work to handle.

"One more thing," Wallander said in closing. "We have to expect that these murders are going to get a lot of press. What we've seen so far is just the tip of the iceberg. As I understand it, people out in the surrounding areas have started to talk again about organising night patrols and a citizen militia. We'll have to wait and see if things develop the way I think they will. For now, it's easier if the chief and I handle the contact with the press. And I'd be grateful if Ann-Britt could help out at our press conferences."

Wallander talked to Chief Holgersson for a while after the meeting. They decided to hold a press conference at 5.30 p.m that day. Wallander went to find Per Åkeson, but he had already left. He went back to his office and called the number Martinsson had given him, remembering as he did so that he still hadn't put Svedberg's note on his desk. Captain Hanzell answered the phone. He had a friendly voice. Wallander introduced himself and asked if he could come out and see him that morning. Hanzell said he was welcome to, and gave him directions.

When Wallander left the station the sky had cleared again. It was windy, but the sun was shining between the scattered clouds. He reminded himself to put a jumper in his car. Though he was in a hurry, he stopped at an estate agent's and stood looking at the properties for sale in the window. One of the houses looked promising. If he'd had more time he would have gone and asked about it. He went back to his car, wondering whether Linda had managed to get on a plane to Stockholm or was still waiting at Sturup.

After taking several wrong turns, he finally found the correct address. He parked the car and walked through the gate of a villa that must have been less than ten years old, but still seemed rather dilapidated. The front door was opened by a man dressed in a tracksuit. He had close-cropped grey hair, a thin moustache, and seemed to be in good physical shape. He smiled and held out his hand in greeting. Wallander introduced himself.

"My wife died years ago," Hanzell said. "Since then I've lived alone. Please forgive the mess. But come on in!"

The first thing Wallander noticed was a large African drum in the hall. Hanzell followed his gaze.

"The year I was in the Congo was the journey of my life. I never travelled again. The children were small and my wife didn't want to. And then one day it was too late."

He invited Wallander into the living room, where coffee cups were set out on a table. There too, African mementos hung on the walls. Wallander sat down on a sofa and said yes to coffee. Actually, he was hungry and could use something to eat. Hanzell had put out a tray of biscuits.

"I bake them myself," he said, nodding at the biscuits. "It's a good pastime for an old soldier."

Wallander wanted to get to the point. He took the photograph of the three men out of his pocket and handed it across the table.

"I want to start by asking whether you recognise any of these men. I can tell you that the picture was taken in the Congo at the time that the Swedish UN force was there."

Hanzell took the photograph and put on a pair of reading glasses. Wallander remembered the visit he would have to make to the optician. Hanzell took the photograph over to the window and looked at it for a long time. Wallander listened to the silence that filled the house. He waited. Then Hanzell came back from the window. Without a word he laid the photograph on the table and left the room. Wallander ate another biscuit. He had almost decided to go and look for Hanzell when he returned with a photograph album in his hand, went back to the window, and starting leafing through it. Wallander kept waiting. Finally Hanzell found what he was looking for. He came back to the table and handed the open album to Wallander.

"Look at the picture at the lower left," Hanzell said. "It's not very clear, I'm afraid. But I think it might interest you."

Wallander looked. He gave an inward start. The photographs showed some dead soldiers. They lay lined up with bloody faces, arms blown off, their torsos torn apart by bullets. The soldiers were black. Behind them stood two white men holding rifles. They stood posing as if for a hunting photograph. The dead soldiers were their trophies.

Wallander recognised one of the white men at once. It was the one standing on the left in the photograph he had found stuffed into the binding of Harald Berggren's diary. There was absolutely no doubt.

"I thought I recognised him," Hanzell said. "But I couldn't be sure. It took me a while to find the right album."

"Who is he? Terry O'Banion or Simon Marchand?"

He saw Hanzell react with surprise.

"Simon Marchand," he replied. "I must admit I'm curious how you knew that."

"I'll explain in a minute. But first tell me how you got hold of these pictures."

Hanzell sat down.

"How much do you know about what was going on in the Congo in those days?" he asked.

"Practically nothing."

"Let me give you some background. I think it's necessary so you can understand."

"Take all the time you need," Wallander said.

"Let me start in 1953. At that time there were four independent countries in Africa that were members of the UN. Seven years later that number had climbed to 26. Which means that the entire African continent was in turmoil. Decolonisation had entered its most dramatic phase. New countries were proclaiming their independence in a steady stream. The birth pangs were often severe. But not always as severe as they were in the Belgian Congo. In 1959, the Belgian government worked out a plan for making the transition to independence. The date for the transfer of power was set for 30 June 1960. The closer that day came, the more the unrest in the country grew. Tribes took different sides, and acts of politically motivated violence happened every day. But independence came, and an experienced politician named Kasavubu became president, while Lumumba became prime minister. Lumumba is a name you've heard before, I presume."

Wallander nodded doubtfully.

"For a few days it looked as though there would be a peaceful transition from colony to independent state, in spite of everything. But then *Force Publique,* the country's regular army, mutinied against their Belgian officers. Belgian paratroopers were dropped in to rescue their own men. The country quickly sank into chaos. The situation became uncontrollable for Kasavubu and Lumumba. At the same time, Katanga province, the southernmost in the country and the richest because of its mineral resources, proclaimed its independence. Their leader was Moise Tshombe.

"Kasavubu and Lumumba requested help from the UN. Dag Hammarskjöld, the General Secretary at the time, quickly mustered an interventionist force of UN troops, including troops from Sweden. Our role was to serve as police only. The Belgians who were left in the Congo supported Tshombe in Katanga. With money from the big mining companies, they hired mercenaries. And that's where this photograph comes in."

Hanzell paused and took a sip of coffee.

"That might give you some idea how tense and complex the situation was."

"I can see it must have been extremely confusing," Wallander replied, waiting impatiently for him to continue.

"Several hundred mercenaries were involved during the conflict in Katanga," Hanzell said. "They came from many different countries: France, Belgium, the French colonies in Africa. It was only 15 years after the end of the Second World War, and there were still plenty of Germans who couldn't accept that the war had ended. They took their revenge on innocent Africans. There were also a number of Scandinavians. Some of them died and were buried in graves that can no longer be located. On one occasion an African came to the Swedish UN encampment. He had the papers and photographs of a number of mercenaries who had fallen. But none were Swedes."

"Why did he come to the Swedish encampment?"

"We were known to be polite and generous. He came

with a cardboard box and wanted to sell the contents. God knows where he had got hold of it."

"And you bought it?"

"I think I paid the equivalent of ten kronor for the box. I threw most of it away. But I kept a few of the photographs. Including this one."

Wallander decided to go one step further.

"Harald Berggren," he said. "One of the other men in the photograph is Swedish and that's his name. He must be either the one in the middle or the one on the right. Does that name mean anything to you?"

Hanzell shook his head.

"No. But on the other hand, that's not so surprising."

"Why?"

"Many of the mercenaries changed their names. Not just the Swedes. You took a new name for the time of your contract. When it was all over and if you were lucky enough to be alive, you could assume your old name again."

"So Harald Berggren could have been in the Congo under a different name?'"

"Exactly."

"And that could also mean that he may have been killed under another name?"

"Yes."

"So it's almost impossible to say whether he's alive or dead, and it would be almost impossible to find him, if he didn't want to be found."

Hanzell nodded. Wallander stared at the tray of biscuits.

"Many of my former colleagues thought differently," Hanzell said, "but for me, the mercenaries were despicable. They killed for money, even if they claimed they were fighting for an ideal: for freedom, against communism. But the truth was something else. They killed indiscriminately, and they took orders from whoever was paying the most at that moment."

"A mercenary must have had considerable difficulty returning to normal life," Wallander said.

"Many of them never managed to. They turned into shadows, on the periphery of society. Often they drank themselves to death. Many were probably mentally unbalanced to start with."

"How do you mean?"

Hanzell's reply was forthright.

"Sadists and psychopaths."

CHAPTER 15

Wallander stayed in Nybrostrand until late in the afternoon. He had left the house at 1 p.m., but when he came out into the autumn air, he felt at a total loss. Instead of returning to Ystad he drove down to the sea. A walk might help him think. But when he got down to the beach and felt the biting wind, he changed his mind and went back to the car. He sat in the front on the passenger side and leaned the seat back as far as it would go. Then he closed his eyes and started going over everything that had taken place since the morning when Sven Tyrén had come into his office and reported Holger Eriksson missing.

Wallander tried to map out the sequence of events. Of all the things he had learned from Rydberg over the years, one of the most important was that the events that occurred first were not necessarily the first in the chain of causality. Eriksson and Runfeldt had both been killed, but were their murders acts of revenge? Or was it a crime committed for gain, even though he couldn't see what kind of gain that might be?

He opened his eyes and looked at a tattered string of flags whipping in the stiff breeze. Eriksson had been impaled in a pit full of sharpened stakes. Runfeldt had been held prisoner and then strangled. Why the explicit display of cruelty? And why was Runfeldt held prisoner before he was killed? Wallander tried to go through the basic assumptions that the investigative team had to start with. The killer must have known both victims. He was familiar with Eriksson's routines. He must have known that Runfeldt was going to Africa. And he wasn't at all concerned that the dead men would be found. The opposite seemed to be the case.

Why put something on display? he wondered. So that somebody will notice what you've done. Did the murderer want other people to see what he had accomplished? If so, what was it he wanted to show? That those two particular men were dead? No, not only that. He also wanted it to be clear that they had been killed in particularly gruesome, premeditated ways.

If that was the case, then the murders of Eriksson and Runfeldt were part of something much bigger. It didn't necessarily mean that more people would die, but it definitely meant that Eriksson, Runfeldt, and the person who had killed them had to be looked for among a larger group of people. Some type of community – such as a group of mercenaries in a remote African war.

Wallander suddenly wished he had a cigarette. Even though it had been unusually easy for him to quit several years back, there were times when he wished he still smoked. He got out of the car and switched to the back seat. Changing seats was like changing perspective. He soon forgot the cigarettes and went back to what he was thinking about.

The most important thing was to find the connection between Eriksson and Runfeldt. He was convinced that there was one. They needed to know more about the two men. Outwardly they had very little in common. The differences began with their ages. They belonged to different generations. Eriksson could have been Runfeldt's father. But somewhere there was a point at which their paths crossed.

The search for that point had to be the focus of the investigation now. Wallander couldn't see any other route to take.

His phone rang. It was Höglund.

"Has something happened?" he asked.

"I have to admit I'm calling out of sheer curiosity," she replied.

"The talk with Captain Hanzell was productive," Wallander said. "One thing I've learned is that Harald Berggren could be living under an assumed name. Mercenaries often use false names when they sign their contracts or make verbal agreements."

"That's going to make it harder for us to find him."

"That was my first thought, too. It's like dropping the needle back into the haystack. But how many people actually change their names during their lifetimes? Even though it's going to be a tedious task, it should be possible to check the records."

"Where are you?"

"At the beach. In Nybrostrand."

"What are you doing there?"

"As a matter of fact, I'm sitting in the car thinking." He noticed the sharpness in his voice, as if he felt the need to defend himself. He wondered why.

"Then I won't bother you," she said.

"You're not bothering me. I'm coming back now. I'm thinking of driving past Lödinge on the way."

"Any special reason?"

"I need to refresh my memory. Later I'm going over to Runfeldt's flat. I'll try to be there by 3 p.m. Could you arrange for Vanja Andersson to meet me there?"

"I'll see to it."

Wallander drove towards Lödinge. In his mind the investigation had been given a sketchy outline.

When he turned into the driveway to Eriksson's house, he was surprised to see two cars there. He wondered who the visitors could be. Reporters devoting an autumn day to taking pictures of a murder scene, perhaps? He had his answer as soon as he entered the courtyard. Standing there was a lawyer whom Wallander had met before. There were also two women, one elderly and one about Wallander's age. The lawyer, whose name was Bjurman, shook hands and said hello.

"I'm overseeing Eriksson's will," he said. "We thought the police were finished with their investigations. I called and asked at the police station."

"We won't be finished until we catch the killer," Wallander replied. "But I have nothing against you going through the house."

Wallander remembered that Bjurman was Eriksson's executor. The lawyer introduced Wallander to the two women. The older one shook his hand with disdain, as if it was beneath her dignity to have anything to do with the police. Wallander, who was extremely sensitive to people's snobbery, was instantly annoyed, but he hid his feelings. The other woman was friendly.

"Mrs Mårtensson and Mrs von Fessler are from the Cultural Association in Lund. Mr Eriksson bequeathed most of his estate to the association. He kept a meticulous record of his property. We were just about to start going through everything."

"Let me know if anything's missing," Wallander said. "Otherwise I won't disturb you. I'm not staying long."

"Is it true the police haven't found the murderer?" said Mrs von Fessler, the older woman. Wallander assumed that she meant this as a criticism.

"That's right," he said. "The police have not."

Knowing that he should end the conversation before he got angry, he turned and walked up to the house, where the front door stood open. To insulate himself from the conversation going on out in the courtyard, he shut the door behind him. A mouse raced right by his feet and disappeared behind an old wardrobe that stood against the wall. It's autumn, thought Wallander. The field mice are making their way into the walls of the house. Winter is on its way.

He went through the house slowly. He wasn't looking for anything in particular; he just wanted to memorise the house. It took him about 20 minutes. Bjurman and the two women were in one of the other two wings when he came outside again. Wallander decided to leave without saying anything. He looked out towards the fields as he walked to his car. The rooks were gone. Just as he reached the car he halted. Bjurman had said something – at first he couldn't recall what it was. He retraced his steps. He pushed open the door, and beckoned to Bjurman.

"What was it you said about the will?" he asked.

"Holger Eriksson bequeathed most of his estate to the Cultural Association in Lund."

"Most? So not everything is going to it?"

"There's a bequest of 100,000 kronor to another beneficiary. That's all."

"What other beneficiary?"

"A church in Berg parish – Svenstavik Church. A gift, to be used in accordance with the wishes of the church authorities."

Wallander had never heard of the place.

"Is Svenstavik in Skåne?" he asked dubiously.

"It's in southern Jämtland," Bjurman replied. "Near the border of Härjadal."

"What did Eriksson have to do with Svenstavik?" Wallander asked in surprise. "I thought he was born here in Ystad."

"Unfortunately I have no information on that," Bjurman replied. "Mr Eriksson was a very secretive man."

"Did he give any explanation for the gift?"

"The will is an exemplary document, brief and precise. No explanations of an emotional nature are included. Svenstavik Church, according to his last wish, is to receive 100,000 kronor. And that is what it shall receive."

When Wallander got back to his car he called the station. Ebba answered. She was the one he wanted to talk to.

"I want you to find the phone number for the parsonage at Svenstavik," he said. "Or it might be in Östersund. I assume that's the nearest city."

"Where is Svenstavik?" she asked.

"Don't you know?" Wallander said. "It's in southern Jåmtland."

"Very funny," she replied.

"When you get the number, let me know," he said. "I'm on my way to Runfeldt's flat now."

"Chief Holgersson wants to talk to you right away," Ebba said. "Reporters keep calling here. But she's postponed the press conference until 6.30 tonight."

"That suits me," Wallander said.

"Your sister called, too," Ebba went on. "She'd like to talk to you before she goes back to Stockholm."

The reminder of his father's death was both swift and harsh, but he couldn't give in to his feelings. At least not right now.

"I'll call her," he said. "But the parsonage in Svenstavik is top priority."

On his way back to Ystad, he stopped and ate a flavourless hamburger at a takeaway restaurant. He was about to get back into his car, but then he turned back and ordered a hot dog. He ate quickly, as if he were committing an illegal act. Then he drove to Västra Vallgatan. Höglund's old car was parked outside Runfeldt's building.

The wind was still blowing hard. Wallander was cold. He hunched up his shoulders as he hurried across the street.

It wasn't Höglund but Svedberg who opened the door to Runfeldt's flat.

"She had to go home," said Svedberg. "One of her children is sick. Her car wouldn't start, so she took mine. But she'll be back."

Wallander went into the living room and looked around.

"Is Nyberg finished already?" he asked in surprise.

Svedberg gave him a baffled look.

"Didn't you hear?" he asked.

"Hear what?"

"About Nyberg's foot."

"I haven't heard a thing," said Wallander. "What happened?"

"He slipped on some oil outside the station. He fell so hard that he tore a muscle or a tendon in his left foot. He's at the hospital right now. He called and said he can still work, but he'll have to use a crutch. He was really pissed off."

Wallander thought about Tyrén's truck. He decided not to mention it.

Vanja Andersson arrived. She was very pale. Wallander nodded to Svedberg, who disappeared into Runfeldt's study. He took her into the living room. She seemed frightened to be in the flat, and hesitated when he invited her to sit down.

"I know this is unpleasant," he said. "But I wouldn't have asked you to come here if it wasn't absolutely necessary."

She nodded. Wallander doubted whether she really understood.

"You've been to this flat before," Wallander said. "And you have a good memory. I know that because you remembered the colour of Mr Runfeldt's suitcase."

"Have you found it?" she asked.

Wallander realised that they hadn't even started looking for it. He excused himself and went to find Svedberg, who was methodically searching the contents of a bookshelf.

"Have you heard anything about Runfeldt's suitcase?"

"Did he have a suitcase?"

Wallander shook his head. "Never mind. I'll talk to Nyberg."

He went back to the living room. Vanja Andersson was sitting uneasily on the sofa. Wallander could see that she wanted to get out as soon as possible. She looked as if she had to force herself to breathe the air in the flat.

"We'll come back to the suitcase," he said. "What I'd like to ask you now is to go through the flat and try to see if anything is missing.

She gave him a terrified look.

"How could I tell? I haven't been here very often."

"I know," Wallander said. "But you still might see that something is missing. Right now everything is important, if we're going to find the person who did this. I'm sure you want that as much as we do."

She burst into tears. Svedberg appeared in the door. As usual in this kind of situation, Wallander felt helpless. He wondered if new officers were better trained in how to comfort people. He must ask Höglund about it.

Svedberg handed Vanja Andersson a tissue. She stopped crying as suddenly as she had started.

"I'm terribly sorry," she said. "It's so difficult."

"I know," Wallander said. "There's nothing to be sorry about. I don't think people cry often enough."

She looked at him.

"That goes for me too," Wallander said.

After a brief pause she got up from the sofa. She was ready to begin.

"Take your time," Wallander told her. "Try to remember how it looked the last time you were here."

He followed her but kept his distance. When he heard Svedberg cursing in the study, he went in and held a finger to his lips. Svedberg nodded; he understood. Wallander had often thought that significant moments in investigations occurred either during conversations or during periods of absolute silence. He had seen it happen countless times. Right now, silence was essential. He could see that she was really making an effort.

Even so, nothing came of it. They returned to the living room. She shook her head.

"Everything looks the same as usual," she said. "I can't see that anything is missing or different."

Wallander was not surprised. He would have noticed if she had paused during her survey of the flat.

"You haven't thought of anything else?" he asked.

"I thought he had gone to Nairobi," she said. "I watered his flowers and took care of the shop."

"You did both of those things very well," Wallander said. "Thank you for coming. We'll be in touch."

He escorted her to the door. Svedberg reappeared just as she left.

"Nothing seems to be missing," Wallander said.

"He seems to have been a complicated man," Svedberg said thoughtfully. "His study is a strange mixture of chaos and order. When it comes to his flowers, there's perfect order. I never imagined there were so many books about orchids. But when it comes to his personal life, his papers are a big mess. In his account books from the shop for this year, I found a tax return from 1969. By the way, in that year he declared a dizzying income of 30,000 kronor."

"I wonder how much we made back then," Wallander said. "Probably not much more than that. Most likely less. I seem to remember that we were getting about 2,000 kronor a month."

They pondered this until Wallander said, "Let's keep searching."

Svedberg went back to what he was doing. Wallander stood by the window and looked out over the harbour. The front door opened. It was Höglund. He met her out in the hall.

"Nothing serious, I hope?"

"An autumn cold," she said. "My husband is in what used to be called the East Indies. My neighbour rescued me."

"I've often wondered about that," said Wallander. "I thought helpful women neighbours became extinct back in the 1950s."

"That's probably true. But I've been lucky. Mine is in her 50s and has no children. Of course she doesn't do it for free. And sometimes she says no."

"Then what do you do?"

She shrugged.

"I improvise. If it's in the evening I might be able to find a babysitter. Sometimes I wonder myself how I cope, and you know that there are times when I come in late. I don't think men really understand what a complicated business it is trying to handle your job when you have a sick child."

"Probably not," Wallander replied. "Maybe we should see to it that your neighbour gets some kind of medal."

"She's been talking about moving," Höglund said gloomily. "What I'll do then, I don't even dare think about."

"Has Vanja Andersson been here?" Höglund asked.

"Nothing seems to have disappeared from the flat," Wallander replied. "But she reminded me of something completely different. Runfeldt's suitcase. I have to admit I forgot all about it."

"Me too," she said. "They didn't find it out in the woods. I talked to Nyberg right before he broke his foot."

"Is it that bad?"

"Well, it's badly sprained, anyway."

"Then he's going to be in a foul mood for a while. Which is not good at all."

"I'll invite him over for dinner," Höglund said cheerfully. "He likes boiled fish."

"How do you know that?" Wallander asked in surprise.

"I've had him over before," she replied. "He's a very nice dinner guest. He talks about all kinds of things, and never about his job."

Wallander wondered briefly whether he would be considered a nice dinner guest. He knew that he tried not to talk about work. But when was the last time he had been invited somewhere for dinner? It was so long ago that he couldn't even remember.

"Runfeldt's children have arrived," Höglund said. "Hansson is looking after them."

They were now in the living room. Wallander looked at the photograph of Runfeldt's wife.

"We should find out what happened to her," he said.

"She drowned."

"I mean the details."

"Hansson understands that. He's usually thorough in his interviews. He'll ask them about their mother."

Wallander knew she was right. Hansson had many bad traits, but one of his best skills was interviewing witnesses. Gathering information. Interviewing parents about their children. Or vice versa, as in this case.

Wallander told Höglund about his conversation with Hanzell, skipping a lot of the details. The most important part was his conclusion that Berggren might be living under a different name. He had mentioned it when they had spoken earlier. He noticed that she had been thinking more about this.

"If he changed his name legally we can track it down through the Registry Office," she said.

"A mercenary soldier wouldn't follow such a formal process," Wallander objected. "But of course we'll look into it, like everything else. It'll be time-consuming."

He told her about his meeting with the women from Lund and the lawyer at Eriksson's farm.

"My husband and I drove through the interior of Norrland once," she said. "I have a distinct memory of passing through Svenstavik."

"Ebba should have called to give me the number of the parsonage," Wallander remembered, taking his phone out of his pocket. It was turned off. He cursed his carelessness. Höglund couldn't conceal her amusement. Wallander realised he was acting like a child. Embarrassed, he called the police station. He borrowed a pen and wrote down the number. Ebba had tried to reach him several times.

At that moment, Svedberg came into the living room with a stack of papers in his hand. Wallander saw that they were receipts.

"This might be something," Svedberg said. "Runfeldt has a place on Harpegatan. He pays rent once a month. As far as I can tell, he keeps it totally separate from any payments that have to do with the shop."

"Harpegatan?" Höglund asked. "Where's that?"

"Over by Nattmanstorg," Wallander replied. "Right in the centre of town."

"Has Vanja Andersson ever mentioned that he had another place?"

"The question is whether she knew about it," said Wallander. "I'll find out right now."

Wallander left the flat and walked the short distance to the shop. He bent over and held his breath in the wind. Vanja Andersson was alone. As before, the scent of flowers was strong. A brief feeling of homelessness came over Wallander as he thought about Rome, and his father. But he pushed the thoughts aside. He was a policeman. He would grieve later, not now.

"I have a question," he said. "You can probably give me a straight yes-or-no answer."

She looked at him with her pale, frightened face. Certain people gave the impression of always being prepared for the worst. Vanja Andersson seemed to be one of those people. Right now he could hardly blame her.

"Did you know that Mr Runfeldt rented a place on Harpegatan?" he asked.

She shook her head.

"Are you sure?"

"Gösta didn't have any other place but this one."

Wallander suddenly felt in a big hurry.

"That's all then," he said. "Thanks."

When he got back to the flat, Svedberg and Höglund had gathered all the keys they could find. They took Svedberg's car to Harpegatan. It was an ordinary block of flats. Runfeldt's name wasn't on the list of residents in the entrance.

"I think it's in the basement," said Svedberg.

They made their way down to the floor below. Wallander noticed the sharp fragrance of winter apples. Svedberg started trying the keys. The twelfth one worked. They went into a hall from which red, steel doors led to what looked like storerooms.

Höglund was the one who found it.

"I think this is it," she said, pointing to a door.

Wallander and Svedberg went to stand next to her. On the door there was a sticker with a floral motif.

"An orchid," Svedberg said.

"A secret room," Wallander replied.

Svedberg tried the keys again. Wallander noticed that an extra lock was set into the door.

Finally the first lock clicked. Wallander felt the tension inside him swell. Svedberg kept on trying the keys. He had only two left when he looked at them and nodded.

"Let's go in," Wallander said.

Svedberg opened the door.

CHAPTER 16

The terror sank into Wallander like a claw. When the thought came it was already too late. Svedberg had opened the door. In that brief instant when terror replaced time, Wallander waited for the explosion to come. But all that happened was that Svedberg felt with one hand along the wall and muttered, wondering where the light switch was. Afterwards, Wallander felt embarrassment at his fear. Why would Runfeldt have booby-trapped his cellar?

Svedberg turned on the light. They entered the room and looked around. Since it was under ground, there was only a thin row of windows along the top of the wall. The first thing Wallander noticed was that the windows had iron gratings on the inside. That was unusual, something Runfeldt must have added himself.

The room was set up as an office. There was a desk, and filing cabinets along the walls. On a small table next to the wall stood a coffee maker and some cups. The room had a telephone, fax machine, and photocopier.

"Should we look around or wait for Nyberg?" Svedberg asked.

Wallander heard him, but waited to reply. He was still trying to understand his first impressions. Why had Runfeldt rented this room? Why hadn't Vanja Andersson known about it? And most important: what did he use the room for?

"No bed," Svedberg continued. "It doesn't seem to be a love nest."

"No woman could get romantic down here," Höglund said.

Wallander still hadn't answered Svedberg. The most important question was why Runfeldt had kept this office secret. It was an office, there was no doubt about that.

He let his gaze wander along the walls. There was another door. He nodded to Svedberg, who walked over and tried the handle. The door was open. He looked inside.

"It looks like a darkroom," Svedberg said.

Wallander wondered if there could be a simple reason for this space. Runfeldt took a lot of photographs. He had a big collection of orchid photographs from all over the world in his flat. Wallander and Höglund went and looked over Svedberg's shoulder. It was indeed a tiny darkroom. Wallander decided they didn't have to wait for Nyberg. They could go through the room themselves.

The first thing he looked for was a suitcase, but there wasn't one. Next he sat down at the desk and started leafing through the papers on the desk. Svedberg and Höglund concentrated on the filing cabinets. Wallander remembered vaguely that Rydberg, way back in the beginning, on one of those frequent evenings when they sat on his balcony drinking whisky, had said that the work of a policeman and an auditor was quite similar. They spent a good deal of their time going through papers. If that's correct, then right now I'm auditing a dead man, he thought.

Wallander pulled out one of the desk drawers and found a laptop computer. Wallander's computer literacy was limited. He often had to ask for help with the computer in his office. Both Svedberg and Höglund were comfortable with computers and viewed them as essential working tools.

"Let's see what's hiding in here," he said, lifting the computer onto the desk.

He got up from the chair. Höglund sat down. After a moment the screen lit up. Svedberg was still going through one of the filing cabinets.

"No passwords," she muttered. "I'm in."

Wallander leaned forward to watch, so closely that he could smell the discreet perfume she wore. He thought about his eyes. He couldn't wait any longer. He had to get reading glasses.

"It's a directory," she said. "A list of names."

"See if Harald Berggren is on it," Wallander said.

She shot him a look of astonishment.

"You think?"

"I don't think anything. But we can try."

Svedberg had left the filing cabinet and now stood next to Wallander while Höglund searched through the directory. Then she shook her head.

"Holger Eriksson?" Svedberg suggested.

Wallander nodded. She searched. Nothing.

"Just browse through the directory at random," said Wallander.

"Here's a man named Lennart Skoglund," she said. "Should we try him?"

"That's Nacka, damn it!" Svedberg exclaimed. "There's a famous soccer player named Lennart Skoglund," said Svedberg. "His nickname is Nacka. Haven't you heard of him?"

Wallander nodded. Höglund didn't know who he was.

"Lennart Skoglund sounds like a common name," Wallander said. "Let's look him up."

She pulled up the record on him. Wallander squinted his eyes and managed to read the brief text.

Lennart Skoglund. Started June 1994. Ended 19 August 1994. No steps taken. Case closed.

"What does that mean?" Svedberg wondered.

"It's almost like one of us had written it," Höglund said.

At that instant Wallander knew what the explanation might be. He thought about the technical equipment Runfeldt had bought. And about the darkroom, and the secret office. The whole thing had seemed improbable, yet now, as they stood leaning over the directory, likely.

Wallander stretched his back.

"The question is whether Runfeldt was interested in other things besides orchids. The question is whether Runfeldt might also have been a private detective. Go through everything you find here. Keep your eyes peeled and don't forget Eriksson. And I want one of you to get hold of Vanja Andersson. Without knowing it, she might have seen or heard things that have to do with this little operation. I'm going back to the station to talk to Runfeldt's children."

"What do we do about the press conference?" Höglund asked. "I promised to be there."

"It's better if you stay here."

Svedberg offered his car keys to Wallander, who shook his head.

"I'll get my own car. I need a walk anyway."

When he reached the street he regretted it at once. The wind was strong and it seemed to be getting colder all the time. He hesitated a moment, wondering whether to go home and get a warmer jumper. But he was in a hurry, and he was uneasy. They had made some new discoveries, but they didn't fit into the picture. Why had Runfeldt been a private detective? Wallander hurried through town and got his car. The fuel gauge was showing empty, but he didn't have time to get petrol. His uneasiness made him impatient.

He reached the police station just before 4.30 p.m. Ebba handed him a pile of phone messages, which he stuffed into his jacket pocket. When he got to his office he called Chief Holgersson. She reminded him about the press conference. Wallander promised to take care of it. It wasn't something he liked to do. He was too easily annoyed by what he regarded as impertinent questions from the reporters. On several occasions there had been complaints about his lack of cooperation, even from Stockholm. This had brought home to Wallander that he was known outside his own circle of colleagues and friends. For better or worse, he had become part of Sweden's national police force.

He gave the chief a quick outline of the discovery of Runfeldt's office, not mentioning his idea that Runfeldt had been operating as a private detective. Then he hung up and called Hansson. Runfeldt's daughter was in his office. They agreed to meet briefly out in the hall.

"I've interviewed the son," Hansson said. "He's back at the Hotel Sekelgården."

Wallander nodded.

"Any luck?"

"Not much. He confirmed the picture of Runfeldt as a man passionately interested in orchids."

"And his mother? Runfeldt's wife?"

"A tragic accident. You want the details?"

"Not now. What does the daughter say?"

"I was just about to talk to her. It took some time with the son. I'm trying to do this as thoroughly as I can. The son lives in Arvika, by the way, and the daughter in Eskilstuna."

Wallander looked at his watch. He should be preparing for the press conference, but he could talk to the daughter for a few minutes first.

"Do you have any objections if I start by asking her a few questions?"

"No, go right ahead."

"I don't have time to explain right now, and the questions might sound strange to you."

They went into Hansson's office. The woman sitting there was young – Wallander guessed no more than 23 or 24. He could see that she resembled her father. She stood up when he came in, and Wallander smiled and shook her hand. Hansson leaned against the doorframe while Wallander sat in his chair.

Hansson had written down a name, Lena Lönnerwall. Wallander gave Hansson a quick glance, and he nodded. He took off his jacket and put it on the floor next to the chair. She followed his movements with her eyes the whole time.

"I should start by saying how sorry we are at what's happened," he said. "My condolences."

"Thank you."

Wallander could see that she was composed. She wasn't about to burst into tears, he noted with some relief.

"Your name is Lena Lönnerwall and you live in Eskilstuna," Wallander said. "You are the daughter of Gösta Runfeldt."

"That's correct."

"All the other personal information that is unfortunately necessary will be taken by Inspector Hansson. I have only a few questions. Are you married?"

"Yes."

"What's your profession?"

"I'm a basketball coach."

Wallander pondered her answer.

"Does that mean you're a PE teacher?"

"It means I'm a basketball coach."

Wallander nodded. He left the follow-up questions to Hansson. He had never met a female basketball coach before.

"Your father was a florist?"

"Yes."

"All his life?"

"In his youth he went to sea. When he and my mother got married he stayed ashore."

"And your mother was drowned?"

"That's right."

The instant of hesitation that preceded her reply hadn't escaped Wallander.

"How long ago did that happen?"

"About ten years ago. I was just 13."

Wallander sensed that she was anxious. He continued cautiously.

"Can you give me a little more detail about what happened, and where?"

"Does this really have something to do with my father?"

"It's police routine to ask for background information," said Wallander, trying to sound authoritative. Hansson stared at him in amazement from his place by the door.

"I don't know that much about it," she said.

Wrong, thought Wallander. You know, but you don't want to talk about it.

"Tell me what you do know," he said.

"It was in the winter. For some reason they took a drive out to Älmhult to take a walk one Sunday. She fell through a hole in the ice. My father tried to save her. But it was no use."

Wallander sat motionless. He was thinking about what she had said. Something was related to the investigation they were working on. Then it occurred to him what it was. It wasn't about Runfeldt, but about Eriksson. A man falls into a hole in the ground and is impaled. Lena Lönnerwall's mother falls through a hole in the ice. Wallander's instinct told him that there was a connection, but he couldn't say what it was. Or why the woman sitting across from him didn't want to talk about her mother's death.

He left the accident and moved on.

"Your father had a florist's shop, and he had a passion for orchids."

"That's the first thing I remember about him. The way he told me and my brother about flowers."

"Why was he such a passionate orchid lover?"

"Why does anyone become passionate about something? Can you answer that?"

Wallander shook his head without replying.

"Did you know that your father was a private detective?"

Over by the door Hansson gave a start. Wallander kept his gaze steady on the woman in front of him. Her astonishment seemed genuine.

"My father was a private detective?"

"Yes. Didn't you know that?"

"That can't be true."

"Why not?"

"I don't understand. I don't even know exactly what a private detective is. Do we really have them in Sweden?"

"That's a different question altogether," Wallander said. "But your father spent time doing business as a private detective."

"Like Ture Sventon? That's the only Swedish detective I've ever heard of."

"Forget about the comic books," Wallander said. "I'm serious about this."

"I am too. I've never heard a word about my father being involved in anything like this. What did he do?"

"It's too early to tell."

Wallander was now convinced that she didn't know what her father had been up to. Of course Wallander might be completely wrong, yet he was almost certain that he was right. The secret room on Harpegatan might lead them on to other secret rooms, but it had shaken up the entire investigation. Everything had been set in motion again.

He got up from the chair. "That's all for now," he said, holding out his hand. "I'm sure we'll meet again."

She gave him a sombre look.

"Who did it?" she asked.

"I don't know," Wallander said. "But I'm convinced we'll catch whoever killed your father."

Hansson followed him out to the hall. "Private detective? Is that some sort of joke?"

"No," Wallander said. "We found a secret office that belonged to Runfeldt. You'll hear more about it later."

Hansson nodded. "Ture Sventon wasn't a comic book character," he said. "He was in a series of mystery novels."

But Wallander had already left. He got a cup of coffee and closed the door to his office. The phone rang. He hung it up without answering. He was dying to get out of that press conference. He had too many other things to think about. With a grimace he pulled over a notebook and wrote down the most important things to tell the press.

He leaned back and looked out the window. The wind was howling.

If the killer speaks a language, than we can attempt to

answer him, he thought. If it's the way I think it is, he wants to show other people what he's doing. So we have to acknowledge that we've seen, but that we haven't let ourselves be scared off.

He made some more notes. Then he got up and went into Chief Holgersson's office. He told her what he had been thinking. She listened carefully and agreed that they would do as he suggested.

The press conference was held in the largest conference room in the station. Wallander felt as though he'd been dragged back to last summer, and that tumultuous press conference that he had stormed out of in a rage. He recognised many of the same faces.

"I'm glad you're handling this," Chief Holgersson whispered. "I'll make the opening remarks. The rest is yours."

They went up to the dais at one end of the room. Lisa Holgersson welcomed everyone and then handed over to Wallander, who could already feel himself starting to sweat.

He gave a thorough description of the murders of Holger Eriksson and Gösta Runfeldt. He told them that these were among the most savage crimes he and his colleagues had ever investigated. The only significant information he held back was the discovery that Runfeldt had probably worked as a private detective. He also didn't mention that they were looking for a man who had once been a mercenary in a remote African war and called himself Harald Berggren.

Instead he said something completely different, something that he and Lisa Holgersson had agreed on. He said that the police had some clear leads to follow. He couldn't go into details at this time, but there were clues and indications. The police were on a specific track that they couldn't talk about yet, for reasons crucial to the investigation.

He'd had this idea when it had seemed to him that the investigation had been shaken up. Movement deep down inside, almost impossible to register, but there nevertheless. The thought that came to him was quite simple. When there is an earthquake, people flee from the epicentre in a hurry. The killer wanted the world to see that the murders were sadistic and well planned. The investigators could confirm that they were aware of this, but they could also give a more detailed answer. They had seen more than what may have been intended.

Wallander wanted to get the killer moving. A person in motion was easier to see than one who kept still and hid in his own shadow. Wallander realised that the whole tactic could backfire. The killer might make himself invisible, but it was worth a try.

He had also received Chief Holgersson's permission to say something that was not altogether true. They had no leads. All they had were unrelated fragments.

When Wallander finished, the questions began. He was ready for most of them. He had heard and replied to them before, and he would keep on hearing them as long as he was a policeman.

Not until it was almost over, when Wallander had started to grow impatient and Chief Holgersson had signalled to him to wind it up, did everything turn in another direction. The man who raised his hand and then stood up had been sitting far back in a corner. Wallander didn't see him and was just about to adjourn the conference when Holgersson drew his attention to the fact that there was one more question.

"I'm from the *Anmärkaren*," the man said. "I have a question."

Wallander searched his memory. He'd never heard of a magazine called the *Anmärkaren*. His impatience was growing.

"What magazine did you say you were from?"

"The *Anmärkaren*."

"I have to admit that I've never heard of your magazine, but what's the question?"

"The *Anmärkaren* has roots that go way back," the man replied, unfazed. "There was a magazine in the early 19th century with that name. A magazine of social criticism. We plan to publish our first issue shortly."

"One question," Wallander said. "When you come out with the first issue I'll answer two questions."

There was tittering in the room. The man had the air of a preacher about him. Wallander wondered whether the *Anmärkaren* might be religious. Or pseudo-religious, he thought. New-age spirituality has finally reached Ystad. The southern plain of Sweden has been conquered, and Österlen is all that's left.

"What do the Ystad police think about the fact that the residents of Lödinge have decided to set up a citizen militia?" asked the man in the corner.

Wallander couldn't see his face clearly.

"I haven't heard that the people of Lödinge have considered committing any collective stupidities," Wallander replied.

"Not only in Lödinge," the man continued calmly. "There are plans to start a people's movement across the whole country. An umbrella organisation for the citizen militia that will protect the populace, which will do everything the police don't want to do. Or can't do. One of the starting points will be the Ystad district."

There was a sudden silence in the room.

"And why was Ystad selected for this honour?" asked Wallander. He was still not sure whether to take the man seriously.

"Within the past few months there have been a large number of brutal murders. The police succeeded in solving the crimes from this summer, but now it seems to have started again. People want to live their lives. The Swedish police have capitulated to the criminal elements that are creeping out of their holes today. That's why the citizen militia is the only way to solve the problem of security."

"It doesn't solve anything for people to take the law into their own hands," Wallander replied. "There can only be one response to this from the Ystad police. And it is clear and unequivocal. No-one can misunderstand it. We will regard all private initiatives to establish a citizen militia as illegal, and participants will be prosecuted."

"Should I interpret that to mean you are against it?" the man asked.

Now Wallander could see his pale, emaciated face. He decided to memorise it.

"Yes," he said. "You can interpret it this way: we are opposed to any attempt to organise a citizen militia."

"Don't you wonder what the people in Lödinge are going to say about that?"

"I may wonder, but I'm not afraid of the answer," he said quickly, and adjourned the press conference.

"Do you think he was serious?" Chief Holgersson asked when they were alone in the room.

"Maybe. We should keep an eye on what's happening in Lödinge. If it's true that people are starting to demand a citizen militia publicly, then there's been a change in the situation. And we might have problems."

It was 7 p.m. Wallander said goodbye to Holgersson and went back to his office. He sat down in his chair. He needed to think. He couldn't remember the last time he had had so little time for reflection and summarising during a criminal investigation.

The phone rang. He picked it up at once. It was Svedberg.

"How did the press conference go?"

"A little worse than usual. How's it going with you two?"

"I think you ought to come over here. We found a camera with a roll of film in it. Nyberg's here. We thought we should develop it."

"Can we establish that he worked as a private detective?"

"We think so. But there's something else too."

Wallander waited tensely for the rest.

"We think the film contains pictures from his last case."

Last, thought Wallander. Not latest.

"I'm coming," he said.

Clouds raced across the sky. As he walked towards his car, he wondered if the migrating birds flew in wind this strong. On the way to Harpegatan he stopped and filled his car with petrol. He felt drained. He wondered when he would have time to look for a house. And think about his father. He wondered when Baiba would come to visit. He looked at his watch. Was it time or his life that was passing? He was too tired to decide which. He started the engine. His watch said 7.40 p.m.

A few minutes later he parked on Harpegatan and went down to the basement.

CHAPTER 17

They watched tensely as the picture began to emerge in the developing bath. Wallander wasn't sure what he was expecting, or hoping for, as he stood with his colleagues in the darkroom. The red light made him feel as though they were waiting for something indecent to happen. Nyberg was developing the film. He was hobbling around with a crutch, and Höglund had warned that he was in an especially grumpy mood.

They had made progress while Wallander had been busy with the reporters. There was no doubt that Runfeldt had been working as a private detective. In the various client records they had discovered, they could see that he'd been doing it for at least ten years.

"His activities were limited," Höglund said. "He had not more than seven or eight cases a year. It seems as though this was something he did in his spare time."

Svedberg had made a swift survey of the types of assignments Runfeldt had taken on.

"About half the cases have to do with suspected infidelity," he said. "Strangely enough, his clients were mostly men who suspected their wives."

"Why is that strange?" Wallander asked.

"I just didn't think it would be that way around," was all Svedberg said. "But what do I know?"

Wallander motioned for him to continue.

"There are about two cases per year in which an employer

suspects an employee of embezzling," Svedberg said. "We've also come across a number of surveillance assignments that are rather vague in nature. In general, quite a tedious picture. His notes aren't particularly extensive. But he was well paid."

"So now we know how he could take those expensive holidays," Wallander said. "It cost him 30,000 kronor for the trip to Nairobi."

"He was working on a case when he died," Höglund said.

She opened a diary on the desk. Wallander thought about those reading glasses. He didn't bother to look at it.

"It seems to have been his usual sort of assignment. Someone referred to only as 'Mrs Svensson' suspects her husband of being unfaithful."

"Here in Ystad?" Wallander asked. "Did he work in other areas too?"

"In 1987 he had a case in Markaryd," Svedberg said. "There's nothing further north than that. Since then only cases in Skåne. In 1991 he went to Denmark twice and once to Kiel. I haven't had time to look into the details, but it had something to do with an engineer on a ferry who was having an affair with a waitress who worked on the ferry too. His wife, in Skanör, had suspected him correctly."

"But otherwise he only took cases in the Ystad area?"

"I wouldn't say that," Svedberg replied. "Southern and eastern Skåne is probably closer to the truth."

"Holger Eriksson?" Wallander asked. "Have you come across his name?"

Höglund looked at Svedberg, who shook his head.

"Harald Berggren?"

"Not him either."

"Have you found anything that might indicate a connection between Eriksson and Runfeldt?"

Again the answer was negative. It has to be there, thought Wallander. It doesn't make sense that there would be two different killers. Just as it doesn't make sense that there would be two random victims. The connection is there. We just haven't found it yet.

"I can't work him out," Höglund said. "He had a passion for flowers, but he spent his spare time working as a private detective."

"People are seldom what you think they are," Wallander replied, wondering suddenly whether this could be said of him.

"He seems to have made a bundle from this work," Svedberg said. "But if I'm not mistaken, he didn't report any of the income when he filed his tax returns. Could the explanation be that simple? He kept it secret so the tax authorities wouldn't find out what he was up to?"

"Hardly," Wallander said. "In the eyes of most people, being a private detective is a rather shady occupation."

"Or childish," Höglund said. "A game for men who have never grown up."

Wallander felt a vague urge to protest. But since he didn't know what to say, he let it drop.

Images of a man in his 50s, with thin, closely cropped hair appeared in the developing tray. The photographs had been taken out of doors. None of them could identify the background. Nyberg guessed that the pictures had been taken from a great distance, since some of the negatives were blurry, suggesting that Runfeldt had used a telephoto lens sensitive to the slightest movement.

"Mrs Svensson contacted him for the first time on 9

September," Höglund said. "Runfeldt noted that he had 'worked on the case' on 14 and 17 September."

"That's only a few days before he was due to leave for Nairobi," Wallander said.

They had come out of the darkroom. Nyberg was sitting at the desk, going through a number of files with photographs in them.

"Who is his client?" Wallander asked. "Mrs Svensson?"

"His client records and notes are vague," Svedberg said. "He seems to have been a detective of few words. There isn't even an address for Mrs Svensson."

"How does a private detective find clients?" Höglund asked. "He must advertise his services somehow."

"I've seen ads in the papers," Wallander said. "Maybe not in *Ystad's Allehanda*, but in national newspapers. It must be possible to track down this Mrs Svensson somehow."

"I talked to the porter," Svedberg said. "He thought Runfeldt just had a storeroom here. He didn't see anyone come to visit."

"So he must have met his clients somewhere else," Wallander said. "This was the secret room in his life."

They mulled this over. Wallander tried to decide what was most important right now, but the press conference was troubling him. The man from the *Anmärkaren* had upset him. Could it really be true that a national citizen militia was being formed? If it was, then Wallander knew it wouldn't be long before these people began seeking vengeance. He felt a need to tell Höglund and Svedberg what had happened, but he stopped himself. It was probably better if they discussed it together at the next team meeting. And Chief Holgersson was really the one who should tell them.

"How can we find Mrs Svensson?" Svedberg asked.

"We'll put a tap on the phone and go through all the papers thoroughly," Wallander said. "We'll find her somewhere. I'm sure of that. I might leave it to you two, while I go and have a talk with Runfeldt's son."

The town seemed deserted. He parked near the post office, and stepped out into the wind again. He saw himself as a pathetic figure, a police officer in a thin jumper, battling the wind in a desolate Swedish town in the autumn. The Swedish criminal justice system, he thought. Or what's left of it. This is how it looks. Freezing officers in flimsy jumpers.

He turned left at the Savings Bank and walked to the Hotel Sekelgården. He checked the son's name – Bo Runfeldt. Wallander nodded to the young man at the reception desk, and realised that he was the oldest son of Björk their former police chief.

"It's been a long time," Wallander said. "How's your father?"

"He's unhappy in Malmö."

He's not unhappy in Malmö, Wallander thought. He's unhappy with his new job.

"What are you reading?" asked Wallander.

"About fractals."

"Fractals?"

"It's a mathematical term. I'm at Lund University. This is just a part-time job."

"That sounds good," Wallander said. "I'm here to talk to one of your guests, Bo Runfeldt."

"He just came in."

"Is there somewhere that we can sit and talk in private?"

"We don't have many guests," the boy said. "You can sit in the breakfast room."

He pointed towards the hall.

"I'll wait there," said Wallander. "Please call his room and tell him that I'm here to see him."

"I read the paper," the boy said. "Why is it that everything is getting so much worse?"

Wallander looked at him with interest.

"What do you mean by that?"

"Worse. More brutal."

"I don't know," Wallander replied. "I honestly don't know why things have got so bad. At the same time, I don't really believe what I just said. I think I do know. I think everybody knows why things are this way."

Björk's son wanted to continue the discussion, but Wallander raised his hand to cut him off and pointed to the phone. Then he went into the breakfast room and sat down. He thought about the unfinished conversation. He knew quite well what the explanation was. The Sweden that was his, the country he had grown up in, that was built after the war, was not as solid as they had thought. Under the surface was quagmire. Even back then the high-rise buildings that had been erected were described as "inhuman". How could people who lived there be expected to keep their "humanity"? Society had grown cruel. People who felt they were unwanted or unwelcome in their own country, reacted with aggression. There was no such thing as meaningless violence. Every violent act had a meaning for the person who committed it. Only when you dared accept this truth could you hope to turn society in another direction.

He also asked himself how it would be possible to be a police officer as things got worse. Many of his colleagues were seriously considering finding other occupations. Martinsson had talked about it, Hansson had mentioned it once. And a few years ago Wallander had cut out an ad for security personnel at a large company in Trelleborg from the paper. He wondered what Ann-Britt thought. She was still young. She could be a police officer for 30 years or more. He would ask her. He needed to know in order to see how he was going to stand it himself.

At the same time he knew that the picture he was drawing was incomplete. Among young people the interest in police jobs had risen sharply in the past few years, and the increase seemed to be steady.

Back in the early 1990s he had often sat on Rydberg's balcony on warm, summer evenings and talked of the future. They continued their discussions even during Rydberg's illness and his last days. They never reached any conclusions, but one thing they did agree on was that police work ultimately had to do with being able to decipher the signs of the times. To understand change and interpret trends in society. And for this reason perhaps the younger generation of police officers were better equipped to deal with modern society.

Now Wallander knew that he had been mistaken about one essential fact. It was no harder being a police officer today than it was in the past. It was harder for him, but that was not the same thing.

Wallander's thoughts were interrupted when he heard steps in the hall. He stood up and greeted Bo Runfeldt. He was a tall, well-built man of about 27 or 28. He had a strong handshake. Wallander invited him to sit down, realising that as usual he had forgotten to bring his notebook. It was doubtful whether he even had a pen. He considered going out to the front desk to borrow some from Björk's son, but decided against it. He would have to rely on his memory. His carelessness was inexcusable, and it annoyed him.

"Let me start by offering my condolences," Wallander began.

Bo Runfeldt nodded. He didn't say anything. His eyes were an intense blue, his gaze rather squinting. Wallander wondered if he was short-sighted.

"I know you've had a long conversation with my colleague, Inspector Hansson," Wallander continued. "But I need to ask you a few questions myself."

Runfeldt remained silent behind his piercing gaze.

"You live in Arvika," said Wallander. "And you're an accountant."

"I work for Price Waterhouse," said Runfeldt. His voice indicated a person who was used to expressing himself.

"That doesn't sound Swedish."

"It's not. Price Waterhouse is one of the world's largest accounting firms. It's easier to list the countries where we don't do business than where we do."

"But you work in Sweden?"

"Not all the time. I often have assignments in Africa and Asia."

"Do they need accountants from Sweden?"

"Not just from Sweden, but from Price Waterhouse. We audit many relief projects. To ensure the money has ended up where it's supposed to."

"And does it?"

"Not always. Is this really relevant to what happened to my father?"

Wallander could see that Bo Runfeldt was finding it difficult to hide his feeling that talking to a policeman was beneath his dignity. Under normal circumstances Wallander would have reacted angrily, but something made him hold back. He wondered fleetingly whether it was because he had inherited the submissiveness that his father had so often exhibited in his life, especially towards the men who had come in their shiny American cars to buy his paintings. Maybe that was his inheritance: a feeling of inferiority.

He regarded the man with the blue eyes.

"Your father was murdered," he said. "Right now I'm the one who decides which questions are relevant."

Bo Runfeldt shrugged. "I have to admit that I don't know much about police work."

"I spoke to your sister earlier," Wallander continued. "One question I asked her may have great significance, and I'm going to ask you too. Did you know that your father, besides being a florist, worked as a private detective?"

Runfeldt burst out laughing.

"That's got to be the most idiotic thing I've heard in a long time," he said.

"Idiotic or not, it's true."

"A private detective?"

"Private investigator, if you prefer. He had an office. He took on various assignments. He'd been doing it for at least ten years."

Runfeldt saw that Wallander was serious. His surprise was genuine.

"He must have started his business about the same time that your mother died."

Wallander noticed an almost imperceptible shift in his features, as though he had encroached on an area that he really should have kept out of. It was the same reaction that the daughter had had.

"You knew that your father was due to go to Nairobi," he continued. "When one of my colleagues spoke to you, you seemed incredulous that he hadn't turned up at Kastrup Airport."

"I talked to him the day before."

"How did he seem?"

"The same as usual. He talked about his trip."

"He didn't seem apprehensive?"

"No."

"You must have been worried about his disappearance. Can you come up with any explanation for why he would miss his trip? Or mislead you?"

"There's no reasonable explanation for it."

"It looks as if he packed his suitcase and left the flat. That's where the trail ends."

"Someone must have picked him up."

Wallander paused before asking the next question.

"Who?"

"I don't know."

"Did your father have any enemies?"

"None that I know of. Not any more."

"What do you mean by that? Not any more?"

"Exactly what I said. I don't think he's had any enemies for a long time."

"Could you explain what you mean?"

Runfeldt took a packet of cigarettes from his pocket. Wallander noticed that his hand was shaking slightly.

"Do you mind if I smoke?"

"Not at all."

Wallander waited. He knew there would be more. He also had a feeling that he was closing in on something important.

"I don't know if my father had any enemies," he said. "But I do know there's one person who had reason to hate him."

"Who?"

"My mother."

Runfeldt waited for Wallander to ask him a question. But it didn't come. He kept on waiting.

"My father sincerely loved orchids," Runfeldt said. "He was a knowledgeable man, a self-taught botanist. But he was also something else."

"What's that?"

"He was a brutal man. He abused my mother throughout their marriage. Sometimes so badly that she had to be hospitalised. We tried to get her to leave him, but she wouldn't. He beat her. Afterwards he would be contrite, and she would give in. It was a nightmare that never seemed to end. The brutality didn't stop until she drowned."

"As I understand it, she fell through a hole in the ice?"

"That's as much as I know, that's what my father told us."

"You don't sound totally convinced."

Runfeldt stubbed out his half-smoked cigarette in an ashtray.

"Maybe she went out there beforehand and sawed a hole in the ice. Maybe she decided to put an end to it all."

"Is that a possibility?"

"She talked about committing suicide. Not often; a few times during the last years of her life. But we didn't believe her. People usually don't. Suicides are fundamentally inexplicable to those who should have paid attention and understood what was happening."

Wallander thought about the pungee pit. The partially sawed-through planks. Gösta Runfeldt had been a brutal man. He had abused his wife. He tried to measure the significance of what Bo Runfeldt was telling him.

"I don't grieve for my father," Runfeldt continued. "I don't think my sister does either. He was a cruel man. He tortured the life out of our mother."

"He was never cruel towards the two of you?"
"Never. Only towards her."
"Why did he mistreat her?"
"I don't know. One shouldn't speak ill of the dead, but he was a monster."
Wallander thought for a moment.
"Has it ever crossed your mind that your father might have killed your mother? That it wasn't an accident?"
"Many times. But there is no way to prove it. There were no witnesses. They were alone on the ice on that winter day."
"What's the name of the lake?"
"Stång Lake. It's not far from Älmhult. In southern Småland."
Wallander thought for a moment. Did he really have any other questions? It felt as if the investigation had taken a stranglehold on itself. There ought to be plenty of questions. And there were. But there was no-one to ask.
"Does the name Harald Berggren mean anything to you?"
Runfeldt gave it careful thought before he answered.
"No. Nothing. But I could be mistaken. It's a common name."
"Has your father ever had contact with mercenaries?"
"Not as far as I know. But I remember that he often talked about the Foreign Legion when I was a child. Never to my sister, only to me."
"What did he tell you?"
"Adventure stories. Maybe joining the Foreign Legion was some kind of teenage dream he'd had. But I'm pretty sure that he never had anything to do with them. Or with mercenaries."
"Holger Eriksson? Have you ever heard that name?"

"The man who was murdered the week before my father? I saw it in the newspapers. As far as I know, my father never had anything to do with him. I could be wrong, of course. We didn't keep in close contact."

"How long are you staying in Ystad?"

"The funeral will be as soon as we can make the necessary arrangements. We have to decide what to do with the shop."

"It's very possible that you'll hear from me again," Wallander said, getting to his feet.

He left the hotel. He was hungry. The wind tugged and pulled at his clothes. He stood in the shelter of a building and tried to decide what to do. He should eat, he knew that, but he also knew that he had to sit down soon and try to collect his thoughts. He was still looking for the point where the lives of Eriksson and Runfeldt intersected. It's there somewhere, in the dim background, he told himself. Maybe I've even seen it already, or walked past it without seeing.

He got his car and drove over to the station. On the way he called Höglund on her mobile phone. She told him that they were still going through the office, but they had sent Nyberg home because his foot was hurting badly.

"I'm on my way to the station. I've just had an interesting conversation with Runfeldt's son," Wallander said. "I need some time to go over it."

"It's not enough for us to shuffle our papers," Höglund replied. "We also need someone to do the thinking."

He wasn't sure if she meant this last remark to be sarcastic, but he pushed the thought aside.

Hansson was sitting in his office going through the reports that were starting to pile up. Wallander stood in the door. He had a coffee cup in his hand.

"Where are the pathologists' reports?" he asked. "They must

have come in by now. At least the one on Holger Eriksson."

"It's probably in Martinsson's office. I seem to recall he mentioned something about it."

"Is he still here?"

"He went home. He copied a file to a disk and was going to keep working on it at home."

"Is that really allowed?" Wallander wondered absent-mindedly. "Taking investigative material home?"

"I don't know," Hansson replied. "For me, it's never come up. I don't even have a computer at home. But maybe that's a breach of regulations these days."

"What's a breach of regulations?"

"Not having a computer at home."

"In that case, we're both guilty," Wallander said. "I'd like to see those reports early tomorrow morning."

"How did it go with Bo Runfeldt?"

"I have to write up my notes tonight, but he said some things that may prove important. And now we know for sure that Gösta Runfeldt spent some of his time working as a private detective."

"Svedberg called in. He told me."

Wallander took his mobile phone out of his pocket.

"What did we do before we had these things?" he asked. "I can hardly remember."

"We did exactly the same thing," Hansson replied. "But it took longer. We searched for phone boxes. We spent a lot more time in our cars. But we did exactly the same things that we do now."

Wallander walked down the hall to his office, nodding to a few officers as they came out of the canteen. He went into his office and sat down. More than ten minutes passed before he pulled over an unused notebook.

* * *

It took him two hours to put together a thorough summary of the two murders. He had been trying to steer two vessels at the same time, while looking for the point of contact that he knew had to exist. After 11 p.m. he threw down his pen and leaned back in his chair. He had reached a point where he could see nothing more. But he was positive. The contact was there. They just hadn't found it yet.

There was something else. Time after time he came back to Höglund's observation. *There's something blatant about the modus operandi.* Both in terms of Eriksson's death, impaled on sharpened bamboo stakes, and Runfeldt, who was strangled and left tied to a tree. I see something, he thought, I just haven't managed to see through it. It was almost midnight when he turned off the light in his office. He stood there in the dark. It was still just a hunch, a vague fear deep inside his brain.

The killer would strike again. He seemed to have detected a signal as he worked at his desk. There was something incomplete about everything that had happened so far. What it was, he didn't know.

But still he was sure.

CHAPTER 18

She waited until 2.30 a.m. From experience she knew that was when the fatigue would creep up on her. She thought back on all the nights when she had been at work. That's how it always was. The greatest danger of dozing off was between 2 a.m. and 4 a.m.

She had been waiting in the linen-supply room since 9 p.m. Just as on her first visit, she had walked right in through the main entrance of the hospital. No-one had noticed her. A nurse in a hurry. No-one had noticed her because there was nothing unusual about her. She had considered disguising herself, maybe changing her hair. But that would have been an unnecessary caution. She'd had plenty of time to think as she'd sat in the linen room, the scent of newly washed and ironed sheets reminding her of childhood. She sat there in the dark until after midnight, and then she took out her torch, the one she always used at work, and read the last letter her mother had written to her. It was unfinished. But it was in this letter that her mother had begun to write about herself. About the events that lay behind her attempt to take her life. She could see that her mother had never got over her bitterness. *I wander around the world like a ship without a captain,* she wrote, *forced to atone for someone else's guilt. I thought that age would create enough distance, that the memories would grow dim, fade, and maybe finally vanish altogether. But now I see that won't happen. Only with death can I put an end to it. And since I don't want to die, not yet, I choose to remember.*

The letter was dated the day before her mother had moved in with the French nuns, the day before shadows had detached themselves from the darkness and murdered her.

After she had read the letter she had turned off the torch. Everything had grown quiet. Someone had walked past in the hall only twice. The linen room was located in a wing that was only partly in use.

She had had plenty of time to think. There were now three free days entered in her timetable. She had some time and she was going to use it. Until now everything had gone the way it was supposed to. Women only made mistakes when they tried to think like men. She had known that for a long time, and in her view she had already proved it.

But there was something that bothered her, something that had thrown her timetable out of kilter. She had followed everything that had been written in the newspapers closely. She listened to the news on the radio and watched it on various TV channels. It was clear that the police didn't understand a thing. And that had been her intention, not to leave any traces, to lead the dogs away from the trails they should be following. But now she was impatient with all this incompetence. The police were never going to solve the crimes. She was adding riddles to the story. In their minds the police would be looking for a male killer. She didn't want it to be that way any longer.

She sat in the dark closet and devised a plan. She would make some minor changes. Nothing that would reveal her timetable, of course. But she would give the riddle a face.

At 2.30 a.m. she left the linen closet. The hall was deserted. She straightened her white uniform and headed for the stairs up to the maternity ward. She knew that there were usually only four people on duty. She had been there in the daytime, asking about a woman that she knew had already gone home with her baby. Over the nurse's shoulder she could see in the log that all the rooms were occupied. She couldn't imagine why women had babies at this time of year, when autumn was turning to winter. But then she knew that few women chose when to have their children, even now.

When she reached the glass doors of the maternity ward, she stopped and took a careful look at the nurses' station. She held the door slightly ajar and heard no voices. That meant the midwives and nurses were busy. It would take her less than 15 seconds to reach the room of the woman she intended to visit. She probably wouldn't run into anybody, but she had to be careful. She pulled the glove out of her pocket. She had sewn it herself and filled the fingers with lead, shaped to follow the contours of her knuckles. She put it on her right hand, opened the door, and quickly entered the ward. The nurses' station was empty; there was a radio playing somewhere. She walked rapidly and soundlessly to the room, slipped inside and closed the door behind her.

Taking off her glove, she approached the woman lying in the bed; she was awake. She stuffed the glove in her pocket, the same pocket where she had put the letter from her mother. She sat down on the edge of the bed. The woman was very pale, and her belly pushed up the sheet. She took the woman's hand.

"Have you decided?" she asked her.

The woman nodded. It didn't surprise her, and yet she

felt a sort of triumph. Even the women who were most cowed could be turned towards life again.

"Eugen Blomberg," the woman said. "He lives in Lund. He's a researcher at the university. I don't know any better way to describe what he does."

She patted the woman's hand.

"I'll take care of it. Don't worry about a thing."

"I hate that man," she said.

"Yes," said the woman sitting on the edge of the bed. "You hate him and you have every right to."

"I would have killed him if I could."

"I know. But you can't. Think of your baby instead."

She leaned forward and stroked the woman's cheek. Then she got up and put on her glove. She had been in the room no more than two minutes. Carefully she pushed open the door. No-one was around. She walked back towards the exit.

Just as she was passing the station a woman came out. It was bad luck. The woman stared at her. It was an older woman, presumably one of the midwives.

She kept walking towards the exit doors. The woman yelled and started running after her. She walked faster. But the woman grabbed her left arm and asked who she was and what she was doing there. It was a shame that this woman had to interfere, she thought. She spun around and hit her with the glove. She didn't want to hurt her badly, and so she took care not to hit her on the temple, which could be fatal. She struck her hard on one cheek – hard enough to knock her out. The woman groaned and fell to the floor.

She turned around to leave, but felt two hands gripping her leg. When she looked back she realised she hadn't struck hard enough. At the same time she heard a door open somewhere in the distance. She was about to lose control of the situation. She yanked her leg away and bent down to deliver another blow. The woman scratched her in the face. Now she struck without worrying if it was too hard or not, right in the temple. The woman sank to the floor.

She fled through the glass doors, her cheek stinging where the midwife's nails had torn her skin. No-one called after her. She wiped her face, and her white sleeve showed streaks of blood. She stuffed the glove in her pocket and took off her clogs so she could run faster. She wondered whether the hospital had an internal alarm system. But she got out without being caught. When she reached her car and looked at her face in the rear-view mirror, she saw that she had only a few scratches.

Things hadn't gone the way she had planned. But you couldn't always expect them to. What was important was that she had succeeded in persuading the woman to reveal the name of the man who had caused her so much grief.

Eugen Blomberg.

She still had 48 hours to begin her investigation and draw up a plan and a timetable. She was in no hurry. It would take as long as necessary. She didn't think she'd need more than a week.

The oven was empty. It was waiting.

Just after 8 a.m. on Thursday morning the investigative team was assembled in the conference room. Wallander had asked Åkeson to attend. As he was about to begin, he noticed someone was missing.

"Where's Svedberg? Didn't he come in today?"

"He's been in, but he left again," Martinsson said. "Evidently there was an assault up at the hospital last night. He said he'd probably be back soon."

A vague memory flitted through Wallander's head, but he couldn't pin it down. Something to do with Svedberg and the hospital.

"This brings the need for additional personnel to a head," Åkeson said. "We can't avoid the issue any longer, I'm afraid."

Wallander knew what he meant. On several earlier occasions he and Åkeson had clashed over whether they should request extra manpower or not.

"We'll take up that question at the end of the meeting," Wallander said. "Let's start with where we actually stand in this mess."

"Stockholm has called a few times," Chief Holgersson said, "and I don't think I need to tell you who it was. These violent events are clouding the image of the friendly local police force."

A mixture of resignation and mirth swept through the room. But no-one commented on what Lisa Holgersson had said. Martinsson yawned audibly. Wallander seized on that as a starting point.

"We're all tired. A policeman's curse is lack of sleep. At least in crises like this."

He was interrupted by the door opening. Nyberg came in. Wallander knew that he had been talking on the phone to the forensic laboratory in Linköping. He hobbled up to the table using his crutch.

"How's your foot?" Wallander asked him.

"It's better than being impaled on bamboo from Thailand," he replied.

Wallander gave him an inquiring look.

"Do we know that for sure? That it's from Thailand?"

"We do. It's imported for making fishing rods and furniture by a company in Bremen. We talked to their Swedish agent. They import more than 100,000 bamboo poles each year. It's impossible to say where they were purchased, but I just talked to Linköping. They can determine how long the bamboo has been in Sweden."

Wallander nodded.

"Anything else?" he asked, still facing Nyberg.

"With regard to Eriksson or Runfeldt?"

"Either one."

Nyberg opened his notebook.

"The planks for Eriksson's bridge came from the Building Warehouse in Ystad. The murder scene is clean of any objects that might have helped us. On the side of the hill where he had his birdwatching tower there's a tractor path that we can assume the killer used, if he came by car, which I'm assuming he did. We've taken impressions of all the tyre tracks we found. But the whole scene is extraordinarily devoid of clues."

"And the house?"

"The problem is, we don't know what we're looking for. Everything seems to be in good order. The break-in he reported a few years ago is a riddle too. The only thing that might be worth noting is that Eriksson had a couple of extra locks installed recently, on the doors leading directly into the living-quarters."

"That might mean he was afraid of something," Wallander said.

"I thought so too. On the other hand, everybody's putting on extra locks these days, aren't they?"

Wallander glanced around the table.

"Neighbours," he said. "Who was Holger Eriksson? Who might have had a reason to kill him? What about Harald Berggren? It's about time we did a complete summary. No matter how long it takes."

Later, Wallander would think back on that Thursday morning as an endless uphill climb. All of them presented the results of their work, and the only conclusion was that there was no sign of a breakthrough. The slope just grew steeper. Eriksson's life seemed impregnable. No-one had seen a thing, no-one even seemed to have known this man who sold cars, watched birds, and wrote poems. Finally Wallander began to wonder whether he was mistaken, whether Eriksson's killer might have selected him at random. But deep inside he knew that this couldn't be true. The killer had spoken a specific language – there was a logic and consistency to his method of killing. Wallander knew he wasn't mistaken. But that was as far as he got.

They were completely bogged down by the time Svedberg returned from the hospital. He appeared like a saviour, because when he sat down at the table and sorted through his notes, the investigation finally seemed to begin to move forward.

Svedberg began by apologising for his absence. Wallander asked what had happened at the hospital.

"The whole thing is pretty weird," Svedberg said. "Just before 3 a.m. a nurse appeared in the maternity ward. One of the midwives, Ylva Brink, who happens to be my cousin, was working there last night. She didn't recognise the nurse and asked her what she was doing there. She was struck to the ground and knocked out. When she came to, the woman was gone. They asked all the patients, but none of them had seen her. I talked to the personnel on duty last night. They were all very upset."

"How's your cousin?" Wallander asked.

"She has concussion."

Wallander was just about to return to Eriksson when

Svedberg spoke up again. He seemed embarrassed and scratched his head nervously.

"What's even stranger is that this woman had been there before, about a week ago. Ylva happened to be working that night too. She's positive that the woman wasn't really a nurse, that she was in disguise."

Wallander frowned, and remembered the note that had been lying on his desk all week.

"You talked to Ylva Brink that time too. And took some notes."

"I threw out that piece of paper," Svedberg said. "Since nothing happened the first time I didn't think it was anything to worry about. We had more important things to do."

"I think it's creepy," said Höglund. "A fake nurse who enters the maternity ward at night. And has no qualms about using violence. It has to mean something."

"My cousin didn't recognise her, but she gave me a very good description. The woman was stocky and obviously very strong."

Wallander said nothing about having Svedberg's note on his desk.

"That sounds odd," was all he said. "What kind of precautions have the hospital taken?"

"For the time being they're hiring a security company. They'll see if the woman shows up again."

They left the night's events behind. Wallander looked at Svedberg, thinking despondently that he was about to reinforce the feeling that the investigation was going nowhere. But Svedberg had some news.

"Last week I talked to one of Eriksson's employees, Ture Karlhammar, who is 73 years old, and lives in Svarte. I wrote up a report about it that you may have read. He worked as a car salesman for Eriksson for more than 30 years. At first he just said how sorry he was about what had happened, and that no-one had anything but good things to say about Eriksson. Karlhammar's wife was making coffee. The door to the kitchen was open. Suddenly she came in, slammed the coffee tray on the table so the cream sloshed over, and said Holger Eriksson was a crook. Then she walked out."

"And then?"

"It was a little embarrassing, of course. But Karlhammar stuck to his story. I went to talk to his wife, but by then she was gone."

"What do you mean, gone?"

"She had taken the car and driven off. Later I called several times, but nobody answered. But this morning I got a letter. I read it before I drove over to the hospital. It's from Karlhammar's wife. And if what she says is correct, then it makes very interesting reading."

"Sum it up for us," Wallander said. "Then you can make copies."

"She claims that Eriksson showed signs of sadism many times in his life. He treated his employees badly. He would harass anyone who quit. She repeats over and over that she could provide as many examples as we need to prove this is true."

Svedberg scanned the letter.

"She says that he had little respect for other people. Towards the end of the letter she indicates that he made trips to Poland quite often. Apparently to visit some women there. According to Mrs Karlhammar, they would be able to tell us stories too. It might all be gossip. How would she know about what he did in Poland?"

“She doesn’t say anything about him being homosexual?” asked Wallander.

“No. And this part about the trips to Poland certainly doesn’t give that impression.”

“And Karlhammar had never heard of anyone named Harald Berggren, I suppose?”

“No.”

Wallander felt a need to get up and stretch his legs. What Svedberg had said about the contents of the letter was important, without a doubt. He realised that this was the second time in 24 hours that he’d heard a man described as brutal.

He suggested a break so they could get some air. Åkeson stayed behind.

“It’s all set now. With the Sudan, I mean.”

Wallander felt a pang of jealousy. Åkeson had made a decision and dared to resign. Why didn’t he do the same thing himself? Why did he settle for looking for a new house? Now that his father was gone, he had nothing to keep him here. Linda could take care of herself.

“They don’t need any policemen to keep order among the refugees, do they? I’ve had some experience in that field here in Ystad.”

Åkeson laughed.

“I can ask. Swedish policemen usually go into the UN special forces. There’s nothing to stop you from putting in an application.”

“Right now I’ve got a murder investigation to take care of. Maybe later. When are you leaving?”

“Between Christmas and New Year. It’ll be great to get away. Sometimes I think I might never come back. I’ll never get to sail to the West Indies in a boat I built myself, but I am going to the Sudan. And I have no idea what'll happen after that."

"Everybody dreams about escape," Wallander said. "People in Sweden are always looking for the next paradise. Sometimes I think I don't even recognise my own country any more."

"Maybe I'm escaping too. But the Sudan is no paradise, believe me."

"At least you're doing the right thing by trying. I hope you write once in a while. I'll miss you."

"That's actually something I'm looking forward to. Writing personal letters, not just official ones. Maybe that way I'll figure out how many friends I actually have: the ones who answer the letters I hope to write."

The short break was over. They all sat down again.

"Let's switch over to Gösta Runfeldt," Wallander said.

Höglund described their discovery of the room on Harpegatan and the fact that Runfeldt was a private detective. After the photographs that Nyberg had developed had made their way around the table, Wallander told them about his conversation with Runfeldt's son. He noticed that the investigative team were now concentrating in a way that they hadn't been when the long meeting had begun.

"I can't shake the feeling that we're close to something crucial," Wallander concluded. "We're still seeking a point of contact. What could be the significance of both Eriksson and Runfeldt having been described as brutal? And why has this never come out before?"

He broke off to allow for comments and questions. No-one said a word.

"It's time we started digging deeper," he went on. "All the material has to be run back and forth between these two men. It's Martinsson's job to see that this gets done. There are a number of items that seem particularly important. I'm thinking about Runfeldt's wife's death. I've got the feeling that this might be crucial. And there's the money that Eriksson donated to the church in Svenstavik. I'll take care of that myself. Which means it might be necessary to take a few trips."

"Where's Svenstavik?" Hansson asked.

"In southern Jämtland. About 50 kilometres from the border of Härjadal."

"What did Eriksson have to do with that place? He was from Skåne, wasn't he?"

"That's precisely what we have to find out," said Wallander. "Why did he choose that particular church to leave money to? There must have been some definite reason."

They had been in the meeting for several hours when Wallander brought up the question of more manpower.

"I have nothing against getting reinforcements. We have plenty to investigate, and it's going to take a lot of time."

"I'll take care of it," Chief Holgersson said.

Åkeson nodded without saying anything. In all the years Wallander had worked with him, he had never known Åkeson to speak unnecessarily. Wallander supposed that this would be an advantage in the Sudan.

"On the other hand, I doubt we need a psychologist," Wallander continued. "I'm the first to agree that Mats Ekholm, who was here in the summer, was helpful. But the situation is different with this case. My suggestion is that we send summaries of the investigative material to him and ask for his comments. Let's leave it at that for now."

They adjourned the meeting at just past 1 p.m. Wallander left the station hastily. The long meeting had left him feeling heavy-headed. He drove to one of the restaurants in the town centre. As he ate, he tried to decide what had actually developed during the meeting. Since he kept coming back to the question of what had happened at the lake outside Älmhult ten years ago, he decided to follow his intuition. When he finished eating he called the Hotel Sekelgården. Bo Runfeldt was in his room. Wallander asked the receptionist to tell him he was coming over shortly. Then he drove back to the police station. He found Martinsson and Hansson and took them to his office. He asked Hansson to call Svenstavik.

"What am I supposed to ask?"

"Get straight to the point. Why did Eriksson make this bequest to them? Was he looking for forgiveness of his sins? If so, what sins? And if they mention confidentiality, tell them we need the information so we can try to prevent more murders."

"You really want me to ask if he was looking for forgiveness for his sins?"

Wallander burst out laughing. "Yes, if necessary. Find out whatever you can. I think I'll take Bo Runfeldt with me to Älmhult. Ask Ebba to book us a couple of hotel rooms there."

Martinsson seemed doubtful. "What do you think you're going to discover by looking at a lake?"

"I honestly don't know," Wallander replied. "But the trip will at least give me time to talk to Runfeldt. I've got a hunch there's some hidden information that's important for us, and that we can get it if we're persistent enough. We have to scrape hard enough to break through the surface. And there might be someone who was there at the time of the accident. I want you to do some background work. Call up our colleagues in Älmhult. It happened about ten years ago. You can find out the exact date from the daughter. A drowning accident. I'll give you a call when I get there."

The wind was still gusting when Wallander walked out to his car. He drove down to the Sekelgården and went into reception. Bo Runfeldt was waiting for him.

"Get your overcoat," Wallander said. "We're going on a field trip."

"Where to?"

"Once you're in the car I'll tell you all about it."

Not until they had passed the turn off to Höör did Wallander tell him where they were going.

CHAPTER 19

It started to rain just after they left Höör. By then Wallander had begun to doubt the whole undertaking. Was it really worth the trouble of driving all the way to Älmhult? What did he actually think he would achieve? Yet deep down he had no doubts. What he wanted was not a solution, but to move a step further in the right direction.

Bo Runfeldt had been angry when Wallander had told him where they were going, asking if this was some kind of joke. What did his mother's death have to do with the murder of his father?

"You and your sister seem reluctant to talk about what happened," he said. "In a way, I can understand it. People don't like to talk about a tragedy. But why don't I believe that it's the tragedy that makes you reluctant to talk about it? If you give me a good answer, we'll turn around and drive back. And don't forget, you're the one who brought up your father's brutality."

"There you have my answer," Runfeldt said. Wallander noticed an almost imperceptible change in his voice. A hint of a defence beginning to crumble.

Wallander cautiously probed deeper as they drove through the monotonous landscape.

"You said that your mother talked about committing suicide?"

It took a while before Runfeldt answered.

"It's strange that she didn't do it earlier. I don't think

you can imagine what hell she was forced to live in. I can't. No-one can."

"Why didn't she divorce him?"

"He threatened to kill her if she left him. She had every reason to believe he would do it. I didn't know anything back then, but later on I understood."

"If the doctors suspect abuse, they're obliged to report it to the police."

"She always had an explanation, and she was convincing. She would say anything to protect him. She might say she was drunk and fell down. My mother never touched alcohol, but of course the doctors didn't know that."

The conversation died as Wallander overtook a bus. He noticed that Runfeldt seemed tense. Wallander wasn't driving fast, but his passenger was clearly nervous in traffic.

"I think what kept her from committing suicide was my sister and me," he said after a while.

"That's natural," Wallander replied. "Let's go back to what you said earlier, that your father had threatened to kill your mother. When a man abuses a woman, he doesn't usually intend to kill her. He does it to control her. Sometimes he hits too hard, and the abuse leads to death. But generally there's a different reason for murder. It's taking it one step further."

Runfeldt replied with a surprising question.

"Are you married?"

"Not any more."

"Did you ever hit your wife?"

"Why would I do that?"

"I just wondered."

"We're not talking about me here."

Runfeldt was silent. Wallander remembered with horrifying clarity the time that he had struck Mona in a moment of uncontrollable rage. She had fallen, hit the back of her head against the doorframe, and blacked out for a few seconds. She almost packed her bags and left, but Linda was still so young. And Wallander had begged and pleaded. They had sat up all night. He had implored her, and in the end she had stayed. The incident was etched in his memory, but he couldn't now recall what they had been fighting about. Where had the rage come from? He didn't know. There were few things in his life that he was more ashamed of. He understood his own reluctance to be reminded of it.

"Let's get back to that day ten years ago," Wallander said. "What happened?"

"It was a Sunday," Runfeldt said. "5 February 1984. It was a beautiful, cold winter's day. They used to go out on excursions every Sunday, to walk in the woods, along the beach, or across the ice on the lake."

"It sounds idyllic," said Wallander. "How am I supposed to make this fit with what you said before?"

"It wasn't idyllic. It was just the opposite. My mother was always terrified. I'm not exaggerating. She had long ago crossed the boundary where fear takes over and dominates your whole life. She must have been mentally exhausted. But he wanted to take a Sunday walk, and so they did. The threat of a clenched fist was ever present. I'm convinced that my father never saw her terror. He probably thought all was forgiven and forgotten each time. I assume he regarded his abuse of her to be chance incidents of rash behaviour. Hardly more than that."

"I think I understand. So what happened?"

"Why they had gone to Småland that Sunday, I don't know. They parked on a logging road. It had been snowing, but it wasn't particularly deep. They walked along the road to the lake, and out onto the ice. Suddenly it gave way and she fell in. He couldn't pull her out. He ran to the car and went to get help. She was dead, of course, when they found her."

"How did you hear about it?"

"He called me himself. I was in Stockholm at the time."

"What do you remember of the phone conversation?"

"Naturally he was very upset."

"In what way?"

"Can you be upset in more than one way?"

"Was he crying? Was he in shock? Try to describe it."

"He wasn't crying. I can only remember my father having tears in his eyes when he talked about rare orchids. It was more that he was trying to convince me he had done everything in his power to rescue her. But that shouldn't be necessary, should it? If someone's in trouble, you do everything you can to help, don't you?"

"What else did he say?"

"He asked me to try to get hold of my sister."

"So he called you first?"

"Yes."

"Then what happened?"

"We came down to Skåne. Just like now. The funeral was a week later. I spoke to a policeman. He said that the ice must have been unexpectedly thin. My mother wasn't a big person."

"Is that what he said? The police officer you spoke to? That the ice must have been 'unexpectedly thin'?"

"I have a good memory for detail. Maybe that's why I'm an accountant."

They passed a café and decided to stop. During the brief meal, Wallander asked Runfeldt about his work in international accounting. He listened without paying much attention. Instead, he went over their conversation in his mind. Something was important, but he couldn't quite pin it down. As they were about to leave the café, his phone rang. It was Martinsson. Runfeldt stepped aside to give Wallander some privacy.

"We seem to be out of luck," Martinsson said. "Of the officers who were working in Älmhult ten years ago, one is dead and the other has retired to Örebro."

Wallander was disappointed. Without a reliable informant, the trip would lose much of its purpose.

"I don't even know how to find the lake," he complained. "Aren't there any ambulance drivers? Wasn't the fire department called in to pull her out?"

"I've located the man who offered to help Gösta Runfeldt," said Martinsson. "I know his name and where he lives. The problem is that he doesn't have a phone."

"Is there really somebody in this country today who doesn't have a phone?"

"Apparently. Do you have a pen?"

Wallander searched his pockets. As usual he didn't have either a pen or paper. He waved over Runfeldt, who handed Wallander a gold-plated pen and one of his business cards.

"Jacob Hoslowski," Martinsson said. "He's an eccentric man who lives alone in a cottage not far from Stång Lake, which is due north of Älmhult. I talked to a woman at the Town Hall who said that there's a sign to Stång Lake next to his driveway. But she couldn't give me exact directions. You'll have to stop at a house and ask."

"Do we have somewhere to stay overnight?"

"IKEA has a hotel, and you have rooms reserved."

"Doesn't IKEA sell furniture?"

"Yes, they do. But they also have a hotel. The IKEA Inn."

"Anything happening?"

"Everyone's really busy, but it sounds as if Hamrén's coming down from Stockholm to help out."

Wallander remembered the two police detectives from Stockholm who had assisted them during the summer. He had nothing against having them again.

"Not Ludwigsson?"

"He was in a car accident; he's in hospital."

"Serious?"

"I'll find out, but I didn't get that impression."

Wallander hung up and returned the pen.

"It looks valuable," he said.

"Being an accountant for Price Waterhouse is one of the best jobs around," Runfeldt said. "At least in terms of salary and future prospects. Wise parents today advise their children to become accountants."

"What's the average salary?" asked Wallander.

"Most people who are employed above a certain level have individual contracts. Which are confidential, of course."

Wallander took this to mean that the salaries were extremely high. His own salary as a detective with many years of experience was quite low. If he had taken a position in the private sector, he could have earned at least double what he was on now, but he had made his choice, he would stay with the police, at least as long as he could survive on his salary.

They reached Älmhult at 5 p.m. Runfeldt asked if it was really necessary to stay the night. Wallander didn't have a good answer. Runfeldt could have taken the train back to Malmö. But Wallander told him that they wouldn't be able to visit the lake until the following day because it would soon be dark, and he wanted Runfeldt to go with him.

After they checked into the hotel, Wallander set off at once to find Jacob Hoslowski's house. He stopped at the road sign posted at the entrance to the town and made a note of Stång Lake's location, then headed away from town. It was already dusk. He turned left and then left again. The forest was dense. The open landscape of Skåne was far behind him. He stopped when he saw a man mending a gate near the road. The man gave him directions, and Wallander drove on. The engine started to knock. His Peugeot was getting old. He wondered how he could afford a new one. He had bought this car after his first one had blown up on the E65 one night. It had also been a Peugeot. Wallander had the feeling that his next car would be the same make. The older he got, the harder it was for him to break his habits.

When he reached the next turn-off, Wallander drove down a rough dirt road. After 100 metres he stopped and parked, afraid that he might get stuck. He got out of the car and started walking. There was a rustling in the trees that stood close together along the narrow road. He walked briskly to keep warm.

The house stood right on the side of the road. It was an old-fashioned cottage. The yard was full of old cars. A solitary rooster was sitting on a stump, staring at him. There was a light in one window. Wallander saw that it was a kerosene lamp. He wondered whether he should postpone his visit until the following day, but he had come so far. He went up to the front door. The rooster sat motionless on the stump. He knocked. After a moment he heard a shuffling sound and the door opened. The man standing there in the dim light was younger than

Wallander had expected, maybe about 40. Wallander introduced himself.

"Jacob Hoslowski," replied the man. Wallander could hear a faint, almost imperceptible accent in his voice. The man was unwashed. He smelled bad. His long hair and beard were matted.

"I wonder if I might disturb you for a few minutes," he said.

Hoslowski smiled and stepped aside.

"Come in. I always let in anyone who knocks on my door."

Wallander stepped inside the dark hall and almost tripped over a cat. The whole house was full of them. He'd never in his life seen so many cats in one place before. It reminded him of the Forum Romanum, but here the stench was appalling. He followed Hoslowski into the larger of the two rooms in the house. There was almost no furniture, just mattresses and cushions, piles of books, and a single kerosene lamp on a stool. And cats, everywhere. Wallander had an uneasy feeling that they were all watching him with alert eyes, ready to hurl themselves at him at any moment.

"I don't often visit a house without electricity," said Wallander.

"I live outside of time," Hoslowski replied simply. "In my next life I'm going to be reincarnated as a cat."

Wallander nodded. "I see," he said. "Were you living here ten years ago?"

"I've lived here ever since I left time behind."

"When did you leave time behind?"

"A long time ago."

Wallander could see this was the most accurate answer he was going to get. With some difficulty he sank down onto one of the cushions, hoping that it wasn't covered with cat piss.

"Ten years ago a woman went out onto the ice at Stång Lake near here and drowned," he went on. "Do you remember the incident? Even though, as you say, you live outside of time?"

Wallander noticed that Hoslowski reacted positively to having his timeless existence accepted.

"A winter Sunday ten years ago," said Wallander. "According to the report, a man came here and asked you for help."

Hoslowski nodded. "A man came and pounded on my door. He wanted to borrow my telephone."

Wallander looked around the room. "But you don't have a phone?"

"Who would I talk to?"

Wallander nodded. "What happened then?"

"I directed him to my nearest neighbours. They have a telephone."

"Did you go with him?"

"I went over to the lake to see if I could pull her out."

Wallander paused and backed up a bit.

"The man who pounded on your door – I presume he was upset?"

"Maybe."

"What do you mean by 'maybe'?"

"I remember him as being oddly calm."

"Did you notice anything else?"

"I forget. It took place in a cosmic dimension that has changed many times since then."

"Let's move on. You went over to the lake. What happened then?"

"The ice was smooth. I saw the hole. I walked over

to it. But I didn't see anything in the water."

"You say that you walked? Weren't you afraid the ice would crack?"

"I know what it can hold. Besides, I can make myself weightless when I have to."

You can't talk sense with a madman, Wallander thought.

"Can you describe the hole in the ice for me?"

"It was probably cut by a fisherman. Maybe it froze over, but the ice hadn't had a chance to get thick."

Wallander thought for a moment.

"Don't ice fishermen drill small holes?"

"This one was almost rectangular. Maybe they had used a saw."

"Are there usually ice fishermen on Stång Lake?"

"The lake is full of fish. I fish there myself. But not in the winter."

"Then what happened? You stood next to the hole in the ice. You didn't see anything. What did you do then?"

"I took off my clothes and got into the water."

Wallander stared at him.

"Why in God's name did you do that?"

"I thought I might be able to feel her body with my feet."

"But you could have frozen to death."

"I can make myself insensitive to extreme cold or heat if necessary."

Wallander realised he should have anticipated this answer.

"But you didn't find her?"

"No. I pulled myself back out of the water and got dressed. Right after that people came running. A car with ladders. Then I left."

Wallander began to get up from the uncomfortable

cushion. The stench in the room was unbearable. He had no further questions and didn't want to stay any longer than he had to. At the same time he had to admit that Hoslowski had been obliging and friendly.

Hoslowski followed him out to the yard.

"They pulled her out later," he said. "My neighbour usually stops by to tell me what he thinks I should know about the outside world. He's a very nice man. He keeps me informed about everything that goes on in the local shooting club. Most of what happens elsewhere in the world he considers less important. That's why I don't know much about what's happening. Maybe you'd permit me to ask whether at the present time there's any kind of extensive war going on?"

"Nothing big," said Wallander. "But lots of small ones."

Hoslowski nodded. Then he pointed.

"My neighbour lives right nearby," he said. "You can't see his house. It's maybe 300 metres from here. Earthly distances are hard to calculate."

Wallander thanked him and left. It was quite dark now. He used his torch to see the way. Lights flickered between the trees. The house he came to seemed relatively new. In front stood a van with the words "Plumbing Services" painted on the side. Wallander rang the bell. A tall, barefoot man wearing a white undershirt wrenched open the door as if Wallander was the latest in an endless line of people who had come to disturb him. But he had an open and friendly face. He could hear a child crying somewhere in the house. Wallander explained briefly who he was.

"And it was Hoslowski who sent you over?" said the man with a smile.

"What makes you think that?"

"I can tell by the smell," said the man. "It goes away with a good airing. Come on in."

Wallander followed him into the kitchen. The crying was coming from upstairs. There was a TV on somewhere too. The man introduced himself as Rune Nilsson. Wallander declined a cup of coffee and told him why he was there.

"You don't forget something like that," Nilsson said. "It was before I was married. There was an old house here that I tore down when I built the new one. Was it really ten years ago that it happened?"

"Exactly ten years ago, give or take a few months."

"He came and pounded on my door. It was the middle of the day."

"How did he seem?"

"He was upset, but in control. He called the police while I put on my coat. Then we took off. We took a shortcut through the woods. I did a lot of fishing back then."

"He gave you the impression of being in control the whole time? What did he say? How did he explain the accident?"

"She had fallen in. The ice broke."

"But the ice was quite thick, wasn't it?"

"You never know about ice. There can be invisible cracks or weaknesses. But it did seem strange."

"Jacob Hoslowski said the hole in the ice was rectangular. He thought it might have been cut with a saw."

"I don't remember whether it was rectangular or not. Only that it was big."

"But the ice around it was strong. You're a big man but you weren't afraid to go out on the ice?"

Nilsson nodded.

"I thought a lot about that afterwards," he said. "It was a strange thing, a woman disappearing into a hole in the ice like that. Why couldn't he have pulled her out?"

"What was his own explanation?"

"He said he tried, but she vanished too fast. Pulled down under the ice."

"Was that true?"

"They found her several metres away from the hole, right under the ice. She hadn't sunk down. I was there when they pulled her out. I'll never forget it. I wouldn't have believed that she could weigh so much."

"What do you mean by that? That she could have 'weighed so much'?"

"I knew Nygren, who was the police officer back then. He's dead now. He told me several times that the man claimed that she weighed almost 80 kilos. That was supposed to explain why the ice broke. I never understood that. But I guess you always brood over accidents."

"That's probably true," Wallander said, standing up. "Thanks for your time. Tomorrow I'd like you to show me where it happened."

"Are we going to walk on water?"

Wallander smiled. "That's not necessary. But maybe Jacob Hoslowski has that power."

Nilsson shook his head.

"He's harmless," he said. "That man and all his cats. Harmless but nuts."

Wallander walked back along the forest road. The kerosene lamp was still burning in Hoslowski's window. Nilsson had promised to be home around 8 a.m. the next morning. He started up his car and headed back to Älmhult. The knocking in the engine was gone now. He was hungry. It might be sensible to suggest to Runfeldt that they have dinner together. For Wallander the trip no longer seemed pointless.

When Wallander reached the hotel there was a message for him at the front desk. Bo Runfeldt had rented a car and gone to Växjö. He had good friends there, and intended to spend the night. He promised to return to Älmhult early the next day. For a moment Wallander felt annoyed. He might have needed Runfeldt for something during the evening. He had left a phone number in Växjö, but Wallander had no reason to call him. He realised that he was relieved that he would have the evening to himself. He went to his room, took a shower, and found that he didn't have a toothbrush with him. He got dressed and went in search of a shop where he could buy what he needed. He ate dinner at a pizzeria, thinking the whole time about the drowning accident. He was slowly piecing together a picture. Back in his hotel room, he called Höglund at home. He hoped her children were in bed asleep. When she answered, he outlined what had happened. What he wanted to know was whether they had succeeded in tracking down Mrs Svensson, Gösta Runfeldt's last client.

"Not yet," she told him.

He kept the conversation short. Then he turned on the TV and watched distractedly for a while. Eventually he fell asleep.

When Wallander woke up just after 6 a.m., he felt well rested. By 7.30 a.m. he had eaten breakfast and paid for his room. He sat down in reception to wait. Runfeldt arrived a few minutes later. Neither of them mentioned his having spent the night in Växjö.

"We're going on an expedition," said Wallander. "To the lake where your mother drowned."

"Has the trip been worth the trouble?" asked Runfeldt. Wallander noticed that he was irritable.

"Yes," he replied. "And your presence has actually been of crucial importance, whether you want to believe it or not."

Wallander wasn't sure of this, of course, but he spoke so firmly that Runfeldt, if not totally convinced, at least looked pensive.

Nilsson was waiting for them. They walked along a path through the woods. There was no wind and the temperature was close to freezing. The water spread out before them. The lake was oblong. Nilsson pointed to a spot in about the middle of the lake. Wallander noticed that Runfeldt looked uncomfortable, and assumed he had never been there before.

"It's hard to imagine the lake covered with ice," said Nilsson. "Everything changes when winter arrives. Especially your sense of distance. What seems far away in the summer can suddenly seem much closer. Or the other way around."

Wallander walked down to the shore. The water was dark. He thought he caught a glimpse of a little fish moving next to a rock. Behind him he could hear Runfeldt asking if the lake was deep. He didn't catch Nilsson's reply.

He asked himself what had happened. Did Gösta Runfeldt plan to drown his wife on that particular Sunday? That's what he must have done. Somehow he must have prepared the hole in the ice. The same way someone had sawed through the planks over the pit at Eriksson's place. And had held Runfeldt prisoner.

Wallander stood there a long time, looking at the lake spread out before them. But what he saw was in his mind.

They walked back through the woods. At the car they said goodbye to Nilsson. Wallander thought they should be back in Ystad well before midday.

He was mistaken. Just south of Älmhult the car stopped, and wouldn't start again. Wallander called the road service he belonged to. The man came in less than 20 minutes, but quickly concluded that the car had a problem that couldn't be repaired on the spot. They would have to leave the car in Älmhult and take the train to Malmö.

Runfeldt offered to buy the tickets and bought first-class seats. Wallander said nothing. At 9.44 a.m., the train left for Hässleholm and Malmö. By then Wallander had called the police station and asked for someone to come to Malmö and pick them up. There was no good connection by train to Ystad. Ebba promised to see to it that someone was there.

"Don't the police have better cars than that?" Runfeldt asked suddenly after the train had left Älmhult behind. "What if there'd been an emergency?"

"That was my own car," Wallander replied. "Our emergency vehicles are in much better shape."

The landscape slid past the window. Wallander thought about Gösta Runfeldt. He was sure that he'd murdered his wife. Now Runfeldt himself was dead. A brutal man, probably a murderer, had now been killed in an equally gruesome way.

The most obvious motive was revenge. But who was taking it? And how did Holger Eriksson fit into the picture? Wallander had no answers.

His thoughts were interrupted by the arrival of the conductor. It was a woman. She smiled and asked for their tickets with a distinct Skåne accent. Wallander felt as though she recognised him. Maybe she'd seen his picture in a newspaper.

"When do we get to Malmö?" he asked.

"12.15," she replied. "Hässleholm 11.13 a.m."

Then she left. She knew the timetable by heart.

CHAPTER 20

Peters was waiting for them at the station in Malmö. Bo Runfeldt excused himself, saying he'd stay in Malmö for a few hours and return to Ystad in the afternoon, so that he and his sister could start going through his father's estate.

On the way back to Ystad, Wallander sat in the back seat and made notes about what had happened in Älmhult. He had bought a pen and a little notebook at the station in Malmö and balanced it on his knee as he wrote. Peters left him alone. It was a sunny, windy day, already 14 October. His father hadn't been in the ground a week. Wallander suspected, or maybe feared, that he hadn't yet begun to grieve.

They went straight to the police station. Wallander had eaten some outrageously expensive sandwiches on the train and didn't need lunch. He stopped at the front desk to tell Ebba what had happened to his car. Her well-kept old Volvo stood in the car park as usual.

"I'm going to have to buy a new car," he said. "But how am I going to afford it?"

"It's shameful how little they pay us," she replied. "But it's best not to think about it."

"I'm not so sure about that," Wallander said. "It's not going to get any better if we just forget about it."

On the way to his office he peeked into his colleagues' rooms. Everyone was out except Nyberg, who had an office at the very end of the hall. He was seldom there. A crutch was leaning against his desk.

"How's the foot?" Wallander asked.

"No better than can be expected," Nyberg answered crossly.

"You didn't happen to find Runfeldt's suitcase, by any chance?"

"No, but we know that it's not in the woods at Marsvinsholm. The dogs would have tracked it down if it were."

"Did you find anything else?"

"We always do, but whether it has anything to do with the murder is another question. We're in the process of comparing tyre tracks from the tractor path behind Eriksson's tower to the ones we found in the woods. I doubt we'll be able to say anything with certainty. It was very muddy at both places."

"Anything else you think I should know about?"

"The shrunken head," said Nyberg. "We got a long, detailed letter from the Ethnographic Museum in Stockholm. I understand about half of what it says. But they're positive it comes from the Belgian Congo. They think it's between 40 and 50 years old."

"That fits," Wallander said.

"The museum is interested in acquiring it."

"That's something the authorities will have to decide after the investigation is over."

Nyberg suddenly gave Wallander an inquiring look.

"Are we going to catch the people who did this?"

"We have to."

Nyberg nodded.

"You said 'the people', but earlier you said it was probably a lone killer."

"Did I say 'the people'?"

"Yes."

"I still think it was someone acting alone. But I can't explain why."

Wallander turned to go. Nyberg stopped him.

"We managed to get Secure, the mail-order company in Borås, to tell us what Runfeldt bought from them. He ordered things on three other occasions. The company hasn't been in business long. He bought night-vision binoculars, several torches, and other unimportant things – nothing illegal. We found the torches at Harpegatan. But the night-vision binoculars weren't there or at the shop."

Wallander thought for a moment.

"Do you think he packed them in his suitcase to take with him to Nairobi? Do people spy on orchids at night?"

"Well, we haven't found them, at any rate," Nyberg said.

Wallander went into his office, sat down at his desk and read through what he had written during the drive from Malmö. He was looking for similarities and differences between the two cases.

Both men had been described as brutal, though in different ways. Eriksson had treated his employees badly; Runfeldt had beaten his wife. There was a similarity. They had both been murdered in a well-planned way. Wallander was convinced that Runfeldt had been held prisoner. There was no other explanation for his long absence. Eriksson, on the other hand, had walked straight to his death. That was a difference.

Why was Runfeldt held prisoner? Why did the murderer wait to kill him? For some reason the killer wanted to wait. Which in turn gave rise to new questions. Could it be that the murderer didn't have the opportunity to kill him right away? If that was the case, why? Or was it part of the plan to hold Runfeldt captive, starving him until he was powerless?

Once again the only motive that Wallander could see was revenge. But for what? They had found no definite clues. He moved on to the killer. They had guessed that it was probably a lone man with great physical strength. They could be wrong, of course; there could be more than one person involved, but Wallander didn't think so. There was something about the planning that pointed to a single killer.

Wallander leaned back in his chair. He tried to understand the uneasiness that he couldn't shake off. There was something about the picture that he wasn't seeing.

After about an hour he went to get a cup of coffee. He called the optician and was told he could come in whenever he liked. After going through his jacket twice, Wallander found the phone number for the garage in Älmhult. The repairs were going to cost a lot, but Wallander had no alternative if he wanted to get anything for the car.

He hung up and called Martinsson.

"I didn't know you were back. How'd it go in Älmhult?"

"I thought we should talk about that. Who's here right now?"

"I just saw Hansson," said Martinsson. "We talked about having a short meeting at 5 p.m."

"So we'll wait till then."

Wallander put down the phone and found himself thinking about Jacob Hoslowski and his cats. He wondered when he would have time to look for a house for himself. Their workload was constantly increasing. In the past there had been times when the pressure eased off, but that almost never happened now. And no-one was talking about it getting any better. He didn't know whether crime was on the rise, but he did know that it was getting more violent. And fewer officers were involved with real police work. More and more of them had administrative jobs. It was impossible for Wallander to think of himself with a desk job. When he did sit there, as he was doing now, it was a break in his routine. They'd never be able to find the killer if they sat around the police station. Forensic science was steadily progressing, but it could never replace field work.

He returned to Älmhult. Had Runfeldt made a murder look like an accident? There were strong indications that he had. Too many details didn't fit with an accident. It should be possible to dig up the investigative work that had been done. It had probably been sloppy, but he couldn't criticise the officers who had carried it out. What could they have suspected? Why would they have had any suspicions at all?

Wallander called Martinsson again and asked him to contact Älmhult and get a copy of the investigative report on the drowning.

"Why didn't you do that yourself?" asked Martinsson in surprise.

"I didn't talk to the police there," Wallander replied, "but I did sit on the floor in a house full of cats, with a man who can make himself weightless whenever he feels like it. It'd be good to get that report as soon as possible."

He hung up before Martinsson could ask questions. It was 3 p.m. It was still nice outside, and he decided to go and see the optician straight away. There wasn't much else he could do before the meeting. His head ached. Ebba was busy on the phone, so he wrote a note saying he'd be back for the meeting and left the station.

He stood in the car park looking for his car for a while, before he remembered it was in the garage. It took him ten minutes to walk to the centre of town. The optician's shop was on Stora Östergatan near Pilgränd.

He was told he had to wait a few minutes. He leafed through the newspapers lying on a table. There was a picture of him that was at least five years old. He hardly recognised himself. There was a lot of coverage of the murders. "The police are following up solid leads." That's what Wallander had told the press, and it wasn't true. He wondered if the killer read the papers. Was he keeping track of the police work? Wallander turned some more pages. He stopped at a story inside, read it with growing astonishment, and studied the pictures. The journalist from the *Anmärkaren*, which hadn't come out yet, had been right. People from all over the country had gathered in Ystad to form a national organisation to create a citizen militia. If necessary, they wouldn't hesitate to commit illegal acts. They supported the work of the police, but they refused to accept any cutbacks. Wallander read on with a growing feeling of bitterness and distaste. Something had happened, all right. These people were coming out into the open. Their names and faces were in the papers and they were gathering right here in Ystad.

Wallander tossed the paper aside. We're going to end up fighting on two fronts, he thought. This is much more serious than the neo-Nazi organisations, whose threat is always exaggerated; or the motorcycle gangs.

When it was his turn, Wallander sat with a strange apparatus in front of his eyes and stared at the blurry letters. He began to worry that he might be going blind. But when the optician set a pair of glasses on his nose and held up a newspaper page on which there was also an article about the citizen militia, he could read the text easily. For a moment this took away the unpleasantness of the article's contents.

"You need reading glasses," said the optician kindly. "Not unusual at your age. Plus 1.5 should be enough. You'll probably have to increase the strength every few years or so."

Wallander went over to look at the display of frames. He was shocked when he saw the prices. When he heard that it was possible to get cheaper plastic frames, he decided on this option.

"How many pairs?" asked the optician. "Two? So you'll have a spare?"

Wallander thought of the pens he was constantly losing. He couldn't stand the thought of having glasses on a string around his neck.

"Five pairs," he said.

When he left the shop it was still only 4 p.m. He strolled over to the estate agent's office. This time he went inside, sat down at a table, and looked through the house listings. Two of the properties interested him. He got copies of the information sheets and promised to let them know if he wanted to see them. He went back outside. He still had some time left, and decided to try to answer a question that had been on his mind ever since Holger Eriksson died. He went into a bookshop near Stortoget and asked for a bookseller he knew. He was told that he was in the stockroom in the basement. He found his acquaintance there unpacking boxes of books. They greeted each other.

"You still owe me 19 kronor," said the bookseller with a smile.

"For what?"

"This summer you woke me up at 6 a.m. because the police needed a map of the Dominican Republic. The officer who came over to get it paid 100 kronor. But it cost 119."

Wallander went to take out his wallet. The bookseller put up his hand to stop him.

"It's on me," he said. "I was just kidding."

"Holger Eriksson's poems," Wallander said, "which he published himself. Who bought them?"

"He was an amateur, of course," the bookseller answered. "But he wasn't a bad poet. The problem was, he wrote only about birds. Or rather, that was the only thing he was any good at writing about. Whenever he tried some other subject, it didn't work."

"So who bought them?"

"He didn't sell many copies through the bookshop. Most of these regional writers don't generate a lot of sales, you know. But they're important for another reason."

"So who did buy them?"

"I honestly don't know. Maybe an occasional tourist? I think some bird lovers discovered his books. Maybe collectors of regional literature."

"Birds," Wallander said. "That means he never wrote anything that people might get upset about."

"Of course not," the bookseller said in surprise. "Did someone say that he had?"

"I was just wondering."

Wallander left the bookshop and went back up the hill to the police station.

When he entered the conference room and sat down in his usual place, he put on his new glasses. A certain merriment was evident in the room, but no-one said a word.

"Who's missing?" he asked.

"Svedberg," Höglund said. "I don't know where he's got to."

She had barely finished her sentence when Svedberg tore open the door of the conference room.

"I've found Mrs Svensson," he said. "The woman we think was Runfeldt's last client."

"Good," Wallander said, feeling the suspense rise.

"I thought that she might have been to the florist's shop," Svedberg continued. "She might have gone to see Runfeldt there. I took along the photograph we developed. Vanja Andersson remembered seeing a picture of the same man in the back room. She also knew that a woman named Svensson had been to the shop a couple of times. Once she bought flowers to be delivered. The rest was simple. Her address and phone number were on file. She lives on Byabacksvägen in Sövestad. I went out there. She runs a little vegetable shop. I took along the picture and told her the truth, that we believed she had hired Runfeldt as a private detective. She admitted at once that I was right."

"What else did she say?"

"I left her there. I thought it'd be better if we interviewed her together."

"I'll talk to her this evening," Wallander said. "Let's keep this meeting as brief as possible."

They were there for half an hour. During the meeting Chief Holgersson came in and sat down at the table. She kept silent. Wallander reported on his trip to Älmhult. He concluded by telling them what he thought, that they couldn't ignore the possibility that Runfeldt had murdered his wife. They should wait for a copy of the investigative report made at the time. Afterwards they would decide how to proceed.

When Wallander stopped talking, no-one had anything

to say. They all could see that he might be right, but what it meant for the investigation was far from clear.

"The trip was important," said Wallander after a moment. "I also think the trip to Svenstavik could be productive."

"With a stop in Gävle," said Höglund. "I don't know whether it means anything, but I asked a good friend in Stockholm to go to a special bookshop and get me a few issues of a paper called *Terminator*. They came today."

"What kind of paper is that?" Wallander asked.

"It's published in the US," she said. "It's a poorly disguised trade paper, you might say. For people looking for contracts as mercenaries or bodyguards, or any kind of assignments as soldiers. It's not a pleasant paper. For one thing, it's extremely racist. But I found a little classified ad that should interest us. There's a man in Gävle who offers to arrange assignments for what he calls 'battle-ready and unbiased men'. I called our colleagues in Gävle. They knew who he was, but have never dealt with him directly. They thought he had contact with men in Sweden who have been mercenaries."

"This could be important," Wallander said. "He's someone we definitely need to talk to. It should be possible to combine a trip to Svenstavik and Gävle."

"I've checked the map," she said. "You can fly to Östersund, then rent a car. Or ask for help from our colleagues up there."

Wallander closed his notebook.

"Get someone to make me a reservation," he said. "If possible, I'd like to go tomorrow."

"On Saturday?" Martinsson asked.

"It won't make a difference to the people I have to see," Wallander said. "There's no time to waste if we can help it. I suggest that we break up the meeting now. Who wants to come along to Sövestad?"

Before anyone could reply, Chief Holgersson tapped her pencil on the table.

"Just a minute," she said. "I don't know whether you realise that there's going to be a meeting of people who have decided to form a national organisation of citizen militia here in Ystad. I think it'd be good if we discussed as soon as possible how we're going to handle this."

"The national police board has sent out flyers about these militia," said Wallander. "I think it's very clear what Swedish law says about vigilante activities."

"No doubt you're right," she replied. "But I have a strong feeling that things are changing. I'm afraid that pretty soon we're going to see a burglar get shot and killed by someone from one of these groups. And then they'll start shooting each other."

Wallander knew she was right. But at that moment he couldn't focus on anything other than the two murder investigations they were working on.

"I agree it's important. In the long run, it's crucial to stamp it out if we don't want people to be playing at being the police all over the country. Let's talk about it on Monday when we meet."

Holgersson let it go at that. The meeting broke up. Höglund and Svedberg were going to accompany Wallander to Sövestad. It was 6 p.m. by the time they left the station. They took Höglund's car. Wallander got into the back seat. He wondered whether he still smelled from his visit to Jacob Hoslowski's house of cats.

"Maria Svensson," Svedberg said. "She's 36 years old and has a little vegetable shop in Sövestad, selling only organic vegetables."

"You didn't ask her why she got in contact with Runfeldt?"

"After she confirmed the connection, I didn't ask her anything else."

"This should be interesting," Wallander said. "In all my years on the force, I've never met anyone who has hired a private detective."

"The photograph was of a man," Höglund said. "Her husband?"

"I've told you everything I know," Svedberg answered.

"Or as little," Wallander corrected him. "We know almost nothing."

They reached Sövestad in about 20 minutes. Wallander had been there once many years ago to cut down a man who had hanged himself. It was the first suicide he had encountered. He thought back on the incident with distaste.

Svedberg stopped the car in front of a building with a shop in the front and a greenhouse next to it. A sign said "Svensson's Produce". They climbed out of the car.

"She lives in the building," said Svedberg. "I assume that she's closed up the shop for the day."

"A florist and a greengrocer," Wallander said. "Does that tell us anything, or is it just a coincidence?"

He didn't expect an answer, and didn't get one. The front door opened.

"That's Maria Svensson," said Svedberg. "She's been waiting for us."

The woman standing on the steps was wearing jeans and a white blouse. She had clogs on her feet. There was something odd about her appearance. Wallander noted that she wore no make-up. Svedberg introduced them and Maria Svensson invited them in. They sat down in her living room. It occurred to Wallander that there was also something odd about her house. As if she wasn't interested in the decor.

"May I offer you coffee?" she asked.

All three of them declined.

"As you know, we've come to find out a little more about your relationship to Gösta Runfeldt."

She gave him a surprised look. "Am I supposed to have had a relationship with him?"

"As a client," Wallander said.

"That's true."

"Gösta Runfeldt has been murdered. It took a while for us to discover that he wasn't only a florist, but that he also worked as a private detective. So my first question is: how did you get in contact with him?"

"I saw an ad in *Arbetet* this past summer."

"How did you first meet?"

"I went to his florist's shop. Later the same day we met at a café near Stortoget in Ystad."

"What was your reason for contacting him?"

"I'd rather not say," she said firmly.

Wallander was surprised because up to that point her answers had been so straightforward.

"I'm afraid that you're going to have to tell us," he said.

"I can assure you that it has nothing to do with his death. I'm just as horrified and shocked as everybody else by what happened."

"Whether it has anything to do with it or not is something for the police to decide," Wallander said. "You'll have to answer the question. You can choose to do so here. Then anything that isn't directly connected with the investigation will just be between us. If we're obliged to take you in for more formal interrogation, it will be more difficult to stop the details from leaking to the press."

She sat in silence for a long time. They waited. Wallander took out the photograph they had developed on Harpegatan. She looked at it without expression.

"Is this your husband?" Wallander asked.

She stared at him. Suddenly she laughed.

"No," she said. "He's not my husband. But he stole my lover away from me."

Wallander didn't understand. Höglund got it at once.

"What's her name?"

"Annika."

"And this man came between you?"

She had regained her composure.

"I was starting to suspect it. I didn't know what to do. That's when I thought of contacting a private detective. I had to find out if she was thinking of leaving me. Or switching. Going with a man. In the end I realised that's what she had done. Gösta Runfeldt came here and told me about it. The next day I wrote to Annika to tell her I never wanted to see her again."

"When did he visit you?"

"September 20th or 21st."

"Did you have any contact with him after that?"

"No. I paid him through his bank account."

"What was your impression of him?"

"He was friendly. He was very fond of orchids. I think we got along well because he seemed just as reserved as I am."

Wallander thought for a moment.

"Can you think of any reason why he was killed? Anything he said or did?"

"No," she replied. "Nothing. And I've thought hard about it."

Wallander glanced at his colleagues and stood up. "Then we won't disturb you any further. And none of this will get out. I promise."

"I'm grateful for that," she said. "I wouldn't want to lose customers."

They said goodbye at the door. She closed it before they reached the street.

"What did she mean by that last remark?" asked Wallander. "That she was afraid of losing her customers?"

"People are conservative out in the country," said Höglund. "Homosexuality is still considered to be something dirty by many people. I think she has all the reason in the world not to want this to get out."

They got into the car.

"Where does that leave us?" Svedberg asked.

"It doesn't lead us backwards or forwards," Wallander said. "The truth about these two investigations is simple. We have a number of loose ends, but we don't have a single good clue to go on."

They sat in the car in silence. For a moment Wallander felt guilty. He felt as if he'd stabbed the investigation in the back. But he knew that what he'd said was the truth.

They had nothing to go on. Absolutely nothing.

CHAPTER 21

That night Wallander had a dream.

He was walking along a street in Rome with his father. The summer was suddenly over and it was autumn, a Roman autumn. They were talking about something, he couldn't remember what, and then all of a sudden his father disappeared. One minute he was right next to him, the next he was gone, swallowed up by the swarm of people on the street.

He woke with a start. In the silence of the night, the dream had seemed perfectly clear. It was his grief over his father's death, over never being able to go on with the conversation they had begun. He couldn't feel sorry for his father, only for himself, left behind.

He couldn't go back to sleep. He had to get up early anyway.

When they had gone back to the station after visiting Maria Svensson in Sövestad, there was a message for Wallander that he'd been booked on the 7 a.m. flight from Sturup the next morning, arriving at Östersund at 9.50 a.m, after changing planes at Arlanda Airport. The itinerary gave him the choice of spending Saturday night in Svenstavik or Gävle. A rental car would be waiting for him at the airport in Frösön. He could decide then where to spend the night. He looked at the map of Sweden hanging on the wall in his office next to the big map of Skåne. That gave him an idea. He went into his office and called

Linda. He got an answering machine for the first time and left his question for her: could she take the train to Gävle, a trip that wouldn't take more than two hours, and spend the night there? Then he went looking for Svedberg, finally finding him in the gym where he usually took a sauna on Friday nights. Wallander asked Svedberg to do him a favour, to book two rooms at a nice hotel in Gävle for Saturday night. The next day he could be reached on his mobile phone.

After that he went home. And when he fell asleep, he dreamt about his father in Rome in the autumn.

At 6 a.m. the taxi he had ordered was waiting outside. He picked up his tickets at Sturup Airport. Since it was Saturday morning, the plane to Stockholm was no more than half full. The plane to Östersund left on time. Wallander had never been there before. His visits to the country north of Stockholm had been few and far between. He was looking forward to the trip. For one thing, it would give him some distance from the dream he'd had during the night.

It was a cool morning in Östersund. The pilot had said it was 1°C. The cold feels different, Wallander thought as he drove across the bridge from Frösön through the beautiful landscape. The town lay along the slope of Storsjön. He headed south. It was liberating to be in a rented car, driving through an unfamiliar landscape.

He reached Svenstavik at 11.30 a.m. He had heard from Svedberg along the way that he was supposed to contact a man named Robert Melander. He was the person in the church administration with whom Eriksson's lawyer, Bjurman, had been in contact. Melander lived in a red house next to the old district courthouse in Svenstavik. Wallander parked his car in the middle of town. It took him a while to work out that the courthouse was on the other side of the new shopping centre. He left his car where it was and walked. It was overcast but not raining. He entered the front yard of Melander's house. A Norwegian elkhound was chained to a kennel. The front door stood open. Wallander knocked. No-one answered, but he thought that he heard sounds from behind the house. He walked around the side and found a large garden with a potato patch and currant bushes. Wallander was surprised to see currants growing so far north. At the back of the house stood a man about Wallander's age, wearing gumboots. He was sawing branches off the trunk of a tree that lay on the ground. When he caught sight of Wallander, he stopped at once and stretched his back, smiled and put down the saw.

"You must be the policeman from Ystad," he said, putting out his hand.

His dialect is quite melodic, thought Wallander, as he greeted the man.

"When'd you leave?" asked Melander. "Last night?"

"This morning."

"Imagine, it can go that fast," said Melander. "I was in Malmö several times back in the 1960s. I'd got it into my head that it might be nice to move around a bit. And there was work at that big shipyard."

"Kockums," said Wallander. "But it doesn't exist any more."

"Nothing exists any more," replied Melander philosophically. "Back then it took four days to drive down there."

"But you didn't stay," said Wallander.

"No, I didn't," replied Melander cheerfully. "It was beautiful and pleasant enough in the south. But it wasn't for me. If I'm going to travel anywhere in my life, it's going to be north. Not south. You don't even have snow down there, they tell me."

"Occasionally we do," Wallander replied. "When it does snow, it snows a lot."

"There's lunch waiting for us inside," said Melander. "My wife works at the welfare centre, but she fixed something for us."

"It's beautiful here," Wallander said.

"Very," Melander replied. "And the beauty remains. Year after year."

They sat down at the kitchen table. Wallander ate heartily. There was plenty of food. Melander was a good talker. He was a man who combined a number of diverse activities to make his living. Among other things, he gave folk-dancing lessons in the winter. Not until they were having coffee did Wallander mention why he was there.

"Of course it came as a great surprise to us," Melander said. "100,000 kronor is a lot of money. Especially when it's a gift from a stranger."

"You mean no-one knows who Holger Eriksson was?"

"He was completely unknown to us. A car dealer from Skåne who was murdered. That was very strange. Those of us who are connected with the church began asking around. We also saw to it that a notice asking for information was placed in the newspapers. But no-one got in touch with us."

Wallander had remembered to bring along a photograph of Eriksson. Melander studied the picture while he filled his pipe. He lit it without taking his eyes off the photograph. Wallander's hopes started to rise. But then Melander shook his head.

"The man is still a stranger to me," he said. "I have a good memory for faces, and I've never seen him before.

Maybe someone else might recognise him, but I don't."

"I'm going to give you two names," Wallander said, "to see if they mean anything to you. The first is Gösta Runfeldt."

Melander thought for a moment. But not for long.

"Runfeldt is not a name from around here," he said. "It almost sounds like an assumed or made-up name."

"Harald Berggren," Wallander said, "is the second."

Melander's pipe had gone out. He put it down on the table.

"Maybe," he said. "Let me make a call."

Wallander felt his excitement rise. What he wanted most of all was to be able to identify the man who had written the diary from the Congo.

Melander asked for a man named Nils.

"I have a guest here from Skåne," he said into the phone. "A man named Kurt who's a policeman. He's asking about someone named Harald Berggren. I don't think there's anyone alive here in Svenstavik by that name. But isn't there someone with that name buried in the cemetery?"

Wallander's heart sank. But not completely. Even a dead Harald Berggren might be of help to them.

Melander listened to the answer and came back to the kitchen table.

"Nils Enman is in charge of the cemetery," he said. "And there's a gravestone with the name Harald Berggren on it. But Nils is young. And the man who took care of the cemetery before is now lying there himself. Maybe we should go over there and have a look?"

Wallander stood up. Melander was surprised by his haste.

"Someone once told me that people from Skåne are relaxed. But that doesn't apply to you."

"I have my bad habits," Wallander said.

They headed out into the clear autumn air. Melander greeted everyone they met. They reached the cemetery.

"His grave is over by the grove of trees," Melander said.

Wallander walked between the graves, following Melander and thinking about the dream he'd had during the night. It seemed unreal to him that his father was dead.

Melander stopped and pointed. The gravestone stood upright, with a gold inscription. Wallander read what it said and realised at once that there was no help to be found here. The man named Harald Berggren who lay buried there had died in 1949. Melander noticed his reaction.

"Not the one?"

"No," replied Wallander. "It's definitely not him. The man we're looking for was still alive at least until 1963."

"A man you're looking for?" Melander said with curiosity. "A man the police are looking for must have committed some type of crime."

"I don't know that. It's too complicated to explain. Often the police look for people who haven't done anything illegal."

"So your trip here was in vain," Melander said. "The church has received a gift of a great deal of money, and we don't know why. We still don't know this Eriksson."

"There must be an explanation," Wallander said.

"Would you like to see the church?" Melander asked suddenly, as if he wanted to give Wallander some encouragement.

Wallander nodded.

"It's a lovely place," Melander said. "I was married there."

They walked up to the church and went inside.

Wallander noted that the door wasn't locked. Light shone in through the side windows.

"It's beautiful," Wallander said.

"Yet I don't think you're particularly religious," said Melander and smiled.

Wallander didn't reply. He sat down on one of the wooden pews. Melander stayed standing in the centre aisle. Wallander searched his mind for some way to proceed. Eriksson wouldn't have left a gift to the church in Svenstavik without a reason.

"Holger Eriksson wrote poetry," Wallander said. "He was what they call a regional poet."

"We have poets like that too," Melander said. "To be quite honest, what they write isn't always very good."

"Eriksson was also a bird lover," continued Wallander. "At night he went out to watch the birds heading south. He couldn't see them. But he knew they were there overhead. Maybe it's possible to hear the rushing of thousands of wings."

"I know some people who keep pigeons," Melander said. "But we've only had one ornithologist."

"Had?" Wallander asked.

Melander sat down on the pew on the other side of the aisle. "It's an odd story," he said. "A story without an ending." He laughed. "Almost like your story. That doesn't have an ending either."

"I'm sure we'll reach a conclusion," said Wallander. "We usually do. So what about your story?"

"Sometime back in the 1960s a Polish woman came here," he said. "Where exactly she came from, I don't think anybody knew. But she worked at the local inn. Rented a room. Kept to herself. Even though she quickly learned to speak Swedish, she didn't seem to have any friends. Later she bought a house. Out towards Sveg. I was young back then, young enough to often think about how beautiful she was. She was interested in birds. At the post office they said she got letters and cards from all over Sweden. They were postcards with information about ringed owls and God knows what else. She wrote lots of cards and letters herself. They had to stock extra postcards for her at the local shop. She didn't care what the picture was of. They bought up postcards that shops in other villages couldn't sell."

"How do you know all this?" Wallander asked.

"In a village you know about a lot of things, whether you want to or not," Melander said. "That's the way it is."

"Then what happened?"

"She disappeared."

"Disappeared?"

"What's that expression? She went up in smoke. Vanished."

Wallander wasn't sure he had understood correctly. "Did she go away somewhere?"

"She travelled a great deal, but she always came back. When she disappeared, she was here. She had gone for a walk through town one afternoon in October. She often took walks. Strolls. After that day she was never seen again. There was a lot written about it back then. She hadn't packed her things. People started to wonder when she didn't show up at the inn. They went over to her house. She was gone. They searched for her. But she was never found. That happened about 25 years ago. They've never found anything. But there have been rumours that she was seen in South America or Alingsås. Or as a ghost in the woods outside Rätansbyn."

"What was her name?" Wallander asked.

"Krista. Her surname was Haberman."

Wallander remembered the case. There'd been a lot of speculation. He vaguely recalled the newspaper headline: "The Polish Beauty".

"So she corresponded with other bird-watchers," he said. "And sometimes she visited them?"

"Yes."

"Do the letters still exist?"

"She was declared dead years ago. A relative from Poland turned up and her belongings disappeared. And the house was later torn down."

Wallander nodded. It would have been too much to expect to find the letters and postcards.

"I have a hazy recollection of the whole thing," he said. "But wasn't there suspicion that she had committed suicide or been the victim of a crime?"

"Of course there were all manner of rumours. I think the police who investigated the case did a good job. They were people from the area who could tell the difference between gossip and the truth. There were rumours about mysterious cars. That she'd had secret visitors in the night. And no-one knew what she did when she went travelling. She disappeared. And she's still missing. If she's alive, she's 25 years older. Everyone gets older. Even people who disappear."

It's happening again, thought Wallander. Something from the past is coming back. I come up here to find out why Holger Eriksson bequeathed his money to the church in Svenstavik. I don't get an answer to my question, but I discover that there was also a bird-watcher here, a woman who disappeared over 25 years ago. Perhaps I've found an answer to my question after all. Even though I don't yet understand it.

"The case material is still in Östersund," Melander said. "It probably weighs several kilos."

They left the church. Wallander looked at a bird sitting on the cemetery wall.

"Have you ever heard of a bird called a middle spotted woodpecker?" he asked.

"Isn't it extinct?" Melander asked. "At least in Sweden?"

"It's close to extinction," said Wallander. "It's been gone from this country for 15 years."

"I may have seen one a few times," Melander said doubtfully. "But any sort of woodpecker is scarce these days. The old trees have disappeared. That's where they usually lived. And on telephone poles, of course."

They had walked back to the shopping centre and stopped at Wallander's car. It was 2.30 p.m.

"Are you going further?" Melander asked. "Or are you heading back to Skåne?"

"I'm going to Gävle," replied Wallander. "How long does it take? Three, four hours?"

"Closer to five. There's no snow and it's not slippery. The roads are good. But it'll take you that long. It's almost 400 kilometres."

"I want to thank you for all your help," said Wallander. "And for the nice lunch."

"But you didn't get any answers to your questions."

"Maybe I did," Wallander said. "We'll see."

"The officer who handled Krista Haberman's disappearance was an old man," said Melander. "He started when he was middle-aged. Stayed with the police until he retired. They say the last thing he talked about on his deathbed was what had happened to her. He could never let it go."

"There's always that danger," Wallander said.

They said goodbye.

"If you ever come south, stop in," Wallander said.

Melander smiled. His pipe had gone out again.

"I think my travels will take me mostly north," he said. "But you never know."

"I'd be grateful if you'd get in touch with me," Wallander said, "if anything happens that might explain why Holger Eriksson left the money to the church."

"It's strange," Melander said. "If he'd seen the church, it might be understandable. It's so beautiful."

"You're right," Wallander replied. "If he'd ever been here, it might make sense."

"Maybe he went through here sometime? Without anyone knowing about it?"

"Or maybe only one person knew," Wallander replied.

Melander looked at him.

"You have something in mind?"

"Yes," Wallander replied. "But I don't know yet what it means."

They shook hands. Wallander got into his car and drove off. In the rear-view mirror he saw Melander standing there, gazing after him.

He drove through endless forests. By the time he reached Gävle it was already dark. He made his way to the hotel that Svedberg had told him about. When he asked at the front desk, he was told that Linda had already arrived.

They found a little restaurant that was cosy and quiet, with only a few guests even though it was Saturday night. He was glad that Linda had agreed to come. Finding themselves in this unfamiliar town encouraged Wallander to talk about his ideas for the future, something he hadn't planned to do.

But first they talked about his father, her grandfather.

"I often wondered about why you were so close," Wallander said. "Maybe it was envy, plain and simple. I saw something that I remembered from my own childhood, but that had totally disappeared."

"Perhaps it's good to have a generation in between," Linda said. "It's not uncommon for grandparents and grandchildren to get along better than parents and children."

"How do you know that?"

"I can see it's true for me. And a lot of my friends say the same thing."

"But I've always had a feeling that the rift was unnecessary," said Wallander. "I've never understood why he couldn't accept the fact that I became a policeman. If only he'd told me why. Or suggested an alternative. But he never did."

"Grandpa was pretty eccentric," she said. "And temperamental. But what would you say if I suddenly came and told you in all seriousness that I was thinking of becoming a policewoman?"

Wallander started to laugh.

"I honestly don't know what I'd say. We've talked about this before."

After dinner they went back to the hotel. On a thermometer ouside a shop, Wallander saw that it was –2°C. They sat down in reception. The hotel didn't have many guests, and they had the place to themselves. Wallander asked Linda cautiously how her acting classes were going. He saw at once that she didn't want to talk about it. He let the topic drop, but it made him uneasy. Over the course of the past few years Linda had changed plans and interests several times. What made Wallander nervous was how quickly she made these changes. It gave him the impression they were rash decisions.

Linda poured herself some tea and suddenly asked him why it was so difficult to live in Sweden.

"Sometimes I think it's because we've stopped darning our socks," Wallander said.

She gave him a perplexed look.

"I mean it," he continued. "When I was growing up, Sweden was still a country where people darned their socks. I even learned how to do it in school myself. Then suddenly one day it was over. Socks with holes in them were thrown out. No-one bothered to repair them. The whole society changed. 'Wear it out and toss it' was the only rule that applied. As long as it was just a matter of our socks, the change didn't make much difference. But then it started to spread, until finally it became a kind of invisible moral code. I think it changed our view of right and wrong, of what you were allowed to do to other people and what you weren't. More and more people, especially young people like you, feel unwelcome in their own country. How do they react? With aggression and contempt. The most frightening thing is that I think we're only at the beginning of something that's going to get a lot worse. A generation is growing up right now, the children who are younger than you, who are going to react with even greater violence. And they have absolutely no memory of a time when we darned our socks. When we didn't throw everything away, whether it was our woollen socks or human beings."

He paused. "Maybe I'm not expressing myself clearly," he said.

"Maybe," she said, "but I still think I know what you're trying to say."

"It's also possible I've got this wrong. Maybe every age seems worse than the ones that came before."

"I never heard Grandpa say anything about it."

"I think he lived in his own world. He painted his pictures so he could decide where the sun would be in the sky. It hung in the same place, above the fields, with or without the grouse, for almost 50 years. Sometimes I don't think he knew what was going on outside that studio of his. He had put up an invisible wall around himself."

"You're wrong," she said. "He knew a lot."

"If he did, he never let me know about it."

"He even wrote poems once in a while."

Wallander looked at her in disbelief. "He wrote poems?"

"He showed me some of them once. Maybe he burned them later on. But he wrote poems."

"Do you write poetry too?" asked Wallander.

"Maybe," she replied. "I don't know whether they're really poems. But sometimes I write. Just for myself. Don't you?"

"No," replied Wallander. "Never. I live in a world of police reports and forensic records, full of unpleasant details. Not to mention all the memos from the national police board."

She changed the subject so fast that afterwards he thought that she must have planned it all out.

"How's it going with Baiba?"

"It's going fine with her. How it's going with us, I'm not so sure. But I'm hoping that she'll come here to live."

"What would she do in Sweden?"

"She'd live with me," Wallander replied in surprise.

Linda slowly shook her head.

"Why wouldn't she?"

"Don't be offended," she said. "But I hope you realise you're a difficult person to live with."

"Why is that?"

"Just think about Mama. Why do you think she wanted to live a different life?"

Wallander didn't answer. In a vague way he felt he was being judged unfairly.

"Now you're angry," she said.

"No, I'm not," he replied. "I'm not angry."

"What, then?"

"I don't know. I guess I'm tired."

She got up from her chair and sat down next to him on the sofa.

"This doesn't mean I don't love you," she said. "It just means that I'm growing up. Our conversations are going to be different."

"I probably just haven't got used to it yet," he said.

When the conversation petered out, they watched a movie on TV. Linda had to go back to Stockholm early the next morning. Wallander thought he had had a glimpse of how the future would be. They would meet whenever they both had time. From now on she would also say what she really thought.

Just before 1 a.m. they said goodnight in the hall. Afterwards Wallander lay in bed for a long time, trying to decide whether he had lost something or gained something. His child was gone. Linda had grown up.

They met for breakfast at 7 a.m., and then he walked her the short distance to the train station. As they stood on the platform, she started to cry. Wallander stood there bewildered. Only a moment ago she hadn't shown any signs of being upset.

"What is it?" he asked. "Did something happen?"

"I miss Grandpa," she replied. "I dream about him every night."

Wallander gave her a hug. "I do too."

The train arrived. He stood on the platform until it pulled away. The station seemed terribly desolate. For a moment he felt like someone who was lost or abandoned, utterly powerless.

He wondered how he could go on.

CHAPTER 22

When Wallander got back to the hotel, there was a message for him from Robert Melander. He went up to his room and dialled the number. Melander's wife answered. Wallander introduced himself, careful to thank her for the nice lunch she had prepared the day before. Melander came to the phone.

"I couldn't help thinking about things some more last night," he said. "I called the old postman too. Ture Emmanuelsson is his name. He told me that Krista Haberman received postcards regularly from Skåne, a lot of them. From Falsterbo, he thought. I don't know if this means anything, but I thought I'd tell you anyway. She had a lot of bird related post."

"How did you find me?" Wallander asked.

"I called the police in Ystad and asked them. It wasn't difficult."

"Skanör and Falsterbo are well-known meeting places for bird-watchers," Wallander said. "That's the only reasonable explanation for why she got so many postcards from there. Thanks for taking the time to call me."

"I just keep wondering," Melander said, "why the car dealer should have left money to our church."

"Sooner or later we'll find out why. But it might take time. Anyway, thanks for calling."

Wallander stayed where he was after he hung up. It wasn't 8 a.m. yet. He thought about the feeling he had experienced at the train station, the feeling that something insurmountable stood before him. He also thought about the conversation with Linda. Most of all, he thought about what Melander had said and what he now faced. He was in Gävle because he had an assignment. It was six hours before his plane left and he had to turn in the rental car at Arlanda.

He got some papers out of his case. Höglund's notes said that he should start by getting in touch with a police inspector named Sten Wenngren. He would be home all day Sunday and was expecting Wallander's call. She had also written down the name of the man who had advertised in *Terminator* magazine: Johan Ekberg, who lived out in Brynäs. Wallander stood by the window. A cold autumn rain had started falling. Wallander wondered whether it would turn to sleet, and if there were snow tyres on the rental car. He thought again about what he had to do in Gävle. With each step he took he felt himself moving further and further away from the heart of the matter.

The feeling that there was something he hadn't discovered; that he had misinterpreted something fundamental in the pattern of the crimes, came back as he stood by the window. Why the deliberate brutality? What is it the killer wants to tell us? The killer's language was the code he hadn't been able to crack.

He shook his head, yawned, and packed his suitcase. Since he didn't know what he would talk to Sten Wenngren about, he decided to go straight to Johan Ekberg. If nothing else, he might be able to get a glimpse into the murky world where soldiers sold themselves to the highest bidder. He took his bag and left the room. At the front desk, he asked how to get to Södra Fältskärsgatan in Brynäs.

When he got into his car he was overcome by that feeling of weakness again. He sat there without starting the engine. Was he coming down with something? He didn't feel sick – not even particularly tired. He realised it had to do with his father. It was a reaction to everything that had happened, to having to adjust to a new life that had been changed in a traumatic way. There was no other explanation. His father's death was causing him to suffer recurrent attacks of powerlessness.

At last he started the engine and drove out of the garage. The desk clerk had given him clear directions, but Wallander got lost immediately. The city was deserted. He felt as though he was driving around in a labyrinth. It took him 20 minutes to find the right street. He stopped outside a block of flats in what he thought must be the old section of Brynäs. Vaguely he wondered whether mercenaries slept late on Sunday mornings. He also wondered if Johan Ekberg was a mercenary himself at all. Just because he advertised in *Terminator* didn't mean he had done any military service.

Wallander sat in the car looking at the building. The rain was falling. October was the most disconsolate month. Everything turned to grey. The colours of autumn faded away.

For a moment he felt like giving up the whole thing and driving away. He might just as well go back to Skåne and ask one of the others to call this Johan Ekberg on the phone. Or he could do it himself. If he left Gävle now he might be able to catch an earlier flight to Sturup.

But of course he didn't leave. Wallander had never been able to conquer the sergeant inside him who made sure he did what he was supposed to do. He hadn't taken this trip at the taxpayer's expense just to sit in his car and stare at the rain. He got out of the car and crossed the street.

Johan Ekberg lived on the top floor. There was no lift in the building. There was cheerful accordion music coming from one of the flats, and someone was singing. Wallander stopped on the stairs and listened. It was a schottische. He smiled to himself. Whoever was playing the accordion wasn't sitting around staring at the miserable rain, he thought, as he continued up the stairs.

Ekberg's door had a steel frame and two extra locks. Wallander rang the bell. He sensed someone looking at him through the peephole, and rang again, as if to announce that he wasn't giving up. The door opened. It had a safety chain. The hall was dark. The man he glimpsed inside was very tall.

"I'm looking for Johan Ekberg," Wallander said. "I'm a detective from Ystad. I need to talk to you, if you are Ekberg. You're not suspected of anything, I just need some information."

The voice that answered him was sharp, almost shrill.

"I don't talk to policemen. Whether they're from Gävle or anywhere else."

Wallander's earlier feeling of powerlessness was gone at once. He reacted instantly to the man's stubborn attitude. He hadn't come this far just to be turned away at the door. He took out his badge and held it up.

"I'm working on solving two murders in Skåne. You probably read about them in the paper. I didn't come all the way up here to stand outside your door and argue. You are fully entitled to refuse me entry. But I'll be back. And then you'll have to come to the Gävle police station with me. Take your pick."

"What do you want to know?"

"Either let me in or else come out into the hall,"

Wallander answered. "I'm not going to talk to you through a crack in the door."

The door closed, then opened. The safety chain was off now. A harsh lamp went on in the hall. It surprised Wallander. It was mounted so that it shined right into the eyes of a visitor. Wallander followed the man, whose face he had still not seen. They came to a living room. The curtains were drawn and the lights were on. Wallander stopped at the door. It was like walking into another era. The room was a relic from the 1950s. There was a Wurlitzer against one wall. Glittering neon colours danced inside its plastic hood. There were movie posters on the walls; one was of James Dean, but the others were mostly war movies. *Men in Action*. American marines fighting the Japanese on the beach. There were weapons hanging on the walls too: bayonets, swords, old cavalry pistols. A black leather sofa and chairs stood against another wall.

Ekberg stood looking at him. He had a crewcut and could have stepped out of one of his posters. He was dressed in khaki shorts and a white T-shirt. He had tattoos on the bulging muscles of his arms. Wallander could see that he was dealing with a serious bodybuilder.

Ekberg's eyes were wary.

"What do you want?"

Wallander pointed inquiringly at one of the chairs. The man nodded. Wallander sat down while Ekberg remained standing. He wondered if Ekberg was even born when Harald Berggren was fighting his despicable war in the Congo.

"How old are you?" he asked.

"Did you come all the way from Skåne to ask me that?"

Wallander made no attempt to hide his irritation. "Among other things," he replied. "If you don't answer my questions we'll stop right now and you can to come to the station."

"Am I suspected of committing a crime?"

"Have you?" Wallander shot back. He knew he was breaking all the rules of police conduct.

"No," said Ekberg.

"Then we'll start again," said Wallander. "How old are you?"

"I'm 32."

So Ekberg wasn't even born when Dag Hammarskjöld's plane crashed outside Ndola.

"I came to talk to you about Swedish mercenaries. I'm here because you've openly advertised in *Terminator*."

"There's no law against that, is there? I advertise in *Combat & Survival* and *Soldier of Fortune* too."

"I didn't say there was. This interview will go a lot faster if you just answer my questions and don't ask any of your own."

Ekberg sat down and lit a cigarette. Wallander saw he smoked non-filters. He lit the cigarette with a Zippo lighter. He wondered whether Johan Ekberg was living in a different era altogether.

"Swedish mercenaries," he repeated. "When did it all start? With the war in the Congo?"

"A little earlier," said Ekberg.

"When?"

"Try the Thirty Years War, for instance."

Wallander realised that he shouldn't be misled by Ekberg's appearance, or by the fact that he seemed to be obsessed with the 1950s. He could well be an expert on this subject, and Wallander had a vague recollection from school that the Thirty Years War was indeed fought by armies made up of mercenary soldiers.

"Let's stick to the years after the Second World War," he said.

"Then it started with the Second World War. There were Swedes who volunteered in all the armies fighting. There were Swedes in German uniforms, Russian uniforms, Japanese, American, British, and Italian."

"I always thought that volunteering wasn't the same as being a mercenary."

"I'm talking about the will to fight," Ekberg said. "There have always been Swedes ready to take up arms."

Wallander sensed something of the hopeless enthusiasm that usually marked men with delusions of a Greater Sweden. He cast a quick glance along the walls to see if he had missed any Nazi insignia, but saw none.

"Forget about volunteers," he said. "I'm talking about mercenaries. Men for hire."

"The Foreign Legion," Ekberg said. "It's the classic starting point. There have always been Swedes enlisted in it. Many of them lie buried in the Sahara."

"The Congo," Wallander said. "Something else started there, right?"

"There weren't many Swedes there, but there were some who fought the whole war on the side of Katanga province."

"Who were they?"

Ekberg gave him a surprised look. "Are you after names?"

"Not yet. I want to know what kind of men they were."

"Former military men. Men looking for adventure. Others convinced they were fighting for a just cause. Here and there, a policeman who'd been kicked off the force."

"What cause?"

"The fight against communism."

"They killed innocent Africans, didn't they?"

Ekberg was instantly on his guard.

"I don't have to answer questions about political views. I know my rights."

"I'm not remotely interested in your views. I just want to know who they were. And why they became mercenaries."

"Why do you want to know that?"

"Let's say it's my only question. And I want an answer to it." Ekberg watched him with his wary eyes.

Wallander had nothing to lose by going straight to the point.

"It's possible that someone with connections to Swedish mercenaries had something to do with at least one of these murders. That's why I'm here. That's why your answers might be significant."

Ekberg nodded. He understood now. "Would you like something to drink?" he asked.

"Such as?"

"Whisky? Beer?"

It was only 10 a.m. He shook his head, although he wouldn't have minded a beer.

"I'll pass."

Ekberg got up and came back a moment later with a glass of whisky.

"What kind of work do you do?" Wallander asked.

Ekberg's reply surprised him. He didn't know what he expected. But certainly not what Ekberg told him.

"I own a consulting firm that specialises in human resources. I concentrate on developing methods for conflict resolution."

"That sounds interesting." Wallander still wasn't sure if Ekberg was pulling his leg or not.

"I also have a stock portfolio that's doing well. My liquidity is stable at the moment."

Wallander decided that Ekberg was telling the truth. He returned to the topic of the mercenaries.

"How is it you're so interested in mercenaries?"

"They stand for some of the best things in our culture, which unfortunately are disappearing."

Wallander felt uneasy at Ekberg's reply. His convictions seemed so unshakable. Wallander wondered how it could be possible. He also wondered whether there were many men playing the Swedish stock market who had tattoos like Ekberg's. It didn't seem likely that the financiers and businessmen of the future would be bodybuilders with vintage jukeboxes in their living rooms.

"How were these men who went to the Congo recruited?"

"There are certain bars in Brussels. In Paris, too. It was all handled very discreetly. It still is, for that matter. Especially after what happened in Angola in 1975."

"What was that?"

"A number of mercenaries didn't get out in time. They were captured at the end of the war. The new regime set up a court martial. Most of them were sentenced to death and shot. It was all very ruthless. And quite unnecessary."

"Why were they sentenced to death?"

"Because they had been recruited. As if that made any difference. Soldiers are always recruited, one way or another."

"But they had nothing to do with that war? They came from outside? They took part in it just to make money?"

Ekberg ignored Wallander's interrruption.

"They were meant to get out of the theatre of combat in time, but they had lost two of their company commanders in the fighting. A plane that was supposed to pick them up landed at the wrong airstrip in the bush. There was a lot of bad luck involved. About 15 of them were captured. The majority managed to get out. Most of them continued on to Southern Rhodesia. On a big farm outside Johannesburg there's a monument to the men who were executed in Angola. Mercenaries from all over the world went to the unveiling."

"Were there any Swedes among the men who were executed?"

"It was mostly British and German soldiers. Their next of kin were given 48 hours to claim their bodies. Almost no-one did."

Wallander thought about the memorial outside Johannesburg.

"So there is a great sense of fellowship among mercenaries from various parts of the world?"

"Every man takes complete responsibility for himself. But yes, there is a sense of fellowship. There has to be."

"So isn't that a reason why many of them would become mercenaries? Because they're looking for fellowship."

"The money comes first. Then the adventure. Then the fellowship. In that order."

"So the truth is that mercenaries kill for money?"

Ekberg nodded. "Of course. But mercenaries aren't monsters. They're human beings."

Wallander felt his disgust rising, but he knew that Ekberg meant every word. It had been a long time since he had met a man with such firm convictions. There was nothing monstrous about these soldiers who would kill anyone for the right amount of money. On the contrary, it was a definition of their humanity. According to Johan Ekberg.

Wallander took out a copy of the photograph and put it on the glass table in front of Ekberg.

"This was taken in what was then called the Belgian

Congo more than 30 years ago. Before you were born. Three mercenaries. And one of them is a Swede."

Ekberg leaned forward and picked up the photograph. Wallander waited.

"Do you recognise any of those men?" he asked after a moment. He mentioned two of the names: Terry O'Banion and Simon Marchand.

Ekberg shook his head.

"Those aren't necessarily their real names."

"In that case, I do recognise those names," said Ekberg.

"The man in the middle is Swedish," Wallander went on. Ekberg stood up and went into an adjacent room. He came back with a magnifying glass in his hand. He studied the picture again.

"His name is Harald Berggren," said Wallander. "And he's the reason I came here."

Ekberg said nothing. He kept looking at the picture.

"Harald Berggren," Wallander said again. "He wrote a diary about that war. Do you recognise him? Do you know who he is?"

Ekberg put down the photograph and the magnifying glass.

"Of course I know who Harald Berggren is."

Wallander gave a start. He didn't know what kind of answer he was expecting, but it certainly wasn't that.

"Where is he now?"

"He's dead. He died seven years ago."

That was a possibility Wallander had considered. Even so, it came as a disappointment.

"What happened?"

"He committed suicide. Which isn't unusual for people with a great deal of courage who have experienced fighting in combat units under difficult conditions."

"Why did he commit suicide?"

Ekberg shrugged. "I think he'd had enough."

"Enough what?"

"What is it you've had enough of when you take your own life? Life itself. The boredom. The weariness that hits you every morning when you look at your face in the mirror."

"What happened?"

"He lived in Sollentuna, north of Stockholm. One Sunday morning he stuck his revolver in his pocket and took a bus to the end of the line. He went into the woods and shot himself."

"How do you know all this?"

"I just know. And that means that he couldn't have been involved with a murder in Skåne. Unless he's a ghost. Or set a time bomb for someone that just went off."

Wallander had left the diary behind in Skåne. Now he thought that this might have been a mistake.

"Harald Berggren wrote a diary in the Congo. We found it in the safe belonging to a car dealer named Holger Eriksson, one of the men who was murdered. Does that name mean anything to you?"

Ekberg shook his head.

"Are you sure?"

"There's nothing wrong with my memory."

"Can you think of any reason why the diary would have ended up there?"

"No."

"Can you think of any reason why these two men might have known each other more than seven years ago?"

"I only met Berggren once. The year before he died. I was living in Stockholm at the time. He came to visit me one evening. He was restless. He told me he was spending his time travelling around the country, working a month here and a month there, while he waited for a new war to start. He had a profession, after all."

Wallander realised that he had overlooked that possibility. Even though it was in the diary, on one of the very first pages.

"You mean the fact that he was a mechanic?"

For the first time Ekberg looked surprised.

"How do you know that?"

"It was in the diary."

"A car dealer might have had use for a mechanic. Maybe Harald passed through Skåne and met this Eriksson."

Wallander nodded. It was a possibility.

"Was Berggren homosexual?" Wallander asked.

Ekberg laughed.

"Very," he said.

"Is that common among mercenaries?"

"It's not unusual. I presume it also occurs among policemen, doesn't it?"

Wallander didn't reply.

"Does it occur among human resources consultants?" he asked instead.

Ekberg was standing next to the jukebox. He smiled at Wallander.

"It does."

"You advertise in *Terminator*. You offer your services. But it doesn't say what those services are."

"I arrange contacts."

"What sort of contacts?"

"With various employers who might possibly be of interest."

"Combat assignments?"

"Sometimes. Bodyguards, transport protection. It varies. If I wanted to, I could supply the newspapers with amazing stories."

"But you don't?"

"I have the trust of my clients."

"I'm not part of the newspaper world."

Ekberg had sat back down in his chair.

"Terre Blanche in South Africa," he said. "The leader of the neo-Nazi party among the Boers. He has two Swedish bodyguards. That's one example. But if you mention it in public I'll deny it, of course."

"I won't say a word," Wallander said.

"Can I have the photograph?" Ekberg asked. "I have a little collection."

"Keep it," Wallander said, getting to his feet. "We've got the original."

"Who has the negative?"

"I wonder that myself."

After Wallander was already out the door it struck him that there was one more question.

"Why do you do all this, anyway?"

"I get postcards from all over the world," he said. "That's all."

Wallander understood that this was the best answer he was going to get.

"I don't believe it. But I might call you up, if I have any more questions."

Ekberg nodded. Then he shut the door.

When Wallander reached the street it was sleeting. It was 11 a.m. He decided that he had nothing else to do in Gävle. He got into his car. Berggren hadn't killed Eriksson, or Runfeldt for that matter. What could have been a lead had dissolved into thin air.

We'll have to start all over again, Wallander thought. We'll have to go back to the beginning and cross out Harald Berggren. We'll forget about shrunken heads and diaries. Then what will we see? It ought to be possible to find Harald Berggren on a list of Eriksson's former employees. And we should also be able to find out if Eriksson was homosexual.

The top layer of the investigation had yielded nothing. They would have to dig deeper.

Wallander started the engine and drove straight to Arlanda Airport. When he arrived he had some trouble finding the place to turn in the rental car. By 2 p.m. he was sitting on a sofa in the departure hall waiting for his plane. He leafed distractedly through a newspaper someone had left behind.

The plane left Arlanda on time. Wallander fell asleep almost as soon as they took off and woke on the descent to Sturup Airport. Next to him sat a woman darning a sock. Wallander looked at her in amazement.

As he got off the plane, he remembered he'd have to call Älmhult to find out how his car was doing. He'd have to take a taxi to Ystad. But as he headed for the airport exit, he discovered Martinsson waiting for him. He knew something must have happened.

Not another one, he thought. Anything but that.

Martinsson saw him coming.

"What's happened?" asked Wallander.

"You must have had your mobile phone turned off," said Martinsson. "It's been impossible to get hold of you."

Wallander waited. He held his breath.

"We found Runfeldt's suitcase," Martinsson said.

"Where?"

"It was left in plain view on the side of the road to Höör."

"Who found it?"

"A man who stopped to take a piss. He saw the suitcase, opened it, and found papers inside with Runfeldt's name on them. He had read about the murder, so he called us. Nyberg is there now."

Good, thought Wallander. Another lead.

"Then let's go there," he said.

"Don't you want to go home first?"

"No. If there's anything I don't want to do, it's that."

Suddenly Wallander was in a hurry.

CHAPTER 23

The suitcase was lying where it had been found. Since this was right by the side of the road, many drivers had stopped out of curiosity at the sight of the two police cars and the group of people. Nyberg was busy taking moulds and photographs of tyre tracks left at the site. One of his assistants held his crutch while he knelt down and pointed at something lying on the ground. He looked up when Wallander approached.

"How was Norrland?" he asked.

"I didn't find a suitcase," Wallander replied. "But it was beautiful. And cold."

"With a little luck we'll be able to say exactly how long it's been lying here," Nyberg said.

Wallander couldn't see any name tag, or any label for "Special Tours" on the case.

"Have you talked to Vanja Andersson?" he asked.

"She's already been here," Martinsson replied. "She recognised it as Runfeldt's. Besides, we've already opened it. The missing night-vision binoculars were right on top. It's definitely his bag."

Wallander thought for a moment. They were on the E13, south of Eneborg. Close by was the intersection where you could take the turn-off to Lödinge. In the opposite direction you could head south around Krageholm Lake and end up not far from Marsvinsholm.

Wallander realised that they stood almost equidistant between the two murder sites.

The suitcase lay on the eastern side of the road. If it had been put there by someone driving a car, then the car must have been on its way north from the Ystad area. But it could also have come from Marsvinsholm, turned off at the Sövestad intersection, and then driven north. Wallander tried to evaluate the alternatives. Nyberg was right: it would be helpful to know how long the suitcase had been lying where they'd found it.

"When can we remove it?" he asked.

"We can take it back to Ystad within an hour," Nyberg replied. "I'm almost done here."

Wallander nodded to Martinsson, and they walked towards his car. On the drive from the airport, Wallander had told him about the trip. They still didn't know why Eriksson had bequeathed the money to the church in Svenstavik. On the other hand, they knew that Harald Berggren was dead. Wallander had no doubts that Ekberg had told the truth. Berggren couldn't have been directly involved in Eriksson's death. They needed to find out whether he had worked for Eriksson, even though they couldn't count on this getting them anywhere. Certain pieces of the puzzle were only valuable because they needed to be put in place before the more important pieces could be fitted together properly. From now on Berggren was that kind of piece in the puzzle.

They got into the car and headed back to Ystad.

"Maybe Eriksson gave unemployed mercenaries odd jobs?" Martinsson said. "Maybe somebody was after Harald Berggren? Someone who suddenly got it into his head to dig a pungee pit for Eriksson, for some reason or other?"

"That's a possibility, of course," Wallander said dubiously.

"But how do we explain what happened to Runfeldt?"

"We can't explain it yet. Should we be concentrating on him?"

"Eriksson died first," Wallander said. "But that doesn't necessarily mean he's the first link in the chain of causality. The problem is not only that we don't have a motive, but that we're missing a real starting point."

Martinsson was silent for a while. They were driving through Sövestad.

"Why would his suitcase end up beside this road?" he asked suddenly. "Runfeldt was going in the opposite direction, towards Copenhagen. Marsvinsholm is in the right direction, heading for Kastrup Airport. What really happened?"

"That's what I'd like to know too," Wallander said.

"We've gone over Runfeldt's car," Martinsson said. "He had a car park behind the building where he lived. He drove a 1993 Opel. Nothing out of the ordinary."

"The car keys?"

"In his flat."

Wallander asked if anyone had found out whether Runfeldt had ordered a taxi for the morning of his departure.

"Hansson talked to the taxi company. Runfeldt ordered a taxi for 5 a.m. It was supposed to take him to Malmö. The taxi company noted that he hadn't shown up. The taxi driver waited. He rang the bell to Runfeldt's place because he thought he might have overslept, but no-one answered. The driver took off. Hansson said that the person he talked to was quite precise about what had happened."

"It seems to have been a well-planned assault," Wallander said.

"Which indicates that there was more than one person," Martinsson said.

"Whoever it was must have had detailed knowledge of Runfeldt's plans, and known when he was planning to leave. Who would know that?"

"The list is rather short. And we already have it, as a matter of fact. I think it was Ann-Britt who put it together. Anita Lagergren at the travel agency knew, and Runfeldt's children. But the daughter only knew what day he was leaving, not that it was early in the morning. Probably nobody else."

"Vanja Andersson?"

"She thought she knew, but she didn't."

Wallander shook his head slowly. "There must be someone else on that list," he said. "That's the person we're looking for."

"We're going through his client files. Altogether we've found 40 or so investigative assignments over the years. In other words, not many. But the person we're looking for might be among them."

"We have to go through them very carefully," Wallander replied. "It's going to be a tedious job. But you could be right."

"I have the feeling that this is going to take a long time."

Wallander thought the same thing.

"We can always hope we're wrong, but it's not very likely."

They were approaching Ystad.

"Apparently they're going to sell the florist's shop," said Martinsson. "The son and daughter have agreed on that. They asked Vanja Andersson if she'd like to take it over but I doubt she has the money."

"Who told you that?"

"Bo Runfeldt called. He wanted to know if he and his sister could leave Ystad after the funeral."

"When is it?"

"On Wednesday."

"Let them go," Wallander said. "We can get in touch with them again if we need to."

They turned in to the car park.

"I talked to a mechanic in Älmhult," Martinsson said. "Your car will be ready by the middle of next week. It's going to be expensive, but I suppose you knew that. He said he'd have the car delivered here to Ystad."

Hansson was sitting in Svedberg's office when they came in. Wallander told him about his trip. Hansson had a terrible cold, and Wallander suggested that he go home.

"Chief Holgersson is sick too," Svedberg said. "I think she's got the flu."

"Is it flu season already?" Wallander said. "That's going to give us big problems here."

"I've only got a cold," Hansson assured him. "With luck I'll feel better tomorrow."

"Both of Ann-Britt's children are sick," Martinsson said. "But her husband's due home tomorrow."

Wallander asked them to let him know when the suitcase arrived, and then left the room. He was thinking of sitting down to write up the report about his trip. Maybe even put together the receipts he needed to submit for his travel expenses. But on the way to his office he changed his mind, and turned around and went back.

"Can I borrow a car?" he asked. "I'll be back in half an hour."

Several sets of car keys were offered to him. He took Martinsson's.

It was dark as he drove down to Västra Vallgatan. There

wasn't a cloud in the sky. The night would be a cold one, maybe below freezing. He parked outside the florist's shop and walked down the street towards the building where Runfeldt had lived. He saw lights in the windows. He assumed that Runfeldt's children were there, going through things in the flat. The police had confirmed that they could pack up and throw out whatever they liked. He suddenly thought about his father, and about Gertrud and his sister Kristina. He hadn't gone out to Löderup to help them go through his father's belongings. Even though his help wasn't really needed, he should still have made an appearance. He couldn't quite decide whether he had avoided it out of distaste or whether he just hadn't had time.

He stopped outside the door to Runfeldt's building. There was no-one about. He stood at the front door and looked around, trying to map out the sequence of events. Then he crossed the street and did the same thing.

Runfeldt is on the street, Wallander thought. The exact time is still not clear. He might have come out of the door in the evening or at night. If so, he wouldn't have had his suitcase with him. Something else made him leave the flat. On the other hand, if he came out in the morning, he would have the suitcase. The street is deserted. He sets the suitcase down on the footpath. Which direction would the taxi come from? Does he wait outside the door, or across the street? Something happens. Runfeldt and his suitcase disappear. The suitcase turns up along the road to Höör. Runfeldt himself is found tied to a tree, dead, in the woods near Marsvinsholm.

Wallander studied the doors on either side of the building. Neither of them was deep enough for someone to hide in. He looked at the streetlights. The ones that lit Runfeldt's door were working.

A car, he thought. A car was waiting here, right by the door. Runfeldt comes down to the street. Someone gets out of the car. Runfeldt was frightened, he would have made some sound. The neighbours would have heard him. If it was a stranger, maybe Runfeldt was just surprised. The man approaches Runfeldt. Does he knock him down? Threaten him? Wallander thought about Vanja Andersson's reaction out in the woods: Runfeldt had grown terribly thin in the brief time since his disappearance. This was because he'd been held captive. Starved.

He carried on. Runfeldt is put into the car by force, unconscious or under duress. Then he is taken away. The suitcase is found on the road to Höör, right beside the road. Wallander's first thought on arriving at the place where the suitcase lay was that it had been put there deliberately so that it would be found.

Wallander went back to the door and started again. Runfeldt comes out to the street. He's about to set out on a journey that he's been looking forward to. He's going to Africa to look at orchids. He began pacing back and forth in front of the door. He thought about the possibility that Runfeldt had killed his wife ten years earlier. Made a hole in the ice and pushed her in. He was a brutal man, who abused the mother of his children. Outwardly he's just a florist with a passion for orchids. And now here he is, taking a trip to Nairobi. Everyone had spoken of his genuine excitement at the holiday. A friendly man who was also a monster.

Wallander thought about the florist's shop, and the break-in. Somebody breaks in. Nothing is stolen. Not even a single flower. There's blood on the floor. Wallander shook his head. There was something he wasn't seeing. One surface was concealing another. Gösta Runfeldt.

Orchid lover, monster. Holger Eriksson. Bird-watcher, poet, and car dealer. He too rumoured to have acted with great brutality. Brutality unites them, thought Wallander. Concealed brutality.

Once more he went back to the door of Runfeldt's block of flats. He comes out to the street. Puts down his suitcase, if it happens in the morning. What does he do then? He waits for a taxi. But when it arrives he has already disappeared.

Wallander stopped mid-stride. Runfeldt waits for a taxi. Could another taxi have arrived? A fake taxi? All Runfeldt knew was that he had ordered a taxi, not which one would come. Or who the driver would be. The driver helps him with his suitcase. He gets into the car and they drive off towards Malmö. But they get no further than Marsvinsholm. Could it have happened like that? Could Runfeldt have been held prisoner near the woods where he was found? But the suitcase was found on the road to Höör in the opposite direction. In the direction of Holger Eriksson's farm.

Wallander didn't know what to think. The only thing that was perfectly clear was that whatever had happened outside Runfeldt's front door had been planned by someone who knew that he was about to leave for Nairobi.

When he got back to the station, he saw Nyberg's car badly parked outside the entrance. The suitcase had arrived.

They had spread out a plastic sheet on the conference table and placed the suitcase on it. The lid was still closed. Nyberg was having coffee with Svedberg and Hansson. Wallander saw that they were waiting for him. Martinsson was on the phone. Wallander could tell that he was talking to one of his children. He handed him his car keys.

"How long was the suitcase lying there?" Wallander asked.

Nyberg's answer surprised him.

"A couple of days," Nyberg replied. "Not more than three."

"So it was kept somewhere else for a long time," Hansson said.

"Why does the killer wait until now to get rid of it?" Wallander asked.

No-one had an answer. Nyberg pulled on a pair of latex gloves and opened the lid. He was about to take out the top layer of clothing when Wallander asked him to wait. He leaned over the table. Something had caught his attention, he wasn't sure what.

"Do we have a photograph of this?" he asked.

"Not of the open suitcase," Nyberg replied.

"Let's take one," Wallander said. Something about the way the suitcase was packed had caught his attention.

Nyberg instructed Svedberg to climb up on a chair and take the pictures, and they unpacked the suitcase. Runfeldt had planned to travel to Africa with little baggage. There were no unexpected items inside. They found his travel documents in a side pocket. There was also a large sum of money in dollars. In the bottom of the case they found several notebooks, literature about orchids, and a camera. They stood in silence and surveyed the various items. Wallander searched his mind for what had caught his attention. Nyberg had opened the toilet bag. He studied the name on a pill bottle.

"Anti-malaria pills," he said. "Runfeldt knew what he'd need in Africa."

Wallander looked carefully at the case, and saw something wedged into the lining of the lid. Nyberg pried it loose. It was a blue plastic name tag holder.

"Maybe Runfeldt went to conferences," Nyberg suggested.

"He was going on a photographic safari," Wallander said. "But of course it might be left there from a previous trip." He picked up a paper napkin from the table and held it around the pin on the back of the holder, and brought it up close to his eyes. He sniffed, noticing a subtle fragrance. He held it out to Svedberg, who was standing next to him.

"Do you know what this smells like?"

"After-shave lotion?"

Wallander shook his head.

"No," he said. "It's perfume."

They took turns sniffing it. They all agreed that it was a woman's perfume. Wallander was even more puzzled. And he had a feeling that he recognised the plastic holder.

"Who's seen this type of holder before?" he asked.

"Isn't that the kind used by the Malmö local authority?" Martinsson said. "Everyone who works in the hospital here has one like it."

"This doesn't make sense," Wallander said. "A plastic holder that smells of perfume is inside Runfeldt's luggage."

At that moment he realised what had troubled him when the lid of the suitcase was opened.

"I'd like Ann-Britt here," he said. "Sick children or not. Maybe her amazing neighbour could help out for half an hour? The police will pay the bill."

Martinsson dialled the number.

"She's on her way," he said.

"Why do you want her?" Hansson asked.

"There's something I want her to do with this suitcase," Wallander said. "That's all."

"Should we put everything back in?" Nyberg asked.

"That's exactly what I want her to do," Wallander replied.

They looked at him in surprise, but no-one said a word. Hansson sniffled. Nyberg sat down on a chair and rested his foot. Martinsson disappeared into his office, presumably to call home. Wallander left the conference room and went to look at the map of the Ystad police district. He studied the roads between Marsvinsholm, Lödinge, and Ystad.

Somewhere there is always a centre, he thought. A junction between various events. A criminal only rarely returns to the scene of the crime. On the other hand, a killer often passes the same point many times.

Höglund came rushing down the hall. Wallander felt guilty for having asked her to come in. But this time he felt he had a good reason for doing so.

"Has something happened?" she asked.

"You know that we found Runfeldt's suitcase?"

"I heard."

They went into the conference room.

"Everything lying here on the table was inside," said Wallander. "I want you to put on some gloves and then pack everything.

"In any particular order?"

"In whatever order comes naturally to you. You've told me several times that you always pack your husband's suitcases. You're experienced, in other words."

She did as he asked. Wallander was grateful that she didn't ask any questions. They watched her. Out of long habit, she selected each item briskly and packed the suitcase. Then she took a step back.

"Should I close the lid?"

"That's not necessary."

They all stood around the table and looked at the results. It was as Wallander had suspected.

"How could you know how Runfeldt had packed his suitcase?" Martinsson wondered.

"Wait with your comments," Wallander interrupted him. "I saw a traffic officer sitting in the canteen. Go and get him."

The traffic officer, whose name was Laurin, came into the room. They had unpacked the suitcase again. Laurin looked tired. Wallander knew that they were working on a drink-driving campaign. He asked Laurin to put on a pair of latex gloves and pack the suitcase. Laurin didn't ask any questions either. Wallander saw that he did not do it sloppily but handled the items of clothing with care. When he was done, Wallander thanked him. He left the room.

"Completely different," Svedberg said.

"I'm not trying to prove something," said Wallander. "I don't think I can, either. But when Nyberg opened the lid of the suitcase I had a feeling that something wasn't right. It's always been my experience that men and women pack suitcases in different ways. It seemed to me that this suitcase had been packed by a woman."

"Vanja Andersson?" Hansson suggested.

"No," Wallander replied. "Not her. It was Runfeldt himself who first packed the suitcase. We can be quite sure of that."

Höglund was the first one to understand.

"So you're saying it was repacked later? By a woman?"

"I'm just trying to think out loud. The suitcase has been lying outside for only a few days. Runfeldt has been gone for a much longer time than that. Where was the suitcase all that time? It might also explain something missing from the contents."

The team remained silent.

"There's no underwear in the suitcase," Wallander continued. "I think it's very odd that Runfeldt would pack for a trip to Africa without taking a single change of underwear."

"It's hardly likely he would have done that," Hansson said.

"Which in turn means that someone repacked his suitcase," Martinsson said. "A woman, perhaps. And during the repacking all of Runfeldt's underwear disappeared."

Wallander could feel the tension in the room.

"There's one more thing," he said slowly. "Runfeldt's underwear has disappeared, but at the same time a foreign object wound up inside the suitcase."

He pointed at the blue plastic holder. Höglund was still wearing gloves.

"Smell it," Wallander said to her.

She did as he asked.

"A woman's perfume," she said.

Nyberg was the one who finally broke the silence.

"Does this mean that there's a woman mixed up in all these atrocities?"

"We have to consider it as a possibility," Wallander replied. "Even if nothing directly indicates it. Apart from this suitcase."

They were all silent again for a long time.

It was 7.30 p.m. on Sunday, 16 October.

She had arrived at the underpass just after 7 p.m. It was cold, and she stamped her feet to stay warm. There was still some time before the man would turn up. At least half an hour, maybe more. But she always arrived with time to spare. With a shudder she remembered the few occasions in her life when she had come late, kept people waiting, stepped into rooms where people stared at her. She would never arrive late again. She had arranged her life around a timetable that allowed margins for error.

She was quite calm. The man didn't deserve to live. She couldn't feel hatred towards him. The woman who had suffered so much misfortune could do the hating. She was just standing here in the dark, waiting to do what was necessary.

She had hesitated over whether she should postpone this. The oven was empty, but her work schedule was complicated over the next few weeks and she didn't want to risk having him die inside it. It would have to be done quickly. And she had no hesitations about how it would be done. The woman who had finally given her his name had talked about a bathtub filled with water. About how it felt to be forced under the water and almost give up breathing, bursting apart from the inside.

She had thought about Sunday school. The fires of hell that awaited the sinner. The terror was still with her. No-one knew how sin was measured. And no-one knew when the punishment would be dealt out. She had never been able to talk about this terror with her mother.

She had wondered about her mother's last moment alive. The police officer, Françoise Bertrand, had written that everything would have happened very fast. She probably didn't suffer. She was probably hardly aware of what was happening to her. But how could Bertrand know that? Had she omitted part of the truth that was too unbearable?

* * *

A train passed overhead. She counted the cars. Then everything was quiet again.

Not with fire, she thought. But with water. With water the sinner shall perish.

She looked at her watch, and noticed that the laces on one of her running shoes were undone. She bent down and retied it, hard. She had strong fingers. The man she was waiting for, the one she had been tailing for the past few days, was short and overweight. He wouldn't cause her any problems. It would be over in a flash.

A man with a dog passed through the underpass on the opposite side. His footsteps reverberated against the footpath, reminding her of an old black-and-white movie. She did what was simplest: pretended to be waiting for someone. She was positive that later he wouldn't remember her. All her life she had taught herself not to be noticed, to make herself invisible. Only now did she realise that it had been in preparation for her future.

The man with the dog disappeared. Her car was parked on the other side of the underpass. The traffic was sparse, even though they were in the centre of Lund. Only the man with the dog and a cyclist had passed. She was ready. Nothing would go wrong.

She saw the man. He came walking along the same side of the street where she was standing. In the distance she could hear a car. She doubled over, as if she was in pain. The man stopped by her side and asked her if she was sick. She fell to her knees, and he did what she had expected. He stepped close and leaned forward. She told him that she was ill. Could he help her to her car? It was right nearby. He put a hand under her arm. She sagged against him. He had to strain to hold her up, just as she had anticipated. He wasn't strong. He helped her over to her car, and asked if he could do anything else, but she said no.

He opened the door for her. She reached for the rag. To prevent the ether from evaporating, she had put it in a plastic bag. It took her only a few seconds to get it out. The street was still deserted. She turned around and pressed the rag hard against his face. He fought back, but she was stronger. When he started to collapse to the ground, she held him up with one arm as she opened the back door. It was easy to shove him inside. She got into the driver's seat. A car passed, followed closely by another cyclist. She leaned over to the back seat and pressed the rag against his face. Soon he was unconscious. He wouldn't wake up in the time it took her to drive to the lake.

She took the road through Svaneholm and Brodda to reach the lake. She turned off near the empty camping ground on the shore, turned off the lights and got out of the car. She listened. Everything was quiet. She pulled the unconscious man out onto the ground. From the boot of the car she took out a sack. The weights inside it clattered against some rocks. It took longer than she had expected to get him into the sack and tie it.

He was still unconscious. She carried the sack out onto the small jetty that jutted into the lake. A bird fluttered past in the dark. She placed the sack at the very end of the jetty. Now there was only a short wait remaining. She lit a cigarette. In the light from the glow she studied her hand. It was steady.

After 20 minutes the man in the sack started to come to life. He began to move around.

* * *

She thought about the bathroom. The woman's story. And she remembered cats being drowned when she was little. They floated away in the sack, still alive, desperately fighting to breathe and survive.

He started shouting. Now he was struggling inside the sack. She put out her cigarette on the jetty. She tried to think, but her mind was empty. She shoved the sack into the water with her foot and walked away.

CHAPTER 24

They stayed at the police station so long that Sunday turned into Monday. Wallander sent Hansson home and later Nyberg too. But the others stayed on, and they began going through the investigative material once again. The suitcase had forced them into a retreat. They sat in the conference room with it on the table in front of them until the meeting ended. Then Martinsson closed the lid and took it with him to his own office.

They went over everything that had happened, working on the assumption that nothing they had done so far could be regarded as wasted effort. In their retreat they needed to take a fresh look at things, stop on various details, and hope to discover something that they had missed earlier.

But they didn't come up with anything that gave them the feeling they had made a breakthrough. The events were still murky, the connection unclear, the motive unknown. The retreat led them back to the beginning, to the fact that two men had been killed in gruesome ways, and that the killer had to be the same person.

It was after midnight when Wallander called a halt. Höglund stayed for the whole meeting. She left the conference room twice for a few minutes. Wallander assumed she was calling home to talk to her neighbour, who was taking care of her children. When the meeting was over, Wallander asked her to stay on. He regretted this at once, knowing that he shouldn't keep her there any longer. But she sat back down, and they waited until the others had left.

"I want you to do something for me," he said. "I want you to go through all of these events from a woman's perspective. Go over the investigative material and imagine that the killer we're looking for is a woman, not a man. Base your work on two assumptions. First, that she was alone. Second, that she had at least one accomplice."

"Do you think there was more than one person involved?"

"Yes. And one of them was a woman. Of course, there might have been several people involved."

She nodded.

"As soon as possible," Wallander told her. "Preferably tomorrow. If you have other important matters that can't wait, turn them over to someone else."

"I think Hamrén will be here tomorrow," she said. "A couple of detectives are coming from Malmö too. I can give my other work to one of them."

Wallander had nothing more to say. They sat there a little longer.

"Do you really think it's a woman?" she asked.

"I don't know," Wallander answered. "It's dangerous to give too much weight to the importance of this suitcase and the perfume. But on the other hand, there's been something funny about this whole investigation right from the start. When we were standing out there by the ditch, with Eriksson on the stakes, you said something that I've been thinking about a lot."

"That the whole thing seemed so deliberate?"

"The killer's language. What we saw smelled of war. Eriksson was executed in a trap for predators."

"Maybe it is war," she said thoughtfully.

"What do you mean by that?"

"I don't know. Maybe we should interpret what we see literally. Pungee pits are used to catch predators. And they're also used in war."

"Go on," he said.

She bit her lip.

"I can't. The woman who's taking care of my children has to get home. I can't ask her to stay any longer. Last time I called home she was pissed off, and it's not going to make any difference if I pay her extra for her time."

Wallander didn't want to cut short the discussion they had started. For a brief moment he felt irritated by her children, or maybe by her husband's absences. But he regretted these thoughts at once.

"You could come to my house," she said. "We can continue talking there."

She was pale and tired, and he knew he shouldn't put such pressure on her. But he said yes. They drove through the deserted town. The babysitter was standing in the door, waiting. Wallander said hello and apologised for her late return. They sat in her living room. He had been there a few times before. He could see that a frequent traveller lived in the house. There were souvenirs from many countries on the walls. There was also a warmth that was completely missing from his own flat. She asked him if he'd like something to drink. He declined.

"The trap for predators and the war," he began. "That's where we left off."

"Men who hunt, men who are soldiers. We also find a shrunken head and a diary written by a mercenary. We see what we see, and we interpret it."

"How do we interpret it?"

"We interpret it correctly. If the killer has a language, then we can clearly read what he writes."

Wallander suddenly thought about something that Linda had said when she was trying to explain to him what acting really was. Reading between the lines, looking for the subtext.

He told Höglund this, and she nodded.

"Maybe I'm not expressing myself well," she said. "But what I'm thinking is that we've seen everything and interpreted everything, and yet it's all wrong."

"We see what the murderer wants us to see?"

"Maybe we're being fooled into looking in the wrong direction."

Wallander thought for a moment. He noticed that his mind was now quite clear. His weariness was gone. They were following a trail that might prove crucial. A trail that had existed before in his consciousness, but he hadn't been able to control it.

"So the deliberateness is an evasive manoeuvre," he said. "Is that what you mean?"

"Yes."

"Go on."

"Maybe the truth is just the opposite."

"What does it look like?"

"I don't know. But if we think we're right, and it's all wrong, then whatever is wrong will have to end up being right in the end."

"I understand," he said. "I understand, and I agree."

"A woman would never impale a man on stakes in a pit," she said. "She would never tie a man to a tree and then strangle him with her bare hands."

Wallander didn't say anything for a long time.

Höglund disappeared upstairs and came back a few minutes later. He saw that she had put on a different pair of shoes.

"The whole time we've had a feeling that it was well planned," said Wallander. "The question now is whether it was well planned in more than one way."

"Of course I can't imagine that a woman could have done this," she said. "But now I realise that it might be true."

"Your summary will be important," Wallander said. "I think we should also talk to Mats Ekholm about this."

"Who?"

"The forensic psychologist who was here last summer."

She shook her head.

"I must be very tired," she said. "I'd forgotten his name."

Wallander stood up. It was 1 a.m.

"I'll see you tomorrow," he said. "Could you call me a taxi?"

"You can take my car," she said. "I'm going to need a long walk in the morning to clear my head." She gave him the keys. "My husband is coming home soon. Things will be easier."

"I think this is the first time I fully realised how hard things are for you," he said. "When Linda was little, Mona was always there. I don't think I ever once had to stay home from work while she was growing up."

She followed him outside. The night was clear. It was below freezing.

"I have no regrets," she said suddenly.

"Regrets about what?"

"About joining the force."

"You're a good police officer," said Wallander. "A very good one. In case you didn't know."

He saw that she was pleased. He nodded, got into her car, and drove off.

The next day, Monday, 17 October, Wallander woke up with a slight headache. He lay in bed and wondered if he was coming down with a cold, but he didn't have any other symptoms. He got up and made coffee, and looked for some aspirin. Through the kitchen window he saw that the wind had picked up. Clouds had moved in over Skåne during the night. The temperature had risen. The thermometer read 4°C.

By 7.15 a.m. he was at the station. He got some coffee and sat down in his office. On his desk was a message from the officer in Göteborg he'd been working with on the investigation into car smuggling. He sat holding the message in his hand for a moment. Then he put it in his drawer. He pulled over a notebook and started looking for a pen. In one of the drawers he came across Svedberg's note. He wondered how many times he had forgotten to give it back.

Annoyed, he stood up and went out to the hall. The door to Svedberg's office was open. He went in and put the paper on the desk, then went back to his own office, closed the door, and spent the next 30 mimutes listing all the questions he wanted answered. He had decided to go over what he and Höglund had discussed when the investigative team met later that morning.

At 7.45 a.m. there was a knock on the door. It was Hamrén from Stockholm, who'd just arrived. They shook hands. Wallander liked him; they'd worked well together during the summer.

"Here already?" he said. "I thought you weren't coming until later in the day."

"I drove down yesterday," Hamrén replied. "I couldn't wait."

"How are things in Stockholm?"

"The same as here. Only bigger."

"I don't know where they plan to put you," Wallander said.

"In with Hansson. It's already been arranged."

"We're going to meet in about half an hour."

"I've got a lot of reading to do before then."

Hamrén left the room. Wallander absentmindedly put his hand on the phone, meaning to call his father. He gave a start. Grief hit him. He no longer had a father he could call. Not today, not tomorrow. Never.

He sat motionless in his chair. Then he leaned forward again and dialled the number. Gertrud answered almost at once. She sounded tired and burst into tears when he asked her how she was. He had a lump in his throat too.

"I'm taking one day at a time," she said, after she had calmed down.

"I'll try to come out for a while this afternoon," Wallander said. "I won't be able to stay long, but I'll try to come."

"There's so much I've been thinking about," she said. "About you and your father. I know so little."

"That goes for me too, but let's see if we can help each other fill in the gaps."

He hung up, knowing that it was unlikely he would make it out to Löderup that day. Why had he said that he would try? Now she would be sitting there waiting.

I spend my life disappointing people, he thought hopelessly. Angrily he broke the pen he was holding and tossed the pieces into the waste-paper basket. One piece missed and he kicked it away with his foot. He suddenly had the urge to escape. When had he last talked to Baiba? She hadn't called him either. Was their relationship dying a natural death? When would he have time to look for a house? Or find a dog? There were moments when he detested his job and this was one of them.

He stood at the window. Wind and autumn clouds, birds on their way south. He thought about Per Åkeson, who had finally decided that there was more to life.

Once, towards the end of summer, as he and Baiba walked along the beach at Skagen, she had said that it seemed as though all the people of the West shared a dream of an enormous yacht that could take the whole continent to the Caribbean. The collapse of the Eastern bloc had opened her eyes. In the impoverished Latvia there were islands of wealth, simple joys. She had discovered great poverty even in the rich countries that she could now visit. There was a sea of dissatisfaction and emptiness everywhere. And that was why people dreamed of escape.

He made a note to call Baiba that evening. He saw that it was 8.15 a.m., and went to the conference room. In addition to Hamrén, there were also two detectives from Malmö, Augustsson and Hartman whom Wallander hadn't met before. They shook hands. Lisa Holgersson arrived and sat down. She welcomed the new arrivals. There wasn't time for anything else. She looked at Wallander and nodded.

He began as he'd decided to do earlier, with the conversation he'd had with Höglund. He noticed at once that the reaction of the others in the room was marked by doubt. That's what he had expected. He shared their doubts.

"I'm not presenting this as anything but one of several possibilities. Since we know nothing, we can ignore nothing."

He nodded to Höglund.

"I've asked for a summary of the investigation from a female perspective," he said. "We've never done anything like this before. But in this case we have to try everything."

The discussion that followed was intense. Wallander had expected that too. Hansson, who seemed to be feeling better this morning, started things off. About halfway through the meeting Nyberg came in. He was walking without the crutch. Wallander met his glance. He had a feeling that Nyberg had something he wanted to say. He gave him an inquiring look, but Nyberg shook his head.

Wallander listened to the discussion without taking an active part in it. Hansson expressed himself clearly and presented good arguments.

Around 9 a.m. they took a short break. Svedberg showed Wallander a picture in the paper of members of the newly created Protective Militia in Lödinge. Several other towns in Skåne were apparently following suit. Chief Holgersson had seen a report about it on the evening news.

"We're going to end up with vigilante groups all over the country," she said. "Imagine a situation where pseudo-policemen outnumber us."

"It might be unavoidable," Hamrén said. "Maybe it's always been true that crime pays. The difference is that today we can prove it. If we brought in ten per cent of all the money that disappears today in financial crimes, we could comfortably afford 3,000 new officers."

This number seemed absurd to Wallander, but Hamrén stood his ground.

"The question is whether we want that kind of society,"

he continued. "House doctors are one thing. But house police? Police everywhere? A society that's divided up into various alarm zones? Keys and codes even to visit your elderly parents?"

"We probably don't need that many new officers," Wallander said. "We just need a different kind of policeman."

"Maybe what we need is a different kind of society," said Martinsson. "With a greater sense of community."

Martinsson's words had taken on the sound of a political campaign speech, but Wallander understood him. He knew that Martinsson worried constantly about his children. That they'd be exposed to drugs. That something would happen to them.

Wallander sat down next to Nyberg, who hadn't left the table.

"It looked like you wanted to say something."

"It's just a small detail," he said. "Do you remember that I found a false nail out in the woods at Marsvinsholm?"

Wallander remembered.

"The one you thought had been there a long time?"

"I didn't think anything of it then, but now I think we can say for certain that it hadn't been there very long."

Wallander nodded. He motioned Höglund over.

"Do you use false nails?" he asked.

"Not often," she replied. "But I have tried them."

"Do they stick on pretty well?"

"They break off easily."

Wallander nodded.

"I thought you should know," Nyberg said.

Svedberg came into the room.

"Thanks for returning the note," he said. "But you could have thrown it out."

"Rydberg used to say that it was an inexcusable sin to throw out a colleague's notes."

"Rydberg said a lot of things."

"They often proved to be right."

Wallander knew that Svedberg hadn't got on with his older colleague. What surprised him was that he still felt that way, even now that Rydberg had been dead for several years.

They reassigned various tasks so that Hamrén and the two detectives from Malmö could get involved in the investigation straight away. At 10.45 a.m., Wallander decided that it was time to adjourn. A phone rang. Martinsson, sitting closest, picked it up. Wallander was thinking that maybe he'd have time to go out to Löderup and see Gertrud later that afternoon after all. Martinsson raised his hand. Everyone stopped talking. Martinsson glanced at Wallander. Not again, he thought. We can't handle this.

Martinsson hung up.

"A body has been found in Krageholm Lake," Martinsson said.

Wallander's first thought was that this didn't have to mean a third murder. Drowning accidents were common enough.

"Where?" he asked.

"There's a small camping ground on the eastern shore. The body was just off the end of a jetty."

Wallander could tell that his feeling of relief was premature.

"The body of a man. Inside a sack," he said.

It has happened again, Wallander thought. The knot in his stomach tightened.

"Who was that on the phone?" Svedberg asked.

"A camper. He was calling on his mobile phone. He

was upset. It sounded like he was throwing up in my ear."

"Nobody would be camping now, would they?" Svedberg asked.

"There are trailers for rent there all year round," Hansson said. "I know where it is."

Wallander felt suddenly incapable of dealing with the situation. Maybe Höglund felt the same way. She helped him out by getting to her feet.

"I guess we'd better go," she said.

"Yes," Wallander said. "We'd probably better leave right now."

Since Hansson knew where they were going, Wallander got into his car. The others followed. Hansson drove recklessly and fast. Wallander braked with his feet. The car phone rang. It was Per Åkeson wanting to talk to Wallander.

"What's this I hear?" he asked. "Is this another one?"

"It's too early to tell. But it may be so. If it was just a body in the water, it might have been a drowning accident or a suicide, but a body in a sack is a murder."

"God damn it to hell," Åkeson said.

"You might say that."

"Keep me posted. Where are you?"

"On our way to Krageholm Lake. We should be there in about 20 minutes."

Wallander hung up. It occurred to him that they were headed towards the place where they had found the suitcase. Hansson seemed to be thinking the same thing.

"The lake is halfway between Lödinge and Marsvinsholm," he said. "It's no great distance."

Wallander grabbed the phone and dialled Martinsson's number. His car was right behind them.

"What else did the man who called say? What's his name?"

"I don't think I got his name, but he had a Skåne accent."

"A body in a sack. How did he know there was a body in the sack? Did he open it?"

"There was a foot with a man's shoe sticking out."

Even though it was a bad connection, Wallander could hear Martinsson's distress. He hung up.

They reached Sövestad and turned left. Wallander thought about Gösta Runfeldt's client. Everywhere there were connections to the events. If there was a geographical centre, then Sövestad was it.

The lake was visible through the trees. Wallander tried to prepare himself for what awaited them. As they drove down towards the camping ground, a man came running towards them. Wallander climbed out of the car before Hansson had even stopped.

"Down there," the man stammered.

Wallander walked slowly down the slope that led to the water. Even at this distance he could make out something in the water, to one side of the jetty. Martinsson came up beside him but stopped at the shore. The others waited in the background. Wallander walked cautiously out onto the jetty. It wobbled under his weight. The water was brown and looked cold. He shivered.

The sack was only partially visible above the water's surface. A foot was indeed sticking out. The shoe was brown and had laces. White skin could be seen through a hole in the trouser leg.

Wallander looked back and motioned to Nyberg to join him. Hansson was talking to the man. Martinsson was waiting further up, and Höglund stood off to one side. It looked like a photograph, Wallander thought.

Reality frozen, suspended. Nothing more would ever happen.

The mood was broken by Nyberg stepping onto the jetty. Reality returned. Wallander squatted down and Nyberg did the same.

"A sack made of jute," Nyberg said. "They're usually strong. But this one has a hole in it. It must be old."

Wallander wished Nyberg were right, but he knew he wasn't. The hole in the sack was new. It looked as though the man had kicked his way through it. The fibres had been pushed out and then ripped apart. Wallander knew what this meant. The man had been alive when he was put in the sack and thrown into the lake. Wallander took a deep breath. He felt sick and dizzy.

Nyberg gave him an inquiring look, but didn't say anything. He waited. Wallander kept on taking deep breaths, one after another.

"He kicked a hole in the sack," Wallander said when he felt able to speak. "He was alive when he was thrown into the lake."

"An execution?" Nyberg asked. "A war between two crime gangs?"

"We could hope for that," Wallander said. "But I don't think so."

"The same killer?"

"It looks like it."

Wallander got to his feet with difficulty. His knees were stiff. He walked back to the shore. Nyberg remained out on the jetty. The forensic technicians had just arrived. Wallander went over to Höglund. She was standing with Chief Holgersson. The others followed. Finally they were all assembled. The man who had discovered the sack was sitting nearby.

"It could be the same killer," Wallander said. "If that's the case, then this time he's drowned a man in a sack."

Disgust passed like a ripple through the team.

"We have to stop this madman," Lisa Holgersson said. "What's become of this country?"

"A pungee pit," Wallander said. "A man tied to a tree and strangled. And now a man tied up in a sack and drowned."

"Do you still think a woman could have done something like this?" Hansson asked aggressively.

Wallander asked himself the same question. What did he really think? In a matter of a few seconds all the events passed through his mind.

"I don't want to believe it, but yes a woman could have done this, or at least be involved."

He looked at Hansson.

"You're asking the wrong question," he said. "It's not about what I think."

Wallander went back to the shore of the lake. A solitary swan was on its way towards the jetty. It glided soundlessly across the surface of the dark water. Wallander watched it for a long time. Then he zipped up his jacket and went to Nyberg, who was already starting his work out on the jetty.

Skåne

17 October – 3 November 1994

CHAPTER 25

Nyberg slowly slit open the sack. Wallander went onto the jetty to look at the dead man's face. The doctor, who had just arrived, went with him.

He didn't recognise the dead man, and of course he hadn't expected to. Wallander guessed that he must have been between 40 and 50 years old.

He looked at the body as it was pulled clear of the sack. He looked for less than a minute; he simply couldn't stand more. He felt dizzy the whole time.

Nyberg was going through the man's pockets.

"He's wearing an expensive suit," Nyberg said. "His shoes aren't cheap either."

They didn't find anything in his pockets. Someone had taken the trouble to remove his identity card, and yet the killer must have assumed that the body would very soon be discovered in Krageholm Lake.

The body had now been pulled free and was on a plastic sheet. Nyberg signalled to Wallander, who had stepped aside.

"This was carefully calculated," he said. "You'd almost think the murderer knew about weight distribution and water resistance."

"What do you mean?" Wallander asked.

Nyberg pointed to several thick seams running along the inside of the sack.

"The sack has weights sewn into it that ensured two

things. One, the weights were light enough so that with the man's body in it the sack wouldn't sink to the bottom. Two, the sack would lie with only a narrow air pocket above the water's surface. Since it was all so carefully calculated, the person who prepared the sack must have known the man's weight. At least approximately. With a margin of error of maybe four to five kilos."

Wallander forced himself to think this over, even though all thoughts of how the man had died made him feel sick.

"So the narrow air pocket guaranteed that the man would actually drown?"

"I'm not a doctor," Nyberg said. "But it's probable that this man was still alive when the sack was put into the water. So he was murdered."

The doctor, who was kneeling down to examine the body, had been listening to their conversation. He stood up and came over to them. The jetty swayed under their weight.

"It's too early to be certain," he said. "But we have to presume that he drowned."

"Not just that he drowned," Wallander said. "But that somebody drowned him."

"The police are the ones who will have to determine whether it was an accident or a murder," the doctor said. "I can only speak about what happened to his body."

"No external marks? No contusions? Or wounds?"

"We'll need to get his clothes off to be able to answer that question. But I can't see anything on the parts of his body that are visible. The autopsy may turn up other results."

Wallander nodded. "I'd like to know as soon as possible if you find any signs of violence."

The doctor went back to his work. Even though

Wallander had met him several times before, he still couldn't remember his name. Wallander went and gathered his colleagues on the shore. Hansson had just finished talking to the man who had discovered the sack.

"We didn't find any identification," Wallander began. "We have to find out who he is. That's the most important thing right now. Until then we can't do anything. We'll start by going through the missing-persons files."

"There's a good chance that he hasn't been missed yet," Hansson said. "Nils Göransson, the man who found him, claims he was here as late as yesterday afternoon. He does shift work at a machine shop in Svedala and usually takes a walk out here because he has trouble sleeping. He was here yesterday. He always walks out on the jetty. And there wasn't any sack. So it must have been thrown into the water during the night."

"Or this morning," Wallander said. "When did Göransson get here?"

Hansson checked his notes.

"At 8.15. He finished his shift at around 7 a.m. and drove here, stopping on the way for breakfast."

"So not much time has passed," Wallander said. "That may give us certain advantages. The difficulty is going to be to find out who he is."

"The sack could have been put into the lake somewhere else," Nyberg said.

Wallander shook his head.

"He hasn't been in the water long. And there's no current here to speak of."

Martinsson kicked at the sand restlessly, as if he were cold.

"Does it really have to be the same man?" he asked. "I think this seems different."

Wallander was as sure about this as he could possibly be.

"No. It's the same killer. We'd better assume that it is, anyway."

He sent them off. There was nothing more for them to do out there on the shore of Krageholm Lake. The cars drove away. Wallander stood and gazed out at the water. The swan was gone. He looked at the men working on the jetty. At the ambulance, the police cars, the crime-scene tape. Everything about it suddenly gave him a sense of depthless unreality. He encountered nature surrounded by plastic tape stretched out to protect crime sites. Everywhere he went there were dead people. He could look at a swan on the water, but in the foreground lay a man who had just been pulled dead out of a sack.

His work was little more than a poorly paid test of endurance. He was being paid to endure this. The plastic tape wound through his life like a snake.

He went over to Nyberg, who was stretching his back.

"We've found a cigarette butt," he said. "That's all. At least out here on the jetty. We've already done a superficial examination of the sand for drag marks. There aren't any. Whoever carried the sack was strong. Unless he lured the man out here and then stuffed him in the sack."

Wallander shook his head.

"Let's assume that the sack was carried," he said. "Carried with its contents."

"Do you think there's any reason to dredge the lake?"

"I don't think so. The man was unconscious when he was brought here. There must have been a car involved. Then the sack was thrown in the water. The car drove off."

"So we'll wait on the dragging," Nyberg said.

"Tell me what you see," Wallander said.

Nyberg grimaced.

"It could be the same man," he said. "The violence, the cruelty, they all look familiar. Even though he varies things."

"Do you think a woman could have done this?"

"I say the same thing you do," Nyberg replied. "I'd rather not believe that. But I can also tell you that she would have to be capable of carrying 80 kilos without difficulty. How many women can do that?"

"I don't know any," said Wallander. "But I'm sure they exist."

Nyberg went back to his work. Wallander was about to leave the jetty when the swan caught his eye. He wished he had a piece of bread. It was pecking at something near the shore. Wallander took a step closer. The swan hissed and turned back towards the lake.

Wallander went over to one of the police cars and asked to be driven to Ystad. On the way back to town he tried to think. What he had feared most had now happened. The killer was not finished. They knew nothing about him. Was he at the end or the beginning of what he had decided to do? They didn't even know whether he had motives for his premeditated acts or was just insane.

It has to be a man, he thought. Anything else goes against all common sense. Women seldom commit murder. Least of all well-planned murders. Ruthless and calculated acts of violence. It has to be a man, or maybe more than one. And we're never going to solve this case unless we find the connection between the victims. Now there are three of them. That increases our chances. But nothing is certain, nothing is going to reveal itself to us.

He leaned his cheek against the car window. The

landscape was brown with a tinge of grey, but the grass was still green. There was a lone tractor working out in a field.

Wallander thought about the pungee pit where he had found Holger Eriksson. The tree that Gösta Runfeldt had been tied to when he was strangled. And now a man was stuffed alive into a sack and tossed into Krageholm Lake to drown.

The only possible motive was revenge, he was sure of that. But this went beyond all reasonable proportions. What was the killer seeking revenge for? Something so horrific that it wasn't enough simply to kill. The victims also had to be conscious of what was happening to them.

There's nothing random about what's behind all this, thought Wallander. Everything has been carefully thought out and chosen. He paused at the last thought. The killer chose. Someone was chosen. Selected from what group or for what reason?

When he reached the station he felt the need for some solitude before he sat down with his colleagues. He took the phone off the hook, pushed aside the phone messages lying on his desk, and put his feet up on a pile of memos from the national police board.

The hardest thing to comprehend was the possibility that the murderer might be a woman. He tried to remember the times he had dealt with female criminals. It hadn't happened often. He could recall all the cases he had ever heard about during his years as a policeman. Once, almost 15 years back, he had caught a woman who had committed murder. Later the district court changed the charge to manslaughter. She was a middle-aged woman who had killed her brother. He had persecuted and molested her ever since they were children. Finally she couldn't take it any more and killed him with his own shotgun. She hadn't really meant to shoot him. She just wanted to scare him, but she was a bad shot. She hit him right in the chest, and he died instantly. In all the other cases that Wallander could remember, the women who had used violence had done so on impulse and in self-defence. It involved their own husbands, or men they were having relationships with. In many cases, alcohol was part of the picture.

Never, in all his experience, had there been a woman who planned in advance to commit a violent act. He got up and walked to the window. What was it that made him unable to let go of the idea that a woman was involved this time? He had no answer to this. He didn't even know whether he believed it was a woman working alone or collaborating with a man. There was nothing to indicate one or the other.

Martinsson knocked on his door and came in.

"The list is almost ready," he said.

"What list is that?" Wallander asked.

"The list of missing persons," Martinsson replied, looking surprised.

Wallander nodded. "Then let's meet," he said, motioning Martinsson ahead of him down the hall.

When they had closed the door of the conference room behind them, his feeling of powerlessness vanished. He remained standing at the head of the table. Usually he sat down. Now he felt as if he didn't have time for that.

"What have we got?" he asked.

"In Ystad no reports of anyone missing during the past few weeks," Svedberg said. "The ones we've been searching for over a longer period don't match with the man we found in Krageholm Lake. There's a couple of teenage girls, and a boy who ran away from a refugee camp. He's very likely on his way back to the Sudan."

"What about the other districts?"

"We've got a couple of people in Malmö," Höglund said. "But they don't match either. In one case the age might be right, but the missing person is from southern Italy."

They went through the bulletins from the closest districts. Wallander was aware that if necessary they might have to cover the whole country and even the rest of Scandinavia. They could only hope that the man had lived somewhere near Ystad.

"Lund took a report late last night," Hansson said. "A woman called to report that her husband hadn't come home from his evening walk. The age is about right. He's a researcher at the university."

"Check it out, of course."

"They're sending us a photograph," Hansson went on. "They'll fax it over as soon as they get it."

Now Wallander sat down. At that moment Per Åkeson came into the room. Wallander wished he hadn't come. It was never easy to report that they were at a standstill. The investigation was stuck with its wheels deep in the mud. And now they had another victim.

Wallander felt uncomfortable, as if he were personally responsible for the fact that they had nothing to go on. Yet he knew they had been working as hard and as steadily as they could. The detectives gathered in the room were intelligent and dedicated.

Wallander pushed aside his annoyance at Åkeson's presence.

"You're here just in time," he said. "I was just thinking about summarising the state of the investigation."

"Does an investigative state even exist?" asked Åkeson.

Wallander knew he didn't mean this as a sarcastic or critical remark. Those who didn't know Åkeson might be put off by his brusque manner. But Wallander had worked with him for so many years that he knew that what he had just said was intended to demonstrate a willingness to help if he could.

Hamrén stared at Åkeson with obvious disapproval. Wallander wondered how the prosecutors in Stockholm behaved.

"There's always an investigative state," Wallander replied. "We have one this time too. But it's extremely hazy. A number of clues we were following are no longer relevant. I think we've reached a point where we have to go back to the beginning. What this new murder means, we can't yet say. It's too early for that."

"Is it the same killer?" Åkeson asked

"I think so," said Wallander.

"Why?"

"The *modus operandi.* The brutality. The cruelty. Of course a sack isn't the same thing as sharpened bamboo stakes. But you have to admit it's a variation on a theme."

"What about the suspicion that a mercenary soldier might be behind all this?"

"That led us to discover that Harald Berggren has been dead for seven years."

Åkeson had no more questions. The door was cautiously pushed open, and a clerk handed in a picture that had arrived by fax.

"It's from Lund," the girl said, and then she closed the door behind her.

Everyone stood up and gathered around Martinsson, who stood holding the picture. Wallander gave a low whistle. There could be no doubt. It was the man they had found in Krageholm Lake.

"Good," he said in a low voice. "We just got a good jump on the murderer's lead."

They sat down again.

"Who is he?" Wallander asked.

Hansson had his papers in order.

"Eugen Blomberg, 51 years old. A research assistant at Lund University. His research has something to do with milk."

"Milk?" Wallander said in surprise.

"That's what it says. 'The relationship between milk allergies and various intestinal diseases.'"

"Who reported him missing?"

"His wife. Kristina Blomberg. She lives on Siriusgatan in Lund."

Wallander knew they had to make the best use of their time. He wanted to make an even bigger dent in the killer's lead.

"Then we'll go there," he said, getting to his feet. "Tell our colleagues that we've identified him. See to it that they track down the wife so I can talk to her. There's a detective in Lund named Birch. Kalle Birch. We know each other. Talk to him, tell him that I'm on my way."

"Can you really talk to her before we have a positive identification?"

"Someone else can identify him. Someone from the university. Another milk researcher. Now we'll have to go through all the material on Eriksson and Runfeldt again. Eugen Blomberg. Is he there somewhere? We need to get through a lot of it today."

Wallander turned to Åkeson. "I think we could safely say that the investigative state has changed."

Åkeson nodded, but said nothing.

Wallander went to get his jacket and the keys to one of the squad cars. It was 2.15 p.m. when he left Ystad. He briefly considered putting on the emergency light, but decided against it. It wouldn't get him there any faster.

He reached Lund at about 3.30 p.m. A police car met him at the entrance to town and escorted him to Siriusgatan, in a residential neighbourhood east of the centre of town. At the entrance to the street the police car pulled over. Another car was parked there. Wallander saw Kalle Birch get out. They had met several years back at a conference of the Southern Sweden Police District held in Tylösand, outside of Halmstad. The purpose of the conference was to improve operational cooperation in the region. Wallander had participated grudgingly. Björk, Ystad's chief of police at the time, had ordered him to go. At the lunch he had sat next to Birch. They discovered that they shared an interest in opera. They had occasionally been in contact since then. From various sources Wallander had heard that Birch was a talented detective who sometimes suffered from deep depression, but he seemed cheerful enough today. They shook hands.

"One of Blomberg's colleagues is on his way to identify the body. They'll let us know by phone."

"And the widow?"

"Not yet informed. We thought that was a little premature."

"That's going to make the interview more difficult," Wallander said. "She'll be shocked, of course."

"I don't think that we can do anything about that."

Birch pointed to a café across the street. "We can wait there," he said. "Besides, I'm hungry."

Wallander hadn't eaten lunch either. They went into the café and had sandwiches and coffee. Wallander gave Birch a summary of the case to date.

"It reminds me of what you were dealing with this summer," he said when Wallander had finished.

"Only because the murderer has killed more than one person," Wallander said. "The method here is quite different."

"What's so different about taking scalps and drowning somebody alive?"

"I might not be able to put it into words," Wallander said hesitantly. "But there's still a big difference."

Birch let the question drop. "We sure as hell never thought about things like this when we joined the force," he said instead.

"I hardly remember what I imagined any more," Wallander said.

"I remember an old commissioner," Birch said. "He's been dead a long time now. Karl-Oscar Fredrick Wilhelm Sunesson. He's practically a legend. At least here in Lund. He saw all of this coming. I remember that he used to talk to us younger detectives and warn us that everything was going to get a lot tougher. The violence would get more widespread and more brutal. He said that this was because Sweden's prosperity was a well-camouflaged quagmire. The decay was underneath it all. He even took the time to put together demographic analyses and explain the connections between various types of crime. He was that rare sort of man who never spoke ill of anyone. He could be critical about politicians, and he could use his arguments to crush suggested changes to the police force. But he never doubted that there were good, albeit confused, intentions behind them. He used to say that good intentions that are not clothed in reason lead to greater disasters than actions built on ill will. I didn't understand it back then. But I do now."

Birch could have been talking about Rydberg.

"That still doesn't explain what we were really thinking when we decided to join the force," he said.

But what Birch had in mind, Wallander never found out. The phone rang. Birch listened without saying anything.

"It's Eugen Blomberg. There's absolutely no doubt about it."

"So let's go in," Wallander said.

"If you want, you can wait until we inform his wife," said Birch. "It's usually rather painful."

"I'll go with you," Wallander said. "It's better than sitting here doing nothing. Besides, it might give me an idea what kind of relationship she had with her husband."

They encountered a woman who was unexpectedly composed. She seemed to understand why they were standing on her doorstep at once. Wallander kept in the background as Birch told her of her husband's death. She sat down on the edge of a chair, as if to bear the brunt of it with her feet, and nodded silently. Wallander assumed that she was about the same age as her husband, but she seemed older, as if she had aged prematurely. She was thin, her skin stretched taut across her cheekbones. Wallander studied her furtively. He didn't think she was going to fall apart. At least not yet.

Birch nodded to Wallander to step forward. Birch had merely said that they had found her husband dead in Krageholm Lake. Nothing about what had happened. This was Wallander's job.

"Krageholm Lake comes under the jurisdiction of the Ystad police," said Birch. "Which is why one of my colleagues from there is with me. This is Kurt Wallander."

Kristina Blomberg looked up. She reminded Wallander of someone, but he couldn't think who it was.

"I recognise your face," she said. "I've seen you in the papers."

"That's quite possible," Wallander said, sitting down on a chair across from her. Birch had taken over Wallander's position in the background. The house was very quiet. Tastefully furnished. But quiet. It occurred to Wallander that he didn't yet know whether they had children.

That was his first question.

"No," she replied. "We don't have any children."

"None from earlier marriages?"

Wallander immediately noticed her uncertainty. She paused before answering; it was barely noticeable but he saw it.

"No," she said. "Not that I know of."

Wallander exchanged a glance with Birch before slowly pressing on.

"When did you last see your husband?"

"He went for a walk last night as he usually did."

"Do you know which way he went?"

She shook her head. "He was often gone for more than an hour. Where he went, I have no idea."

"Was everything normal last night?"

"Yes."

Wallander again sensed a shadow of uncertainty in her answer. He continued cautiously.

"So he didn't come back? What did you do then?"

"At 2 a.m. I called the police."

"But didn't you think he might have gone to see some friends?"

"He didn't have many friends. I called them before I contacted the police. He wasn't with them."

She looked at him. Still composed. Wallander realised that he couldn't wait any longer.

"Your husband was found dead in Krageholm Lake. We have determined that he was murdered. I regret this very much, but I have to tell you the truth."

Wallander studied her face. She's not surprised, he thought. About him being dead, or that he was murdered.

"Of course it's important that we catch the person or persons who did this. Did your husband have any enemies?"

"I don't know," she replied. "I didn't know my husband very well."

Wallander paused to think before he continued. Her answer made him uneasy.

"I don't know how to interpret your answer."

"Is it really so difficult? I didn't know my husband very well. Once upon a time, a long time ago, I thought I did. But that was back then."

"What happened? What changed things?"

She shook her head. Wallander saw something he interpreted as bitterness in her expression. He waited.

"Nothing happened," she said. "We grew apart. We live in the same house, but we have separate bedrooms. He has his own life, and I have mine."

Then she corrected herself. "He had his own life. And I have mine."

"And he was a researcher at the university?"

"Yes."

"Milk allergies? Is that right?"

"Yes."

"Do you work there too?"

"I'm a teacher."

Wallander nodded. "So you wouldn't know whether your husband had any enemies?"

"No."

"And few friends?"

"That's right."

"And you can't imagine anyone who would want to kill him? Or why?"

Her face was strained. Wallander felt as if she were looking right through him.

"No-one except me," she replied. "But I didn't kill him."

Wallander looked at her for a long time, without saying anything. Birch had stepped forward to stand next to him.

"Why would you want to kill him?" Wallander asked.

She stood up and tore off her blouse with such force that it ripped. It happened so fast that Wallander and Birch didn't understand what was going on. Then she held out her arms. They were covered with scars.

"He did this to me," she said. "And a lot of other things that I won't even talk about."

She left the room with the torn blouse in her hand. Wallander and Birch looked at each other.

"He abused her," Birch said. "Do you think she was the one who did it?"

"No," Wallander answered. "It wasn't her."

They waited in silence. After a few minutes she came back wearing a new shirt.

"I'm not going to grieve for him," she said. "I don't know who did it. I don't think I want to know, either. But I realise that you have to catch him."

"Yes," Wallander said. "We do. And we need all the help we can get."

She looked at him, and all of a sudden her expression was completely helpless.

"I didn't know anything about him," she said. "I can't help you."

It was quite likely that she was telling the truth. But she had already helped them. When Wallander saw her arms, he lost his last shred of doubt.

He knew that they were looking for a woman.

CHAPTER 26

It was raining when they left the house on Siriusgatan. They stopped at Wallander's car. He felt restless.

"I don't think I've ever met a widow who took the loss of her husband so lightly," Birch said, his voice grim with distaste.

"And yet it's something we have to bear in mind," Wallander replied.

He didn't take the trouble to explain his answer. Instead he tried to think ahead through the next few hours. His feeling of urgency was intense.

"We have to go through his belongings both at home and at the university. That's your job, of course. But I'd like someone from Ystad to be here too. We don't know what we're looking for, but this way we might discover something of interest more quickly."

Birch nodded. "You're not staying yourself?"

"No. I'll ask Martinsson and Svedberg to come over. I'll have them leave right away."

Wallander dialled the number of the Ystad police, and asked for Martinsson, telling him quickly what had happened. Martinsson said that they would leave immediately. Wallander told him to meet Birch at the police station in Lund. He had to spell the name for Martinsson. Birch smiled.

"I would have stayed," Wallander said, "but I have to start working backwards through the investigation. I've got a hunch that the solution to Blomberg's murder is in there somewhere, though we haven't seen it yet. The solution to all three murders is there in a complex system of caverns."

"It would be good if we could prevent any more deaths," Birch said. "Enough have died as it is."

They said goodbye. Wallander drove back towards Ystad. Rain showers came and went. When he passed Sturup Airport there was a plane coming in to land. As he drove he went over the case again. He didn't know how many times he had done it so far.

He arrived back at 5.45 p.m. In reception he stopped and asked Ebba if Höglund was in.

"She and Hansson came back an hour ago."

Wallander hurried on. He found Höglund in her office. She was on the phone. Wallander signalled to her and then waited out in the hall. As soon as he heard her hang up, he went back in.

"I think we should go to my office," he said. "We need to do a thorough overview."

"Shall I bring anything?" She pointed at the papers and folders strewn across her desk.

"No. If we need anything you can come back and get it."

She followed him to his office. Wallander told the switchboard to hold his calls.

"You remember that I asked you to go through everything that's happened and look for female characteristics," he said.

"I've done that," she replied.

"We have to go over all the material again," he went on. "I'm convinced that there's a point where we can make a breakthrough. It's just that we haven't seen it yet. We've walked right past it. We've gone back and forth, and it's been there the whole time, but we just haven't been looking in the right direction. And now I'm certain that a woman must be involved."

"Why do you think that?"

He told her about his conversation with Kristina Blomberg and about how she had ripped off her blouse and showed them her scars.

"You're talking about an abused woman," she said. "Not about a woman who murders people."

"It might be the same thing," Wallander said. "In any case, I have to find out if I'm right or wrong."

"Where do we start?"

"From the beginning. Like with a story. And the first thing that happened was that someone prepared a pungee pit for Holger Eriksson in a ditch in Lödinge. Imagine that it was a woman. What do you see?"

"It's not impossible, of course. Nothing was too heavy or too large."

"Why did she choose this particular *modus operandi*?"

"So it would look like it was done by a man."

"She wanted to throw us off the track?"

"Not necessarily. She may have wanted to demonstrate how violence comes back, like a boomerang. Or, why not both reasons?"

Wallander thought about that. Her explanation was certainly possible.

"The motive," he continued. "Who wanted to kill Holger Eriksson?"

"With Gösta Runfeldt there are a number of candidates. But with Eriksson we still don't know enough about him. It's as if his life is a no trespassing zone."

He knew right away that she was saying something important.

"How do you mean?"

"Just what I said. We should know more about a man who's 80 years old and has lived his whole life in Skåne. A well-known man. We know so little that it's unnatural."

"What's the explanation?"

"I don't know."

"Are people scared to talk about him?"

"No."

"Then what is it?"

"We were searching for a mercenary," she said. "We found a man who's dead. We've learned that these men often use assumed names. It struck me that the same might apply to Holger Eriksson."

"That he could have been a mercenary?"

"No, I don't think so. But he could have used an assumed name. He mightn't always have been Holger Eriksson. That might be one explanation as to why we know so little about his private life. Maybe sometimes he was someone else."

Wallander recalled some of Eriksson's earliest poetry books. He had published them under a pseudonym, later using his real name.

"I have a hard time accepting what you're saying," Wallander said. "Mostly because I don't see any reasonable motive. Why does someone use an assumed name?"

"So that he can do something in secret."

Wallander looked at her. "You mean that he might have used an alias because he was homosexual? In a time when it was best to keep it secret?"

"That's one possibility."

Wallander nodded, but he was still dubious. "We've got the gift to the church in Jämtland. That must mean something. Why did he do it? And the Polish woman who disappeared. There's something that makes her special. Have you thought what it might be?"

Höglund shook her head.

"The fact that she's the only woman who appears in the investigative material on Holger Eriksson," he said.

"Copies of the material on her were sent from Östersund. But I don't think anyone has started going through it yet. Besides, she's just on the periphery. We have no proof that she and Eriksson knew each other."

Wallander was suddenly determined.

"That's right. We have to do that as soon as possible. Find out whether there's a connection."

"Who's going to do it?"

"Hansson. He reads faster than any of us. He usually goes right to the heart of the matter."

She made a note. Then they left the topic of Holger Eriksson for the moment.

"Gösta Runfeldt was a brutal man," Wallander said. "We know that for sure. On that point there's a similarity with Eriksson. Now it turns out that it applies to Eugen Blomberg too. Runfeldt abused his wife, just like Blomberg. Where does this lead us?"

"To three men with violent tendencies, at least two of them who abused women."

"It might also be true of Eriksson. We don't know yet."

"The Polish woman? Krista Haberman?"

"For example. And it might also be true that Runfeldt killed his wife. Prepared a hole in the ice for her to fall into and drown."

They both knew that they were onto something. Wallander went back through the investigation again.

"The pungee pit," he said. "What was it?"

"Prepared, well planned. A death trap."

"More than that. A way to kill someone slowly."

Wallander searched for a paper on his desk.

"According to the pathologist in Lund, Eriksson may have hung there impaled on the bamboo stakes for several hours before he died."

He put down the paper in disgust.

"Runfeldt," he said. "Emaciated, strangled, hanging tied to a tree. What does that tell us?"

"That he was held captive. He wasn't hanging in a pungee pit."

Wallander raised his hand. She didn't say a word. He was thinking, recalling the visit to Stång Lake, how they'd found her under the ice.

"Drowning under ice," he said. "I've always imagined that would be one of the most horrifying ways to die. To be beneath the ice and not be able to break through. Maybe even see the light through it."

"Held captive under the ice," she said.

"Precisely. That's just what I was thinking."

"Do you mean that this killer has invented methods of killing that are linked to the event that's being avenged?"

"Something like that. It's a possibility, anyway."

"In that case, what happened to Eugen Blomberg looks more like what happened to Runfeldt's wife."

"I know," Wallander said. "Maybe we can figure that out too if we keep at it a while longer."

They went on. They discussed the suitcase. Wallander mentioned the false nail that Nyberg had found out in the woods near Marsvinsholm. Then they started on Blomberg. The pattern was repeated.

"The plan was to drown him, but not too fast. He had to be aware of what was happening to him."

Wallander leaned back in his chair and looked at her across his desk.

"Tell me what you see."

"A revenge motive is taking shape. At any rate, it runs through each crime as a possible link. Men who use force against women are attacked in return by a calculated violence of a masculine kind. As if they were being forced to feel their hands on their own bodies."

"That's a good way of putting it," Wallander said. "Go on."

"It could also be a way of hiding the fact that a woman committed the crimes. It took a long time for us to even imagine that a woman was involved. And when we did think of it, we rejected it immediately."

"What is there to contradict the idea that the killer might be a woman?"

"We still know very little. Women almost never use violence unless they're defending themselves or their children. And then it's not premeditated violence, but instinctive, acts done in self-defence. A woman would not normally dig a pungee pit. Or hold a man captive. Or throw a man in the lake inside a sack."

Wallander looked at her intently.

"Normally," he said. "Your word."

"If a woman is involved in this, then she must be very sick indeed."

Wallander stood up and went to the window. "There's one more thing," he said, "which could knock down this whole house of cards we're building. She isn't avenging herself. She's avenging others. Runfeldt's wife is dead. Blomberg's wife didn't do it, I'm sure of that. Eriksson has no woman. If this is revenge and if it's a woman, then she's taking revenge for others. And that doesn't sound likely. If it's true, I've never come across anything like it."

"It could be more than one woman," Höglund said hesitantly.

"A number of angels of death? A group of women? A cult?"

"That doesn't sound plausible."

"No," Wallander said, "it doesn't."

He sat down again in his chair. "I'd like you to do just the opposite," he said. "Go over all the material again. And then give me the reasons why it isn't a woman who did this."

"Wouldn't it be better to wait until we know more about what happened to Blomberg?"

"Maybe. But I don't think we have time."

"You are thinking that it could happen again?"

Wallander wanted to give her an honest answer. He sat silently for a moment before he replied.

"There is no beginning," he said. "At least none we can see. That makes it less likely that there will be an end. It could happen again. And we don't have any idea what direction to look in."

They didn't get any further. Wallander felt impatient that neither Martinsson nor Svedberg had called. Then he remembered that he had blocked all his calls. He checked with the switchboard. Neither Martinsson nor Svedberg had rung in. He asked for their calls to be allowed through.

"The break-ins," Höglund said suddenly. "At the florist's shop and at Eriksson's house. How do they fit into the picture?"

"I don't know," he replied. "Or the blood on the floor. I thought I had an explanation, and now I don't."

"I've been thinking about it," she said.

Wallander could see that she was excited. He nodded to her to continue.

"We're talking about having to distinguish what we can see from what has happened," she began. "Holger Eriksson reported a break-in where nothing was stolen. Why did he report it at all?"

"I've thought about that too," Wallander said. "He may have just been upset that someone broke into his house."

"In that case it fits in with the pattern."

Wallander didn't understand immediately what she was getting at.

"There's always the possibility that someone broke in to make him nervous. Not to steal anything."

"A first warning?" he asked. "Is that what you mean?"

"Yes."

"And the florist's shop?"

"Runfeldt leaves his flat. Or he's lured out. Or else it's early in the morning. He goes down to the street to wait for a taxi. There he vanishes without a trace. What if he went to the shop? It only takes a few minutes. He could have left his suitcase inside the front door. Or carried it with him. It wasn't heavy."

"Why would he have gone to the shop?"

"I don't know. Maybe he forgot something."

"You mean he might have been attacked there?"

"I know it's not a great idea. But it's what I've been thinking."

"It's no worse than lots of others," said Wallander. He looked at her.

"Has anyone checked if the blood on the floor was Runfeldt's?"

"I don't think it was ever done. If not, I'm to blame."

"If we had to keep track of who was responsible for all

the mistakes made during criminal investigations, there wouldn't be time for anything else," Wallander said. "I assume there aren't any samples left?"

"I'll find out. We'll check it out just to be sure."

She got up and left the room. Wallander was tired. They had had a good talk, but his anxiety had increased. They were as far from the heart of the matter as they could be. The investigation still lacked a gravitational force drawing them in a specific direction.

Someone was complaining loudly out in the hall. He started thinking of Baiba, but forced himself to concentrate on the investigation again. He got up and went for some coffee. Another officer asked him if he'd had time to decide whether it was proper for a local association to call itself "Friends of the Axe". He said no. Went back to his office. The rain had stopped. The clouds hung motionless in the sky over the water tower.

The phone rang. It was Martinsson. Wallander listened for signs in his voice that something important had happened, but he heard nothing.

"Svedberg just came back from the university. Eugen Blomberg seems to have been the type of person that blended into the woodwork. He wasn't a particularly prominent researcher. He was loosely affiliated with the children's clinic in Lund, but what he was working on was considered quite rudimentary. That's what Svedberg claims, at least."

"Go on," Wallander said, not hiding his impatience.

"I have a hard time understanding how a man could be so utterly devoid of interests," Martinsson said. "He seems to have been completely preoccupied with his damned milk. And nothing else. Except for one thing."

Wallander waited.

"He was having a relationship with another woman. I found some letters. The initials K.A. keep showing up. What's interesting about all this is that she seems to have been pregnant."

"How did you find that out?"

"From the letters. In the most recent it says that she was near the end of her pregnancy."

"When was it dated?"

"There isn't any date. But she mentions that she saw a movie on TV she liked. And if I remember correctly, it ran a few months back. Of course we'll have to check that out more exactly."

"Does she have an address?"

"It doesn't say."

"Not even whether it's in Lund?"

"No. But she's probably from somewhere in Skåne. She uses several expressions that indicate as much."

"Did you ask the widow about this?"

"That's what I wanted to talk to you about. Whether it's appropriate to do so, or whether I should wait."

"Ask her," Wallander said. "We can't wait. Besides, I have a strong feeling that she knows about it already. We need that woman's name and address as fast as we can damn well get it, in fact. Let me know as soon as you've got something."

Afterwards Wallander sat with his hand on the telephone. A cold wave of aversion passed through him. What Martinsson had said reminded him of something. It had to do with Svedberg, but he couldn't recall what it was.

As he waited for Martinsson to call back, Hansson appeared at the door and said he was going to get started on the investigative material from Östersund that evening.

"There's eleven kilos of it," he said. "Just so you know."

"Did you weigh it?" Wallander asked, surprised.

"I didn't, but the courier did. Want to know what it cost?"

"I'd rather not."

Hansson left. Wallander imagined a black Labrador sleeping next to his bed. It was 7.40 p.m. He still hadn't heard from Martinsson. Nyberg called in and said he thought he'd call it a night. Why had Nyberg let him know? So that he could be found at home, or because he wanted to be left in peace?

Finally Martinsson called.

"She was asleep," he said. "I didn't really want to wake her. That's why it took so long."

Wallander said nothing. He wouldn't have hesitated to wake Kristina Blomberg.

"What did she say?"

"You were right. She knew her husband had other women. But the initials K.A. didn't mean anything to her."

"Does she know where she lives?"

"She claims she doesn't. I'm inclined to believe her."

"But she must have known if he went out of town."

"I asked about that. She said no. Besides, he didn't have a car. He didn't even have a driver's licence."

"That sounds like she must live nearby."

"That's what I was thinking too."

"A woman with the initials K.A. We have to find her. Drop everything else for the time being. Is Birch there?"

"He drove back to the station a while ago."

"Where's Svedberg?"

"He was supposed to talk to someone who knew Blomberg best."

"Tell him to concentrate on finding out who the woman is with the initials K.A."

"I'm not sure I can get hold of him," Martinsson replied. "He left his phone here with me."

Wallander swore.

"The widow must know who her husband's best friend was. It's important to tell Svedberg."

"I'll see what I can do."

Wallander put down the receiver, then thought better of it, but it was too late. What he had forgotten had suddenly come back to him. He looked up the phone number of the police station in Lund, and got hold of Birch almost at once.

"I think we might have hit on something," Wallander said.

"Martinsson spoke to Ehrén, who's working with him at Siriusgatan," Birch said. "As I understand it, we're looking for an unknown woman who might have the initials K.A."

"Not 'might', they are her initials," Wallander said. "Karin Andersson, Katrina Alström . . . we have to find her, whatever her name is. And there's one detail that I think is important."

"That she was pregnant?"

Birch was thinking fast.

"Precisely," said Wallander. "We should contact the maternity ward in Lund and check up on women who have had children recently or will soon. With the initials K.A."

"I'll take care of it myself," Birch said. "This sort of thing is always a little sensitive."

Wallander said goodbye. He had started to sweat. Something had started moving. He went out into the hall. It was empty. When the phone rang he gave a start. It was Höglund. She was at Runfeldt's shop.

"There's no blood here," she said. "Vanja Andersson

scrubbed the floor herself. She thought the stain was upsetting."

"What about the rag?"

"She threw it out. And the rubbish was collected long ago, of course."

Wallander knew that only the tiniest amount was needed to carry out an analysis.

"Her shoes," he said. "What shoes was she wearing that day? There might be a little bit on the sole."

"I'll ask her."

Wallander waited.

"She had on a pair of clogs," Höglund said. "But they're back at her flat."

"Go and get them. Bring them here, and call Nyberg at home. He can at least tell us if there's any blood on them."

During the conversation Hamrén appeared at his door. Wallander hadn't seen much of him since he arrived in Ystad. He wondered what the two detectives from Malmö were working on.

"I've taken over matching the data between Eriksson and Runfeldt now that Martinsson's in Lund. So far there are no matches," he said. "But I don't think their paths ever crossed."

"Still, it's important to do a thorough job on it," Wallander said. "Somewhere these investigations are going to merge. I'm convinced of that."

"And Blomberg?"

"He'll find a place in the pattern too. Anything else is just implausible."

"When was police work ever a matter of plausibility?" Hamrén said with a smile.

"You're right, of course. But we can hope."

Hamrén stood there with his pipe in his hand.

"I'm going out for a smoke. It clears my brain."

He left. It was just past 8 p.m. Wallander waited for Svedberg to report in. He got a cup of coffee and some biscuits. Wallander wandered into the canteen and absent-mindedly watched the TV for a while. Beautiful pictures from the Comoro Islands. He wondered where those islands were. At 8.45 p.m. he was back in his chair. Birch called. They had started looking for women who had given birth in recent months or would give birth in the next two months. So far they hadn't found any with the initials K.A. After he hung up, Wallander thought he might as well go home. They could call him on his mobile phone if they wanted him. He tried to get hold of Martinsson, without success. Then Svedberg called. It was 9.10 p.m.

"There's nobody with the initials K.A.," he said. "At least not known to the man who claims to have been Blomberg's best friend."

"So at least we know that," Wallander said, not hiding his disappointment.

"I'm heading home now," Svedberg said.

Wallander had hardly hung up before the phone rang again. It was Birch.

"Unfortunately," he said, "there's no-one with the initials K.A."

"Shit," said Wallander.

Both of them thought for a moment.

"She could have given birth somewhere else," Birch said. "It doesn't have to have been in Lund."

"You're right," Wallander said. "We'll have to keep at it tomorrow." He hung up.

Now he knew what it was that was connected with Svedberg. A piece of paper that had landed on his desk by mistake. About something going on at night in the Ystad maternity ward. Had it been an attack? Something about a fake nurse?

He called Svedberg, who answered from his car.

"Where are you?" Wallander asked.

"I haven't even made it to Staffanstorp."

"Come to the station. There's something we have to check out."

"All right," Svedberg said. "I'm on my way."

It took him exactly 45 minutes. It was just before 10 p.m. when Svedberg showed up in the door of Wallander's office. By that time Wallander had already started to doubt his own idea.

It was all too probable that he was just imagining things.

CHAPTER 27

He didn't fully comprehend what had happened until the door closed behind him. He went down the few steps to his car and got in behind the wheel. Then he said his own name out loud: Åke Davidsson.

From now on Åke Davidsson was going to be a very lonely man. He hadn't expected this to happen to him. He had never thought that the woman he had been in a relationship with for so many years, even though they didn't live together, would tell him that it was over, and throw him out of her house.

He started to cry. It hurt. He didn't understand. But she had been quite firm, telling him to leave and never come back. She'd met another man who wanted to move in with her.

It was almost midnight on Monday, 17 October. He peered into the darkness. He knew that he shouldn't drive after dark. His eyes weren't strong enough. He could really only drive in daylight, with special glasses. He squinted through the windscreen. He could only just make out the contours of the road. But he had no choice, he couldn't stay here all night. He had to go back to Malmö.

He started the engine and turned onto the road, still feeling upset. He was really having trouble seeing. Maybe it would get easier when he got on to the motorway. But first he had to get out of Lödinge.

He took a wrong turn. There were so many side roads, and they all looked alike in the dark. After half an hour he knew that he was completely lost. He reached a courtyard where the road seemed to come to a dead end, and started to turn around. Suddenly he caught sight of a shadow in his headlights. Someone was coming towards the car. He felt relieved at once. There was someone out there who would tell him which way to go. He opened the car door and got out.

Then everything went black.

It took Svedberg a quarter of an hour to find the paper Wallander wanted to see. Wallander had made himself quite clear when Svedberg arrived back just before 10 p.m.

"This might be a shot in the dark," Wallander had told him. "But we're looking for a woman with the initials K.A. who recently gave birth or will soon give birth somewhere in Skåne. We thought she was in Lund, but that turned out to be wrong. Maybe she's here in Ystad instead. I've been told that Ystad's maternity ward is known even outside the country for its practices. Something strange has occurred there one night, and then a second time, and I want to know what happened."

When Svedberg had found the paper, he went back to Wallander, who was waiting impatiently.

"Ylva Brink," Svedberg said. "She's my cousin, a distant cousin. And she's a midwife at the maternity ward. She came here to report that an unknown woman had showed up one night in her ward. It made her nervous."

"Why is that?"

"It's simply not normal for a stranger to be in the maternity ward at night."

"We need to take a good look at this," Wallander said. "When was the first time it happened?"

"The night of 30 September."

"And it made her nervous?"

"She came over here the following day, a Saturday. I talked with her for a while. That's when I made these notes."

"When was the second time?"

"The night of 13 October. Ylva happened to be working that night too. That's when she was knocked to the ground. I was called out there in the morning."

"What happened?"

"The woman showed up again. When Ylva tried to stop her, she was knocked down. Ylva said it felt like being kicked by a horse."

"She'd never seen this woman before?"

"Just that one other time."

"She was wearing a uniform?"

"Yes. But Ylva was positive she wasn't on the nursing staff."

"How could she be sure? There must be a lot of people she wouldn't recognise who work at the hospital."

"She was positive. I'm afraid that I didn't ask her why."

"This woman had an interest in the maternity ward between 30 September and 13 October," Wallander said. "She made two visits late at night, not hesitating to knock down a midwife. So what was she really up to?"

"That's what Ylva wants to know too."

"She has no answer?"

"They went over the ward both times, but everything was in order."

Wallander looked at his watch. It was almost 10.45 p.m.

"I want you to call your cousin," he said. "Even if you have to wake her up."

Svedberg nodded. Wallander pointed at his phone. He knew that Svedberg, generally forgetful, had a good memory for phone numbers. He dialled the number. It rang and rang. No answer.

"If she's not home, that means she's working," Svedberg said.

Wallander jumped up.

"Even better," he said. "I haven't been back to the maternity ward since Linda was born."

"The old wing was torn down," Svedberg said. "The whole place is new."

It took them only a few minutes to drive to the hospital. Wallander remembered the night several years ago when he'd woken up with violent pains in his chest and thought he was having a heart attack. Since then the hospital had been remodelled. They rang the bell and a guard came at once and opened the door. Wallander showed him his identification, and they took the stairs to the maternity ward. A woman was waiting for them at the door to the ward.

"My cousin," Svedberg said. "Ylva Brink."

Wallander shook her hand, catching a glimpse of a nurse in the background. Ylva took them to a small office.

"It's calm right now," she said. "But that can change at any minute."

"I'll get right to the point," Wallander said. "I know that all information on patients is confidential, and I'm not intending to challenge that rule. The only thing I want to know is whether between 30 September and 13 October a woman gave birth here whose initials were K.A. K as in Karin and A as in Andersson."

The woman looked uneasy.

"Has something happened?"

"No," Wallander said. "I just need to identify someone, that's all."

"I can't tell you," she said. "That information is confidential unless the patient has signed a release form allowing details about her to be divulged. I'm certain that the rule must also apply to initials."

"My question will be answered sooner or later," Wallander said. "My problem is that I need to know right now."

"I still can't help you."

Svedberg had been sitting in silence. Wallander saw that he was frowning.

"Is there a men's room here?" he asked.

"Around the corner."

Svedberg nodded to Wallander.

"You said that you needed to go."

Wallander understood. He got up and left the room.

He waited for five minutes before he went back. Ylva Brink was not there. Svedberg stood leaning over several papers lying on the desk.

"What did you say to her?" Wallander asked.

"That she shouldn't embarrass the family," Svedberg replied. "I also explained that she could spend a year in jail."

"For what?" Wallander asked in surprise.

"Obstructing the discharge of official duties."

"There isn't such an offence, is there?"

"She doesn't know that. Here are all the names. I think we'd better read fast."

They went through the list. None of the women had the initials K.A. Wallander realised it was as he had feared. Another dead end.

"Maybe those weren't someone's initials," Svedberg said thoughtfully. "Maybe K.A. means something else."

"What would that be?"

"There's a Katarina Taxell here," Svedberg replied, pointing. "Maybe the letters K.A. are just an abbreviation of Katarina."

Wallander looked at the name. He went through the list again. There was no other name with the combination K.A. No Karin, no Karolina.

"You may be right," he said. "Write down the address."

"It's not here," he said. "Only her name. Maybe you'd better wait downstairs while I talk to Ylva one more time."

"Stick with the line that she shouldn't embarrass the family," Wallander said. "Don't mention bringing charges. That could cause us trouble later on. I want to know if Katarina Taxell is still here. I want to know if she's had any visitors. I want to know if there's anything special about her. Family relationships, that sort of thing. But especially, I want to know where she lives."

"This is going to take a while," Svedberg said. "Ylva is busy with a birth."

"I'll wait," Wallander said. "All night if I have to."

He took a biscuit from a plate and left the ward. When he passed the casualty ward downstairs he caught sight of a drunk man, covered in blood, who was being brought in from an ambulance. Wallander recognised him. His name was Niklasson, and he owned a junkyard outside Ystad. Normally he was sober, but occasionally he went on binges and got into fights.

Wallander knew the two medics bringing him in.

"Is it bad?" he asked them.

"Niklasson is tough," said the older of the two. "He'll

survive. He got into a fight in a pub in Sandskogen."

Wallander went out to the car park. It was chilly. They'd also have to find out if there was a Karin or Katarina in Lund. Birch could handle that. It was 11.30 p.m. He tried the doors of Svedberg's car. It was locked. He wondered if he should go back and ask for the keys. He might have to wait a long time. Instead, he began pacing back and forth in the car park.

Suddenly he was back in Rome again. Ahead of him, in the distance, was his father, out on a secret midnight excursion towards an unknown destination. A son tailing his own father. The Spanish Steps, then the fountain. His eyes glistened. An old man alone in Rome. Did he know that he was going to die soon?

Wallander stopped. He had a lump in his throat. When would he ever have the peace and quiet that he needed to work through his grief over his father? Life tossed him back and forth. He would soon be 50. It was autumn now. Night. And he was walking around in a hospital car park, freezing. What he feared most was that the world would become so hostile and alien that he'd no longer be able to handle it. What would be left then? Retire early? Ask for a desk job? End up spending 15 years going around to schools giving talks about drugs and traffic accidents?

The house, he thought. And the dog. And maybe Baiba too. An outward change is necessary. I'll start with that. Later we'll see what happens with me. My workload is too heavy. I can't continue like this.

It was past midnight. He paced the car park. The ambulance had left. Everything was quiet. He knew there were a lot of things he needed to think through, but he was too tired. The only thing he could manage to do was wait. And keep moving so he wouldn't freeze.

Finally Svedberg appeared. He was walking fast. Wallander could see that he had news.

"Katarina Taxell is from Lund," he said.

Wallander felt his excitement rise.

"Is she here?"

"She had her baby on 15 October. She's gone home already."

"Do you have the address?"

"I've got more than that. She's a single mother, there's no father listed in the records. And she didn't have any visitors while she was here."

Wallander realised that he was holding his breath. "Then it could be her," he said. "The woman called K.A."

They hurried back to the station. At the entrance Svedberg braked hard to avoid hitting a hare that had wandered into town. They sat down in the empty canteen. The phone rang in the duty officers' room. Wallander filled a cup with bitter coffee.

"She couldn't be the one who stuffed Blomberg in a sack," Svedberg said, scratching his scalp with a coffee spoon. "There's no way that a new mother would go out and kill someone."

"She's a link," Wallander said. "If what I'm thinking is true. She fits in between Blomberg and the person who seems most important right now.

"The nurse who knocked Ylva down?"

"That's the one."

Svedberg strained to follow Wallander's thoughts.

"So you think this nurse showed up at the maternity ward to see her?"

"Yes."

"But why did she come at night? Why didn't she come during normal visiting hours? There must be visiting hours, surely? And no-one writes down who visits patients, or who has visitors, do they?"

Wallander saw that Svedberg's questions were important. He had to answer them before they could continue.

"She didn't want to be seen," he said. "That's the only conceivable explanation."

"Seen by whom?" Svedberg said stubbornly. "Was she afraid of being recognised? Did she not want even Katarina Taxell to see her? Did she visit the hospital at night to look at a woman asleep?"

"I don't know," Wallander said. "It's strange, I agree."

"There's only one conceivable explanation," Svedberg continued. "She comes at night because she could be recognised in the daytime."

Wallander pondered this. "So you're saying that someone who works there during the day might have recognised her?"

"You can't ignore the fact that she has twice visited the maternity ward at night. And then she gets involved in a situation where it's necessary to assault my cousin, who was doing nothing wrong."

"There might be an alternative explanation," Wallander said

"What's that?"

"Night could be the only time she is able to visit the maternity ward."

Svedberg nodded thoughtfully.

"That's possible, of course. But why?"

"There could be lots of reasons. Where she lives. Her work. Maybe she wants to make these visits in secret."

Svedberg pushed his coffee cup away.

"Her visits must have been important. She went there twice."

"We can put together a timetable," Wallander said. "The first time she came was on the night of 30 September. At the hour when everyone is at their most tired, and least alert. She stays a few minutes and then disappears. Two weeks later she repeats the whole thing. At the same hour. This time she's stopped by Ylva Brink, who is knocked down. Then she disappears without a trace."

"Katarina Taxell has her child several days later."

"And the woman doesn't come back. On the other hand, Eugen Blomberg is murdered."

"Do you think a nurse is behind all this?"

They looked at each other without saying anything.

Wallander suddenly realised that he had forgotten to tell Svedberg to ask Ylva Brink about an important detail.

"Do you remember the plastic holder we found in Gösta Runfeldt's suitcase?" he said. "The kind used by the hospital staff?"

Svedberg nodded. He remembered.

"Call the maternity ward," Wallander said. "Ask Ylva if she remembers whether the woman who knocked her down was wearing a name tag."

Svedberg got up to use the phone. The conversation was brief.

"She's positive that she was wearing a name tag," he said. "Both times."

"Could she read the name on the tag?"

"She isn't sure that there was a name."

Wallander thought a moment.

"She might have lost the badge the first time," he said. "Somewhere she got hold of a hospital uniform, so she could also have got a new plastic holder."

"It'd be impossible to find any fingerprints at the hospital," Svedberg said. "It's always being cleaned. Besides, we don't even know if she touched anything."

"She wasn't wearing gloves, at least," Wallander asked. "Ylva would have noticed that."

Svedberg tapped his forehead with the coffee spoon.

"Maybe so," he said. "Ylva said that the woman grabbed hold of her when she hit her."

"She only grabbed her clothes," Wallander said. "And we won't find anything on them."

For a moment he felt discouraged.

"Even so, we should talk to Nyberg," he said. "Maybe she touched the bed that Katarina Taxell was lying in. We have to try. If we can find fingerprints that match with those that we found in Runfeldt's suitcase, the investigation would take a big leap forward. Then we could look for the same fingerprints on Eriksson and Blomberg."

Svedberg pushed across his notes on Katarina Taxell. Wallander saw that she was 33, and self-employed, although it didn't say what her occupation was. She lived in central Lund.

"We'll go there first thing tomorrow morning," he said. "Since the two of us have been working on it tonight, we might as well continue. Now I think it'd be smart for us to get a few hours sleep."

"It's strange," Svedberg said. "First we're looking for a mercenary soldier, and now we're looking for a nurse."

"Who presumably isn't really a nurse," Wallander interjected.

"We don't know that for sure," Svedberg replied. "Just because Ylva didn't recognise her doesn't mean that she's not a nurse."

"You're right. We can't exclude that possibility." He got up.

"I'll drive you home," Svedberg said. "How is your car?"

"I really should get a new one, but I don't know how I'm going to afford it."

One of the duty officers rushed into the room.

"I knew you were here," he said. "I think something has happened."

Wallander felt the knot in his stomach. Not again, he thought.

"There's a man lying badly injured on the side of the road between Sövestad and Lödinge. A lorry driver found him. We don't know whether he was run over or attacked. An ambulance is on the way out there, but I thought that since it was close to Lödinge . . . "

He never finished his sentence. Svedberg and Wallander were already on their way out of the room.

They arrived just as the medics were lifting the injured man onto a stretcher. Wallander recognised them as the ones he had spoken to outside the hospital earlier.

"Like ships passing in the night," said one of them.

"Was it a car accident?" Wallander asked him.

"If so, it was a hit-and-run. But it looks more like an assault."

Wallander looked around. The stretch of road was deserted.

"Who would be walking around here in the middle of the night?" he asked.

The man's face was covered in blood. He wheezed faintly.

"We're going now," the medic said. "We've got to hurry. He might have internal injuries."

The ambulance left. They searched the site in the

headlights of Svedberg's car. A few minutes later a squad car arrived from Ystad. Svedberg and Wallander hadn't found anything. Not even any skid marks. Svedberg told the officers what had happened, and then they set off back to the station. It was getting windy. The thermometer in Svedberg's car read 3°C.

"This is probably not related," Wallander said. "If you drop me off at the hospital, you can go home and get some sleep. At least one of us should be awake in the morning."

"Where should I pick you up?" Svedberg asked.

"At Mariagatan. Let's say 6 a.m. Martinsson gets up early. Call him and tell him what happened. Ask him to talk to Nyberg about the plastic holder. And tell him that we're going to Lund."

For the second time that night Wallander found himself outside the hospital. When he arrived at the casualty ward, the man was being treated. Wallander sat down and waited. He was exhausted. He couldn't stop himself from falling asleep. He woke abruptly when someone said his name, and at first he didn't know where he was. He'd been dreaming that he was walking along dark streets, searching for his father, but he couldn't find him.

A doctor was standing in front of him. Wallander was instantly wide awake.

"He's going to make it," the doctor said. "But he was severely beaten."

"So it wasn't a car accident?"

"No. An assault. As far as we can tell, he hasn't suffered any internal injuries."

"Did he have any papers on him?"

The doctor gave him an envelope. Wallander took out a wallet, which contained a driver's licence, among other things. The man's name was Åke Davidsson. Wallander noticed that he wasn't supposed to drive at night.

"Can I talk to him?"

"I think it'd be better to wait."

Wallander decided to ask Hansson or Höglund to follow it up. If this was an assault case, they'd have to leave it in someone else's hands for the time being. They just didn't have the time.

Wallander got up to leave.

"We found something that I think might interest you," the doctor said.

He handed him a piece of paper. Wallander read the scrawled message: "A burglar neutralised by the night guards."

"What night guards?" he asked.

"I read in the papers about a citizen militia being formed," said the doctor. "Isn't it possible that they would call themselves the night guards?"

Wallander stared at the message in disbelief.

"There's something else that points to it," the doctor continued. "The paper was attached to his body. It was stapled to his skin."

Wallander shook his head.

"This is fucking incredible," he said.

"Yes," the doctor said. "It's incredible that it's gone this far."

Wallander never liked to call a taxi. He walked home through the empty streets. He thought about Katarina Taxell. And Åke Davidsson.

When he got home, he stretched out on the sofa with a blanket over him, taking off only his jacket and shoes. The alarm clock was set. But he found that he couldn't sleep. He was starting to get a headache. He went out to the kitchen and took some aspirin. The streetlight swayed in the wind outside his window. Eventually he lay down again, and dozed uneasily until his alarm went off. When he sat up on the sofa he felt more tired than he had on lying down. He went to the bathroom, washed his face with cold water, and then changed his shirt. While he waited for the coffee to brew, he called Hansson at home. It took a long time before he answered. Wallander knew that he had woken him up.

"I'm not done with the Östersund papers," Hansson said. "I was up until 2 a.m. I have about four kilos left."

"We'll talk about that later," Wallander interrupted him. "I need you to go to the hospital and talk to a man named Åke Davidsson. He was assaulted somewhere near Lödinge last night and left lying by the side of the road, by people who are probably part of a citizen militia. I want you to look after it."

"What should I do about the Östersund papers?"

"You'll have to deal with those at the same time. Svedberg and I are going to Lund. I'll tell you more later."

He hung up before Hansson could ask any questions. He didn't have the energy to answer them.

At 6 a.m. Svedberg was parked outside. Wallander stood at the kitchen window with his coffee cup and watched him pull up.

"I talked to Martinsson," Svedberg said when Wallander got into the car. "He was going to ask Nyberg to start work on the plastic holder."

"Did Martinsson understand what we came up with?"

"I think so."

"Then let's go."

Wallander leaned back and closed his eyes. The best thing he could do on the way to Lund was sleep.

* * *

Katarina Taxell lived in a block of flats on a square that Wallander wasn't familiar with.

"It might be best if we call Birch," Wallander said. "So there won't be any trouble later on."

Svedberg reached him at home. He handed the phone to Wallander, who explained what had developed. Birch said he'd be there within 20 minutes. They sat in the car and waited. The sky was grey, and the wind had picked up. Birch drew up behind them and they went inside.

"I'll stay in the background," Birch said. "You can conduct the conversation."

Svedberg rang the bell of a flat on the third floor. The door opened almost at once. A woman wearing a dressing gown stood in front of them. She had dark circles under her eyes. She reminded Wallander of Ann-Britt.

Wallander tried to sound as friendly as possible. But he noted her reaction when he said that he was a police officer from Ystad. They went into the flat, which was small and cramped. Everywhere were signs that she had just had a baby. It reminded Wallander of how his own home had looked when Linda was just born. They went into a living room with light-coloured, wooden furniture. On the table lay a brochure that caught Wallander's attention. "Taxell's Hair Products".

"I apologise for coming so early in the morning," he said as they sat down. "But this can't wait."

He wasn't sure how to continue. She sat across from him and didn't take her eyes off his face.

"You've just had a child at Ystad's maternity ward," he said.

"A boy," she replied. "He was born on 15 October."

"My congratulations," Wallander said. Svedberg and Birch murmured something similar.

"About two weeks before that," Wallander continued, "or to be precise, on the night of 30 September, I wonder if you had a visitor sometime after midnight?"

She gave him a look of incomprehension. "Who would that have been?"

"A nurse who you might not have seen before?"

"I knew all of the nurses who worked at night."

"This woman came back two weeks later," he continued. "And we think she was there to visit you."

"At night?"

"Yes. Sometime after 2 a.m."

"No-one visited me. And besides, I'm a sound sleeper."

Wallander nodded slowly. Birch was standing behind the sofa. Svedberg was sitting on a chair against the wall. All of a sudden it was quiet. They were waiting for Wallander to go on, and he planned to do so in a moment. But first he wanted to collect himself. He was still tired. He really should ask her why she was in the maternity ward for so long. Were there complications with her pregnancy? But he didn't ask her this. Something else was more important.

She wasn't telling the truth, he knew it. He was convinced that she'd had a visitor, and that she knew the woman who'd been to see her.

CHAPTER 28

Suddenly a child started to cry.

Katarina Taxell got up and left the room. At that moment Wallander decided how he would proceed with the interview. He had sensed that she was being evasive. His years as a policeman had taught him to tell when someone was lying. He stood up and went over to the window where Birch was standing. Svedberg followed. Wallander spoke in a low voice, keeping his eye on the door.

"She's not telling the truth," he said.

The others didn't seem to have noticed anything, or weren't as convinced as he was, but they made no objections.

"This may take some time," Wallander went on. "But since in my opinion she's crucial for us, I'm not going to give up. She knows who that woman is, and I'm more convinced than ever that she's important."

Birch suddenly seemed to understand the connection.

"You mean there might be a woman behind all this? The killer is a woman?" He sounded almost frightened by his own words.

"She doesn't necessarily have to be the killer," Wallander said. "But there is a woman somewhere near the heart of this investigation. I'm certain of that. At the very least she's blocking our view of what's behind all this. Which is why we have to get to her as soon as possible. We have to find out who she is."

The crying stopped. Svedberg and Wallander returned quickly to their places in the room. A minute went by. Katarina Taxell came back and sat down on the sofa. Wallander could see that she was very much on her guard.

"Let's return to the maternity ward in Ystad," Wallander said in a friendly voice. "You say that you were asleep. And nobody visited you there at night?"

"That's right."

"You live here in Lund. Yet you choose to give birth in Ystad. Why?"

"I prefer the methods they practise there."

"I understand," Wallander said. "My own daughter was born in Ystad."

She didn't respond. Wallander sensed that she wanted only to answer the questions. She wasn't going to say anything voluntarily.

"I have to ask you some questions of a personal nature," he continued. "Since this is not an interrogation, you can choose not to answer. But then I must warn you that we may have to take you down to the police station and arrange a formal interrogation. We came here because we're looking for information connected with a number of extremely brutal and violent crimes."

Still she didn't react. Her gaze was fixed on his face. It felt as if she was staring straight into his head. Something about her eyes made him nervous.

"Did you understand what I said?"

"I understand. I'm not stupid."

"Do you agree that I can ask you some questions of a personal nature?"

"I won't know until I hear them."

"It seems that you live alone in this flat. You're not married?"

"No."

The reply came very swiftly and hard, Wallander thought, as if she was hitting something.

"May I ask who the father of your child is?"

"I don't think I'll answer that. It's of no concern to anyone but myself. And the child."

"If the child's father has been the victim of a violent crime, I would say it has something to do with the matter that I am concerned with."

"That would mean that you knew who the father of my child is. But you don't. So the question is unreasonable."

Wallander saw that she was right. There was nothing wrong with her mind.

"Let me ask another question. Do you know a man named Eugen Blomberg?"

"Yes."

"In what way do you know him?"

"I know him."

"Do you know that he was murdered?"

"Yes."

"How do you know that?"

"I saw it in the paper this morning."

"Is he the father of your child?"

"No."

She's a good liar, thought Wallander. But not good enough.

"You and Eugen Blomberg had a relationship, didn't you?"

"That's correct."

"But he isn't the father of your child?"

"No."

"How long did you have this relationship?"

"For two and a half years."

"It must have been kept secret, since he was married."

"He lied to me. I didn't find out about that until much later."

"What happened then?"

"I ended it."

"When did that happen?"

"About a year ago."

"After that you never met again?"

"That's right."

Wallander seized the moment and went on the attack.

"We've found letters at his house that you wrote to him as recently as a few months ago."

She stood her ground.

"We wrote letters, but we didn't meet."

"The whole thing seems rather strange."

"He wrote letters. I answered them. He wanted us to meet again. I didn't."

"Because you had met another man?"

"Because I was pregnant."

"And you won't tell us the father's name?"

"No."

Wallander cast a glance at Svedberg, who was staring at the floor. Birch was looking out the window. Wallander knew they were both on tenterhooks.

"Who do you think might have killed Eugen Blomberg?"

Wallander sent off the question at full force. Birch moved at the window. The floor creaked under his weight. Svedberg switched to staring at his hands.

"I don't know who would have wanted to kill him."

The child started fretting again. She got up at once and left them. Wallander looked at the others. Birch shook his head. Wallander tried to evaluate the situation. It would create big trouble if he took a woman with a three-day-old baby in for interrogation. And she wasn't suspected of a particular crime. He made a quick decision. They huddled at the window once again.

"I'll stop the questions there," Wallander said. "But I want her put under surveillance. And I want to know everything you can possibly dig up on her. She seems to have a business that sells hair products. I want to know all about her parents, her friends, what she did earlier in her life. Run her through all the databases. I want her life completely mapped out."

"We'll take care of it," Birch said.

"Svedberg will stay here in Lund. We need someone who's familiar with the earlier murders."

"Actually, I'd prefer to go home," Svedberg said. "You know that I don't do well outside Ystad."

"I know that," Wallander answered. "I'm afraid that right now it can't be helped. I'll ask someone to relieve you when I get back to Ystad. But we can't have people driving back and forth unnecessarily."

Suddenly the woman was standing at the door, holding the baby. Wallander smiled. They went over and looked at the boy. Svedberg, who liked children even though he didn't have any of his own, started playing with him.

Something struck Wallander. He thought back to when Linda was a baby, when Mona had carried her around and when he had done it himself, always terrified of dropping her. Then it came to him. She wasn't holding the baby against her body. It was as if the baby was something that didn't really belong to her. He was getting angry, but he managed to hide it.

"We won't trouble you any longer," he said. "But we'll be in touch again, no doubt."

"I hope you catch the person who murdered Eugen," she said.

Wallander looked at her carefully. Then he nodded.

"Yes, we're going to solve this. I can promise you that."

When the three men reached the street, the wind had picked up.

"What do you think of her?" Birch asked.

"She's not telling the truth, of course," Wallander said. "But it didn't seem like she was lying, either."

Birch gave him a quizzical look.

"How am I supposed to take that? That it's as though she was lying and telling the truth at the same time?"

"Something like that. What it means I don't know."

"I noticed a little detail," Svedberg said suddenly. "She said she hoped we caught 'the person', not 'the man' who murdered Eugen Blomberg."

Wallander nodded. He had noticed it too.

"Does that necessarily mean anything?" Birch asked sceptically.

"No," Wallander said. "But both Svedberg and I noticed it. And that might mean something in itself."

They decided that Wallander would drive back to Ystad in Svedberg's car. He promised to send someone to relieve Svedberg in Lund as soon as he could.

"This is important," he told Birch once again. "Katarina Taxell had a visit at the hospital from this woman. We have to find out who she is. The midwife she knocked down gave a good description."

"Give me the description," said Birch. "She might show up at her home too."

"She was quite tall," said Wallander. "Ylva Brink herself is five-nine. She thought this woman was about five-eleven. Dark, straight, shoulder-length hair. Blue eyes, pointed nose, thin lips. She was stocky without looking overweight. No prominent bust. The power of her blow shows that she's strong. And we can assume that she's in good physical shape."

"That description fits quite a few people," Birch said.

"All descriptions do," Wallander said. "Even so, you know right away when you find the right person."

"Did the woman say anything? What was her voice like?"

"She didn't say a word. She just knocked her to the ground."

"Did she notice the woman's teeth?"

Wallander looked at Svedberg, who shook his head.

"Was she wearing make-up?"

"Nothing out of the ordinary."

"What did her hands look like? Was she wearing false nails?"

"We know for certain that she wasn't. Ylva said she would have noticed."

Birch had made some notes. He nodded.

"We'll see what we can come up with," he said. "We'll do the surveillance very discreetly. She's going to be on her guard."

They said goodbye. Svedberg gave Wallander his car keys. On the way to Ystad Wallander tried to comprehend why Katarina Taxell didn't want to reveal that she'd had night-time visits while she was in the Ystad maternity ward. Who was the woman? How was she connected to Taxell and Blomberg? Where did the threads lead from there? What did the chain of events look like that led to his murder?

He was afraid that he might be on a completely wrong track, leading the investigation way off course. Nothing caused him more torment. Prevented him from sleeping, gave him an upset stomach. The thought that he could be heading at full speed towards the collapse of a criminal investigation. He'd been through it all before, the moment when an investigation suddenly shattered. There would be nothing to do but start again from the beginning. And it would be his fault.

It was 9.30 a.m. when he parked outside the Ystad police station. Ebba stopped him in reception.

"It's total chaos here," she said.

"What happened?"

"Chief Holgersson wants to speak to you right away. It's about that man you and Svedberg found on the road last night."

"I'll go and talk to her," Wallander said.

"Do it now," Ebba said.

He went straight to her office. The door was open. Hansson was sitting inside, looking pale. Lisa Holgersson was more upset than he had ever seen her. She motioned him to a chair.

"I think you should hear what Hansson has to say."

Wallander took off his jacket and sat down.

"I had a long conversation with Åke Davidsson this morning."

"How is he?" Wallander said.

"It looks worse than it really is. It's still bad, but nowhere near as bad as the story he had to tell."

Afterwards he knew that Hansson hadn't been exaggerating. Wallander listened first in surprise, then with growing indignation. Hansson was clear and to the point. Wallander could hardly believe what he was hearing; it was something he never thought could happen. Now they'd have to live with it. Sweden was steadily changing. Usually these changes were subtle, nothing obvious at the time. But sometimes Wallander, when he observed these changes as a policeman, felt a shudder pass through the entire framework of society. Hansson's story about Åke Davidsson was one such shudder, and it shook Wallander to the core.

Åke Davidsson was a civil servant in the social welfare office in Malmö. He was classified as partially disabled because of bad eyesight. After struggling for many years, he had finally got a restricted driver's licence. Since the late 1970s, Davidsson had a relationship with a woman in Lödinge. It had ended the previous evening. Usually Davidsson would sleep over in Lödinge, since he wasn't allowed to drive in the dark. But this time he had no choice. He got lost, and finally stopped to ask directions. He was attacked by a night patrol of volunteers who had gathered in Lödinge. They accused him of being a burglar and refused to believe his explanation. His glasses vanished; maybe they were crushed. He was beaten senseless and didn't wake up until the ambulance men lifted him onto the stretcher.

There was more.

"Davidsson is a peaceful man who suffers from high blood pressure. I spoke with some of his colleagues in Malmö, and they were deeply distressed. One of them told me something that Davidsson hadn't mentioned."

Wallander was listening intently.

"Davidsson is a dedicated and active member of Amnesty International," Hansson said. "Now that organisation might begin to take an interest in Sweden, if this rise of the citizen militia and attacks on people isn't stopped."

Wallander was speechless. He felt sick and dizzy.

"These thugs have a leader," Hansson went on. "His

name is Eskil Bengtsson, and he owns a lorry company in Lödinge."

"We've got to put a stop to this," Chief Holgersson said. "Even though we're up to our necks in murder investigations. At least we have to plan what to do."

"It's quite simple," Wallander said, getting to his feet. "We drive out and arrest Eskil Bengtsson. And we also bring in everyone who's mixed up in this militia. Åke Davidsson will have to identify them, one by one."

"But his eyesight is terrible," Holgersson said.

"People who don't see well often have excellent hearing," Wallander replied. "You said that the men were talking while they were beating him."

"I wonder if this will hold up," she said doubtfully. "What kind of proof have we got?"

"It holds up for me," Wallander said. "Of course you can always order me not to leave the station."

She shook her head. "Go ahead. The sooner the better."

Wallander nodded to Hansson. They went out into the hall.

"I want two squad cars," Wallander said, poking Hansson on the shoulder with his finger for emphasis. "They should drive there with lights flashing and sirens going, both when we leave Ystad and when we enter Lödinge. It wouldn't hurt to let the press know about this either."

"We can't do that," Hansson said, looking anxious.

"Of course we can't," Wallander said. "We're leaving in ten minutes. We can talk about your Östersund work in the car."

"I've got a kilo of papers left," Hansson said. "It's an incredible amount of research. Layer after layer. There's even a son who took over from his father as investigator."

"In the car," Wallander interrupted him. "Not here."

Wallander went out to reception. He said something to Ebba in a low voice. She nodded and promised to do what he'd asked. Five minutes later they were on their way. They left Ystad with lights flashing and sirens on.

"What are we going to arrest Bengtsson for?" Hansson asked.

"He's suspected of aggravated assault," Wallander replied. "Instigating violence. Davidsson must have been transported to the road, so we'll try kidnapping too. And inciting a riot."

"You're going to have Åkeson on your back for this."

"I'm not so sure about that," Wallander said.

"It feels as though we're on our way to arrest some pretty dangerous men," Hansson said.

"You're right. We're after dangerous people. Right now I have a hard time thinking of anything that is more dangerous for the rule of law in this country."

They pulled up at Eskil Bengtsson's farmhouse, which lay on the road into the village. There were two trucks and a digger parked nearby. A dog was barking furiously.

"Let's get him," Wallander said.

Just as they reached the front door it was opened by a stocky man with a pot belly. Wallander glanced at Hansson, who nodded.

"Inspector Wallander of the Ystad Police," he introduced himself. "Get your jacket. You're coming with us."

"Where the hell to?"

The man's arrogance almost made Wallander lose control. Hansson noticed this and poked him in the arm.

"You're coming to Ystad," Wallander said with icy calm. "And you damn well know why."

"I haven't done anything," Bengtsson said.

"Yes, you have," Wallander said. "In fact, you've done way too much. If you don't get your jacket you'll have to come along without it."

A small, thin woman appeared at the man's side.

"What's going on?" she yelled in a high-pitched, piercing voice. "What did he do?"

"You keep out of this," the man said, shoving her back inside the house.

"That does it, handcuff him," Wallander said.

Hansson stared at him uncomprehendingly.

"Why?"

Wallander's patience was at an end. He turned to one of the officers and took his handcuffs. He told Bengtsson to stick out his hands, and snapped the cuffs on him. It happened so fast that Bengtsson didn't think to resist. At the same time there was a flash from a camera. A photographer who had just hopped out of his car had taken a picture.

"How the hell does the press know we're here?" Hansson asked.

"No idea," Wallander said. Ebba was reliable and fast. "Let's go."

The woman came outside again. Suddenly she jumped on Hansson and started hitting him with her fists. The photographer took more pictures. Wallander escorted Bengtsson to the car.

"You're going to get shit for this," Bengtsson said.

Wallander smiled. "Maybe. But nothing compared to what you're going to get. You want to start with the names right now? The men who were with you last night?"

Bengtsson said nothing more. Wallander pushed him hard into the back seat. Hansson had finally managed to get away from the hysterical woman.

"Goddamn it, she's the one who should be in the kennel."

He was shaking. He had a deep scratch on one cheek.

"We're leaving now," Wallander said. "Get in the other car and drive over to the hospital. I want to know if Davidsson heard any names. Or whether he saw anyone who could have been Eskil Bengtsson."

Hansson nodded and left. The photographer came over to Wallander.

"We got an anonymous tip-off," he said. "What's going on?"

"A number of individuals attacked and battered an innocent man last night. They seem to be part of some sort of citizen militia. The man was guilty of nothing more than taking a wrong turn. They claimed he was a burglar. They almost beat him to death."

"And the man in the car?"

"He's suspected of having participated," Wallander said. "We know that he's behind this militia. We're not going to have vigilantes in Sweden. Here in Skåne or anywhere else in the country."

The photographer wanted to ask another question, but Wallander raised his hand to stop him.

"There'll be a press conference later. We're leaving now."

Wallander told the officers that he wanted sirens on the way back too. Several cars full of curiosity-seekers had stopped outside the farmhouse. Wallander squeezed into the back seat next to Eskil Bengtsson.

"Shall we start with the names?" he asked. "It'll save a lot of time. Both yours and mine."

Bengtsson didn't answer. Wallander could smell the strong odour of his sweat.

* * *

It took Wallander three hours to get Bengtsson to admit that he had taken part in the assault on Davidsson. Then everything happened quickly. Bengtsson told him the names of the three other men who'd been with him. Wallander had them all brought in at once. Åke Davidsson's car, which had been left in an abandoned shed, was discovered. Just after 3 p.m. Wallander convinced Åkeson to keep the four men in custody. He went straight from his talk with Åkeson to the room where several reporters were waiting. Chief Holgersson had already informed them of the events of the previous night. For once Wallander was actually looking forward to meeting the press. Although he knew that the chief had already given them the background, he recounted the sequence of events for them.

"Four men have just been indicted by the prosecutor," he said. "We have absolutely no doubt that they are guilty of assault. But what's even more serious is that there are another five or six men involved in the group, a vigilante guard out in Lödinge. These are individuals who have decided to put themselves above the law. We can see what that leads to in this case: an innocent man, with poor eyesight and high blood pressure, is almost murdered when he gets lost. Is this the way we want it to be? That you might be risking your life when you make a wrong turn? Is that how things stand? That from now on we're all thieves, rapists, and killers in one another's eyes? I can't make it any plainer. Some of the people who are lured into joining these illegal and dangerous militias probably don't understand what they're getting involved with. They can be excused if they resign immediately. But those who joined and were fully conscious of what they were doing, are indefensible. These four men that we arrested today unfortunately belong to the latter group. We can only hope they receive sentences that will serve as deterrents to others."

Wallander put force into his words. The reporters immediately bombarded him with questions, but there weren't many in attendance, and they only wanted details clarified. Höglund and Hansson were standing at the back of the room. Wallander searched through the group for the man from the *Anmärkaren*, but he wasn't there.

After less than half an hour the press conference was over.

"You handled it extremely well," Chief Holgersson said.

"There was only one way to handle it," Wallander replied.

Höglund and Hansson applauded when he came over to them. Wallander was not amused. He was hungry, and he needed some air. He looked at the clock.

"Give me an hour. Let's meet at 5 p.m. Is Svedberg back yet?"

"He's on his way."

"Who's relieving him?"

"Augustsson."

"Who's that?" Wallander asked.

"One of the policemen from Malmö."

Wallander had forgotten his name. He nodded.

"We'll meet at 5 p.m.," he repeated. "We've got a lot to do."

He stopped in reception and thanked Ebba for her help. She smiled.

Wallander walked to the centre of town. It was windy. He sat down in the café by the bus station and had a couple of sandwiches and felt better. His head was empty. On his way back to the police station he stopped and bought a hamburger. He tossed the napkin in the rubbish bin and started thinking about Katarina Taxell again. Eskil Bengtsson no longer existed for him. He knew they'd have another confrontation with the local citizen militia. What had happened to Åke Davidsson was only the beginning.

They gathered in the conference room at the appointed time. Wallander began by telling the group everything that they had discovered about Katarina Taxell. He noticed that everyone in the room was listening with great attention. For the first time during the investigation he felt as though they were getting close to something that might be a breakthrough. This was reinforced by what Hansson had to say.

"The amount of investigative material on Krista Haberman is huge," he said. "I haven't had much time, and it's possible I may have missed something important. But I did find one thing that might be of interest."

He leafed through his notes until he found the right place.

"At some point in the 1960s Krista Haberman visited Skåne on three occasions. She had made contact with a bird-watcher who lived in Falsterbo. Many years later, long after she'd disappeared, a police officer named Fredrik Nilsson travelled from Östersund to talk to this man in Falsterbo. He took the train the whole way. The man in Falsterbo is named Tandvall. Erik Gustav Tandvall. He confirmed without hesitation that he'd received visits from Krista Haberman. It seemed as though they'd had a relationship. Detective Nilsson didn't find anything suspicious in this. The relationship between Haberman and Tandvall ended long before she vanished. Tandvall had nothing to do with her disappearance. So he was removed from the investigation and never reappears."

Up to this point Hansson had been reading from his notes. Now he looked up at everyone listening around the table.

"There was something familiar about the name," he said. "Tandvall. An unusual name. I got the feeling I'd seen it before. It took me a while before I remembered where. It was in a list of men who had worked as car salesmen for Holger Eriksson."

There was total silence in the room. The tension was high. Hansson had made an important connection.

"The car salesman's name wasn't Erik Tandvall," he continued. "His first name was Göte, Göte Tandvall. And right before this meeting I got a confirmation that he's Erik Tandvall's son. I should probably also mention that Erik Tandvall died several years ago. I haven't been able to locate the son yet."

Hansson was done. No-one said anything for a long time.

"So there's a possibility that Holger Eriksson met Krista Haberman," Wallander said slowly. "A woman who has disappeared without a trace. A woman from Svenstavik, where there is a church that has received a bequest in accordance with Eriksson's will."

Everyone knew what this meant. A connection was finally beginning to emerge.

CHAPTER 29

Just before midnight Wallander realised that they were too tired to do any more. The meeting had been going on since 5 p.m., and they had only taken short breaks to air out the conference room. Hansson had given them the opening they needed. A connection was established. The contours of a person who moved like a shadow among the three men who had been killed were being to appear. Even though they were still cautious about stating that there was a definite motive, they now had a strong feeling that they were skirting the edges of a series of events connected by revenge.

Wallander had called them together to make a unified advance through difficult terrain. Hansson had given them a direction. But they still had no map to follow. At first there was still a lingering feeling of doubt among the team. Could this really be right? That a mysterious disappearance so many years ago, revealed in kilos of investigative materials from police officers in Jämtland who were no longer alive, might help them unmask a killer who had set a trap made of sharpened bamboo stakes in a ditch in Skåne?

It was when the door opened and Nyberg came in, several minutes after 6 p.m., that all doubt was dispelled. He didn't even bother to take his usual place at the far end of the table. For once he was excited, something no-one could remember ever having seen before.

“There was a cigarette butt on the jetty,” he said. “We were able to identify a fingerprint on it.”

Wallander gave him a surprised look.

“Is that really possible? Fingerprints on a cigarette butt?”

“We were lucky,” Nyberg said. “You’re right that it’s not usually possible. But there’s one exception: if the cigarette is rolled by hand. And this one was.”

First Hansson had discovered a plausible and even likely link between a long-vanished Polish woman and Holger Eriksson, and now Nyberg told them that a fingerprint on Runfeldt’s suitcase matched one at the site where Blomberg’s body was found.

Silence fell over the room. It almost felt like too much to handle in such a short time. An investigation that had been dragging along without direction was now starting to pick up speed in earnest.

After presenting his news, Nyberg sat down.

“A killer who smokes,” Martinsson said. “That’ll be easier to find today than it was 20 years ago.”

Wallander nodded thoughtfully. “We need to find other points of intersection between these murders,” he said. “With three people dead, we need at least nine combinations. Fingerprints, times, anything that will prove that there’s a common denominator.”

He looked around the room.

“We need to put together a proper sequence of events,” he said. “We know that the person or persons behind these killings acts with appalling cruelty. We’ve discovered a deliberate element in the way the victims have been killed. But we haven’t succeeded in reading the killer’s language, the code we discussed earlier. We have a feeling that the murderer is talking to us. But what is he or she trying to say? We don’t know. The question is whether there are more patterns to the whole thing that we haven't yet found."

"You mean something like whether the killer strikes when there's a full moon?" Svedberg asked.

"That sort of thing. The symbolic full moon. What does it look like in this case? Does it exist? I'd like someone to put together a timetable. Is there anything there that might give us another lead?"

Martinsson undertook to put together what information they had. Wallander knew that – on his own initiative – Martinsson had obtained several computer programmes developed by the F.B.I. headquarters in Washington, D.C. He assumed that Martinsson saw an opportunity to make use of them.

Then they started talking about whether there actually was a geographical centre to the crimes. Höglund put a map on the slide projector, and Wallander stationed himself at the edge of the image.

"It starts in Lödinge," he said, pointing. "A person begins surveillance of Holger Eriksson's farm. We can assume that he travels by car and that he uses the tractor path on the hill behind Eriksson's tower. A year earlier someone, maybe the same person, broke into his house, without stealing anything. Possibly to warn him, leave him a sign. We don't know, but it doesn't have to be the same person."

Wallander pointed at Ystad.

"Gösta Runfeldt is looking forward to his trip to Nairobi. Everything is ready. His suitcase is packed, money changed, the tickets collected. He has even ordered a taxi for early on the morning of the day of his departure. But he never takes the trip. He disappears without a trace for three weeks."

Wallander moves his finger again. “Now to the woods west of Marsvinsholm. An orienteer training at night finds him tied to a tree, strangled, emaciated. He must have been held captive in some way during the time he was missing. So, two murders at different places, with Ystad as a kind of midpoint.”

His finger moved northeast.

“We find a suitcase along the road to Höör, not far from a point where you can turn off towards Holger Eriksson’s farm. The suitcase is lying at the side of the road as though it was placed there to be found. We can ask ourselves the question: why that particular spot? Because the road is convenient for the killer? We don’t know. This question may be more important than we’ve realised up until now.”

Wallander moved his hand again. To the southwest, to Krageholm Lake.

“Here we find Eugen Blomberg. This means we have a defined area that isn’t particularly large, only 30 or 40 kilometres between the outer points. It’s no more than half an hour by car between each site.”

He sat down.

“Let’s draw up some tentative and preliminary conclusions,” he went on. “What does this indicate?”

“Familiarity with the local area,” Höglund said. “The site in the woods at Marsvinsholm was well chosen. The suitcase was placed at a spot where there are no houses from which you could see a driver stop and leave something behind.”

“How do you know that?” Martinsson asked.

“Because I checked.”

“You can either be familiar with an area yourself, or else you can find out about it from someone else,” Wallander said. “Which seems likely in this case?”

They couldn't agree. Hansson thought that a stranger could easily have decided on each of the sites. Svedberg thought the opposite, that the place where they had found Runfeldt indicated beyond a doubt that the killer was extremely familiar with the area. Wallander had his doubts. Earlier he had tended to think of a person who was an outsider. He was no longer so sure. They didn't come to any agreement on this, and they couldn't pinpoint an obvious centre, either. It was most likely to be near to where Runfeldt's suitcase was found, but that didn't get them any further.

During the evening they kept returning to the suitcase. Why had it been put there, next to the road? And why had it been repacked, probably by a woman? They also couldn't come up with a reasonable explanation for why the underwear was missing. Hansson had suggested that Runfeldt might be the type of person who didn't wear any. No-one took that seriously. There had to be some other explanation.

At 9 p.m. they took a break to get some air. Martinsson disappeared into his office to call home, Svedberg put on his jacket to take a walk. Wallander went to the bathroom and washed his face. He looked at himself in the mirror. Suddenly he had a feeling that his appearance had changed since his father's death. What the difference was, he couldn't tell. He shook his head at his reflection. Soon he would have to make time to think about what had happened. His father had been dead for several weeks. He also thought about Baiba, the woman he cared so much about but never called.

He doubted that a policeman could combine his job with anything else. But Martinsson had an excellent relationship with his family, and Höglund had almost total responsibility for her two children. It was Wallander who didn't seem able to combine the two things.

He yawned at himself in the mirror. From the hall he could hear that they had started to reconvene. He decided that now they would have to talk about the woman who could be glimpsed in the background. They had to try to picture her and the role that she had actually played. This was the first thing he said when they closed the door.

"There's a woman involved somewhere in all of this," he said. "For the rest of this meeting, as long as we can keep at it, we have to go over the background. We talk about a motive of revenge. But we're not being very precise. Does that mean we're thinking incorrectly? That we're on the wrong track? That there might be a completely different explanation?"

They waited in silence for him to continue. Even though they all looked exhausted, he could see that they were still concentrating. He started by going back to Katarina Taxell in Lund.

"She gave birth here in Ystad," he said. "On two nights she had a visitor. I'm convinced that this woman did visit her, even though she denies it. So she's lying. Why? Who was the woman? Why won't Taxell reveal her identity? I think that we can assume that Eugen Blomberg is the father of Katarina Taxell's child – she's lying about this. I'm sure that she lied about everything during our meeting in Lund. I don't know why, but I think that we can probably assume that she holds a crucial key to this whole mess."

"Why don't we just bring her in?" Hansson asked with some vehemence.

"On what grounds?" Wallander replied. "She's a new

mother. We have to treat her carefully. And I doubt that she would tell us more than she has already if we interrogate her at Lund police station. We'll have to try to go around her, smoke out the truth another way."

Hansson nodded reluctantly.

"The third woman linked to Eugen Blomberg is his widow," Wallander continued. "She gave us a lot of important information. Probably the fact that she doesn't seem to mourn his death at all is most significant. He abused her, for a long time, and quite severely judging by her scars. She also confirms, indirectly, our theory about Katarina Taxell, since she says he has had extramarital affairs."

As he said these last words, he thought he sounded like an old-fashioned preacher. He wondered what term Höglund would have used.

"Let's say that the details surrounding Blomberg form a pattern," he said. "Which we'll come back to later."

He switched to Runfeldt. He was moving backwards, towards the first killing.

"Gösta Runfeldt was known to be a brutal man. Both his son and daughter confirm this. Behind the orchid lover, a whole different person was concealed. He was a private detective, something that we don't have a good explanation for. Was he looking for excitement? Weren't orchids enough for him?"

He switched to Runfeldt's wife.

"I made a trip to a lake outside Älmhult without knowing for sure what I would find. I don't have any proof, but I can imagine that Runfeldt actually killed his wife. We'll never know what happened out there on the ice. The main players are dead. There were no witnesses, but I still have a hunch that someone outside the family knew about it.

For lack of anything better, we have to consider the possibility that the death of his wife had something to do with Runfeldt's fate."

Wallander paused for a moment and then continued.

"So, he's taking a trip to Africa. He doesn't go. Something prevents him. How he disappears, we don't know. On the other hand, we can pinpoint the date. But we have no explanation for the break-in at his shop. We don't know where he was held prisoner. The suitcase may, of course, provide a clue. For some reason it was repacked by a woman. If so, by the same woman who smoked a hand-rolled cigarette on the jetty where Blomberg was thrown into the water."

"There could be two people," Höglund objected. "One who smoked the cigarette and left a fingerprint on the suitcase. Someone else could have repacked it."

"You're right," Wallander said. "Let's say that at least one person was present." He glanced at Nyberg.

"We're looking," Nyberg said. "We're going through Holger Eriksson's place. We've found lots of fingerprints. But so far none that match."

"The name tag," Wallander said. "The one we found in Runfeldt's suitcase. Did it have any fingerprints on it?"

Nyberg shook his head.

"It should have had," said Wallander in surprise. "You use your fingers to put it on or take it off, don't you?"

No-one had an explanation for this.

"So far we've talked about a number of women, one of whom keeps appearing," he continued. "We also have spousal abuse and possibly an undetected murder. The question we have to ask ourselves is: who would have known about these things? Who would have had a reason to seek revenge? If the motive is revenge, that is."

"There might be another thing," Svedberg said, scratching the back of his neck. "We have two old police investigations that were both archived, unsolved. One in Östersund and one in Älmhult."

Wallander nodded.

"That leaves Eriksson," he went on. "Another brutal man. After a lot of effort, or rather a lot of luck, we find a woman in his background too. A Polish woman who's been missing for 30 years or so."

He looked around the table before he concluded.

"In other words, there's a pattern," he said. "Brutal men and abused, missing, and maybe murdered women. And one step behind, a shadow that follows in the tracks of these events. A shadow that might be a woman. A woman who smokes."

Hansson dropped his pencil on the table and shook his head.

"It doesn't seem possible," he said. "Let's imagine that there's a woman involved, who seems to have enormous physical strength and a macabre imagination when it comes to methods of murder. Why would she have an interest in what happened to these women? Is she a friend of theirs? How did all these people cross paths?"

"That's not just an important question," Wallander said. "It could be crucial. How did these people come into contact with each other? Where should we start looking? Among men or among women? A car dealer, regional poet and bird-watcher; an orchid lover, private detective, and florist; and an allergy researcher. Blomberg, at any rate, doesn't seem to have had any special interests. Or should we start with the women? A mother who lies about the father of her newborn child? A woman who drowned in Stång Lake outside Älmhult ten years ago? A woman from Poland who lived in Jämtland and was interested in birds, missing for 30 years? And finally, this woman who sneaks around in the Ystad maternity ward at night and knocks down midwives? Where are the points of connection?"

The silence lasted a long time. Everyone tried to find an answer. Wallander waited. This was a key moment. He was hoping that someone would come up with an unexpected conclusion. Rydberg had told him many times that the most important task of the leader of an investigation was to stimulate his colleagues to think the unexpected. Had he been successful?

It was Höglund who at last broke the silence.

"There are some occupations that are dominated by women," she said. "Nursing is one of them."

"Patients come from all different places," Martinsson continued. "If we assume that the woman we're looking for works in an emergency room, she would have seen lots of abused women pass through. None of them knew each other. But she knew them. Their names, their patient records."

Höglund and Martinsson had come up with something that might fit.

"We don't know whether she really is a nurse," Wallander said. "All we know is that she doesn't work in the maternity ward in Ystad."

"She could work somewhere else in the hospital," Svedberg suggested.

Wallander nodded slowly. Could it really be so simple? A nurse at Ystad General Hospital?

"It should be relatively easy to find out," Hansson said. "Even though patient records are confidential, it should be possible to find out if Gösta Runfeldt's wife was treated there. And why not Krista Haberman, for that matter?"

Wallander took a new tack.

"Have Runfeldt and Eriksson ever been charged with assault? That's easily checked."

"There are also other possibilities," Höglund said, as though she felt the need to question her own previous suggestions. "There are other occcupations in which women dominate. There are crisis groups for women. Even the female officers in Skåne have their own network."

"We have to investigate all these," Wallander said. "It will take a long time and I think we have to accept that this investigation is heading in many directions at once. Especially in terms of time."

They spent the last two hours before midnight planning various strategies to be explored simultaneously, until at last they ran out of steam.

Hansson put the final question into words, the one they had all been waiting for the whole evening.

"Is it going to happen again?"

"I don't know," Wallander said. "I have a sense of incompleteness about what's happened so far. Don't ask me why. That's all I can say. Something as unprofessional as a feeling. Intuition, maybe."

"I have the same feeling," Svedberg said. He said this with such force that everyone was surprised. "Isn't it possible that we can expect a series of murders that go on indefinitely? If it's someone pointing a vengeful finger at men who have mistreated women, then it's never going to stop."

Wallander knew it was likely that Svedberg was right. He'd been trying to avoid the thought himself all along.

"There is that risk," he said. "Which in turn means that we have to catch the killer fast."

"Reinforcements," said Nyberg, who had barely uttered a word the past two hours. "Otherwise it won't work."

"Yes," Wallander said. "I agree that we're going to need them. Especially after what we've talked about tonight. We can't manage without extra help to do much more than we already are."

Hamrén raised his hand to signal that he wanted to say something. He was sitting next to the two detectives from Malmö near the far end of the long table.

"I'd like to underline that last comment," he said. "I've rarely if ever taken part in such efficient police work with so few personnel. Since I was here in the summer too, I can say with certainty that it's the rule, not the exception. If you request reinforcements, no reasonable person is going to refuse you."

The detectives from Malmö nodded in agreement.

"I'll take it up with Chief Holgersson tomorrow," Wallander said. "I'm also thinking of trying to get a few more female officers. If nothing else, it might boost morale."

The weary mood lifted for a moment. Wallander seized the opportunity and stood up. It was important to know when to end a meeting. Now was the time. They wouldn't make any more progress. They needed sleep.

Wallander went to his office. He leafed through the steadily growing stack of phone messages. Instead of putting on his jacket, he sat down in his chair. Footsteps disappeared down the hall. Soon it was quiet. He twisted the lamp down to shine on the desk. The rest of the room was dark.

It was 12.30. Without thinking he grabbed the phone and

dialled Baiba in Riga. She had irregular sleeping habits, just as he did. Sometimes she went to bed early, but just as often she stayed up half the night. She answered almost at once. She was awake. As always he tried to hear from her tone of voice whether she was glad he had called. He never felt sure ahead of time. This time he sensed that she was wary. He was instantly insecure. He wanted reassurance that everything was the way it should be. He asked her how she was, told her about the exhausting investigation. She asked a few questions. Then he didn't know how to continue. Silence began wandering back and forth between Ystad and Riga.

"When are you coming over?" he asked at last.

Her response surprised him, even though it shouldn't have.

"Do you really want me to come?"

"Why wouldn't I?"

"You never call. And when you do call, you say you really don't have time to talk to me. So how are you going to have any time to spend with me if I come to Ystad?"

"That's not how it is."

"Then how is it?"

Where his reaction came from, he had no idea. Not then or later. He tried to stop his own impulse, but he couldn't. He slammed the receiver down hard and stared at the phone. Then he got up and left the station. Even before he got to reception, he regretted it. But he knew Baiba well enough to know that she wouldn't answer if he called her back.

He stepped out into the night air. A police car rolled past and vanished in the direction of the water tower. There was no wind. The night air was chilly, the sky clear.

He didn't understand his own reaction. What would have happened if she had been there, right next to him?

He thought about the murdered men. It was as if he suddenly saw something he hadn't seen before. Part of himself was hidden in all the brutality that surrounded him. He was a part of it. Only the degree was different. Nothing else.

He shook his head. He knew he ought to call Baiba early in the morning. It didn't have to be so terrible. She understood. Fatigue could make her irritable too.

It was 1 a.m. He should go home to bed, ask an officer to drive him home. But instead he started walking. Somewhere a car skidded, tyres screeching. Then silence. He walked down the hill towards the hospital.

The investigative team had sat in the meeting for seven hours. Nothing had really happened, and yet the evening had been eventful. Clarity arises in the spaces in between, Rydberg had said once when he was quite drunk. Wallander, who was at least as drunk, had understood. He'd never forgotten it, either. They were sitting on Rydberg's balcony. Five, maybe six years ago. Rydberg was not yet ill. It was an evening in June, right before Midsummer. They were celebrating something, Wallander had forgotten what it was.

Clarity arises in the spaces in between.

He had reached the hospital. He stopped. He hesitated, but only briefly. Then he walked round the side of the hospital and rang the night bell. When a voice answered he said who he was and asked whether the midwife Ylva Brink was on duty. She was.

She met him outside the glass doors of her ward. He could see by her face that she was nervous. He smiled, but her unease didn't diminish. Maybe his smile didn't look genuine. Or the light was bad. They went inside. She asked if he'd like some coffee. He shook his head.

"I'll only stay for a moment," he said. "You must be busy."

"Yes," she replied. "But I can spare a few minutes. If it can't wait until tomorrow?"

"It probably could," Wallander replied. "But I was passing on my way home."

They went into the office. A nurse on her way in stopped when she saw Wallander.

"It can wait," she said and left.

Wallander leaned against the desk. Ylva Brink sat down.

"You must have wondered," he began, "about the woman who knocked you down. Who she was. Why she was here. Why she did what she did. You must have thought long and hard about it. You've given us a good description of her face. Maybe there's some detail you thought of afterwards."

"You're right, I've been thinking about it. But I've told you everything I can remember about her face."

He believed her.

"It doesn't have to be her face. She might have had a certain way of moving. Or a scar on her hand. A human being is a combination of so many different details. We think we can trust our memory, and that all of the details are there, just like that. Actually it's just the opposite. Imagine an object that can almost float, that sinks through water extremely slowly. That's the way memory works."

She shook her head.

"It happened so fast. I don't remember anything except what I've already told you. And I've really tried."

Wallander nodded. He hadn't really expected anything else.

"What has she done?" Ylva asked.

"She knocked you down. We're looking for her. We think she might have some important information for us. That's all I can tell you."

A clock on the wall read 1.27 a.m. He put out his hand to say goodbye, and they left the office.

Suddenly she stopped him.

"There might be something else," she said hesitantly.

"What is it?"

"I didn't think about it then, when I went towards her and she knocked me down. It wasn't until afterwards."

"What?"

"She was wearing a perfume that was special."

"In what way?"

She gave him almost an imploring look.

"I don't know. How does one describe a scent?"

"That's one of the hardest things to do. But give it a try."

He could see that she was making a real effort.

"No," she said. "I can't find the words. I just know that it was special. Maybe you could say that it was harsh."

"More like after-shave lotion?"

She looked at him in surprise.

"Yes," she said. "How did you know that?"

"It was just a thought."

"Maybe I shouldn't have said anything. Since I can't express myself clearly."

"Oh no," he replied. "This could turn out to be valuable. We never know ahead of time."

They parted at the glass doors. Wallander took the lift down and left the hospital. He walked fast. Now he had to get some sleep. He thought about what she had said. If there were any traces of perfume left on the name tag holder, she would be asked to smell it early the next morning. He already knew that it would be the same. They were looking for a woman. Her perfume was special. But would they ever find her?

CHAPTER 30

At 7.35 a.m. her shift ended. She was in a hurry, driven by a sudden restlessness. It was a cold, wet morning in Malmö. She hurried towards the car park. Normally she would have driven straight home and gone to bed. Now she knew that she had to go to Lund. She tossed the bag in the back and got in. When she took the steering wheel she could feel that her hands were sweating.

She never had been able to trust Katarina Taxell. The woman was too weak. There had always been the risk that she would cave in. Taxell was the sort of person who bruised easily. So far, she had judged her control over Taxell to be sufficient. Now she was less sure.

I have to get her out of there, she had thought all night long. At least until she begins to put some distance between herself and what happened. It shouldn't be difficult to persuade her to leave her flat for the time being. There was nothing unusual in a woman developing psychological problems in connection with the birth of a child.

It was raining when she arrived in Lund. Her uneasiness persisted. She parked in a side street and started walking towards the square where Katarina Taxell's building was. Suddenly she stopped. She took a few wary steps back, as if a predator had abruptly appeared in front of her. She stood next to the wall of a building and observed the front door of Taxell's block of flats.

There was a car parked outside with a man, or maybe two, sitting in it. She was instantly sure they were policemen. Katarina Taxell was being watched.

The panic came out of nowhere. She couldn't see it, but she knew that her face was flaming red. She was having palpitations. The thoughts swirled in her head like confused nocturnal animals in a room when a light is turned on. What had Katarina said? Why were they sitting outside her front door?

Or was it only her imagination? She stood motionless and tried to think calmly. She could be certain that Katarina hadn't told them anything. Otherwise they wouldn't be watching her. They would have taken her down to the station. So it wasn't too late after all. But she probably didn't have much time. Not that she needed much. She knew what she had to do.

She lit a cigarette that she had rolled during the night. According to her timetable, it was at least an hour too early. Now she broke with routine. This day was going to be special. There was no getting around it.

She stood there for several minutes more and watched the car by the front door. Then she put out the cigarette and walked quickly away.

When Wallander woke up just after 6 a.m. on Wednesday morning, he was still tired. His sleep deprivation was huge. The powerlessness was like a lead weight deep in his consciousness. He lay in bed with his eyes open. A human being is an animal who lives to endure, he thought. But right now, it seems I can't handle it any more.

He sat up on the edge of his bed. The floor was cold beneath his feet. He looked at his toenails. They needed cutting. His whole body needed an overhaul. A month earlier he had been in Rome, storing up new energy. It was all used up. He forced himself to stand up. He went into the bathroom. The cold water was like a slap in the face. Someday he'd have to quit doing this – using cold water to get himself going. He dried off, put on his dressing gown, and went to the kitchen. Always the same routine. The coffee, then the window, the thermometer. It was raining and it was 4°C. Autumn, and the cold already had a firm grip. Someone at the police station had predicted a long winter. That was what he feared.

When the coffee was ready, he sat at the kitchen table, after having picked up the morning paper from outside his door. On the front page was a photograph taken at Lödinge. He took a few sips of coffee. Already he had moved beyond the first and highest threshold of fatigue. His mornings were sometimes like an obstacle course. It was time for him to call Baiba.

She answered on the second ring. It was the way he'd imagined it during the night. Things were different now.

"I'm exhausted," he excused himself.

"I know," she replied. "But my question still stands."

"Whether I want you to come?"

"Yes."

"There's nothing that I want more."

She believed him. Maybe she could come in early November. She would start looking into the possibility that day.

They didn't need to talk long. Neither of them liked the telephone. Afterwards, when Wallander returned to his cup of coffee, he thought that this time he'd have to have a serious talk with her about whether she would move to Sweden. About the new house. Maybe he'd even tell her about the dog.

He sat there a long time without even opening the newspaper. He didn't get dressed until almost 7.30 a.m. He had to search for a long time before he found a clean shirt. It was his last. He had to sign up to use the laundry room today. As he was on his way out, the phone rang. It was the garage in Älmhult. He flinched when he heard the total bill for the repairs, but he said nothing. The mechanic promised that the car would be in Ystad later in the day. He had a brother who could drive it down and then take the train home. All he'd be charged for was the price of the train ticket.

When Wallander reached the street, he saw it was raining harder than it had looked. He went back inside and called the police station. Ebba said she would send a squad car to pick him up. Five minutes later it pulled up outside. By 8 a.m. he was in his office.

He had barely managed to take off his jacket when everything seemed to start to happen at once. Höglund was standing in his door. She was pale.

"Did you hear?"

Wallander gave a start. Again? Another man murdered?

"I just got in. What is it?"

"Martinsson's daughter has been attacked."

"Terese?"

"Yes."

"What happened?"

"She was attacked outside her school. Martinsson's just left. If I understood Svedberg correctly, it had to do with Martinsson being a police officer."

Wallander was thunderstruck. "Is she seriously hurt?"

"She was pushed and punched in the head, and kicked too, apparently. She wasn't badly injured, but she's certainly had a shock."

"Who did it?"

"Other students. Older than her."

Wallander sat down in his chair. "That's outrageous! But why?"

"I don't know everything that happened. The students have been talking about the citizen militia too, saying that the police aren't doing anything. That we've given up."

"So they jump on Martinsson's daughter?"

"Right."

Wallander felt a lump in his throat. Terese was 13 years old, and Martinsson talked about her constantly.

"Why would they attack an innocent girl?"

"Did you see the paper?" she asked.

"No, why?"

"You ought to. People are talking about Eskil Bengtsson and the others. The arrests are being described as scandalous. They're claiming that Åke Davidsson fought back. There's a big story about it with pictures, and placards at the newsstands that say: 'Whose side are the police on, anyway?'"

"I don't need to read that crap," Wallander said in disgust. "What's happening at the school?"

"Hansson drove over there. Martinsson took his daughter home."

"So it was some boys at the school who did this?"

"As far as I know."

"Go over there," Wallander decided quickly. "Find out everything you can. Talk to the boys. I think it's best if I stay out of it. I might fly off the handle."

"Hansson's already there. They don't need anybody else."

"I don't agree," Wallander said "I'd really like you to go. I'm sure Hansson can handle it himself, but I still want you to find out, in your own way, what actually happened and why. If more of us show up, it will prove we're taking it seriously. I think I'll drive over to Martinsson's house. Everything else can wait till later. The worst thing you can do in this country, like everywhere else, is to kill a policeman. The next-worst thing is to attack a policeman's child."

"I heard that other students stood around laughing," she said.

Wallander threw up his hands. He didn't want to hear any more. He got up from his chair and grabbed his jacket.

"Eskil Bengtsson and the others are going to be released today," she said as they walked down the hall. "But Åkeson is going to prosecute."

"What will they get?"

"People in the area are already talking about taking up a collection, in case there are fines. We can always hope for jail terms. At least for some of them."

"How is Åke Davidsson?"

"He's back home in Malmö. On sick leave."

Wallander stopped and looked at her.

"What would have happened if they'd killed him? Would they have been given fines then too?"

He didn't wait for an answer.

A police car drove Wallander to Martinsson's house, in a development on the eastern side of town. Wallander had only been there a few times before. The house was plain, but Martinsson and his wife had put a lot of love into their garden. He rang the bell. Martinsson's wife Maria opened the door. Wallander saw that she had been crying. Terese was their oldest child and only daughter. One of their two sons, Rikard, stood behind her. Wallander smiled and patted him on the head.

"How's it going?" he asked. "I just heard about it and rushed right over."

"She's sitting on her bed crying. She won't speak to anyone but her father."

Wallander went inside and took off his jacket and shoes. One of his socks had a hole in it. Maria asked if he wanted some coffee. He gratefully accepted. At the same moment Martinsson came down the stairs. Usually he was a cheerful man. Now Wallander saw a grey mask of bitterness. And fear too.

"I heard what happened," Wallander said. "I came at once."

They sat down in the living room.

"How is she?" Wallander asked.

Martinsson just shook his head. Wallander thought he was going to burst into tears. It wouldn't be the first time.

"I'm quitting," Martinsson said. "I'm going to talk to the chief today."

Wallander didn't know what to say. Martinsson had good reason to be upset. He could easily imagine reacting the same way if it had been Linda who was attacked. Even so, he would have to play the devil's advocate. The last thing he wanted was for Martinsson to quit. He also realised that Martinsson would have to make up his own mind. But it was still too soon. He could see how shocked Martinsson was.

Maria came in with coffee. Martinsson shook his head. He didn't want any.

"It's not worth it," he said, "when it starts to affect your family."

"No," Wallander said, "it's not worth it."

Martinsson didn't say any more. Nor did Wallander. Martinsson got up and went back upstairs. Wallander knew there was nothing he could do just then.

Martinsson's wife followed him to the door.

"Say hello to her from me," Wallander said.

"Are they going to come after us again?"

"No. I know that what I'm going to tell you may sound odd. As if I were trying to make light of this situation. But that's not my intention at all. It's just that we can't lose our sense of proportion and start drawing the wrong conclusions. These boys were probably only a couple of years older than Terese. They're not bad children. They probably didn't know what they were doing. This has happened because men like Eskil Bengtsson and those others out in Lödinge are starting to organise citizen militias and incite people against the police."

"I know," she said. "I've heard that people are talking about it in this area too."

"I know it's hard to think clearly when your own child is the target of something like this, but we have to try and hold on to our common sense."

"All this violence," she said. "Where does it come from?"

"There aren't many people who are truly evil," Wallander replied. "At least I think they're few and far between. On the other hand, there are evil circumstances, which trigger all this violence. It's those circumstances that we have to tackle."

"Won't it just get worse and worse?"

"Maybe," Wallander said hesitantly. "If that happens then it's because the circumstances are changing. Not because there are more evil people."

"This country has turned so cold-hearted."

"You're right," he said.

He shook hands with her and walked towards the waiting police car.

"How's Terese doing?" asked the officer who had driven him.

"She's upset. And her parents are, too."

"Doesn't it make you furious?"

"Yes," Wallander said. "It does."

Wallander returned to the police station. Hansson and Höglund were still at the school where Terese had been attacked. Wallander discovered that Chief Holgersson was in Stockholm. For a moment it made him angry. But she had been informed about what happened, and she was coming back to Ystad that afternoon. Wallander got hold of Svedberg and Hamrén. Nyberg was out at Eriksson's farm searching for fingerprints. The detectives from Malmö had gone off in different directions. Wallander sat down with Svedberg and Hamrén in the conference room. They were all upset about what had happened to Martinsson's daughter. They had a brief conversation, and then went back to work. They had divided up all the assignments the night before. Wallander called Nyberg on his mobile phone.

"How's it going?" he asked.

"It's tough," Nyberg said. "But we think we may have found an indistinct print on the bottom of the railing of Eriksson's tower that might not be his. We'll keep looking."

Wallander thought for a moment.

"You mean the killer might have been up in the tower?"

"Why not?"

"You may be right. In that case, there might be cigarette butts too."

"If there were any, we would have found them on our first pass. Now it's definitely too late."

Wallander changed the subject and told him about his visit to see Ylva Brink at the hospital.

"The name tag is in a plastic bag," Nyberg said. "If she has a good nose maybe she will recognise the scent."

"I want that tried out as soon as possible. You can call her yourself. Svedberg has her number."

Nyberg said that he'd arrange for it. Wallander found a letter from the Registry Office on his desk. It reported that no-one had officially changed his name to or from Harald Berggren. Wallander put it aside. It was 10 a.m. and still raining. He thought about the meeting the night before. Again he felt uneasy. Were they really on the right track? Or were they going down a path that would lead them straight into a vacuum? He went to stand by the window. His eyes fell on the water tower. Katarina Taxell is our main lead. She has met the woman. Why else would someone be in a maternity ward in the middle of the night?

He went back to his desk and called Birch in Lund. It took almost ten minutes before they managed to locate him.

"Everything's quiet outside her building," Birch said. "No visits except a woman we can positively identify – her mother. Katarina went out shopping for groceries once. That was when her mother was there watching her baby. There's a supermarket nearby. The only thing of interest was that she bought a lot of newspapers."

"She probably wanted to read about the murder. Do you think she knows we're in the vicinity?"

"I don't think so. She seems tense. But she never looks around. I don't think she suspects we've got her under surveillance."

"It's important that she doesn't discover it."

"We keep changing officers."

Wallander leaned over his desk and opened his notebook.

"How is the profile of her coming along? Who is she?"

"She's 33 years old," Birch said. "That makes an age difference of 18 years to Blomberg."

"It's her first child," Wallander said. "She started late. Women in a hurry might not be so particular about age differences."

"According to her, Blomberg isn't the child's father anyway."

"That's a lie," Wallander said, wondering how he really dared to be so certain. "What else have you got?"

"Katarina Taxell was born in Arlöv," Birch continued. "Her father was an engineer at the sugar refinery. He died when she was little. His car was hit by a train, outside Landskrona. She has no siblings. She and her mother moved to Lund after the father died. The mother worked part-time at the city library. Katarina Taxell got good grades in school and went on to study geography and foreign languages at the university. A somewhat unusual combination. Then she went to teacher training college, and she's been a teacher ever since. At the same time she has built up a small business selling hair products. She's said to be quite industrious. Of course she's not in any of our records."

"Well, that was certainly fast work," Wallander said, impressed.

"I did what you said," Birch replied. "I put a lot of people on the case."

"Obviously she doesn't know about it yet. She'd be looking over her shoulder if she knew we were profiling her."

"We'll have to see how long that lasts. The question is whether we shouldn't lean on her a little."

"I've been thinking the same thing," Wallander said.

"Should we bring her in?"

"No. But I think I'll drive over to Lund. Then you and I can start by talking to her one more time."

"What about? If you don't ask any meaningful questions she'll get suspicious."

"I'll think of something on the way there. Shall we say we'll meet outside her building at midday?"

Wallander signed out a car and drove out of Ystad. He stopped at Sturup Airport and had a sandwich. As usual he was shocked at the price. While he ate he tried to come up with some questions to ask Katarina Taxell. He couldn't show up and ask the same things as last time.

He decided to start with Eugen Blomberg. He was the one who was murdered, after all. They needed all the information they could get on him. Taxell was only one of the people they were questioning, he would tell her.

Just before midday, Wallander finally managed to find a parking place in the centre of Lund. The rain had stopped, and he walked through the city. After a while he saw Birch in the distance.

"I heard the news about Martinsson and his daughter," he said. "It's awful."

"What isn't awful these days?" Wallander said.

"How's the girl handling it?"

"Let's just hope she can forget all about it. But Martinsson told me that he's quitting the force. I have to try and prevent that."

"If he really means it, deep down, nobody will be able to stop him."

"I don't think he'll do it."

"I took a rock on my head once," Birch said. "I got so angry I tore after the man who threw it. It turned out that

I'd arrested his brother once and so he thought he was completely justified in throwing a rock at me."

"A policeman is always a policeman," Wallander said. "At least if you believe the rock throwers."

Birch changed the subject.

"What are you going to ask her about?"

"Eugen Blomberg. How they met. I have to make her think I'm asking her the same questions I ask everyone else. Routine matters, more or less."

"What do you hope to achieve?"

"I don't know. But I still think it's necessary."

They went into the building. Wallander suddenly had a premonition that something was wrong. He stopped on the stairs. Birch looked at him.

"What is it?"

"I don't know. Maybe nothing."

They continued up to the third floor. Birch rang the bell. They waited. He rang again. The bell echoed inside the flat. They looked at each other. Wallander bent down and opened the letter slot. Everything was silent. Birch rang again. Long, repetitive rings. No-one came to the door.

"She's got to be home," he said. "No-one reported that she went out."

"Then she went up the chimney," Wallander said. "Because she's not here."

They ran down the stairs. Birch tore open the door to the police car. The man at the wheel sat reading a magazine.

"Did she go out?" he asked.

"She's inside."

"Guess again."

"Is there a back door?" Wallander asked.

"Not that I know of."

"That's no answer," Birch said angrily. "Either there's a back door or there isn't."

They went back inside the building and down a flight of stairs. The door to the basement level was locked.

"Is there a caretaker?" Wallander asked.

"We don't have time for that," Birch said.

He examined the hinges on the door. They were rusty.

"We can try," Birch muttered to himself.

He took a running start and threw himself against the door. It was ripped off its hinges.

"You know what it means to break the regulations," Wallander said without irony.

They went inside. The hall between a row of locked storage rooms led to a door at the end. Birch opened it. They were at the bottom of some stairs leading up to the street.

"So she got out the back way," he said. "And nobody even took the trouble to see if there was one."

"She might still be in the flat," Wallander said.

Birch understood.

"Suicide?"

"I doubt it. But we have to go in. And we don't have time to wait for a locksmith."

"I'm pretty good at picking locks," Birch said. "I'll just have to get some tools."

When he came back he was out of breath. In the meantime Wallander had gone back to Katarina Taxell's door and was ringing the bell. An elderly man next door came out and asked what was going on. Wallander got angry. He took out his badge and held it right up to the man's face.

"We'd appreciate it if you'd shut your door," he said. "Now. And keep it shut until we tell you."

The man retreated. Wallander heard him putting on the safety chain.

Birch picked the lock in less than five minutes. They went in. The flat was empty. Taxell had taken her baby with her. Birch shook his head.

"Somebody's going to answer for this," he said.

They went through the flat. Wallander got the feeling that she had left in a big hurry. He stopped in front of a baby buggy in the kitchen.

"She must have been picked up by car," he said. "There's a petrol station across the street. Maybe someone there saw a woman with a baby leave the building."

Birch left to find out. Wallander went through the flat one more time. He tried to imagine what had happened. Why does a woman leave her flat with a newborn baby? Taking the back way meant that she wanted to leave in secret. It also meant that she knew the building was being watched.

She or someone else, Wallander thought. Someone might have seen the surveillance from outside and then called her to arrange her escape. He sat down on a chair in the kitchen. There was one more question he needed to consider. Were Katarina Taxell and her baby in danger? Or had their flight from the flat been voluntary? Someone would have noticed if she had put up a struggle, he thought. So she must have left of her own volition. There was only one reason for that. She didn't want to answer questions from the police.

He stood up and went over to the window. Birch was talking with one of the attendants at the petrol station. Then the phone rang. Wallander gave a start. He went into the living room. It rang again. He picked up the receiver.

"Katarina?" asked a woman's voice.

"She's not here," he said. "Who's calling?"

"Who are you?" asked the woman. "I'm Katarina's mother."

"My name is Kurt Wallander. I'm a police officer. Nothing has happened. But Katarina isn't here. And her baby is gone too."

"That's impossible."

"It seems strange, but she isn't here. Maybe you have some idea where she might have gone."

"She wouldn't have left without telling me."

Wallander made a quick decision.

"It would be good if you could come over here. I understand you don't live far away."

"It'll take me less than ten minutes," she replied. "What's happened?"

He could hear the fear in her voice.

"I'm sure there's an explanation. We can talk about it when you get here."

He heard Birch coming in the door as he hung up.

"We're in luck," Birch said. "I talked to a man who works at the petrol station. A man who keeps his eyes opened."

He had made some notes on a piece of paper spotted with oil.

"A red Golf stopped here this morning, sometime between 9 a.m. and 10 a.m. A woman came out the back door of the building. She was carrying a baby. They got into the car."

Wallander felt the tension rising. "Did he notice who was driving?"

"The driver didn't get out of the car."

"So he doesn't know whether it was a man or woman?"

"I asked him. He gave an interesting answer. He said the car drove off as if a man was behind the wheel."

Wallander was surprised. "How did he figure that out?"

"Because the car started with a roar and tore off. Women seldom drive that way."

"Did he notice anything else?"

"No. But maybe he can remember more with a little help. As I said, he seemed very observant."

Wallander told him that Taxell's mother was on her way over. Then they stood in silence.

"What do you think has happened here?" Birch asked.

"I don't know."

"Do you think she's in danger?"

"I don't think so, but I could be wrong."

They went into the living room. There was a baby's sock on the floor. Wallander looked around the room. Birch followed his gaze.

"There's a solution somewhere here," Wallander said. "There's something in this flat that will lead us to the woman we're looking for. When we find her, we'll also find Katarina Taxell. There's something here that will tell us which way to turn. We're going to find it if we have to tear up the floorboards."

Birch said nothing.

They heard the door lock click. So she had her own key. Katarina Taxell's mother walked into the room.

CHAPTER 31

Walland stayed in Lund for the rest of the day. With every hour that passed he grew more certain that they would find who had murdered the three men through Katarina Taxell. They were looking for a woman who was beyond all doubt deeply involved in some way. But they didn't know whether she was acting alone, or what her motive was.

The talk with Katarina Taxell's mother had got them nowhere. She started rushing hysterically around the flat, looking for her missing daughter and grandchild. Finally she became so agitated that they had to get a doctor to see her. Wallander was convinced by then that she didn't know where her daughter had gone. The few women friends she had who her mother thought might have come to get her were contacted at once. Each seemed puzzled. But Wallander didn't trust what he heard over the phone. At his request, Birch followed closely in his tracks and called on each person Wallander had spoken to.

Wallander went downstairs and across the street to the petrol station. He had asked the attendant, Jonas Hader, to repeat his account of what he had seen. It was like meeting the perfect witness. Hader seemed to look at the world around him as if his observations might at any time be transformed into crucial testimony.

The red Golf had stopped outside the building at the same time as a lorry carrying newspapers had left the petrol station. They got hold of the driver, who was positive that he had left the petrol station at 9.30 a.m. sharp. Hader had noticed lots of details, including a big sticker on the rear window of the car, but it was too far away for him to see what it was. He insisted that the car had roared off, that it was driven in what he considered a masculine way. The only thing he hadn't seen was the driver. It was raining, and the windscreen wipers were going. He couldn't have seen anything even if he'd tried. On the other hand, he was convinced that Taxell was wearing a light green coat, that she'd had a big sports bag, and that the child was wrapped in a blue blanket. She came out the door just as the car drew up. The back door was opened from the inside and she put the child in and then put her bag in the boot. Then she opened the back door on the other side and climbed into the car. The driver gunned the engine before Taxell had even closed her door. Hader couldn't catch the licence-plate number, although Wallander had a feeling that he had tried. He had never seen a car stop at the back door before.

Wallander returned to the building with a feeling that he'd had something confirmed, although he wasn't sure what it was. It seemed to have been a hurried escape, but how long had it been planned? And why?

In the meantime Birch had talked to the officers who had taken turns keeping the building under surveillance. Wallander specifically asked them to say whether they had seen a woman near the building who had come and gone, or showed up more than once. But unlike Jonas Hader, the officers had made few observations. They had concentrated on the front door. Wallander insisted that they identify every person they noticed. Since 14 families lived in the building, the whole afternoon had been filled with policemen checking up on the residents.

This was how Birch found someone who might have seen something important. It was a man who lived two floors above Katarina Taxell. He was a retired musician, and according to Birch he described his life as "standing for hours at the window, staring out at the rain, and hearing in my mind music I will never play again". That morning he'd seen a woman on the other side of the square. A woman on foot, who had suddenly stopped, took several steps back, and then stood motionless and studied the building, before turning around and disappearing. When Birch brought this news, Wallander immediately thought that this could be the woman they were looking for. Someone had come, and noticed the car parked right outside the door. Someone had come to visit Katarina Taxell. In the same way that she'd had a visitor in the hospital.

Wallander became energetic and determined. He asked Birch to contact Taxell's friends again and ask if any of them had been on their way to visit her that morning. The answer was unequivocal. No-one had. Birch had tried to coax a description of the woman out of the musician, but the only thing that he could say with certainty was that it was a woman. It had been around 8 a.m. This wasn't confirmed, though, because the three clocks in his flat all showed different times.

Wallander's energy on that day was inexhaustible. He sent Birch out on various tasks. Birch didn't seem at all put out that Wallander was giving him orders as if to a subordinate. Meanwhile Wallander began a methodical search of Taxell's flat. The first thing he asked Birch was whether he could have his forensic technicians secure fingerprints.

He kept in constant contact with Ystad. On four separate occasions he talked to Nyberg. Ylva Brink had smelled the name tag holder, which still had a faint trace of perfume. It might have been the same scent she noticed on that night in the maternity ward, but she wasn't positive.

Twice during the day he talked to Martinsson at home. Terese was still scared and depressed, of course, and Martinsson was determined to quit the force. But Wallander managed to get him to promise to wait at least until the next day before he wrote his letter of resignation. Wallander gave him a detailed account of what had happened. He was sure that Martinsson was listening, although he made few comments. But Wallander knew that he had to keep Martinsson involved with the investigation. He didn't want to risk having him make a decision he would later regret. He talked to Chief Holgersson several times. Hansson and Höglund had taken firm action at the school where Terese was attacked. They interviewed the three boys who were involved, one after the other. They had been in contact with the parents and the teachers. According to Höglund, Hansson had done an excellent job when all the students had been assembled and told about what happened. The students were upset, and she didn't think it would happen again.

Eskil Bengtsson and the other men had been released, but Åkeson was going to prosecute. Maybe what had happened to Martinsson's daughter would make some people reconsider, Höglund said, but Wallander had his doubts. They would have to use a great deal of energy in the future to combat the private militias.

The most important news of the day came from Hamrén, who had taken over some of Hansson's assignments. He had managed to locate Göte Tandvall, and called Wallander at once.

"He has an antique shop in Simrishamn," Hamrén said. "He also travels around and buys antiques, which he exports to Norway and other places."

"Is that legal?"

"I don't think it is strictly illegal," Hamrén replied. "The prices are probably higher there. Then of course it depends on what kind of antiques they are."

"I want you to pay him a visit," Wallander said. "Go to Simrishamn. The thing we need to know is whether a relationship really existed between Holger Eriksson and Krista Haberman. And Tandvall might have other information for us."

Hamrén called back three hours later. He was in his car outside Simrishamn. He had met Tandvall. Wallander waited tensely.

"Tandvall is an extremely precise individual," Hamrén said. "He seems to have a complicated sort of memory. Some things he couldn't remember at all, but on other matters he was crystal clear."

"Krista Haberman?"

"He remembered her. I got a feeling that she must have been rather beautiful. He was positive that Eriksson had met her on a couple of occasions. He remembered them watching returning geese one morning on the pier at Falsterbo. Or maybe it was cranes. On that point he was unclear."

"Is he a bird-watcher too?"

"He was dragged along by his father."

"So now we know the most important thing," Wallander said.

"It does look as if it all fits. Krista Haberman, Holger Eriksson."

Wallander felt a sudden wave of disgust. It came to him with horrifying clarity what he was now starting to believe.

"I want you to return to Ystad," he said. "Go through all the material on Haberman's actual disappearance. When and where was she last seen? I want you to put together a summary of that part of the investigation."

"It sounds as though you have something in mind," Hamrén said.

"She disappeared," Wallander said. "She was never found. What does that indicate?"

"That she's dead."

"More than that. Don't forget that we're skirting the edges of an investigation in which both men and women are subjected to the most brutal violence imaginable."

"Do you believe that she was murdered?"

"Hansson gave me a summary of the investigation. The possibility of murder has been there from the start, but since there was nothing to suggest that this had happened, it wasn't allowed to outweigh other possible explanations for her disappearance. That's correct police procedure. No hasty conclusions."

"You think that Eriksson killed her?"

Wallander could hear that this idea was occurring to Hamrén for the first time.

"I am not certain of it," said Wallander. "But it's a possibility that we can't ignore."

Wallander left Katarina Taxell's flat. He had to have something to eat. He found a pizzeria close by. He ate too fast and immediately got a stomach ache.

Since there was nothing to indicate that the series of killings was over, they were working against time. And they didn't know how much time they had. He reminded himself that Martinsson had promised to put together a timetable of everything that had happened so far. He was supposed to have done that on the day that Terese was attacked. On his way back to Taxell's flat, Wallander decided it couldn't wait. He stopped in a bus shelter and called Ystad. He was in luck. Höglund was there. She had already talked to Hamrén and knew that they had positive confirmation that Krista Haberman and Holger Eriksson had met. Wallander asked her to make the timetable of events.

"I have no idea whether it's important," he said. "But we know too little about how this woman moves around. Maybe the geographical centre will become clear if we make a timetable."

"Now you're saying 'she'," Höglund said.

"Yes, I am. But we don't know if she's alone. We also don't know what role she plays."

"What do you think has happened to Katarina Taxell?"

"She's run away, in a hurry, when she discovered that the building was being watched. She's run away because she has something to hide."

"Is it possible that she killed Blomberg?"

"Taxell is a link in the chain. She doesn't represent a beginning or an end. I can't imagine her killing anyone. She presumably belongs to the group of women who have been victims of abuse."

"Was she abused too? I didn't know that." Höglund sounded genuinely surprised.

"She might not have been beaten up or cut with a knife," Wallander said. "But I suspect that she's been victimised in some other way."

"Psychologically?"

"Something like that."

"By Blomberg?"

"Yes."

"But she still had his child? If what you think about the father is true."

"I described to you the way she held her baby. But of course there are still a lot of holes," Wallander admitted. "Police work is a question of piecing together tentative solutions. We have to make the gaps speak and the pieces tell us about things that have hidden meanings. We have to try to see through the events, turn them on their heads in order to set them on their feet."

"Nobody at the police academy ever talked about this. Weren't you invited to give a lecture there?"

"Never," Wallander said. "I can't give lectures."

"That's exactly what you can do," she replied. "You just refuse to admit it. And besides, I think you'd actually enjoy doing it."

"That's neither here nor there," Wallander said.

Afterwards he thought about what she had said. Did he really want to speak to trainee police officers? In the past he was convinced that his reluctance was genuine. Now he wasn't so sure.

He left the bus shelter and hurried on through the rain. It was starting to get windy. Back at Taxell's flat, he continued to search methodically. In a box in the back of a cupboard he found a large number of diaries. She had started the first one when she was twelve. Wallander noticed with surprise that it had a beautiful orchid on the cover. She had kept on writing the diaries through her teenage years and into adulthood. The last diary he found was from 1993. But there were no entries after September. He kept searching, without finding another. But he was certain that it existed. He enlisted the help of Birch, who had finished interviewing the other residents in the building.

Birch found the keys to Taxell's basement storage room. It took him an hour to go through it. There weren't any diaries there either. Wallander was convinced that she had taken it with her. They were in the bag that Hader had seen her put in the boot of the car.

Finally only her desk was left. He had quickly gone through the drawers earlier, now he would do it more thoroughly. He sat down on an old chair with the heads of dragons carved into the armrests. The desk was a small secretary in which the top folded down to make a desk surface. On top of the desk there were framed photographs of Katarina Taxell as a child. Katarina sitting on a lawn, with white garden furniture and blurry figures in the background. Katarina sitting next to a big dog, looking straight at the camera with a bow in her hair. Katarina with her mother and her father, the engineer at the sugar refinery. He had a moustache, and seemed to exude self-confidence. Katarina looked more like her father than her mother. Wallander took down the photograph and looked on the back. There was no date. The picture had been taken in a studio in Lund. There was a graduation photograph of Katarina with her white cap, flowers around her neck. She was thin, and had grown pale. Now Katarina was living in a different world. The last picture was an old photograph, the contours faded. It was of a barren landscape by the sea. An old couple gazed stiffly at the camera. In the distance was a three-master, anchored, sails furled. Wallander thought the picture could be from Öland, taken sometime at the end of the last century. Perhaps the couple were Katarina's great-grandparents. There was nothing written on the back of that one either. He put the photographs back. There was no sign of Blomberg. That might be understandable, but no other man either. Did that mean anything? Everything means something, he thought. The question was what.

One by one he pulled out the small drawers. Letters, documents, bills. Old report cards. Her highest marks were in geography, she had done poorly in physics and maths. In the next drawer he found pictures taken in a photographic booth. Three girls, crowded together, making faces. Another picture, this time of the pedestrian street in Copenhagen. The same three girls were sitting on a bench, laughing. Katarina was on the far right. There was another drawer full of letters, some from as far back as 1972. A stamp with a picture of the man-of-war *Wasa*. If the secretary contains Taxell's innermost secrets, thought Wallander, then she doesn't have many. An impersonal life. No passions, no summer adventures on Greek islands, but high marks in geography. He continued going through the drawers, but nothing caught his attention. He moved on to the three larger drawers below. Still no diaries. Wallander didn't feel like digging through layer after layer of impersonal mementos. He couldn't see the woman behind them. Had she even been able to see herself?

He pushed back the chair and closed the last drawer. Nothing. He didn't know much more than he had before. He frowned. Something didn't add up. If her decision to leave was sudden, and he was convinced that it had been, then she wouldn't have had time to take along everything that might give away her secrets. She had the diaries within easy reach. But there is almost always a messy side to a person's life. Here there was nothing. He stood up and cautiously moved the desk away from the wall. Nothing was fastened to the back. He sat down in the chair again, thinking hard. There was something he had noticed. Something that only now came back to him. He tried to coax the image out. Not the photographs. Not the letters either. What was it then? The report cards? The rental contract? The bills from her credit card company? None of those. What was left?

There's nothing else but the furniture, he thought. Then it came to him. It was something about the small drawers. He pulled one of them out again, then the next, and compared them. Then he took them all the way out and looked inside. There was nothing there either. He put the drawers back in and pulled out the one on the top left, and then the second. That's when he discovered it. The drawers were not equally deep. He pulled out the smaller one and turned it around. There was another opening. It was a double drawer. It had a secret compartment in the back. There was only one thing inside. He took it out and put it on the desk.

It was a timetable for Swedish Railways, from the spring of 1991. The trains between Malmö and Stockholm. He took out the other drawers, one by one. He found another secret compartment. It was empty. He leaned back in his chair and thought about the timetable. Why was it important? It was even harder to understand why it had been put into a secret compartment. But it couldn't have ended up there by mistake.

Birch came into the room.

"Take a look at this," Wallander said, pointing at the timetable. "This was in Katarina Taxell's secret hiding place."

"A timetable?"

Wallander nodded. "I don't get it," he said.

He leafed through it, page by page. Birch had pulled up a chair and sat down next to him. Wallander turned the pages. Nothing was written on it, no page had been pressed down and fell open by itself. It was only when he came to the next to last page that he stopped. Birch saw it too. A departure time from Nässjö was underlined. Nässjö to Malmö. Departure at 16.00. Arrival in Lund at 18.42, Malmö at 18.57. Nässjö 16.00. Someone had underlined the whole row.

Wallander looked at Birch. "Does that tell you anything?"

"Not a thing."

Wallander put down the timetable.

"Does Katarina Taxell have something to do with Nässjö?" Birch asked.

"Not as far as I know," Wallander said. "But it's possible that she does. Our biggest problem right now is that everything seems to be possible. We can't tell what is important and what isn't."

Wallander had acquired several plastic bags from the forensic technicians who had gone through the flat earlier in the day, searching for fingerprints that didn't belong to Katarina Taxell or her mother. He put the timetable in one of them.

"I'm taking this along," he said, "if you have no objections."

Birch shrugged.

"You can't even use it to tell when the trains go," he said. "It expired three years ago."

"I rarely take the train," Wallander said.

"It can be relaxing," Birch said. "I prefer taking the train to flying. You get time to yourself."

Wallander thought about his most recent train trip, from Älmhult. Birch was right. During the journey he had managed to fall asleep for a while.

"I think it's time for me to go back to Ystad."

"We're not going to put out an APB for Katarina Taxell and her baby?"

"Not yet."

They left the flat. Birch locked up. The wind was coming in gusts, and it was cold. They said goodbye at Wallander's car.

"What should we do about her surveillance?" Birch asked.

Wallander thought for a moment.

"Keep it up for the time being," he said. "Only don't forget the back this time."

"What do you think might happen?"

"I don't know. But someone who has run away might decide to return."

He drove out of the city. Autumn pressed in all around the car. He switched on the heater, but he was still cold.

What are we going to do now? he asked himself. Katarina Taxell is missing. After a long day in Lund I'm going back to Ystad with an old Swedish Railways timetable in a plastic bag.

But he knew that they had taken an important step forward that day. Eriksson did know Krista Haberman. They knew that there was a connection between the three men who had been murdered. Involuntarily he accelerated. He wanted to find out what Hamrén had discovered. When he reached the exit for Sturup Airport he called Ystad. He got hold of Svedberg. The first thing he asked about was Terese.

"She's getting a lot of support from the school," Svedberg said. "Especially from the other students. But it's going to take time."

"And Martinsson?"

"He's depressed. He's talking about quitting."

"I know."

"You're the only one who can talk him out of it."

"I will."

He asked if anything important had happened. Svedberg had just arrived at the station himself after sitting in on a meeting with Åkeson about obtaining the investigative material on the drowning of Runfeldt's wife in Älmhult.

Wallander asked him to call a meeting of the investigative team for 10 p.m.

"Have you seen Hamrén?" was his last question.

"He's sitting with Hansson going over the material on Krista Haberman. That was apparently something you said was urgent."

"If they could finish by 10 p.m., I'd be grateful."

"Are they supposed to find Krista Haberman by then?" Svedberg asked.

"Not exactly. But not far from it, either."

Wallander put the phone down on the seat next to him. He thought about Katarina Taxell's secret drawer, which contained an old timetable. He didn't understand it. Not at all.

At 10 p.m. they were all assembled. Only Martinsson was missing. They began by talking about what had happened that morning. Everyone knew by then that Martinsson had decided to resign from the force.

"I'll talk to him," Wallander said. "I'll find out if he's really made up his mind. If he has, then of course no-one is going to stop him."

Wallander gave a brief summary of what had happened in Lund. They considered various explanations as to why Taxell had run away. They also asked themselves if it might be possible to track down the red car. How many red Golfs were there in Skåne?

"A woman with a newborn baby can't disappear

without a trace," Wallander said at last. "It'd be best for us to be patient."

He looked at Hansson and Hamrén.

"The disappearance of Krista Haberman," he said.

Hansson nodded to Hamrén.

"You wanted to know the details surrounding the disappearance itself," he said. "The last time she was seen was in Svenstavik on Tuesday, 22 October 1967. She went for a walk through town. It wasn't unusual for her to be out walking. A lumberjack coming from the station on his bike saw her. It was about 5 p.m. and it was already dark. There are several witnesses who said they'd seen a strange car in town that evening. That's all."

They sat in silence.

"Did anyone mention the make of the car?" Wallander asked at last.

Hamrén searched through the papers. He shook his head and left the room. When he came back he had another stack of papers in his hand. Finally he found what he was looking for.

"One of the witnesses claimed it was a dark blue Chevrolet. He was positive about it. There was a taxi in Svenstavik that was the same make only it was light blue."

Wallander nodded. "Svenstavik and Lödinge are a long way from each other," he said softly. "But I seem to remember that Holger Eriksson was selling Chevrolets back then. Is it possible that Eriksson made the long drive to Svenstavik, and that Krista Haberman went back with him?"

He turned to Svedberg.

"Did Eriksson own his farm then?"

Svedberg nodded.

Wallander looked around the room.

"Eriksson was impaled in a pungee pit," he said. "If the murderer takes the lives of his or her victims in a way that mirrors crimes that were committed earlier, then I think we can imagine our way to a very unpleasant conclusion."

He wished he was mistaken, but he doubted that he was.

"I think we have to start searching Eriksson's fields," he said. "Krista Haberman might be buried there somewhere."

CHAPTER 32

They went out to the farm in the early dawn. Wallander took Nyberg, Hamrén and Hansson along with him. They all drove separately, Wallander in his own car, which was finally back from Älmhult. They parked at the entrance to the empty house, which stood like a deserted ship out there in the fog.

On that particular morning, Thursday, 20 October, the fog was thick. It had come in from the sea and now lay motionless over the landscape. They had agreed to meet at 6.30 a.m., but they were all late because visibility was practically nil. Wallander was the last to arrive. When he got out of his car it occurred to him that it looked like a hunting club had gathered. The only thing missing was their guns. He was dreading the task that awaited them. Somewhere on Eriksson's property a murdered woman might lie buried. Whatever they found – if they found anything at all – would be skeletal remains. Nothing else, 27 years was a long time.

Shivering, they greeted each other. Hansson had brought a surveyor's map of the farm and the adjacent fields. Wallander wondered fleetingly what the Cultural Association of Lund would think if they really did find the remains of a body. It would probably increase the number of visitors to the farm, he thought gloomily. There were few tourist attractions that could compete with the scene of a crime.

They spread the map out on the bonnet of Nyberg's car and gathered around it.

"In 1967 the fields were laid out differently," Hansson said, pointing. "Eriksson didn't buy all the fields to the south until the mid-1970s."

This reduced the relevant area of land by a third, but what remained was still large. They would never be able to dig up the whole area.

"The fog is making things harder for us," Wallander said. "I thought we could try to get an overview of the terrain. It seems to me that it should be possible to eliminate certain areas. I assume that a person would choose the spot carefully for burying someone he killed."

"You'd probably pick the spot where you thought it least likely anyone would look," Nyberg said. "A study was done on it. In the US, of course. But it sounds reasonable."

"It's a big area," Hansson said.

"That's why we have to make it smaller," Wallander said. "Nyberg is right. He wouldn't bury her just anywhere. I imagine, for instance, that you wouldn't want a body lying in the ground right outside your front door. Unless you're completely insane, and there's nothing to indicate that Eriksson was."

"Besides, there are cobblestones there," Hansson said. "I think we can eliminate the courtyard."

They went up to the farmhouse. Wallander wondered whether they should return to Ystad and come back when the fog was gone. Since there was no wind, it could last all day. In the end he decided that they should spend a while trying to gain an overview.

They walked over to the large garden that lay behind the house. The soft ground was covered with fallen, rotten apples. A magpie fluttered up from a tree. They stopped and looked around. Not here either, Wallander thought. A man who murders someone in the city and has only his garden might bury the body there, but not a man who lives out in the country.

He told the others what he was thinking. No-one had any objections.

They started walking out to the fields. The fog was still thick. Hares popped up against all the whiteness and then vanished. They headed towards the northern border of the property.

"A dog wouldn't be able to find anything, I guess?" Hamrén asked.

"Not after 27 years," Nyberg replied.

The mud was sticking to their gumboots. They tried to balance their way along the narrow ridges of mown grass that formed the boundary of Eriksson's property. A rusty hoe stood mired in the earth. It wasn't just their task that bothered Wallander. The fog and the damp grey earth also oppressed him. He was fond of the landscape of Skåne, where he had been born and raised, but he could do without the autumn. At least on days like this.

They reached a pond that lay in a hollow. Hansson pointed on the map to where they were. They looked at the pond. It was about 100 metres wide.

"This is full of water all year round," Nyberg said. "At the middle it's probably between two and three metres deep."

"It's a possibility, of course," Wallander said. "He could have sunk the body with weights."

"Or a sack," Hansson said.

Wallander nodded. There was the mirror image again. But he wasn't sure.

"A body can float to the surface. Would Eriksson choose to sink a corpse in a pond when he has thousands of square metres of land to dig a grave in?"

"Who actually worked all this land?" Hansson asked. "Surely not Eriksson. He didn't have it leased out. But this land is well tended." Hansson had grown up on a farm outside of Ystad and knew what he was talking about.

"That's an important question," Wallander said. "We have to find out."

"It might also give us the answer to another question," Hamrén said. "Whether any changes have occurred on the land. If you dig in one place, a mound appears somewhere else. I'm not thinking about a grave. But a ditch, for example. Or something else."

"We're talking about something that happened almost 30 years ago," Nyberg said. "Who would remember that far back?"

"It happens," Wallander said. "But of course we'll have to look into it. So who worked Holger Eriksson's land?"

"There could well have been more than one person," Hansson said.

"Then we'll talk to all of them," Wallander replied. "If we can find them. If they're still alive."

They moved on. Wallander remembered that he had seen several old aerial photographs of the farm inside the house. He asked Hansson to call the Cultural Association in Lund and get someone to bring the keys out.

"It's unlikely anyone would be there this early in the morning."

"Call Höglund," Wallander said. "Ask her to contact the lawyer who was the executor of Eriksson's will. He might still have a set of keys."

"Lawyers might be morning people," Hansson said doubtfully as he dialled the number.

"I want to see those aerial shots," Wallander said. "As soon as possible."

They kept walking while Hansson talked to Höglund. The field now sloped downwards. The fog was still just as thick. In the distance they heard a tractor engine dying away. Hansson's phone rang. Höglund had spoken to the lawyer. He had turned in his keys. She was trying to get hold of someone in Lund who could help. She would get back to them.

It took them almost 20 minutes to reach the next boundary marker. Hansson pointed to the map. They were now at the southwest corner. The property stretched another 500 metres, but Eriksson hadn't bought this section until 1976. They walked east, now approaching the ditch and the hill with the bird tower. Wallander felt his uneasiness growing. He thought he could sense the same silent reaction from the others.

It was turning into an image of his life, he thought. My life as a policeman during the last part of the 20th century in Sweden. An early morning, dawn. Autumn, fog, a damp chill. Four men slogging around in the mud. They approach a ditch where a man was trapped, impaled on bamboo stakes. At the same time they're searching for the burial site of a Polish woman who disappeared 27 years ago.

I'm going to end up trudging around in this mud until I collapse. Out there in the fog people are huddled around their kitchen tables, organising vigilante militias. Anyone who takes a wrong turn in the fog runs the risk of being beaten to death.

He was carrying on a conversation with Rydberg as he

walked along. He saw Rydberg sitting on his balcony towards the end of his illness. The balcony hovered before Wallander's eyes like an airship in the fog. Rydberg didn't speak, but listened to Wallander with a wry smile, his face already heavily marked by illness.

They reached the pungee pit. A torn remnant of crime-scene tape was caught under one of the collapsed planks. We didn't clean up very well, Wallander thought. The bamboo stakes were gone. He wondered where they were. In the basement of the police station? At the forensic laboratory in Linköping? The tower was on their right, barely visible in the fog.

Wallander took a few steps to the side and nearly slipped in the mud. Nyberg stood staring into the ditch. Hamrén and Hansson were discussing a detail on the map in low voices.

Someone keeps an eye on Holger Eriksson and his farm, thought Wallander, an idea developing slowly in his mind. This person knows what happened to Krista Haberman, a woman, missing for 27 years, declared dead – a woman who is buried here somewhere. Eriksson's time is being measured out. A grave with sharpened stakes is prepared. Another grave in the mud.

He went over to Hamrén and Hansson. He told them what he'd just been thinking. Nyberg had disappeared in the fog.

"Let's assume that the killer knew where Krista Haberman was buried. On several occasions we've talked about the murderer having a language – that he or she is trying to tell us something. We've only had partial success in breaking the code. Eriksson was killed with what can only be described as deliberate brutality. His body was intended to be found. It's also possible that this place was chosen for another reason, as a challenge to us to keep searching right here. And if we do, we'll also find Krista Haberman."

Nyberg reappeared out of the fog. Wallander repeated what he'd said. They made their way over the ditch and up to the tower. The woods below were shrouded in fog.

"Too many roots," Nyberg said. "I don't think it's that grove of trees."

They turned around and continued eastwards until they were back where they had started. It was close to 8 a.m., and the fog was just as thick. Höglund called to say that the keys were on the way. Everyone was cold and wet. Wallander didn't want to keep them there unnecessarily. Hansson would devote the next few hours trying to find out who had worked the land.

"An unexpected change 27 years ago," Wallander emphasised. "That's what we want to know about. But don't mention that we think there's a body buried here. Then there'll be an invasion."

Hansson nodded. He understood.

"We'll go over this again sometime when there's no fog," Wallander continued. "But I think it's useful to have been out here already."

They all left. Wallander remained behind. He got into his car and turned on the heater. It didn't seem to be working. The repairs had cost an incredible amount of money, but apparently didn't cover the heating system. He wondered when he'd have the time and money to trade it in for another car. When was this one going to fall apart again?

He waited, thinking about the women. Krista Haberman, Eva Runfeldt, and Katarina Taxell. Plus the fourth one who didn't have a name. What was the common point of contact? He had a feeling it was so close that he was looking at it without seeing it.

He went back over his thoughts. Abused, maybe murdered women. A vast stretch of time arched like a vault over the whole thing.

As he sat in his car he realised that there was one other possible conclusion. They hadn't seen everything. The events they were trying to understand were part of something bigger. It was important for them to find the connection between the women, but they also had to consider the possibility that the connection was coincidental. Someone was making choices. But what were the choices based on? Circumstances? Coincidences? Available opportunities? Eriksson lived alone on a farm. Didn't socialise, watched birds at night. He was someone it was possible to get near. Runfeldt was leaving on an orchid safari for two weeks. That provided an opportunity. He also lived alone. Eugen Blomberg took walks by himself in the evening.

Wallander shook his head at his own thoughts. He couldn't make any progress. Was he thinking in the right direction or not? He didn't know.

It was cold in the car. He got out to move around. The keys should be arriving soon. He walked across the courtyard, remembering the first time he had come here, the flock of rooks in the ditch. He looked at his hands. His tan was gone. Even the memory of the sun in the garden of the Villa Borghese was gone. And so was his father.

He let his gaze wander over the courtyard. The house was well cared for. Once a man named Holger Eriksson sat here and composed poems about birds. One day he got into a dark blue Chevrolet and drove all the way to Jämtland. Was he driven by passion? Or something else?

Krista Haberman was a beautiful woman. Did she go with him willingly? She must have.

They drive back to Skåne. Then she disappears. Eriksson lives alone. He digs a grave. She's gone. The investigation never catches up with him. Until now, when Hansson finds a connection.

Wallander was standing and looking at the deserted kennel. At first he wasn't aware of what he was thinking. The image of Krista Haberman slowly slipped away. He frowned. Why wasn't there a dog? No-one had asked that question before. He hadn't either. When had the dog disappeared? Did that have any significance at all? These were questions he wanted to have answered.

A car braked outside the house. A moment later a boy who couldn't be more than 20 came into the courtyard. He walked over to Wallander.

"Are you the policeman that needs the key?"

"Yes, I am."

The boy regarded him doubtfully.

"How can I be sure? You could be anybody."

Wallander felt annoyed, but he realised that the boy's doubts were justified. He had mud all over his trousers. He took out his identification. The boy nodded and gave him the set of keys.

"I'll see to it that they get back to Lund," Wallander said.

The boy nodded. Wallander heard the car roar off as he looked through the keys for the one to the front door. He thought fleetingly about what Jonas Hader had said about the red Golf outside Katarina Taxell's building. Don't women gun their engines? Mona drives faster than I do. Baiba always stamps on the accelerator. But maybe they don't gun their engines.

He opened the door and went inside. It smelled musty.

He sat down on a bench and pulled off his muddy gumboots. When he went into the main room he noticed to his surprise that the poem about the woodpecker was still on the desk. The night of 21 September. Tomorrow it would be a month since then. Were they really any closer to a solution? They had two more murders to solve. And the mystery of woman who had disappeared, who might be buried out in Eriksson's fields.

He stood motionless in the silence. The fog outside the windows was still dense. He felt uneasy. The objects in the room were watching him. He walked over to the wall where the two aerial photographs hung in their frames. He searched his pockets for his glasses, put them on and leaned forwards. One of the photographs was black-and-white, the other a faded colour shot. The black-and-white picture was taken in 1949, two years before Holger Eriksson had bought the farm. The colour photograph was from 1965.

Wallander opened a curtain to let in more light, and saw a lone deer grazing among the trees in the garden. He stood quite still. The deer raised its head and looked at him. Then it calmly went on grazing. Wallander stayed where he was. He had a feeling that he would never forget that deer. How long he stood there and watched it, he didn't know. Finally a sound that he himself didn't notice caught the deer's attention. It vanished. Wallander kept on looking out the window for a time and then went back to the two photographs. The plane carrying the camera had come in from due south. All the details were clear. In 1965 Eriksson hadn't yet built his tower, but the hill was there and so was the ditch. He couldn't make out a bridge. He followed the contours of the fields. The picture was taken early in the spring. The fields had been ploughed, but nothing was growing yet. The pond was quite clear in the photograph. A grove of trees stood next to a narrow tractor path separating two of the fields. He frowned. He couldn't remember those trees. This morning he wouldn't have seen them because of the fog, but he didn't remember them from his previous visits. The trees looked tall. He studied the house, which was in the centre of the picture. An outbuilding that might have been used as a pigsty had been torn down. The approach road was wider. But otherwise everything was much the same. He took off his glasses and sat down in a leather armchair. Silence surrounded him.

A Chevrolet goes to Svenstavik. A woman comes back to Skåne. Then she vanishes and 27 years later the man who may have gone to Svenstavik to get her is murdered. Now they were looking for no less than three different women. Krista Haberman, Katarina Taxell, and one without a name. One who drives a red Golf, smokes hand-rolled cigarettes and might wear false nails.

He wondered whether two of the women could be in fact be one and the same, whether Krista Haberman, in spite of everything, was still alive. If so, she would be 65 years old by now, and the woman who knocked down Ylva Brink was a lot younger.

It didn't add up. Nothing did.

He looked at his watch. It was 8.45 a.m. He stood up and left the house. The fog was still just as thick. He thought about the deserted kennel. Then he locked up and drove away.

At 10 a.m. Wallander called the investigative team together for a meeting. Martinsson was still away, but he had promised to come in that afternoon after he had been at Terese's school. Höglund said that he'd called her late the night before. She thought he sounded drunk, which was out of the ordinary. Wallander felt vaguely jealous. Why had Martinsson called her and not him? It was the two of them who had worked together all these years.

"He still seems determined to quit," she said. "But I got the feeling that he also wished I would talk him out of it."

"I'll talk to him," Wallander said.

They closed the door to the conference room. Per Åkeson and Chief Holgersson were the last ones to arrive. Wallander had a feeling that they had just completed their own meeting. Lisa Holgersson took the floor as soon as the room was quiet.

"The whole country is talking about the citizen militia," she said. "From now on Lödinge is firmly on the map. We've had a request for Kurt to participate in a discussion programme on TV tonight, to be broadcast from Göteborg."

"Not on your life," Wallander replied, horrified. "What would I say?"

"I've turned them down on your behalf already," she replied with a smile. "But I'm thinking of asking for a favour in return later on."

Wallander realised that she was referring to the lectures at the police academy.

"There is a huge debate taking place," she went on. "We can only hope that something good comes out of it, now that the issues are actually being discussed."

"It might also force the senior members of the police administration in this country to be a little more self-critical," Hansson said. "We're not entirely without blame for the way things have developed."

"What are you suggesting?" Wallander asked, curious. Hansson rarely participated in discussions about the police force.

"I'm thinking about the scandals in which the police have been involved," Hansson said. "Maybe they've always existed, but not as often as they do now."

"That's something we should neither exaggerate nor ignore," Per Åkeson said. "The big problem is the gradual shift in what the police and the courts see as a crime. What would have brought a conviction yesterday is suddenly considered a trifle today, and the police often don't even bother to investigate. I think that's offensive to the national sense of justice, which has always been strong in this country."

"They're probably related," Wallander said. "But I have strong doubts that a discussion of the citizen militia will have any effect on this, even though I'd like to believe otherwise."

"I'm thinking of prosecuting these men with as serious charges as I can," Åkeson said. "The assault was vicious, that's something I can emphasise. There were four men involved and I think I can convict at least three of them. I should also tell you that the chief prosecutor wants to be kept informed. I consider that quite surprising, but it indicates that at least this is being taken seriously at a high level."

"Åke Davidsson sounds intelligent and articulate in an interview in *Arbetet*," said Svedberg. "He's not going to have any permanent injuries by the way."

"Then there's Terese and her father," Wallander said. "And the boys at the school."

"Is it true that Martinsson is thinking of resigning?" Åkeson asked.

"That was his first reaction," Wallander replied. "Which seems both reasonable and natural. But I'm not sure he's really going to go through with it."

"He's a good policeman," Hansson said. "Doesn't he know that?"

"Yes," Wallander said. "The question is whether that's enough. Other things can come up when something like this happens. Especially with our workload."

"I know," Chief Holgersson said. "And that's not going to get any better."

Wallander remembered that he still hadn't done what he had promised Nyberg: talk to Holgersson about his workload. He made a note of it.

"We'll have to take up this discussion later," he said.

"I just wanted to inform you," Holgersson said. "That's all, except that Björk called to wish you luck. He was sorry to hear about what happened to Martinsson's daughter."

"He resigned in time," Svedberg said. "What did we give him as a leaving present? A fishing rod? If he was still working here, he wouldn't have time to use it."

"He probably has a lot on his hands now too," Holgersson said.

"Björk was a good chief," Wallander said. "Now let's move on."

They started with Höglund's timetable. Next to his notepad Wallander had placed the plastic bag containing the Swedish Railways timetable that he had found in Katarina Taxell's desk.

Höglund had done a thorough job. The times of the various events were mapped out and listed in relation to each other. Wallander knew that this was an assignment he wouldn't have done as well. In all probability he would have been sloppy. All policemen are different, he thought. It's only when we can work with something that brings out our strengths that we're of any real use.

"I don't really see a pattern emerging," Höglund said as

she neared the end of her presentation. "The pathologists in Lund have established the time of Eriksson's death as late on the evening of 21 September. Runfeldt also died at night. The times of death correspond, but one can't draw any conclusions from this. There's no correspondence in terms of the days of the week. If we add the two visits to the Ystad maternity ward and the murder of Blomberg, there might be a fragment of a pattern."

She broke off and looked around the table. Neither Wallander nor anyone else seemed to understand what she meant.

"It's almost pure mathematics," she said. "But it seems as if our killer acts according to a pattern that is so irregular that it's interesting. On 21 September Eriksson dies. On the night of 30 September, Katarina Taxell is visited at the Ystad maternity ward. On 11 October Gösta Runfeldt dies. On the night of 13 October the woman is back at the maternity ward and knocks down Svedberg's cousin. Finally, on 17 October Eugen Blomberg is found dead. To this we can also add the day that Runfeldt probably disappeared. There is no regularity whatsoever. Which might be surprising, since everything else seems to be minutely planned and prepared. This is a killer who takes the time to sew weights into a sack that are carefully balanced to the victim's weight. So we could say that perhaps the irregularity is caused by something out of the killer's control. And then we have to ask: what?"

Wallander wasn't quite following her.

"One more time," he said. "Slowly."

She repeated what she had said. This time Wallander understood what she meant.

"Maybe we can just say that it doesn't have to be a coincidence," she concluded. "I won't try to stretch it further than that."

Wallander started to see the picture more clearly.

"Let's assume that there is a pattern," he said. "Then what's your interpretation? What factors affect a killer's timetable?"

"There could be various explanations. The killer doesn't live in Skåne, but makes regular visits here. Or perhaps he or she has a job that follows a certain rhythm."

"So you think these dates could be days off? If we could follow them for another month, would it be clearer?"

"That's possible. The killer has a job that follows a rotating schedule. The days off don't always occur on Saturdays and Sundays."

"That might turn out to be important," Wallander said hesitantly. "But I find it difficult to believe it."

"Otherwise I couldn't manage to read much from the times," she said.

Wallander held up the plastic bag.

"Now that we're talking about timetables, I found this in a secret compartment in Katarina Taxell's desk, as if this were her most important possession, that she hid from the world. A timetable for Swedish Railways' inter-city trains for the spring of 1991. With a departure time underlined: Nässjö 16.00. It goes every day."

He pushed the plastic bag over to Nyberg.

"Fingerprints," he said.

Then he moved on to Krista Haberman and told them about the morning visit in the fog. There was no mistaking the sombre mood in the room.

"So I think we have to start digging," he concluded. "When the fog lifts and Hansson has had a chance to find out who worked the land, and whether any changes took place after 1967."

For a long time there was complete silence as everyone

evaluated what Wallander had just said. It was Åkeson who spoke.

"This sounds both incredible and at the same time highly plausible," he said. "I assume that we have to take this possibility seriously."

"It would be good if this didn't get out," Chief Holgersson said. "There's nothing people like better than having old, unsolved missing-person cases come up again."

They had made a decision. Wallander decided to end the meeting as quickly as possible because everyone had a lot of work to do.

"Katarina Taxell has disappeared," he said. "Left her home in a red Golf with an unknown driver. Her departure was hasty. Her mother wants us to put out an APB on her, which we can hardly refuse since she's the next of kin. But I think we should wait, at least a few more days."

"Why?" Åkeson asked.

"I have a suspicion that she'll make contact," Wallander said. "Not with us, of course. But with her mother, who she knows will be worried. She'll call to reassure her. Unfortunately she probably won't say where she is. Or who she's with."

Wallander now turned to face Åkeson.

"I want someone to stay with Taxell's mother and record the conversation. Sooner or later it'll come."

"If it hasn't happened already," Hansson said, getting to his feet. "Give me Birch's phone number."

He got it from Höglund and quickly left the room.

"There's nothing more for now," Wallander said. "Let's say we'll meet again at 5 p.m. if nothing else happens before then."

* * *

When Wallander got to his own office, the phone was ringing. It was Martinsson, wanting to know if Wallander could meet him at his house at 2 p.m. Wallander promised to be there. He left the station and ate lunch at the Hotel Continental. He knew that he couldn't afford it, but he was hungry and didn't have much time. He sat alone at a window table, nodding to people passing by, surprised and hurt that no-one stopped to offer condolences at the death of his father. It was in the papers. News of a death travels fast, and Ystad was a small town. He ate halibut and drank a light beer. The waitress was young and blushed every time he looked at her. He wondered sympathetically how she was going to stand her job.

At 2 p.m. he rang Martinsson's bell, and they went and sat in the kitchen. Martinsson was home alone. Wallander asked about Terese. She had gone back to school. Martinsson looked pale and dejected. Wallander had never seen him so depressed.

"What should I do?" Martinsson asked.

"What does your wife say? What does Terese say?"

"That I should keep working, of course. They're not the ones who want me to quit. I'm the one."

Wallander waited. But Martinsson didn't say anything.

"Remember a few years back?" Wallander began. "When I shot a man in the fog near Kåseberga and killed him? And then ran over another one on the Öland Bridge? I was gone almost a year. All of you thought that I had quit. Then there was that case with the two lawyers named Torstensson, and suddenly everything changed. I was about to sign my letter of resignation, but instead I went back on duty."

Martinsson nodded. He remembered.

"Now, after the fact, I'm glad that I did what I did. The

only advice I can give you is that you shouldn't do anything rash. Wait to make up your mind. Work one day at a time. Decide later. I'm not asking you to forget, I'm asking you to be patient. Everyone misses you. You're a good policeman. Everyone notices when you're not there."

Martinsson threw out his arms.

"I'm not that important. Sure, I know a few things. But you can't tell me that I'm in any way irreplaceable."

"You are irreplaceable," Wallander said. "That's just what I'm trying to tell you."

Wallander had expected the conversation to take a long time. Martinsson sat in silence for a few minutes. Then he got up and left the kitchen. When he came back he had his jacket on.

"Shall we go?" he asked.

"Yes," said Wallander. "We've got a lot of work to do."

In the car on the way to the station, Wallander gave him a brief summary of the events of the past few days. Martinsson listened in silence. When they entered reception, Ebba stopped them. Since she didn't take the time to welcome Martinsson back, Wallander knew at once that something had happened.

"Ann-Britt is trying to get hold of you two," she said. "It's important."

"What's happened?"

"Someone named Katarina Taxell called her mother."

Wallander looked at Martinsson. So he had been right, but it had happened faster than he had expected.

CHAPTER 33

They weren't too late. Birch had managed to be there in time. In just over an hour the tape of the conversation was in Ystad. They gathered in Wallander's office, where Svedberg had set up a tape recorder, and listened tensely to the brief conversation. The first thing that occurred to Wallander was that Katarina Taxell didn't want to talk any longer than necessary.

They listened to it once, then a second time. Svedberg handed Wallander a pair of earphones so that he could listen to the two voices more closely.

"Mama? It's me."

"Dear God. Where on earth are you? What happened?"

"Nothing happened, we're fine."

"Where on earth are you?"

"With a good friend."

"Who?"

"A good friend. I just wanted to call and tell you everything's fine."

"What happened? Why did you disappear?"

"I'll explain some other time."

"Who are you staying with?"

"You don't know her."

"Don't hang up. What's your phone number?"

"I'm going now. I just wanted to call so you wouldn't worry."

Her mother tried to say something else, but Katarina hung up.

They listened to the tape at least 20 times. Svedberg wrote down what was said on a piece of paper.

"It's the eleventh line that interests us," Wallander said. "'You don't know her.' What does she mean by that?"

"Just what she says," Höglund said.

"That's not what I'm getting at," Wallander answered. "'You don't know her.' That could mean two things. Either that her mother has never met her or that her mother doesn't understand what she means to Katarina."

"The first one is the most plausible," Höglund said.

While they talked Nyberg put on the earphones and listened again. The sounds seeping out told them that he had the volume turned up high.

"There's something audible in the background," Nyberg said. "A banging noise."

Wallander put on the earphones. Nyberg was right. There was a steady pounding in the background. The others took turns listening. No-one could say for sure what it was.

"Where is she?" asked Wallander. "She's arrived somewhere. She's staying with the woman who came to pick her up. And somewhere in the background something is banging."

"Could it be near a construction site?" Martinsson suggested. It was the first thing he had said since returning to work.

"That's a possibility," Wallander said.

They listened again. It was definitely a banging sound.

"Send the tape to Linköping," he said. "If we can identify the sound, it might help us."

"How many construction sites are there in Skåne alone?" Hamrén said.

"It could be something else," Wallander said. "Something that might give us an idea where she is."

Nyberg left. They stayed in Wallander's office, leaning against the walls and desk.

"Three things are important from now on," Wallander said. "For the time being we'll have to put aside certain aspects of the investigation. We have to keep mapping out Katarina Taxell's life. Who is she? Who are her friends? That's the first thing. The second thing is: who is she staying with?"

He paused before he went on.

"We'll wait until Hansson comes back from Lödinge, but I think our third task will be to start digging at Eriksson's place."

The meeting broke up. Wallander had to go to Lund, and he was thinking of taking Höglund with him. It was already late afternoon.

"Do you have a babysitter?" he asked when they were alone in his office.

"Yes," she said. "My neighbour needs the money, thank God."

"How can you afford it on a police salary?" Wallander asked.

"I can't," she said. "But my husband makes a good living. That's what saves us. We're one of the lucky families today."

Wallander called Birch and told him that they were on their way. He let Höglund take her car. He no longer trusted his own car, in spite of the expensive repairs. The landscape slowly vanished into the twilight. A cold wind blew across the fields.

"We'll start at Taxell's mother's house," he said. "Later we'll go back to her flat."

"What do you think you might find? You've already gone over the flat. And you're usually thorough."

"Maybe nothing new. But maybe a connection between two details that I didn't see before."

She drove fast.

"Do you usually rev the engine when you start the car?" Wallander asked suddenly.

She gave him a quick look. "Sometimes. Why do you ask?"

"Because I wonder if it was a woman driving the red Golf that picked up Taxell and the baby."

"Don't we know that for sure?"

"No," Wallander said firmly. "We hardly know anything for sure."

He looked out the window. They were passing Marsvinsholm.

"There's something else we don't know with certainty," he said after a while. "Though I'm becoming more and more convinced of it."

"What's that?"

"She's alone. There's no man anywhere near her. There's no-one at all. We're not looking for a woman who might give us a possible lead. There's nothing behind her. There's just her. No-one else."

"So she's the one who committed the murders? Dug the pungee pit? Strangled Runfeldt after holding him captive? Tossed Blomberg in the lake, alive in a sack?"

Wallander replied by asking another question.

"Do you remember, early on, when we talked about the killer's language? That he or she wanted to tell us something? About the deliberateness of the *modus operandi*?"

She remembered.

"It strikes me now that from the start we saw things correctly. But we were thinking wrong."

"Because a woman was behaving like a man?"

"Maybe not exactly the behaviour. But she committed deeds that made us think of brutal men."

"So we were supposed to think about the victims? It was they who were brutal?"

"Exactly. Them and not the killer. We read the wrong message into what we saw."

"But here's where it gets difficult," she said. "To believe that a woman can be capable of this. I'm not talking about physical strength. I'm just as strong as my husband, for example. He has trouble beating me at arm wrestling."

Wallander looked at her in surprise. She noticed and laughed.

"People amuse themselves in different ways."

Wallander nodded.

"I remember having a finger-pulling match with my mother when I was little," he said. "I think I was the winner."

"Maybe she let you win."

They turned off towards Sturup.

"I don't know what motivation this woman has for her actions," Wallander said. "But if we find her, I think we'll be dealing with someone the likes of whom we've never encountered before."

"A female monster?"

"Maybe. But that's not certain either."

The phone interrupted their conversation. Wallander answered. It was Birch. He gave them directions to Katarina Taxell's mother's house.

"What's her first name?" Wallander asked.

"Hedwig. Hedwig Taxell."

They would be there in about half an hour. The twilight wrapped around them.

Birch was on the steps to receive them. Hedwig Taxell lived at the end of a row of terrace houses on the outskirts of Lund. Wallander guessed that the houses had been built in the early 1960s. Flat roofs, square boxes facing onto small courtyards. He recalled having read that the roofs sometimes caved in during heavy snowfalls.

"They almost started talking before I got the machine set up," he said.

"We haven't exactly been overwhelmed with good luck," Wallander replied. "What's your impression of Hedwig Taxell?"

"She's worried about her daughter and grandson. But she seems more composed than before."

"Do you think she'll help us? Or is she protecting her daughter?"

"I think she wants to know where she is."

He let them into the living room. Without being able to define it, Wallander had a feeling that the room was somehow similar to Katarina Taxell's flat. Hedwig Taxell came in and greeted them. As usual, Birch stayed in the background. Wallander studied her. She was pale. Her eyes shifted restlessly. Wallander was expecting this. Her voice on the tape had been nervous and tense, close to breaking point. He had brought Höglund along because she had a great ability to reassure nervous people. Mrs Taxell didn't seem to be on her guard. He had a feeling that she was glad not to be alone. They sat down. Wallander had prepared his first questions.

"Mrs Taxell, we need your help. Can you answer some questions about Katarina for us?"

"How could she know anything about those horrible murders? She just had a baby, you know."

"We don't think she's in any way involved," Wallander said in a friendly voice. "But we have to look for information from many different sources."

"What's she supposed to know?"

"That's what I'm hoping to find out."

"Can't you try to find her instead? I don't understand what's happened."

"I'm sure she's in no danger," Wallander said, but he wasn't entirely successful in hiding his doubt.

"She's never done a thing like this before."

"So you have no idea where she is, Mrs Taxell?"

"My name is Hedwig."

"You have no idea where she is?"

"No. I can't quite believe what is happening."

"Does Katarina have a lot of friends?"

"No, she doesn't, but the ones she has are close friends. I don't know where she'd be other than with one of them."

"Maybe there's someone she didn't see very often? Or someone she has met recently?"

"Who would that be?"

"Or maybe someone she met earlier? Someone she had started seeing again recently?"

"I would have known about it. We have a good relationship. Much better than most mothers and daughters."

"I'm not implying that you had any secrets from each other," Wallander said patiently. "But it's rare that someone knows everything about another person. Do you know, for instance, who the father of her child is?"

Wallander hadn't meant to throw the question in her face like that. She flinched.

"I've tried to get her to talk about it," she said. "But she refuses."

"So you don't know who he is? You can't even guess?"

"I didn't even know she was seeing anyone."

"You knew that she had a relationship with Eugen Blomberg?"

"I knew about it. I didn't like him."

"Why not? Was it because he was already married?"

"I didn't know that until I saw the obituary in the paper. It was a shock."

"Why didn't you like him?"

"I don't know. He was unpleasant."

"Did you know that he had abused Katarina?"

Her horror was genuine. For a moment Wallander felt sorry for her. Her world was threatening to collapse. She was being forced to admit that there was a lot she didn't know about her daughter, that the intimacy she thought they shared was hardly more than a shell.

"Did he hit her?"

"Worse than that. He abused her in many different ways."

She stared at him in disbelief, but saw that he was telling the truth. She couldn't defend herself.

"It's possible that Eugen Blomberg is the father of her child, even though they weren't seeing each other."

She shook her head slowly and said nothing. Wallander looked at Höglund. She nodded. He took this to mean that he should go on. Birch stood motionless in the background.

"Her friends," Wallander said. "We need to talk to them."

"I've already told you who they are. And you've already talked to them."

She rattled off three names. Birch nodded in the background.

"There are no others?"

"No."

"Does she belong to any clubs?"

"No."

"Has she taken any holidays abroad?"

"We usually go somewhere once a year, in February. To Madeira, Morocco, Tunisia."

"Does she have any hobbies?"

"She reads a lot, she likes to listen to music. Her hair products business takes up most of her time. She works hard."

"Nothing else?"

"Sometimes she plays badminton."

"Who with? One of the three girlfriends?"

"With a teacher. I think her name is Carlman. But I've never met her."

Wallander didn't know if this was important. At least it was a new name.

"Do they work at the same school?"

"Not any more. They did in the past, a few years ago."

"You don't remember her first name?"

"I've never met her."

"Where did they usually play?"

"At Victoria Stadium. It's within walking distance of her flat."

Birch discreetly went into the hall. Wallander knew that he would trace the woman named Carlman. It took him less than five minutes. He came back and signalled to Wallander, who stood up and went out to the hall. In the meantime Höglund tried to clarify what Mrs Taxell really knew about her daughter's relationship with Eugen Blomberg.

"That was easy," Birch said. "Annika Carlman. She's

the one who reserves and pays for the court. I have her address. It's not far from here."

"Let's go there," Wallander said.

He went back into the room.

"Your daughter's friend's name is Annika Carlman," he said. "She lives on Bankgatan."

"I've never heard her first name before," Mrs Taxell said.

"We'll leave you two alone for a while," Wallander went on. "We need to talk to her right away."

It took less than ten minutes to get there. It was 6.30 p.m. Annika Carlman lived in a turn-of-the-century block of flats. Birch picked up the security phone. A man's voice answered, and Birch identified himself. The door opened. A door on the second floor stood open. A man stood there waiting for them. He introduced himself.

"I'm Annika's husband," he said. "What's happened?"

"Nothing," Birch said. "We just need to ask a few questions."

He invited them in. The flat was big and lavishly furnished. Somewhere in another room they could hear music and children's voices. A moment later Annika Carlman came in. She was tall, and was dressed in gym gear.

"These police officers want to talk to you."

"We need to ask some questions about Katarina Taxell," Wallander said.

They sat down in a room lined with books. Wallander wondered whether Annika Carlman's husband was also a teacher.

He got right to the point.

"How well do you know Katarina Taxell?"

"We played badminton together, but we didn't socialise."

"But you do know that she just had a baby?"

"We haven't played badminton for five months for precisely that reason."

"Were you going to start up again?"

"We'd agreed she would give me a call."

Wallander mentioned the names of Katarina's three girlfriends.

"I don't know them. We just played badminton."

"When did you start playing?"

"About five years ago. We were teachers at the same school."

"Is it really possible to play badminton regularly with someone for five years without getting to know her?"

"Perfectly possible, yes."

Wallander pondered how to continue. Annika Carlman gave clear, concise answers. And yet he could feel that they were moving away from something.

"You never saw her together with anyone else?"

"Man or woman?"

"Let's start with a man."

"No."

"Not even when you were working together?"

"She kept to herself. There was one teacher who seemed interested in her. She acted very cold towards him, you might almost say hostile. But she was good with the students. She was smart. A stubborn and smart teacher."

"Did you ever see her with a woman?"

Wallander had given up hope in the value of that question before he even asked it. But he had resigned himself too soon.

"Yes, as a matter of fact," she replied. "About three years ago."

"Who was it?"

"I don't know her name. But I know what she does. It was a very peculiar situation."

"What does she do?"

"What she's doing now, I don't know. But back in those days she was a waitress in a dining car on a train."

Wallander frowned.

"You ran into Katarina Taxell on a train?"

"I just happened to catch sight of her in town with another woman. I was walking on the other side of the street. We didn't even say hello to each other. A few days later I took the train to Stockholm. I went into the dining car somewhere after Alvesta. When I was paying the bill I recognised the woman working there. I'd seen her with Katarina."

"You say you don't know what her name is?"

"No."

"But you mentioned this to Katarina later on?"

"Actually, I didn't. I forgot all about it. Is it important?"

Wallander suddenly thought about the timetable he had found in Taxell's desk.

"Maybe. What day was it? Which train?"

"How would I remember that?" she said in surprise. "It was three years ago."

"Do you happen to have an old calendar? We'd like you to try and remember."

Her husband, who had been sitting quietly and listening, stood up.

"I'll get the calendar," he said. "Was it 1991 or 1992?"

She thought for a moment.

"1991. In February or March."

Several minutes passed as they waited tensely. The music from somewhere in the flat had been replaced by sounds from a TV. The husband came back and handed her an old black calendar. She leafed through a few months. Then she found the right place.

"I went to Stockholm on 19 February 1991. On a train that left at 7.12 a.m. Three days later I came back. I'd been to see my sister."

"You didn't see this woman on your return trip?"

"I've haven't seen her since."

"But you're positive that it was the same woman as the one you'd seen on the street here in Lund with Katarina?"

"Yes."

Wallander regarded her thoughtfully.

"There's nothing else you think might be important for us?"

She shook her head.

"I realise how little I know about Katarina. But she's a good badminton player."

"How would you describe her as a person?"

"That's hard. Maybe that describes her right there. A hard-to-describe person. She's temperamental. She can be depressed. But that time I saw her on the street with the waitress she was happy and laughing."

"There's nothing else you think might be important?"

Wallander saw that she was making an effort to be helpful.

"I think she misses her father," she said after a moment.

"Why do you think that?"

"It's just a feeling I got. Something to do with the way she acted towards men who were old enough to be her father."

"How did she act?"

"She'd stop behaving naturally, as if unsure of herself."

Wallander thought about Katarina's father, who had died when she was still young. He also wondered if what Annika

Carlman had said could explain her relationship with Eugen Blomberg.

He looked at her again. "Anything else?"

"No."

Wallander nodded to Birch and stood up.

"We won't bother you any more," he said.

"I'm curious, of course," she said. "Why are the police asking questions if nothing has happened?"

"A lot has happened," Wallander said. "But not to Katarina. I'm afraid that's all the answer I can give you."

They left the flat.

"We have to find this waitress," Wallander said.

"Swedish Railways must have lists of employees," Birch said. "But I wonder if we're going to find out anything more tonight. It was three years ago, after all."

"We have to try," Wallander said. "Of course I can't ask you to do it. We can handle it from Ystad."

"You have enough to do," Birch replied. "I'll take care of it."

Wallander could tell that Birch was sincere. It was no sacrifice.

They drove back to Hedwig Taxell's house. Birch dropped Wallander off and continued on to the police station to start looking for the waitress. Wallander wondered whether it was an impossible task.

Just as he rang the bell, his phone rang. It was Martinsson. Wallander could hear from his voice that he was managing to pull himself out of his depression. It was going better than Wallander had dared hope.

"How are things?" Martinsson asked. "Are you still in Lund?"

"We're trying to trace a waitress who works for Swedish Railways," Wallander replied.

Martinsson was wise enough not to ask any further questions.

"A lot's been going on here," he said. "Svedberg managed to get hold of the person who printed Eriksson's poetry books. He was a very old man, but his mind was sharp. And he didn't mind telling us what he thought of Eriksson. Apparently he had trouble getting paid for his work."

"Did he tell us anything new?"

"Eriksson seems to have made regular trips to Poland since the war. He took advantage of the poverty there to buy women. When he came home, he would boast about his conquests. That old printer really told us what he thought of him."

Wallander remembered what Sven Tyrén had told him during one of their first conversations. Now it had been confirmed. So Krista Haberman wasn't the only Polish woman in Eriksson's life.

"Svedberg wondered whether it would be worth contacting the Polish police," Martinsson said.

"Maybe," Wallander replied. "But for the time being, I think we'll wait on that."

"There's more," Martinsson said. "I'll let you talk to Hansson now."

Hansson came on the phone.

"I think I have a clear picture of who worked Eriksson's land," he said. "It all seems to be distinguished by one thing."

"What?"

"An unsolved crime. If I can believe my source, Eriksson had an incredible ability to make enemies. You'd think that his life's great passion was to make new enemies."

"The fields," Wallander said impatiently.

He could hear how Hansson's voice changed when he replied. He sounded more serious.

"The ditch," Hansson said. "Where we found Eriksson hanging on the stakes."

"What about it?"

"It was dug some years back. It wasn't there to start with. Nobody really understood why Eriksson needed to put it in. It wasn't necessary for drainage. The mud was shovelled out, and made the hill taller where the tower is."

"A ditch isn't what I had in mind," Wallander said. "It doesn't seem believable that it could have anything to do with a grave."

"That was my first thought too," Hansson said. "But then I heard something that made me change my mind."

Wallander held his breath.

"The ditch was dug in 1967. The farmer I talked to was sure about that. It was dug in the late autumn of 1967."

"So that means the ditch was dug about the same time that Krista Haberman disappeared."

"My farmer was even more specific. He was certain that the ditch was dug at the end of October. He remembered because of a wedding in Lödinge on the last day of October that year. The times match exactly. Krista Haberman goes on a car ride from Svenstavik. He kills her. Buries her. A ditch appears. A ditch that wasn't really necessary."

"Good," Wallander said. "This means something."

"If she's there, then I know where we should start searching," Hansson said. "The farmer claimed that they started digging the ditch just southeast of the hill. Eriksson had rented a digger. The first few days he did the digging himself, then he let others finish."

"Then that's where we'll start digging," Wallander said, noticing his feeling of unease growing. "We'll start tomorrow," he went on. "I want you to make all the preparations."

"It's going to be impossible to keep this secret," Hansson said.

"We have to try, at least," Wallander said. "I want you to talk to Chief Holgersson about it. And Per Åkeson, and the others."

"There's one thing that puzzles me," Hansson said hesitantly. "If we do find her, what does it really prove? That Holger Eriksson killed her? We can assume so, even if we can never prove a dead man's guilt. But what will it really mean for the murder investigation we're doing right now?"

It was a reasonable question.

"Most of all it'll tell us that we're on the right track," Wallander said. "That the motive connecting these murders is revenge."

"And you still think it's a woman behind this?"

"Yes," replied Wallander. "Now more than ever."

When the conversation was over, Wallander remained standing outside in the autumn night. The sky was cloudless. A faint breeze blew on his face. They were slowly approaching something – the centre he had spent exactly one month searching for. He still didn't know what they would find there.

The woman he tried to visualise kept slipping away, yet at the same time he sensed that in some way he might be able to understand her.

Cautiously she opened the door to where they were sleeping. The child lay in the bassinet she had bought that day. Katarina Taxell was curled up in a foetal position on the edge of the bed. She stood still and looked at them. *It was as if she were looking at herself. Or maybe it was her sister lying in the crib.*

Suddenly she couldn't see. She was completely surrounded by blood. It's not just a child who is born in blood. Life itself had its source in the blood that ran out when the skin was cut. Blood that remembered the arteries it had once flowed through. She could see it clearly. Her mother screaming and the man standing over her as she lay on a table with her legs spread. Even though it was 40 years ago, time came rushing towards her from the past. All her life she had tried to escape, but she couldn't. The memories always caught up with her. But she knew that she no longer needed to fear these memories. Now that her mother was dead, and she was free to do what she wanted, what she had to do to keep the memories at bay.

The feeling of dizziness passed as quickly as it had come. Cautiously she approached the bed and looked at the sleeping child. It wasn't her sister. This child already had a face. Her sister hadn't lived long enough to have anything. This was Katarina's newborn baby. Not her mother's. Katarina's child, who would never have to be tormented, haunted by memories.

She felt quite calm again. The images were gone. What she was doing was right. She was preventing people from being tormented as she had been. She had forced those men who had committed violent acts that had gone unpunished, to take the harshest of all roads. Or so she imagined. A man whose life was taken by a woman would never be able to understand what had happened to him.

It was quiet. That was the most important thing. It was the right thing for her to go and get the woman and child.

Speak calmly, listen, and tell her that everything that had happened was for the best. Eugen Blomberg had drowned. What it said in the papers about a sack was rumour and exaggeration. Eugen Blomberg was gone. Whether he had stumbled or tripped and then drowned, nobody was to blame. Fate had decided. And fate was just. That's what she had repeated over and over again, and it seemed as if Katarina was now starting to accept it.

Yesterday she'd had to tell the women that they would have to miss their meeting this week. She didn't like interrupting her timetable. It created disorder and made it hard for her to sleep. But it was necessary. It wasn't possible to plan everything.

As long as Katarina and her child stayed with her, she would live at the house in Vollsjö. She had brought along only the essentials from her flat in Ystad: her uniforms and the small box in which she kept her slips of paper and the book of names. Now that Katarina and her child were asleep, she didn't have to wait any longer. She dumped the slips of paper onto the top of the baking oven, shuffled them, and then began picking them up.

The ninth slip she unfolded had the black cross on it. She opened the ledger and slowly scanned the list, stopped at number 9 and read the name. Tore Grundén. She stood motionless and stared straight ahead. His picture slowly materialised. First as a vague shadow, a few barely visible contours. Then a face, an identity. Now she remembered him. Who he was, and what he had done.

It was more than ten years ago. She was working at the hospital in Malmö. One evening right before Christmas she was working in the casualty ward. The woman in the ambulance was dead on arrival. She had died in a car accident. Her husband had come with her. He was upset, and yet composed, and she was immediately suspicious. She had seen it so many times. Since the woman was dead, there was nothing they could do. But she had taken one of the policemen aside and asked him what happened. It was a tragic accident. Her husband had backed out of the garage without noticing that she was standing behind the car. He had run over her, and her head was crushed under one of the back wheels of the car. It was an accident that shouldn't have happened. In a moment when she wasn't being observed, she had pulled the sheet away and looked at the dead woman. She wasn't a doctor, but she was convinced that the woman had been run over more than once. Later she started investigating. The woman who now lay dead on the stretcher had been admitted to the hospital several times before. Once she had fallen from a ladder. Another time she hit her head hard on a cement floor when she tripped in the basement.

She wrote an anonymous letter to the police. She talked to the doctors who examined the body. But nothing happened. The man was given a fine, or maybe a suspended sentence, for gross negligence. Nothing else happened. Now everything would be made right again. Everything except the life of the dead woman. She couldn't bring her back.

She started planning how it would take place, but something bothered her. The men who were watching Katarina's house. They had come to stop her. They were trying to get to her through Katarina. Maybe they had started to suspect that a woman was behind all that had happened. She was counting on that. First they would think it was a man. Then they would begin to have doubts. Finally they would see that they had been looking in the wrong direction.

They would never find her. Never. She looked at the baking oven and thought about Tore Grundén. He lived in Hässleholm and worked in Malmö. Then it came to her how it would happen. It was almost embarrassingly easy. She could do it on the job. During working hours. With pay.

CHAPTER 34

They started digging early on the morning of Friday, 21 October. The light was still quite dim. Wallander and Hansson had marked off the first quadrant with crime-scene tape. The officers, dressed in overalls and gumboots, knew what they were looking for. Their apprehension seemed in tune with the cool morning air. Wallander felt as though he were in a cemetery. Somewhere in the earth they might come upon the remains of a body.

He had put Hansson in charge of the digging. Wallander was going to work with Birch to track down the waitress who had once made Katarina Taxell laugh on a street in Lund. For half an hour, he stayed out in the mud where the men had started digging. Then he walked up the path to the farm where his car was waiting. He called Birch and caught him at home. Birch had managed to discover that they might be able to find the name of the waitress they were looking for in Malmö. Birch was having coffee when Wallander called. They agreed to meet outside the station in Malmö.

This is the fourth woman involved in the investigation. There was Krista Haberman, then Eva Runfeldt and then Katarina Taxell. The waitress was the fourth woman. Was there another woman, a fifth one? Was she the one they were looking for? Or had they reached their goal if they succeeded in finding the waitress? Was she the one who made the night-time visits to Ystad's maternity ward? Without being able to explain why, he doubted that the waitress was the woman they were really searching for. Maybe she could give them a lead, but he couldn't hope for much more than that.

He drove through the grey autumn countryside in his old car, wondering absentmindedly how the winter would be. When had they had snow for Christmas in the past few years? It was so long ago he couldn't remember.

He reached Malmö station, and found a carpark next to the main entrance. He thought of getting a cup of coffee before Birch arrived, but time was tight.

He found Birch on the other side of the canal, on his way across the bridge. He must have parked up by the square. They shook hands. Birch was wearing a knitted cap that was much too small. He was unshaven and looked as though he hadn't had enough sleep.

"Have you started digging?" he asked.

"At 7 a.m.," Wallander replied.

Birch nodded gloomily. He pointed at the station.

"We're supposed to meet a man named Karl-Henrik Bergstrand," he said. "Normally he doesn't get in this early. He promised to be here today to meet us."

They went into the administrative offices of Swedish Railways. Bergstrand was already there. He was in his early 30s. Wallander assumed that he represented the new, youthful image of the company. They introduced themselves.

"Your request is unusual," Bergstrand said and laughed. "But we'll see if we can help you."

He invited them into his spacious office. Wallander

found his self-confidence extraordinary. When Wallander had been 30, he was still insecure about almost everything.

Bergstrand sat down behind his big desk. Wallander looked at the furniture in the room. Maybe that explained why their tickets were so expensive.

"We're looking for a dining car attendant," Birch began. "A woman."

"An overwhelming majority of the people working in train service are women," Bergstrand replied. "It would have been significantly easier to find a man."

"We don't know her name," Birch said. "All we know is what she looks like."

Bergstrand gave him a surprised look.

"Do you really have to try to find someone you know so little about?"

"We do," Wallander interjected.

"We know which train she worked on," said Birch.

He gave Bergstrand the information they had from Annika Carlman. Bergstrand shook his head.

"This was three years ago," he said.

"We know that," said Wallander. "But I assume that you have personnel records?"

"That's really not something I can answer," Bergstrand said. "Swedish Railways is divided into many enterprises. The restaurants are a subsidiary. They have their own personnel administration. They're the ones who can answer your questions."

Wallander was starting to get both impatient and annoyed. "Let's get one thing clear," he interrupted. "We're not looking for this waitress just for the fun of it. We want to find her because she may have important information relating to a complicated murder investigation. So we don't care who answers our questions. But we're anxious to get it done as fast as possible. I assume you can get hold of someone who can help us," he said. "We'll sit here and wait."

"Is it about the murders in the Ystad area?" Bergstrand asked with interest.

"Exactly. And this waitress might know something that's important."

"Is she a suspect?"

"No," Wallander replied. "She's not a suspect. No shadow will be cast on either the train or the sandwiches."

Bergstrand got up and left the room.

"He seemed a little arrogant," Birch said. "It was good what you said to him."

"It'd be even better if he could give us an answer," Wallander said.

While they waited, Wallander called Hansson in Lödinge. They were digging towards the middle of the first quadrant. They hadn't found anything.

"Unfortunately it's already leaked out," Hansson said. "We've had a number of people hanging around up at the farm."

"Keep them at a distance," Wallander told him. "I guess that's all we can do."

"Nyberg wants to talk to you. It's about that tape recording of Katarina Taxell and her mother."

"Were they able to identify the noise in the background?"

"I think not, but it's better if you talk to him yourself."

"They couldn't say anything at all?"

"They thought someone near the phone was pounding on the floor or the wall. But what good does that do us?"

Wallander had started to hope too soon.

"It couldn't very well be Taxell's newborn baby," Hansson said.

"Apparently we have access to an expert who might be able to work out whether the phone call came from far away or close by. But it's a complicated process. Nyberg said it would take at least a couple of days."

"We'll have to settle for that," Wallander said.

Bergstrand came back into the office and Wallander quickly ended his conversation.

"It'll take a while," Bergstrand said. "We have to get hold of a personnel list that's three years old and the company has undergone a lot of changes since then. But I've explained that it's important. They're getting right onto it."

"We'll wait," Wallander said.

Bergstrand didn't seem overly enthusiastic about having two police officers sitting in his office, but he didn't say anything.

"Coffee's one of your specialities, isn't it?" Birch asked. "Can we get some?"

Bergstrand left the room.

"I don't think he's used to getting the coffee himself," Birch said gleefully.

Wallander didn't reply.

Bergstrand returned with a tray. Then he excused himself, saying that he had an urgent meeting. They stayed where they were. Wallander drank the coffee and felt his impatience growing. He thought about Hansson and wondered whether he should leave Birch to wait for the waitress to be identified. He decided to stay half an hour. No more.

"I've been trying to get abreast of everything that's happened," Birch said after a while. "I admit I've never been involved in anything like this before. Could the killer really be a woman?"

"We can't ignore what we know," Wallander replied.

At the same time the feeling that kept plaguing him returned. The fear that he was steering the whole investigation into terrain that consisted of nothing but pitfalls. At any moment the trap door could open under their feet.

"We haven't had many female serial killers in this country," he said.

"If any," Wallander said. "Besides, we don't know if she's committed the murders. Our clues will either lead us to her alone or to someone who is working behind her."

"And you think she regularly serves coffee on trains between Stockholm and Malmö?"

Birch's doubt was unmistakable.

"No," Wallander replied. "I don't think she serves coffee. The waitress is probably just the fourth step along the way."

Birch stopped asking questions. Wallander looked at the clock and wondered if he should call Hansson again. The half hour was almost up. Bergstrand was still busy with his meeting. Birch was reading a brochure.

Another 30 minutes passed. Wallander's patience was running out.

Bergstrand came back.

"It looks like we're going to solve it," he said brightly. "But it'll take a little while longer."

"How long?"

Wallander didn't hide his irritation. It probably wasn't justified, but he couldn't help it.

"Maybe half an hour. They're driving the files over here. That takes time."

They continued to wait. Birch put down his brochure and dozed off. Wallander went over to the window and looked out at Malmö. To the right he caught a glimpse of the hydrofoil terminal. He thought about the times he had stood there waiting for Baiba. How many? Twice. It felt more than that. He called Hansson. Nothing. The digging was going to take time. Hansson also said it had started to rain. Wallander gloomily realised the extent of this depressing work.

The whole thing is going to hell, he thought suddenly. I've steered the whole investigation right into perdition. Birch started snoring. Wallander kept on checking his watch. Bergstrand came back. Birch woke up with a start. Bergstrand had a piece of paper in his hand.

"Margareta Nystedt," he said. "That's probably the person you're looking for. She was the only one handling the serving that day for the departure in question."

Wallander jumped up from his chair. "Where is she now?"

"I don't actually know. She stopped working for us about a year ago."

"Damn," Wallander said.

"But we have her address," Bergstrand went on. "She might not have moved just because she stopped working for us."

Wallander grabbed the piece of paper. It was an address in Malmö.

"Carl Gustaf's Road," Wallander said. "Where's that?"

"Near Pildamm Park," replied Bergstrand.

Wallander saw that there was a phone number, but he decided not to call it. He would go there himself.

"Thanks for your help," he said to Bergstrand. "Can I count on this information being correct? Was she the only one on duty that day?"

"Swedish Railways is known for its reliability," said

Bergstrand. "That means that we take care to keep track of our employees. Both in the administration and in the subsidiaries."

Wallander didn't understand the connection, but he didn't have time to ask. "Then let's go," he said to Birch.

They left the station. Birch went in Wallander's car. It took them less than ten minutes to find the address. It was a five-storey block of flats. Margareta Nystedt lived on the fifth floor. They took the lift. Wallander rang the bell before Birch was even out of the lift, waited, and then rang again. No answer. He swore to himself, then he made a quick decision. He rang the bell next door. The door opened almost at once. An elderly man gave Wallander a stern look. His shirt was unbuttoned over his paunch and he was holding a betting form.

He took out his identification. "We're looking for Margareta Nystedt," he said.

"What has she done?" the man asked. "She's a very friendly young woman. Her husband too."

"We just need some information," Wallander said. "She's not home. No-one came to the door. Do you happen to know where we could find her?"

"She works on the hydrofoil," replied the man. "She's a waitress."

Wallander looked at Birch.

"Thanks for your help," said Wallander. "Good luck with the horses."

Ten minutes later they braked in front of the hydrofoil terminal.

"I don't think we can park here," Birch said.

"To hell with it," said Wallander.

He felt as if he was running, and that everything would fall apart if he stopped. It took them only a few minutes to find out that Margareta Nystedt was working that morning on *Springaren*. It had just left Copenhagen and was expected to dock in half an hour. Wallander used the time to move his car. Birch sat on a bench in the departure hall and read a tattered newspaper. The terminal manager came over and said they could wait in the staff room. He wondered whether they wanted him to contact the boat.

"How much time does she have?" Wallander asked.

"She's really supposed to go back to Copenhagen on the next trip."

"That won't be possible."

The man was helpful. He promised to see to it that Margareta Nystedt could stay ashore. Wallander assured him that she wasn't suspected of any crime. He went out onto the dock as the boat pulled in. The passengers struggled against the wind. Wallander was surprised that so many people were travelling across the Sound on a weekday. He waited impatiently. The last passenger was a man on crutches, and then a woman wearing a uniform came out onto the deck. The manager pointed her out to Wallander. She was blonde, with her hair cropped very short, and she was younger than Wallander had expected. She stopped in front of him and crossed her arms. She was cold.

"Are you the one who wants to talk to me?" she asked.

"Margareta Nystedt?"

"That's me."

"Let's go inside. We don't have to stand out here freezing."

"I don't have much time."

"More than you think. You're not going back on the next trip."

She stopped.

"Why not? Who decided that?"

"I have to talk to you. But you have nothing to worry about."

He suddenly had a feeling that she was scared. For a brief moment he started to think he was mistaken. That she was the one they were looking for. That he already had the fifth woman at his side, without having met the fourth. Then he realised just as quickly that he was wrong. Margareta Nystedt was young and slender. She wasn't strong enough. And something about her whole presence told him she wasn't the murderer.

They went into the terminal building where Birch was waiting, went into the staff room and sat down. The room was empty. Birch introduced himself. She shook hands with him. Her hand was fragile. Like a bird's foot, Wallander thought to himself.

He studied her face. She was about 27 or 28. Her dress was short, and she had nice legs. She was wearing harsh make-up. He got the impression that she had painted over something on her face that she didn't like. She was nervous.

"I'm sorry we had to contact you like this," Wallander said. "But sometimes there are things that can't wait."

"Like my boat, for instance," she replied. Her voice had a strangely hard sound to it. Wallander hadn't expected that.

"It's not a problem. I've talked to your supervisor about it."

"What have I done?"

Wallander looked at her thoughtfully. She had no idea why he and Birch were there. There was no doubt about that. The trap door of his doubt creaked and groaned under his feet.

She repeated her question. What had she done?

Wallander glanced at Birch, who was surreptitiously looking at her legs.

"Katarina Taxell," Wallander said. "Do you know her?"

"I know who she is. Whether I know her is a different story."

"How did you meet her? What have you had to do with her?"

Suddenly she gave a start. "Has something happened to her?"

"No. Answer my questions."

"Answer mine! I only have one. Why are you asking me about her?"

Wallander saw that he had been too impatient. He had moved too fast. Her aggression was understandable.

"Nothing has happened to Katarina. And she's not suspected of committing any crime. Nor are you. But we need to get some information about her. That's all I can tell you. After you've answered my questions, I'll leave and you can go back to work."

She gave him a searching look. She was starting to believe him.

"About three years ago you spent time with her. Back then you were working as a waitress on the railway dining cars."

She seemed surprised that he knew about her past. Wallander had the impression that she was on her guard, which in turn made him sharpen his attention.

"Is that true?"

"Of course it's true. Why would I deny it?"

"And you knew Katarina Taxell?"

"Yes."

"How did you meet her?"

"We worked together."

Wallander gave her a surprised look before he continued.

"Isn't she a teacher?"

"She was taking a break. That's when she worked on the train."

Wallander looked at Birch, who shook his head. He hadn't heard about this either.

"When was this?"

"In the spring of 1991. I can't be any more specific than that."

"And you worked together?"

"Not always. But often."

"And you also spent time together when you were off?"

"Sometimes. But we weren't close friends. We had fun. That's all."

"When did you last see her?"

"We drifted apart when she stopped waitressing. It wasn't a close friendship."

Wallander saw that she was telling the truth. Her wariness was gone.

"Did Katarina have a steady boyfriend during that time?"

"I actually don't know," she replied.

"If you worked together and also spent time together, wouldn't you have known that?"

"I don't remember her ever mentioning anyone."

"And you never saw her with any men?"

"Never."

"Did she have any girlfriends she spent time with?"

Margareta Nystedt thought for a moment. Then she

gave Wallander three names. The same names Wallander already had.

"No-one else?"

"Not as far as I know."

"Have you ever heard the name Eugen Blomberg before?"

She thought about it.

"Wasn't he the man who was murdered?"

"That's right. Can you remember Katarina ever talking about him?"

She suddenly gave him a serious look.

"Was she the one who did it?"

Wallander pounced on her question.

"Do you think she could have killed anyone?"

"No. Katarina was a very gentle person."

"You went back and forth between Malmö and Stockholm," he said. "I'm sure you had a lot of work to do, but you must have talked to each other. Are you positive she never mentioned any other girlfriend? It's important."

"No," she said. "I can't remember anyone."

At that moment Wallander noticed her hesitate for a split second. She saw that he had noticed.

"Maybe," she said.

"What?"

"It must have been just before she quit. I'd been sick for a week with the flu. When I came back she was different."

Wallander was on tenterhooks now. Birch had also noticed that something was up.

"Different in what way?"

"I don't know how to explain it. Her mood seemed to swing between gloom and exhilaration. She had changed."

"Try to describe the change. This could be crucial."

"Usually when we didn't have anything to do we would sit in the little kitchen in the restaurant car. We talked and looked through magazines. But when I came back we didn't do that any more."

"What happened instead?"

"She left."

Wallander waited for her to go on. But she didn't.

"She left the dining car? She couldn't very well have left the train. What did she say she was going to do?"

"She didn't say anything."

"But you must have asked her. She was different? She didn't sit and talk any more?"

"Maybe I asked. I don't remember. But she didn't say anything. She just left."

"Did this always happen?"

"No. Just before she quit she was different. She seemed completely closed off."

"Do you think she was meeting someone on the train? A passenger who was on board each time? It sounds strange."

"I don't know."

Wallander had no more questions. He looked at Birch, who had nothing more to add either.

The hydrofoil was just about to leave the harbour.

"You can have a break now," Wallander said. "I want you to contact me if you think of anything else."

He wrote his name and phone number on a piece of paper and handed it to her.

She stood up and left.

"Who would meet Katarina on a train?" Birch asked. "A passenger who travels back and forth between Malmö and Stockholm? Besides, they can't be serving all the time on the same train. That doesn't sound logical."

Wallander was only half listening to what Birch said. An idea had occurred to him that he didn't want to lose. It couldn't be a passenger. So it had to be someone else who was on the train for the same reason she was.

Wallander looked at Birch.

"Who works on a train?" he asked.

"I assume there's an engine driver."

"Who else?"

"Conductors. One or more."

Wallander nodded. He thought about what Höglund had discovered. The faint glimmer of a pattern. A person who had irregular but recurring days off. Like people who work on trains. And then there was the timetable in the secret compartment. He stood up.

"I think we'll go back and see Bergstrand," he said.

"Are you looking for more waitresses?"

Wallander didn't reply. He was already on his way out of the terminal building.

Bergstrand did not look at all happy to see Wallander and Birch again. Wallander moved fast, practically shoving him through the door to his office.

"During the same time period," he said. "The spring of 1991, there was a woman named Katarina Taxell working for you. I want you to get out all the documents on conductors and engine drivers who worked the shifts when Katarina Taxell was working. I'm especially interested in a week during the spring of 1991 when Margareta Nystedt called in sick. Do you understand what I'm saying?"

"You can't be serious," Bergstrand said. "It's an impossible job to piece together all that information. It'll take months."

"Let's say you have a couple of hours," Wallander replied

in a friendly voice. "If necessary, I'll ask the national police commissioner to call up his colleague, the general manager of Swedish Railways. And I'll ask him to complain about the lack of cooperation by an employee in Malmö named Karl-Henrik Bergstrand."

Bergstrand smiled grimly. "So let's do the impossible," he said. "But it's going to take hours."

"If you work as fast as you can, then you can have as long as you need," Wallander replied.

"You can spend the night in one of our dormitory rooms at the station," said Bergstrand. "Or at the Hotel Prize, with which we have an agreement."

"No thanks," Wallander said. "When you have the information I've asked for, send it to me by fax at the police station in Ystad."

"So you think there is someone else who worked for Swedish Railways back then?" Birch asked.

"There has to be. There's no other reasonable explanation."

Birch put on his knitted cap. "That means we wait."

"You in Lund and me in Ystad. Keep monitoring Hedwig Taxell's phone. Katarina might call again."

They parted outside the station building. Wallander got into his car and drove through the city. He wondered whether he had reached the innermost Chinese box. What would he find inside?

He turned into a petrol station right before the last roundabout on the road to Ystad. He filled up the car and went inside to pay. When he came out he heard his phone ringing. He yanked open the door and grabbed the phone. It was Hansson.

"Where are you?" Hansson asked.

"On my way to Ystad."

"I think you'd better come out here."

Wallander gave a start. He almost dropped the phone.

"Did you find her?"

"I think so."

Wallander drove straight to Lödinge.

The wind had picked up and shifted direction until it was blowing from the north.

CHAPTER 35

They had found a thighbone. That was all. It took several more hours before they found any more skeletal remains. There was a cold, blustery wind blowing that day, a wind that cut right through their clothes and magnified the dreariness and horror of the situation.

The femur lay on a plastic sheet. They had dug up an area no larger than 20 square metres, and were surprisingly close to the surface when a spade had struck the bone.

A doctor came and examined it. Naturally he couldn't say anything except that it was human. But Wallander didn't need any additional confirmation. In his mind there was no doubt that it was part of Krista Haberman's remains. They had to keep digging. Maybe they would find the rest of her skeleton, and maybe then they could determine how she had been killed.

Wallander felt tired and melancholy on that endless afternoon. It didn't help that he had been right. It was as though he was looking straight into a terrible story that he would rather not deal with. The whole time he was waiting tensely for what Karl-Henrik Bergstrand could tell them. He spent two long hours out in the mud with Hansson and the other policemen doing the excavation, then returned to the station, after explaining to Hansson what had happened in Malmö.

When he got to the police station he gathered all the

colleagues he could find and repeated his account of what had happened. Now all they had to do was wait for the paper to start coming out of the fax machine. While they were sitting in the conference room, Hansson called to say they had also found a shinbone. The discomfort around the table was palpable. They were sitting there waiting for a skull to appear in the mud.

It was a long afternoon. The first autumn storm was building over Skåne. Leaves whirled across the car park outside the station. They stayed in the conference room even though there was nothing for them to discuss as a group. All of them had many other assignments waiting on their desks, but Wallander thought that what they needed most right now was to gather their strength. If the information coming from Malmö gave them the breakthrough that he was hoping for, then they would have to do a lot in a very short space of time. That's why they were slumped in their chairs around the conference table, resting.

Birch called and told him that Hedwig Taxell had never heard of Margareta Nystedt. She also said that she couldn't understand how she'd managed to forget that her daughter had worked as a waitress on the trains for a while. Birch thought she was telling the truth.

Martinsson kept leaving the room to call home, allowing Wallander to check with Höglund. She thought that everything was already going much better for Terese. Martinsson had said no more about wanting to resign. Even that discussion had to be put on hold for the time being. Investigating serious crimes meant putting the rest of one's life on hold.

At 4 p.m. Hansson called to say they had found a middle finger. Soon after that he called again The skull had been uncovered. Wallander asked him if he wanted to be relieved, but he said he might as well stay.

An icy ripple of revulsion passed through the conference room when Wallander announced this latest news. Svedberg quickly put down the half-eaten sandwich he had in his hand.

Wallander had been through this before. A skeleton meant little without the skull. Only then was it possible to imagine the person who had once existed. In this mood of weary anticipation, the members of the team sat around the table like little isolated islands. Conversations were started from time to time. Someone would ask a question. An answer was given, something was clarified, and then silence would fall again.

Svedberg brought up Svenstavik.

"Eriksson must have been a strange man. First he entices a Polish woman to come with him down to Skåne. God knows what he promised her. Marriage? Wealth? The chance to be a car-dealer's princess? Then he kills her almost at once. But when he feels his own death approaching, he buys a letter of indulgence by bequeathing money to the church up there in Jämtland."

"I've read his poems," Martinsson said. "You can't deny that he occasionally shows some sensitivity."

"For animals," Höglund said. "For birds. But not for human beings."

Wallander remembered the abandoned kennel. He wondered how long it had been empty. Hamrén grabbed a phone and got hold of Sven Tyrén and they got the answer. Eriksson's last dog was found dead in the kennel one morning a few weeks before Eriksson was murdered. Tyrén had been told this by his wife, who in turn had heard it from the postwoman. What the dog died of he didn't know, but it was pretty old. Wallander guessed that someone must have killed the dog so it wouldn't bark. And that person was the one they were looking for. They had come up with one more explanation. But they still lacked an overall framework. Nothing had been fully clarified yet.

At 4.30 p.m. Wallander called Malmö. Bergstrand came to the phone. They would be able to fax over the names and other information Wallander had requested shortly.

The waiting continued. A reporter called and asked what they were digging for at Eriksson's farm. Wallander told him that the enquiry was progressing, but that he wasn't able to provide details at this stage. He was as friendly as possible. Chief Holgersson sat with them for most of the time. She also drove out to Lödinge with Åkeson. Unlike their former chief, Björk, she didn't say much. The two of them were quite different. Björk would have taken the opportunity to complain about the latest memo from the national police board, managing to connect it with the investigation that was under way. Lisa Holgersson was different. Wallander decided that they were both good in their own ways.

Hamrén was doing a crossword, Svedberg was searching for any remaining hairs on his scalp, and Höglund was sitting with her eyes closed. Now and then Wallander got up and took a walk down the hall. He was very tired. He wondered why Katarina Taxell hadn't made contact. Should they start to search for her? He was afraid they would scare off the woman who had come to get her. He heard the phone ringing in the conference room, and hurried back to stand in the door. Svedberg had picked it up.

Wallander mouthed the question "Malmö?" Svedberg shook his head. It was Hansson again.

"A rib this time," Svedberg said when he'd hung up. "Does he have to call here every time they find a bone?"

Wallander sat down at the table. The phone rang again. Svedberg picked it up. He listened briefly and then handed it to Wallander.

"You'll have it by fax in a few minutes," Bergstrand said. "I think we've found all the information you wanted."

"Then you've done a good job," Wallander said. "If there is any additional information I'll call you back."

"I'm sure you will," Bergstrand said. "I get the impression you aren't the type to give up."

They all gathered around the fax machine. After a few minutes pages started to be transmitted. Wallander saw instantly that there were many more names than he had imagined. When the transmission was completed he made copies for everyone. Back in the conference room they studied them in silence. Wallander counted 32 names, 17 of them women. He didn't recognise any of them. The lists of hours of service and the various combinations seemed endless. He searched for a long time before he found the week when Margareta Nystedt's name wasn't included. Eleven women conductors had been on duty on the days that Katarina Taxell was working as a waitress.

For a moment Wallander felt his powerlessness return. Then he forced it aside and tapped his pen on the table.

"There are a lot of people listed here," he said. "We have to concentrate on the eleven female conductors. Does anyone recognise any of the names?"

They bent their heads over the pages. No-one could remember any of the names from other parts of the investigation. Wallander missed Hansson's presence. He was the one with the best memory. He asked one of the detectives from Malmö to make a copy and see to it that someone drove it out to him.

"Then let's get started," he said when the detective left the room. "Eleven women. We have to look at every one of them. Let's hope that somewhere we'll find a point of connection with this investigation. We'll divide them up. And we'll start now. It's going to be a long night."

They divided up the names. Wallander knew the hunt was on. The waiting was finally over.

Many hours later, when it was almost 11 p.m., Wallander started to despair again. They had got no further than eliminating two of the names from the list. One of the women had died in a car accident long before they found Eriksson's body, and the other had already transferred to an administrative job in Malmö. Bergstrand had discovered the mistake and called Wallander at once. They were searching for points of intersection but found none. Höglund came into Wallander's office.

"What should I do with this one?" she asked, shaking a paper she had in her hand.

"What about her?"

"Anneli Olsson, 39 years old, married with four children. She lives in Ängelholm with her husband who is a vicar. She's deeply religious. She works on trains, takes care of her family, and spends the little free time she has on handicrafts and various efforts for the mission. What should I do with her? Call her in for an interview? Ask her if she killed three men in the past month? If she knows where Katarina Taxell and her newborn baby are?"

"Put her aside," Wallander said. "That's a step in the right direction too."

Hansson had come back from Lödinge when the rain

and wind made it impossible to keep working. He told Wallander that from tomorrow he'd need more people on the job. Then he set to work on the eight remaining women. Wallander tried in vain to send him home, at least to change out of his wet clothes. But he refused, and Wallander could see that he wanted to shake off the unpleasant experience of standing out in the mud digging for Krista Haberman's remains as soon as possible.

Just after 11 p.m., Wallander was on the phone trying to track down a relative of a female conductor named Wedin. She had moved five times in the past year. She had gone through a messy divorce and was on the sick list often. He was just dialling Information when Martinsson appeared at the door. Wallander could see by Martinsson's face that something had happened and he hung up quickly.

"I think I've found her," he said softly. "Yvonne Ander."

"Why do you think she's the one?"

"She actually lives here in Ystad. She has an address on Liregatan."

"What else?"

"She seems strange in many ways. Elusive, like this whole investigation. But she has a background that should interest us. She has worked both as an assistant nurse and an ambulance medic."

Wallander looked at him for a moment in silence. Then he got up quickly.

"Get the others," he said. "Now, right away."

In a few minutes they were gathered in the conference room.

"Martinsson may have found her," Wallander said. "And she lives here in Ystad."

Martinsson went over everything he had managed to find out about Yvonne Ander.

"She's 47 years old," he began. "She was born in Stockholm and came to Skåne 15 years ago. The first few years she lived in Malmö before moving here to Ystad. She's worked for Swedish Railways for the past ten years. But before that, when she was younger, she studied to be an assistant nurse and worked for many years in health care. She has also worked as an ambulance medic. And for long periods she doesn't seem to have worked at all."

"What was she doing then?" Wallander asked.

"There are big gaps."

"Is she married?"

"She's single."

"Divorced?"

"There are no children in the picture. I don't think she's ever been married. But the times that she was working on the trains match Katarina Taxell's."

Martinsson had been reading from his notebook. Now he dropped it on the table.

"There's one more thing. She's active in the Swedish Railways Recreational Association in Malmö. I think a lot of people are. But what surprised me was that she was interested in weight training."

It got very quiet in the room.

"So she's presumably strong," Martinsson continued. "And isn't it a woman with great physical strength that we're looking for?"

Wallander made a quick decision.

"We'll put all the other names aside for the time being and work on Yvonne Ander. Take it from the beginning one more time. Slowly."

Martinsson repeated his summary. They came up with new questions. Many of the answers were missing. Wallander looked at his watch. It was just before midnight.

"I think we should talk to her tonight."

"If she's not working," Höglund said. "She works on the night train occasionally. The other conductors work days or nights, never both."

"Either she's home or she's not," Wallander said.

"What are we actually going to talk to her about?"

The question came from Hamrén. It was legitimate.

"I think it's possible that Katarina Taxell might be there," Wallander said. "If nothing else, we can use that as an excuse. Her mother is worried. We can start with that. We have no evidence against her. We don't have a thing. But I want to get some fingerprints."

"So we're not sending a whole team," Svedberg said.

Wallander nodded at Höglund.

"I thought the two of us should visit her. We can have another car follow as backup. In case something happens."

"Like what?" Martinsson asked.

"I don't know."

"Isn't that a little irresponsible?" Svedberg said. "We do suspect she's involved in murder."

"We'll be armed," Wallander said.

They were interrupted by a man from the dispatch centre knocking on the door.

"There's a message from a doctor in Lund," he said. "He did a preliminary examination of the skeletal remains you found. He thinks they're from a woman. And they've been in the ground a long time."

"So we know that," Wallander said. "If nothing else, we're on our way to solving a 27-year-old case."

The officer left the room.

"I don't anticipate any trouble," Wallander said.

"How are we going to explain it if Taxell isn't there?

After all, we're thinking of knocking on her door in the middle of the night."

"We'll ask for Katarina," Wallander said. "We're looking for her. That's all."

"What happens if she's not home?"

Wallander didn't have to think it over.

"Then we go in. And the officers acting as backup will watch in case she's on her way home. In the meantime I'd like to ask the rest of you to wait here. I know it's late, but it can't be helped."

No-one had any objections.

They left the police station just after midnight. The wind was now at gale force. Wallander and Höglund took her car. Martinsson and Svedberg were in the backup car. Liregatan was right in the middle of Ystad. They parked a block away. The streets were almost deserted. They met only one other car, one of the police night patrols. Wallander wondered if the planned new cycle commando unit would be able to handle patrol duty when it was blowing as hard as it was now.

Yvonne Ander lived in a flat in a restored wood and brick building. Hers was the middle of three flats, with her door facing the street. Apart from a light on in a window to the far left, the whole building was in darkness.

"Either she's asleep or she's not home," Wallander said. "But we have to assume she's there."

The wind was blowing hard.

"Is she the one?" Höglund asked.

Wallander was freezing cold and out of sorts. Was it because they were now hunting a woman?

"Yes," he replied, "I think she is."

They crossed the street. To their left was Martinsson

and Svedberg's car, the headlights turned off. Höglund rang the bell. Wallander pressed his ear to the door and could hear the bell ringing inside. They waited tensely. He nodded to her to ring again. Still nothing. Then a third time, with the same result.

"Do you think she's asleep?" Höglund asked.

"No," Wallander said, "I don't think she's home."

He tried the door. It was locked. He took a step into the street and waved at the car. Martinsson came walking up. He was the best at opening locked doors without using force. He had a torch and a bundle of tools with him. Wallander held the light while Martinsson worked. It took him more than ten minutes. Finally he got the lock to open. He took the torch and went back to the car.

Wallander looked around. There was no-one about. He and Höglund went inside. They stood listening to the silence. There was no window in the hall. Wallander turned on a lamp. To the left was a living room with a low ceiling, to the right a kitchen. Straight ahead a narrow staircase led to an upper floor. It creaked under their feet. There were three bedrooms, all empty. There was no-one in the flat.

He tried to take stock of the situation. Could they count on the woman who lived there coming back during the night? He thought it highly unlikely. Especially since she had Taxell and her baby with her. Would she move them around at night?

Wallander walked up to a glass door in one of the bedrooms and discovered a balcony outside. Big flowerpots filled almost the entire space. But there were no flowers in them, just soil. The balcony and the empty flowerpots filled him with sudden dismay. He left the room quickly. They returned to the hall.

"Get Martinsson," he said. "And ask Svedberg to drive back to the station. They have to keep looking. I think Yvonne Ander has another residence besides this flat. Maybe a house."

"Shouldn't we have some surveillance on the street?"

"She won't come back tonight. But you're right, we should have. Ask Svedberg to take care of it."

Höglund was just about to leave when he held her back. Then he looked around. He went into the kitchen and lit the lamp over the bench. There were two dirty cups there. He wrapped them in a handkerchief and handed them to her.

"Prints," he said. "Get Svedberg to give them to Nyberg. This could be crucial."

He went back upstairs, hearing Höglund shut the front door behind her. He stood still in the dark, then did something that surprised even him. He went in the bathroom, picked up a towel, and sniffed it. He smelled the faint scent of a special perfume. But the smell reminded him of something else. He tried to capture the mental image. The memory of a scent. He sniffed the towel again, but he couldn't pin it down. Even though he knew he was close. He had smelled that scent somewhere else. He couldn't remember where or when, but it had been quite recently. He jumped when he heard the door open. Martinsson and Höglund appeared on the stairs.

"Now we have to start looking," said Wallander. "We're searching not only for something to connect her to the murders, but for something that indicates where she has another residence."

"Why should she have?" Martinsson asked.

They were whispering, as if the person they were looking for was close by and might hear them.

"Katarina Taxell," Wallander said. "Her baby. And we've believed all along that Runfeldt was held captive for three weeks. I'm sure that it wasn't here, in the middle of Ystad."

Martinsson and Höglund started work upstairs. Wallander closed the curtains in the living room and turned on some lamps. Then he stood in the middle of the room and turned slowly. The woman who lived here had beautiful furniture. And she smoked. He saw an ashtray on a little table next to a leather sofa. There were no cigarette butts in it, but there were faint traces of ashes. Paintings and photographs hung on the walls. Still lifes, vases of flowers, not very well done. Down in the lower right corner of one was a signature: *Anna Ander 1958*. A relative. Ander was an unusual surname. It figured in the history of Swedish crime, although he couldn't recall how. He looked at one of the framed photographs. A Scanian farm. The picture was taken from above at an angle. Wallander guessed that the photographer had been standing on a roof or a tall ladder. He walked around the room, trying to feel her presence. He wondered why it was so difficult. Everything gave an impression of abandonment, he thought. A prim, pedantic abandonment. She isn't here very often. She spends her time somewhere else.

He went over to her little desk next to the wall. Through the gap in the curtain he glimpsed a small yard. The window was draughty. He pulled out the chair, sat down and tried the biggest drawer. It was unlocked. A car passed by. Wallander saw the headlights catch a window and disappear. Then only the wind remained.

In the drawer were bundles of letters. He found his glasses and took out the top bundle. The sender was A. Ander, and the letter was sent from an address in Spain. He took out the letter and quickly scanned it. It was clear at once that Anna Ander was her mother. She was describing a trip. On the last page she wrote that she was on her way to Africa. The letter was dated April 1993. He put back the letter on the top of the bundle. The floorboards upstairs were creaking. He stuck one hand inside the drawer. Nothing. He started to go through the other drawers. Even paper can feel abandoned, he thought. He found nothing to make him take notice. It was too empty to be natural. Now he was convinced that she lived somewhere else. He kept going through the drawers. The floor upstairs creaked. It was 1.30 a.m.

She was driving through the night, feeling very tired. She had been listening to Katarina for hours. She often wondered about the weakness of these women. They let themselves be tortured, abused, murdered. Then if they survived, they sat night after night moaning about it. She didn't understand them. As she drove through the night she actually felt contempt for them. They didn't fight back.

It was 1 a.m. Normally she would have been asleep by now. She had to go to work early the next day. She had planned to sleep at Vollsjö, but in the end she dared to leave Katarina alone with her baby. She had convinced her to stay where she was just for a few more days, maybe a week. Tomorrow night they would call her mother again. Katarina would call and she would sit next to her. She didn't think Katarina would say anything she wasn't supposed to, but she wanted to be there anyway.

It was 1.10 a.m. when she drove into Ystad. She sensed the danger as soon as she turned down Liregatan and saw the parked car with its headlights off. She couldn't turn around, she had to keep going. There were two men in the car, and she thought she could see a light in her flat too. Furious, she accelerated. The car leaped ahead, and she braked just as suddenly when she'd turned the corner. So they had found her. The ones who were watching Katarina's house were in her flat. She felt dizzy, but she wasn't afraid. There was nothing there that could lead them to Vollsjö. Nothing that told them who she was, nothing but her name.

She sat motionless. The wind tore at the car. She had turned off the engine and the headlights. She would have to return to Vollsjö. Now she knew why she had come here – to see if the men who were following her had got into her flat. But she was still way ahead of them. They would never catch up with her. She would keep unfolding her slips of paper as long as there was a single name left in the ledger.

She started the car, and decided to drive past her building one more time. The car was still parked there. She stopped 20 metres behind it without shutting off the engine. Even though it was some distance and the angle was difficult, she could see that the curtains in her house were drawn. Whoever was inside had turned on the light. They were searching but they wouldn't find anything.

She forced herself to drive off slowly, without gunning the engine as she usually did. When she got back to Vollsjö, Katarina and her baby were asleep. Nothing would change. Everything would continue according to plan.

Wallander had returned to the bundle of letters when he heard quick steps on the stairs. He got up from his chair. It was Martinsson with Höglund right behind.

"I think you'd better take a look at this," Martinsson said. He was pale, his voice shaky.

He placed a worn notebook with a black cover on the desk. It was open. Wallander leaned over and put on his glasses. There was a column of names. Each had a number in the margin. He frowned.

"Go forward a few pages," Martinsson said.

Wallander did as he said. The column of names was repeated. There were arrows, deletions, and changes, and it looked as if it was a draft of something.

"A couple more pages," Martinsson said.

Wallander could hear he was shaken.

The column of names appeared again. This time there were fewer changes and deletions. Then he saw it.

He recognised the first name. Gösta Runfeldt. Then he found the others, Holger Eriksson and Eugen Blomberg. At the end of the rows there were dates written in. The dates of their deaths. Wallander looked up at Martinsson and Höglund. Both of them were pale. There was no longer any doubt. They had come to the right place.

"There are more than 40 names here," Wallander said. "You think she intends to kill them all?"

"At least we know who might be next," Höglund said. She pointed to a name.

Tore Grundén. Next to his name was a red exclamation mark. But there was no date in the margin.

"In the back there's a loose sheet of paper," Höglund said.

Wallander carefully took it out. There were meticulously written notes on it. The handwriting reminded him of Mona's. The letters were rounded, the lines even and regular, without deletions and changes. But what was written there was hard to interpret. There were numbers, the word Hässleholm, and something that could be from a timetable: 07.50, Saturday, 22 October. Tomorrow's date.

"What the hell does this mean?" Wallander asked. "Is Tore Grundén getting off the train in Hässleholm at 07.50?"

"Maybe he's getting on a train," Höglund said.

Wallander understood. He didn't hesitate.

"Call Birch in Lund. He's got the phone number of a man named Karl-Henrik Bergstrand in Malmö. Get the answer to this question. Is Yvonne Ander working on the train that stops in or leaves from Hässleholm at 7.50 a.m. tomorrow?"

Martinsson pulled out his phone. Wallander stared at the open notebook.

"Where is she?" Höglund asked. "Right now? We know where she'll probably be tomorrow morning."

Wallander looked at her. In the background he saw the paintings and photographs. Suddenly he knew. He should have realised it at once. He went over to the wall and unhooked the framed picture of the farm. Turned it over. *Hansgården in Vollsjö, 1965*, someone had written in ink.

"That's where she lives. And that's where she probably is right now."

"What should we do?" she asked.

"We'll go out there and bring her in."

Martinsson had got hold of Birch. They waited. The conversation was brief.

"He'll chase down Bergstrand for us," Martinsson said.

Wallander stood with the notebook in his hand.

"Let's go, then. We'll pick up the others on the way."

"Do we know where Hansgården is?" she asked.

"We can find it in the database," Martinsson said. "It won't take me ten minutes."

Now they were in a real hurry. They were back at the station just after 2 a.m. They gathered their weary colleagues. It took longer than Martinsson thought to find

Hansgården. He didn't find it until almost 3 a.m. It was on the outskirts of Malmö.

"Should we be armed?" Svedberg asked.

"Yes," Wallander said. "But don't forget that Katarina Taxell and her baby are there too."

Nyberg came into the conference room. His hair was standing on end and his eyes were bloodshot.

"We found what we were looking for on one of the cups," he said. "The fingerprint matches the ones on the suitcase and the cigarette butt. Because it's not a thumbprint, I can't say whether it's the same one we found on the tower. That print seems to have been made later as if she had been there a second time. But it's probably a match. Who is she?"

"Yvonne Ander," Wallander said. "And now we're going to bring her in. If only Bergstrand had called."

"Do we really have to wait for him?" Martinsson said.

"Half an hour, at the most." Wallander said.

They waited. Martinsson left the room to check that the flat on Liregatan was still under surveillance. Bergstrand called after 20 minutes.

"Yvonne Ander is working on the northbound train from Malmö tomorrow morning," he said.

"So, we know that much," Wallander said simply.

It was 3.45 a.m. when they left Ystad. The storm had reached its peak.

The final thing Wallander did was make two calls. First to Lisa Holgersson, then to Per Åkeson. They agreed that they would arrest her as soon as humanly possible.

CHAPTER 36

At just after 5 a.m. they were gathered at Hansgården in a hard, gusting gale. They were all freezing. They had surrounded the house in a shadow-like manoeuvre. It had been decided that Wallander and Höglund should go in. The others had taken up positions where they each had close contact with at least one colleague.

They had left the cars out of sight of the farmhouse and approached the last stretch on foot. Wallander spotted the red Golf parked in front of the house. On the ride up to Vollsjö he had worried that she might have already left. But her car was there. She was still home. The house was dark and quiet. Wallander couldn't see a dog.

It all went very fast. They took up their positions. Wallander asked Höglund to announce over their radios that they would wait a few more minutes before going in.

Wait for what? She didn't understand why. Wallander couldn't explain it either. Maybe it was because he had to prepare himself. Or did he need to create a space for himself for a few minutes so that he could think through everything that had happened? He stood there bitterly cold, everything seeming totally unreal. They had been pursuing a strange, elusive shadow for a month. Now they were close to their goal, at the point where the pounce would conclude the hunt. It was as if he had to free himself from the feeling of unreality that surrounded everything that had happened, especially in relation to the woman in the house, whom they had to arrest. For all this he needed breathing space. That's why he said they would wait.

He stood with Höglund in a windbreak next to a dilapidated barn. The front door was about 25 metres away. Time passed. Soon it would be dawn. They couldn't wait any longer.

Wallander had approved the use of guns, but he wanted everything to proceed slowly, especially since Katarina Taxell and her baby were inside. Nothing must go wrong. The most important thing was for them to stay calm.

"Now we go," he said finally. "Pass it on."

Höglund spoke softly into the radio and received a series of acknowledgments from the others. She took out her revolver. Wallander shook his head.

"Keep it in your pocket," he said. "But remember which one."

The house was still quiet. No movement. They approached, Wallander in the lead, Höglund behind him to the right. The wind was blowing hard. Wallander took another quick look at his watch. It was 5.19 a.m. Yvonne Ander should be up by now if she was going to make it to work. They stopped outside the door. Wallander took a deep breath, knocked on the door and took a step backwards. He had his hand on the revolver in his pocket. Nothing happened. He took a step forwards and knocked again. He tried the latch. The door was locked. He knocked again. Suddenly he felt uneasy. He pounded on the door. Still no reaction. Something was wrong.

"We'll have to break in," he said. "Tell the others. Who has the crowbar? Why didn't we bring it along?"

Höglund spoke with a firm voice into the radio. She turned her back to the wind. Wallander kept an eye on the windows next to the door. Svedberg came running with the crowbar. Wallander asked him to return to his position at once. Then he stuck in the crowbar and started prying, putting all his strength into it. The door sprang open at the lock. There was a light on in the hall. He drew his revolver, and Höglund quickly followed his lead. Wallander crouched and went in. She stood to one side behind him and covered him with her revolver. Everything was quiet.

"Police!" Wallander yelled. "We're looking for Yvonne Ander."

Nothing happened. He yelled again. Cautiously he moved towards the room straight ahead of him. Höglund followed at his flank. The sense of unreality returned. He stepped quickly into a large, open room, sweeping over it with his revolver. It was completely empty. He let his arm drop. Höglund was on the other side of the door. A huge baking oven stood against one wall.

Suddenly a door opened across the room. Wallander gave a start and raised his revolver again, and Höglund went down on one knee. Katarina Taxell came through the door dressed in a nightgown. She looked terrified.

Wallander lowered his revolver, and Höglund did too. At that moment Wallander knew that Yvonne Ander wasn't in the house.

"What's happening?" Taxell asked.

Wallander went quickly up to her.

"Where's Yvonne Ander?"

"She's not here."

"Where is she?"

"I assume she's on her way to work."

Wallander was now in a big hurry.

"Who came and picked her up?"

"She always drives herself."

"But her car is still parked outside the house."

"She has two cars."

So simple, thought Wallander. Not just the red Golf.

"Are you feeling all right?" he asked. "And your baby?"

"Why shouldn't I feel all right?"

Wallander took a quick look around the room. Then he asked Höglund to call in the others. They didn't have much time.

"Get Nyberg here," he said. "The house has to be gone over from the rafters to the cellar."

The freezing police officers gathered in the big white room.

"She's gone," Wallander said. "She's on her way to Hässleholm. At least there's no reason to believe otherwise. She's supposed to start her shift there. A passenger named Tore Grundén will be getting on too. He's the next one on her hit list."

"Is she really going to kill him on the train?" Martinsson asked, incredulous.

"We don't know. But we don't want any more murders. We have to catch her."

"We'll have to warn our colleagues in Hässleholm," Hansson said.

"We'll do that on the way," Wallander said. "I think Hansson and Martinsson should come with me. The rest of you start on the house. And talk to Katarina Taxell."

He nodded at her. She was standing next to the wall. The light was grey. She almost blended in with the wall, dissolved, faded. Could a person become so pale that she was no longer visible?

They took off. Hansson drove. Martinsson was just about to call Hässleholm when Wallander told him to wait.

"I think it's best we do this ourselves," he said. "If there's chaos, we don't know what will happen. She could be dangerous. I understand that now. Dangerous for us too."

"Of course she is," Hansson said in surprise. "She's killed three people. Impaled them on stakes, strangled them, drowned them. If a person like that isn't dangerous then I don't know who is."

"We don't even know what Grundén looks like," Martinsson said. "Are we going to page him at the station? And she'll probably be in uniform."

"Maybe," Wallander said. "We'll see when we get there. Put on the lights. We've got no time to lose."

Hansson drove fast. Time was tight. With about 20 minutes to go, Wallander realised that they wouldn't make it. One of their tyres blew. Hansson swore and braked. When they saw that the left rear tyre had to be changed, Martinsson wanted to call Hässleholm. If nothing else, they could send a car for them. But Wallander said no. He had made up his mind. They would make it.

They changed the tyre at lightning speed while the wind tore at their clothes. Then they were on the road again. Hansson drove very fast. Time was running out and Wallander tried to decide what they should do. He couldn't believe that Yvonne Ander would kill Tore Grundén in plain sight of the passengers. It didn't fit with her previous *modus operandi.* For the time being they'd have to forget about Grundén. They would look for her, a woman in uniform, and they would grab her as discreetly as possible.

They reached Hässleholm and Hansson started to head in the wrong direction, even though he claimed to know the way. Now Wallander was agitated too, and by the time they reached the station they were almost yelling at each other. They jumped out of the car, its lights flashing and ran towards the platform. We look as though we're about to rob the ticket office, Wallander thought. They had exactly three minutes left. The train was announced, but Wallander couldn't hear if it was just arriving or was already there.

He told Martinsson and Hansson that now they had to calm down. They should walk out onto the platform a little apart from each other. When they found her they should grab her from both sides. They couldn't be sure how she would react. They should be prepared, not with revolvers, but with their hands. Yvonne Ander didn't use weapons. They should be prepared, but they had to take her without firing a shot.

The wind was still blowing hard. The train hadn't arrived. The passengers were huddled in whatever shelter from the wind they could find. The station was crowded. They went out onto the platform, Wallander first, Hansson right behind him, and Martinsson out by the track. Wallander spotted a male conductor standing smoking a cigarette. He felt the tension making him sweat. He couldn't see Yvonne Ander. No women in uniform. Quickly he scanned the crowd for a man who might be Tore Grundén, but it was hopeless. The man had no face. He was just a name in a macabre notebook.

He exchanged glances with Hansson and Martinsson. He looked back towards the entrance to see if she was coming from that direction. At the same time the train came into the station. He knew that something was going very wrong. He couldn't believe that she intended to kill Grundén on the platform. But he couldn't be entirely sure. He'd seen the most calculating individuals suddenly lose control and act impulsively when they felt threatened. The passengers started picking up their belongings. Wallander no longer had any choice. He had to talk to the conductor and ask whether Yvonne Ander was already on the train.

The train came to a halt, its brakes shrieking. Wallander had to push his way through the passengers who were hurrying to board the train and get out of the wind. Suddenly he noticed a lone man standing further down the platform. He was just picking up his bag. Next to him stood a woman, wearing a long overcoat that was being whipped by the wind. A train was coming in from the other direction. Wallander was never sure whether he consciously understood the situation, but he reacted as though everything was perfectly clear. He shoved aside the passengers in his way. Hansson and Martinsson came behind him, without knowing exactly where they were going. Wallander saw the woman grab the man from behind. She almost lifted him off the ground. Wallander sensed more than understood that she intended to throw him in front of the train coming in on the other track. Since he couldn't reach them in time, he screamed at her. Despite the roar of the engines she heard him. One instant of hesitation was enough. She looked at Wallander. Martinsson and Hansson appeared at his side. They sprinted towards the woman, who had let go of the man. The long coat had blown up, and Wallander caught a glimpse of her uniform underneath. Suddenly she raised her hand and did something that made both Hansson and Martinsson stop in their tracks. She ripped off her hair. It was caught at once by the wind and flew down the platform. Under the wig her hair was short. They started running again.

Grundén didn't seem to understand what had happened to him.

"Yvonne Ander!" Wallander shouted. "Police!"

Martinsson was now almost upon her. Wallander saw him stretch out his arms to grab her. She jabbed with her right fist, hard and accurate. The blow struck Martinsson on the left cheek. He dropped to the platform without a sound. Behind Wallander someone was shouting. A passenger had seen what was going on. Hansson went to draw his revolver, but it was already too late. She grabbed his jacket and kneed him hard in the groin. For a moment she leaned over him as he buckled forwards. Then she started running down the platform. She tore off the overcoat. It fluttered and then blew away on a gust of wind. Wallander stopped beside Martinsson and Hansson. Martinsson was out cold. Hansson was moaning and white in the face. When Wallander looked up she was gone. He took off down the platform running as fast as he could, and caught sight of her just before she vanished across the tracks. He knew the chances of catching up with her were small. And he didn't know how badly Martinsson was hurt. He turned back and saw that Tore Grundén was gone. Several railway workers came running up. No-one realised in the confusion what had happened.

Afterwards Wallander would recall the next few hours as an eternal chaos. He had to try to handle a lot of things at once. On the platform, no-one understood what he was talking about. Passengers were swarming around him. Slowly Hansson began to recover, but Martinsson was still unconscious. Wallander raged at the ambulance that took so long to arrive, and not until some bewildered Hässleholm police appeared on the platform did he start to make some sense of the situation.

Martinsson's breathing was steady. By the time the ambulance attendants carried him off, Hansson had managed to get to his feet again, and he went with them to the hospital. Wallander explained to the police officers that they had been trying to arrest a female conductor, but that she had escaped.

By that time the train had left. Wallander wondered whether Grundén had boarded it. Did he have any idea how close to death he had come? Wallander realised that no-one understood what he was talking about. Only his identification made them accept that he was a policeman and not a lunatic.

Now he had to find where Yvonne Ander had gone. He called Höglund and told her what had happened. She would see to it that they were prepared if she came back to Vollsjö. The flat in Ystad was already under surveillance, but Wallander didn't think that she would go there. They were hot on her heels, and they wouldn't give up until they caught her. Where could she go? He couldn't ignore the possibility that she would simply take flight, but it didn't seem likely. She planned everything. Wallander told Höglund to ask Katarina Taxell one question. Did Yvonne Ander have another hideout?

"I think she always has an escape route," Wallander said. "She may have mentioned an address, a location."

"What about Taxell's flat in Lund?"

Wallander saw that she might be right.

"Call up Birch. Ask him to check."

"She has keys to it," Höglund said. "Katarina told me so."

Wallander was escorted to the hospital by a police car. Hansson lay on a stretcher. His scrotum was swollen and he would be kept in for observation. Martinsson was still unconscious. A doctor diagnosed a severe concussion.

"The man who hit him must have been extremely strong," the doctor said.

"You're right," said Wallander, "except that the man was a woman."

He left the hospital. Where had she gone? Something was nagging at Wallander's subconscious. Something that could give him the answer to where she was or at least where she might be headed. Then he remembered what it was. He stood quite still outside the hospital. Nyberg had been absolutely clear on something. *The fingerprints in the tower must have been put there later*. Yvonne Ander might be similar to him. In tense situations she sought out solitude. A place where she could take stock, come to a decision. All her actions gave the impression of detailed planning and precise timetables. Now her ordered life had come crashing down around her. He decided it was worth a try. The site was sealed off, of course, but Hansson had told him that the work wouldn't be resumed until they got the extra help they needed. Wallander knew that she could reach the spot by the same route she had used before.

Wallander said goodbye to the police who had helped him and promised to give them a full report on the investigation later that day. No real damage had been done. The officers who had been admitted to the hospital would soon be on their feet again.

Wallander got into his car and called Höglund again. He didn't tell her what it was about, just that he wanted her to meet him at the turn-off to Eriksson's farm.

It was after 10 a.m. when Wallander arrived in Lödinge. Höglund was standing by her car waiting for him. They drove the last stretch up to the farmhouse in Wallander's car. He stopped 100 metres from the house.

"I might be wrong," he said. "But there's a chance she might come back here to the bird tower. She's been here before." He reminded her of what Nyberg said about the fingerprints.

"What would she be doing here?" she asked.

"I don't know, but she's on the run. She needs to make some kind of decision. And we know that she's been here before."

They got out of the car. The wind was biting.

"We found the hospital uniform," she said. "And a plastic bag with underpants in it. We can assume that Runfeldt was held captive at Vollsjö."

They were approaching the house.

"What do we do if she's up in the tower?"

"We take her. I'll go around the other side of the hill. If she comes here, that's where she'll park her car. You walk down the path. This time we'll have our guns drawn."

"I don't think she'll come," Höglund said.

Wallander didn't reply. He knew there was a good chance she was right.

They found some shelter in the courtyard. The crime-scene tape around the ditch where they had been digging for Krista Haberman's remains had been torn away in the wind. The tower was empty. It stood out sharply in the autumn light.

"Let's wait a while anyway," Wallander said. "If she comes it'll be soon."

"There's an APB out for her," she said. "If we don't find her, she'll be hunted all over the country." They stood silent for a moment. The wind tore at their clothes.

"What is it that drives her?" she asked.

"She's probably the only one who can answer that question. But shouldn't we assume that she was abused too?"

Höglund didn't reply.

"I believe she's a lonely person," Wallander said. "And she thinks the purpose of her life is a calling to kill on behalf of others."

"Once I thought we were out after a mercenary," she said. "And now we're waiting for a female conductor to appear in a tower built for watching birds."

"That mercenary angle might not have been so far-fetched," Wallander said thoughtfully. "She's a woman, and she doesn't get paid for killing as far as we know. But there's something that reminds me of what we initially believed that we were dealing with."

"Katarina Taxell said that she got to know her through a group of women who met at Vollsjö. But their first encounter was on a train. You were right about that. Apparently she asked about a bruise Taxell had on her temple. It was Eugen Blomberg who had abused her. I never found out exactly how it all happened, but she confirmed that Yvonne Ander had previously worked in a hospital and also as an ambulance medic. She saw plenty of abused women. Later she got in contact with them and invited them to Vollsjö. You might call it an extremely informal support group. She found out the names of the men who had abused the women. Katarina acknowledged that it was Yvonne Ander who visited her at the hospital. On the second visit she gave Ander the father's name. Eugen Blomberg."

"That signed his death warrant," Wallander said. "I also think she's been preparing this for a long time. Something happened that triggered it all. And neither you nor I can know what that was."

"Does she know it herself?"

"We have to suppose that she does. If she isn't completely insane."

They waited. The wind came and went in strong gusts. A police car drove up to the entrance of the courtyard. Wallander asked them not to come back until further notice. He gave no explanation, but he was unequivocal. They kept on waiting. Neither of them had anything to say.

At 10.45 a.m. Wallander cautiously put a hand on her shoulder.

"There she is," he whispered.

Höglund looked. A person had appeared up by the hill. It had to be Yvonne Ander. She stood there and looked around. Then she began to climb the stairs to the tower.

"It'll take me 20 minutes to go around to the back of the tower," Wallander said. "Then you start to walk down the path. I'll be behind her if she tries to escape."

"What happens if she attacks me? Then I'll have to shoot."

"I'll make sure that doesn't happen. I'll be there."

He ran to the car and drove as fast as he could to the tractor path that led up the back of the hill. He didn't dare drive all the way, so he go out and ran. It took longer than he had calculated. A car was parked at the top of the tractor path. Also a Golf, but a black one. The phone rang in Wallander's jacket pocket. He stopped. It might be Höglund. He answered and kept walking along the tractor path.

It was Svedberg.

"Where are you? What the hell is going on?"

"We're at Eriksson's farm. I can't go into it right now. It would be good if you could come out here with someone. Hamrén, perhaps. I can't talk right now."

"I called because I have a message," Svedberg said. "Hansson called from Hässleholm. Both he and Martinsson are feeling better. Martinsson is conscious again, anyway. But Hansson wondered if you had picked up his revolver."

Wallander froze.

"His revolver?"

"He said it was lost."

"I don't have it."

"It couldn't still be lying on the platform, could it?"

At that instant Wallander could see the events played out clearly before him. Ander grabs hold of Hansson's jacket and knees him hard in the groin. Then she quickly bends over him, and that's when she takes the revolver.

"Shit!" Wallander yelled.

Before Svedberg could answer he had hung up and stuffed the phone back in his pocket. He had put Höglund in mortal danger. The woman in the tower was armed.

Wallander ran. His heart pounded like a hammer in his chest. He saw by his watch that she must already be on her way down the path. He stopped and dialled her phone number. No connection. He started running again. His only chance was to get there first. Höglund didn't know that Ander was armed. His terror made him run faster. He had reached the back of the hill. She must be almost to the ditch now. Walk slowly, he tried to tell her in his mind. Trip and fall, slip, anything. Don't hurry. Walk slowly. He had pulled out his gun and was stumbling up the slope behind the bird tower. When he reached the top he saw Höglund at the ditch. She had her revolver in her hand. The woman in the tower hadn't seen her. He shouted.

"Ann-Britt, she's got a gun! Get out of there!"

He aimed his revolver at the woman standing with her back to him up there in the tower. In the same instant a shot rang out. He saw Höglund jerk and fall backwards into the mud. Wallander felt as if someone had thrust a sword right through him. He stared at the motionless body in the mud and sensed that the woman in the tower had turned around. Then he dived to the side and fired towards the top of the tower. The third shot hit home. Ander lurched and dropped Hansson's gun.

Wallander rushed down into the mud. He stumbled into the ditch and scrambled up the other side. When he saw Höglund on her back in the mud he thought she was dead. She had been killed by Hansson's revolver and it was all his fault.

For a split second he saw no way out but to shoot himself. Right where he stood, a few metres from her. Then he saw her moving feebly. He fell to his knees by her side. The whole front of her jacket was bloody. She was deathly pale and stared at him with fear in her eyes.

"It'll be all right," he said. "It will be all right."

"She was armed," she mumbled. "Why didn't we know that?"

Wallander could feel the tears running down his face. He called for an ambulance. Later he would remember that while he waited, he had steadily murmured a confused prayer to a god he didn't really believe in. In a haze he was aware that Svedberg and Hamrén had arrived. Ann-Britt was carried away on a stretcher. Wallander was sitting in the mud. They couldn't get him to stand up. A photographer who had raced after the ambulance when it drove off from Ystad took a picture of Wallander as he sat there. Dirty, forlorn, hopeless. The photographer managed to take that one picture before Svedberg, in a rage, chased him off. Under pressure from Chief Holgersson the photograph was never published.

Meanwhile, Svedberg and Hamrén brought Ander down from the tower. Wallander had hit her high on the thigh. She was bleeding profusely, but her life was not in danger. She too was taken away in an ambulance. Svedberg and Hamrén finally managed to get Wallander up from the mud and helped him up to the farmhouse. The first report came in from the Ystad hospital. Ann-Britt Höglund had been shot in the abdomen. The wound was severe, and her condition was critical.

Wallander rode with Svedberg to get his car. Svedberg was unsure about letting Wallander drive alone to Ystad, but Wallander assured him that he would be OK. He drove straight to the hospital and then sat in the hall waiting for news of Ann-Britt's condition. He still hadn't had time to get cleaned up. He didn't leave the hospital until many hours later, when the doctors assured him that her condition had stabilised.

All of a sudden he was gone. No-one had noticed him leave. Svedberg began to worry, but he thought he knew Wallander well enough: he just wanted to be alone.

Wallander left the hospital right before midnight. The wind was still blowing hard, and it would freeze overnight. He got into his car and drove to the cemetery where his father lay buried. He found his way to the grave and stood there, completely empty inside, still caked with mud.

Around 1 a.m. he got home and called Baiba. They talked for a long time. Then he finally undressed and took a hot bath. Afterwards he dressed and returned to the hospital. Just after 3 a.m. he went into the room where Yvonne Ander lay, under guard. She was asleep when he entered the room cautiously. He stood for a long time looking at her face. Then he left without saying a word.

After an hour he was back. At dawn Lisa Holgersson came to the hospital and said they had reached Höglund's husband, in Dubai. He would arrive at Kastrup Airport later that day.

No-one knew if Wallander was listening to anything anyone said to him. He sat motionless on a chair, or stood at a window staring into the gale. When a nurse wanted to give him a cup of coffee he burst into tears and locked himself in the bathroom. But most of the time he sat unmoving on his chair and looked at his hands.

At about the same time Höglund's husband landed at Kastrup, a doctor gave them the news they had all been waiting for. She was going to make it, and probably wouldn't have any permanent injury. She was lucky. All the same, her recovery would take time and the convalescence would be long. Wallander stood as he listened to the doctor, as if he were receiving a sentence in court. Afterwards he walked out of the hospital and disappeared somewhere in the wind.

On Monday, 24 October, Yvonne Ander was indicted for murder. She was still in hospital. So far she hadn't spoken a single word, not even to the lawyer appointed to act for her. Wallander had tried to question her that afternoon. She just stared at him. As he was about to leave, he turned in the door and told her that Ann-Britt Höglund was going to recover. He thought he saw a reaction from her; that she looked relieved, maybe glad.

Martinsson was still off work with his concussion. Hansson went back on duty, even though he had a hard time walking and sitting for several weeks.

Their primary focus during this period was to complete the laborious task of establishing exactly what had happened. One thing they hadn't managed to find conclusive evidence for was whether it was the remains of Krista Haberman that they had dug up in Eriksson's field. There was nothing to disprove it, but no hard evidence either. And yet they were certain. A crack in the skull told them how Eriksson had killed her more than 25 years earlier. Everything else began to be cleared up, although slowly. There was another question mark. Had Runfeldt killed his wife? The only one who might give them the answer was Ander, and she still wasn't talking. They explored Ander's life in detail and uncovered a story that only partially told them who she was and why she might have acted as she did.

One afternoon, as they were sitting in a long meeting, Wallander abruptly concluded it by saying something he had been thinking for a long time.

"Yvonne Ander is the first person I've ever met who is both intelligent and insane."

He didn't explain any further. No-one doubted that he believed it.

Every day during this period Wallander went to visit Ann-Britt at the hospital. He couldn't get over what he was convinced was his responsibility. Nothing anyone said made any difference. He regarded the blame for what had happened as his alone. It was something he would have to live with.

Yvonne Ander kept silent. One evening Wallander sat in his office late, reading through the extensive collection of letters she had exchanged with her mother. The next day he visited her in jail. That day, she finally started to talk.

It was 3 November 1994, and frost lay over the countryside around Ystad.

Skåne

4 – 5 December 1994

EPILOGUE

On the afternoon of 4 December, Kurt Wallander spoke with Yvonne Ander for the last time. He didn't know then that it would be the last, although they didn't make an appointment to meet again.

They had come to an end. There was nothing more to add. Nothing to ask about, no reply to give. And after that the long and complex investigation began to slip out of his consciousness for the first time. Although more than a month had passed since they captured her, the case had continued to dominate his life. In all his years as a detective, he had never had such an intense need to understand. Criminal acts were always just the surface, and sometimes, once the surface of a crime had been cracked, chasms opened that no-one could have imagined. This was the case with Yvonne Ander. Wallander punched through the surface and immediately looked down into a bottomless pit. He had decided to climb down into it. He didn't know where it would lead, for her or for him.

The first step had been to get her to break her silence. He was successful when he read again the letters that she had exchanged all her adult life with her mother and kept so carefully. Wallander sensed that it was here he could start to break through her aloofness. And he was right. That was 3 November, more than a month earlier. He was still shattered by the fact that Ann-Britt had been shot. He knew by then that she would survive and even regain full health, but the guilt weighed so heavily that it threatened to suffocate him. His best support during that period was Linda. She came to Ystad, even though she didn't really have time, and took care of him, forcing him to accept that circumstances were to blame, not him. With her help he managed to crawl through the first terrible weeks of November. Aside from the sheer effort of functioning normally, he spent all of his time on Yvonne Ander. She was the one who had shot and nearly killed Ann-Britt. In the beginning he often felt like hitting her. Later it became more important to try and understand her. He managed to break through her silence and get her to start talking. He knotted the rope around himself and started down into the pit.

What was it he found down there? For a long time he was unsure whether she was insane or not, whether all she said about herself were confused dreams and sick, deformed fantasies. He didn't trust his own judgement during this time, and he could hardly disguise his wariness of her. But somehow he sensed that she was telling him the truth. Yvonne Ander was that rare type of person who couldn't lie.

In the last bundle of letters from her mother was one from a police officer in Africa named Françoise Bertrand. At first couldn't decipher its contents. It was with a number of unfinished letters from her mother. They were all from the same North African country, written the year before. Françoise Bertrand had sent her letter to Yvonne Ander in August 1993. Finally he understood. Yvonne Ander's mother Anna had been murdered by mistake, and the police had covered the whole thing up. Politics were clearly behind the killing, although Wallander felt incapable of fully understanding what was involved. But Françoise Bertrand had in all confidence written the letter, outlining what had really happened. Without any help from Ander at this point, he discussed with Chief Holgersson what had happened to the mother. The chief listened and then contacted the national police. The matter was thus removed from Wallander's responsibility. But he read through all the letters one more time.

Wallander conducted his meetings with Yvonne Ander in jail. She slowly came to understand that he was a man who wasn't hunting her. He was different from the others, the men who populated the world. He was introverted, seemed to sleep very little, and was also tormented by worry. For the first time in her life Ander discovered that she could trust a man. She told him this at one of their last meetings.

She never asked him straight out, but she still believed she knew the answer. He had probably never struck a woman. If he had, it happened only once. No more, never again.

On 3 November Ann-Britt underwent the last of the three operations. Everything went well, and her convalescence could finally begin. During this entire month Wallander set up a routine. After his talks with Ander he would drive straight to the hospital. He seldom stayed long, but Ann-Britt became the discussion partner he needed in order to help him understand how to penetrate the depths he had begun to plumb.

His first question to Ander was about the events in Africa. Who was Françoise Bertrand? What had actually happened? A pale light was falling through the window into the room. They sat facing each other at a table. In the distance a radio could be heard. The first sentences she uttered he didn't catch. It was like a powerful roar when her silence finally broke. He just listened to her voice. Then he started to listen to what she was saying. He seldom took notes during their meetings, and he didn't use a tape recorder.

"Somewhere there's a man who killed my mother. Who's looking for him?"

"Not me," he had replied. "But if you tell me what happened, and if a Swedish citizen has been killed overseas, we will take steps to see that justice is done."

He didn't mention the conversation he had had a few days before with Chief Holgersson, that her mother's death was already being investigated.

"Nobody knows who killed my mother," she continued. "Fate selected her as a victim. Her killer didn't even know her. He thought he was justified. He believed he could kill anybody he wanted to. Even an innocent woman who spent her retirement taking all the trips she never had the time or the money to take before."

She made no attempt to conceal her bitter rage.

"Why was she staying with the nuns?" he asked.

Suddenly she looked up from the table, straight into his eyes.

"Who gave you the right to read my letters?"

"No-one. But they belong to you, a person who has committed several atrocious murders. Otherwise I never would have read them."

She turned away again.

"The nuns," Wallander repeated. "Why was she staying with them?"

"She didn't have much money. She stayed wherever it was cheap. She never imagined it would lead to her death."

"This happened more than a year ago. How did you react when the letter arrived?"

"There was no reason for me to wait any longer. How could I justify doing nothing when no-one else seemed to care?"

"Care about what?"

She didn't reply. He waited. Then he changed the question.

"Wait to do what?"

She answered without looking at him.

"To kill them."

"Who?"

"The ones who went free in spite of all they had done."

He realised he had guessed correctly. It was when she received Françoise Bertrand's letter that a force locked inside her had been released. She had harboured thoughts of revenge, but she could still control herself. Then the dam broke. She decided to take the law into her own hands.

Later Wallander came to see that there really wasn't much difference from what had happened in Lödinge. She had been her own citizen militia. She had placed herself outside the law and dispensed her own justice.

"Is that how it was?" he asked. "You wanted to dispense justice? You wanted to punish those who should have been brought before a court of law but never were?"

"Who's looking for the man who killed my mother? Who?"

She fell silent again. Wallander could see how it had all begun. Some months after the letter came from Africa she broke into Holger Eriksson's house. That was the first step. When he asked her point blank if it was true, she didn't even act surprised. She took it for granted that he knew.

"I heard about Krista Haberman," she said. "That it was the car dealer who killed her."

"Who did you hear it from?"

"A Polish woman in the hospital in Malmö. That was many years ago."

"You were working at the hospital then?"

"I worked there several different times. I often talked to women who had been abused. She had a friend who used to know Krista Haberman."

"Why did you break into Eriksson's house?"

"I wanted to prove to myself that it was possible, and I was looking for signs that Krista Haberman had been there."

"Why did you dig the pit? Why the stakes? Did the woman who knew Krista Haberman suspect that the body was buried near that ditch?"

She didn't answer. But Wallander understood anyway. Despite the fact that the investigation had always been hard to grasp, Wallander and his colleagues had been on the right track without knowing it. Ander had echoed the men's brutality in her methods of killing them.

During the five or six meetings Wallander had with Ander, he went methodically through the three murders, clearing up details and piecing together the connections that had previously been so vague. He continued to talk to her without a tape recorder. After the meetings he would sit in his car and make notes from memory. Then he would have them typed up. A copy went to Per Åkeson, who was preparing the indictment, which would inevitably lead to a conviction on three counts. Yet the whole time, Wallander knew he was just scraping the surface. The real descent hadn't even started yet. The evidence would send her to prison. But he wouldn't find the actual truth he sought until he reached the deepest depths of the pit.

She had to undergo a psychiatric evaluation, of course. Wallander knew it was unavoidable, but he insisted that it be postponed. Right now the most important thing was that he be able to talk to her in peace. No-one objected to this. They understood that she would probably clam up again if she was upset. She was ready to talk to him and him alone.

They went further, slowly, step by step, day by day. Outside the jail the autumn was deepening and drawing them towards winter. Wallander never found out why Eriksson had driven up to get Krista Haberman in Svenstavik and then killed her. Presumably it was because she had denied him something he was used to getting. Maybe an argument turned violent.

He moved on to Gösta Runfeldt. She was convinced that Runfeldt had murdered his wife, drowned her in Stång Lake. And even if he hadn't done it, he still deserved his fate. He had abused her so severely that she actually wanted to die. Höglund was right when she sensed that Runfeldt had been attacked in the florist's shop. Ander had found out that he would be leaving for Nairobi and lured him to the shop by telling him that she had to buy flowers for a reception early the next morning. Then she knocked him to the ground. The blood on the floor was indeed his. The broken window was a diversion to fool the police into believing it was a break-in.

Then came a description of what for Wallander was the most terrifying element. Until that point he had tried to understand her without letting his emotional reactions take over. But then he couldn't go any further. She recounted with utter calm how she had undressed Gösta Runfeldt, tied him up, and forced him into the baking oven. When he could no longer control his bodily functions she took away his underwear and laid him on a plastic sheet.

Later she led him out to the woods. By that time he was quite powerless. She tied him to the tree and strangled him. It was at that moment that she turned into a monster in Wallander's eyes. It didn't matter if she was a man or a woman. She became a monster, and he could only be thankful that they had stopped her before she killed Tore Grundén or anyone else on the list she had made.

The list was also her only mistake – she hadn't destroyed the notebook in which she drew up her plans before she copied them into the ledger she kept in Vollsjö. Wallander never asked her why. Even she admitted it was a mistake. That was the only one of her actions she couldn't explain. Later Wallander pondered whether she had actually wanted to leave a clue, that deep inside she wanted to be discovered and stopped. Sometimes he thought this was true, sometimes he didn't.

She didn't have much to say about Eugen Blomberg. She described how she shuffled the slips of paper. She let chance decide who would be next, just as chance had killed her mother. This was one of the times he interrupted her. Normally he let her speak freely, prompting her with questions when she couldn't decide how to go on. But now he stopped her.

"So you did the same thing as the men who killed your mother," he said. "You let chance select your victim."

"It's not comparable," she replied. "All those men whose names I had written down deserved their death. I gave them time with my slips of paper. I prolonged their lives."

He pursued it no further, since he realised that in an

obscure way she was right. Reluctantly he admitted to himself that she had her own peculiar sort of truth.

When he read through the transcripts of the notes he made from memory, he could see that what he had was a confession, but it was also an exceedingly incomplete account. Did he succeed with what he intended? Afterwards, Wallander found it difficult to speak about Yvonne Ander. He always referred people who questioned him to the notes.

As it turned out, what became Yvonne Ander's last will and testament was her story of the terrifying experiences of her childhood. Wallander was almost the same age as Ander, and he thought time after time that the era he was living in was concerned with one single decisive question: what are we actually doing with our children? She had told him how her mother was frequently abused by her stepfather, who had replaced her biological father. The stepfather had forced her mother to have an abortion. She had never had the chance to have the sister her mother was carrying. She couldn't have known if it really was a sister – maybe it was a brother – but to her it was a sister, brutally ripped from her mother's womb against her will one night in the early 1950s. She remembered that night as a bloody hell. When she was telling Wallander about it, she raised her eyes from the table and looked straight into his. Her mother had lain on a sheet on the kitchen table, the abortionist was drunk, her stepfather locked in the cellar, probably drunk too. That night she was robbed of her sister and for all time learned to view the future as darkness, with threatening men lurking round every corner, violence lurking behind every friendly smile, every word.

She had barricaded her memories into a secret interior

room. She had been educated, become a nurse, and she had always harboured the vague notion that someday she would avenge the sister she never had, and the mother who wasn't allowed to give birth to her. She collected the stories from abused women, she tracked down the dead women in muddy fields and Småland lakes, she entered names in a ledger, shuffled her slips of paper.

And then her mother had been murdered.

She described it almost poetically to Wallander. *Like a silent tidal wave*, she said. *No more than that. I knew that it was time. I let a year pass. I planned, completed the timetable that had kept me alive all those years. Then I dug in a ditch at night.*

Precisely those words. *Then I dug in a ditch at night.* Maybe they best summed up Wallander's experience of his many conversations with Yvonne Ander that autumn. It was like a picture of the time he was living in. What ditch was *he* digging?

One question was never answered: why she suddenly, in the mid-1980s, changed professions and became a conductor. Wallander had understood that the train timetable was the liturgy she lived by, her handbook. But the trains remained her private world. Maybe the only one; maybe the last one.

Did she feel guilt? Åkeson asked him about that many times. Lisa Holgersson asked less often, his colleagues almost never. The only person besides Åkeson who really insisted on knowing was Ann-Britt Höglund. Wallander told her the truth: he didn't know.

"Ander reminds me of a coiled spring," he told her. "I can't express it better than that. I can't say whether guilt is part of it, or whether it's gone."

On 4 December it was over. Wallander had nothing more

to ask, and Yvonne Ander had nothing more to say. The confession was complete. Wallander knew he had reached the end of the long descent. Now he could return to the surface. The psychiatric examination could begin, the defence lawyer could sharpen his pencils, and only Wallander had any idea what would happen.

He knew that Yvonne Ander would fall silent again, with the determined will of someone who has nothing more to say. Just before he left, he asked her about two more things he didn't have answers to. The first was a detail that no longer had any significance, but he needed to satisfy his own curiosity.

"When Katarina Taxell called her mother from the house in Vollsjö, something was making a banging noise," he said. "We couldn't work out where that sound was coming from."

She gave him a baffled look. Then her face broke open in a smile, the only one Wallander saw in all his talks with her.

"A farmer's tractor had broken down in the field next to us. He was hitting it with a big hammer to get something loose from the undercarriage. Could you really hear that on the phone?"

Wallander nodded. He was already thinking of his last question.

"I think we actually met once," he said. "On a train."

She nodded.

"South of Älmhult? I asked you when we would get to Malmö."

"I recognised you from the newspapers. From last summer."

"Did you already know then that we'd catch you?"

"Why should I?"

“A policeman from Ystad gets on a train in Älmhult. What’s he doing there? Unless he’s following the trail of what happened to Gösta Runfeldt’s wife?”

She shook her head. “I never thought about that. I should have.”

Wallander had nothing more to ask. He had found out everything he wanted to know. He stood up, muttered goodbye, and left.

That afternoon Wallander visited the hospital as usual. Ann-Britt was asleep when he arrived, but he spoke to a doctor who told him that in six months she could return to work. He left the hospital just after 5 p.m. It was already dark, just below freezing, no wind. He drove out to the cemetery and went to his father’s grave. Withered flowers had frozen solid to the ground. It was still less than three months since they had come back from Rome. The holiday was vivid in his mind as he stood by the grave, wondering what his father had actually been thinking when he took his night-time walk to the Spanish Steps, to the fountain, with that gleam in his eyes.

It was as if Yvonne Ander and his father could have stood on either side of a river and waved to each other, even though they had nothing in common. Or did they? Wallander wondered what he himself had in common with her. He had no answer.

That night, out by the grave in the dark cemetery, the investigation came to an end for him. There would still be papers he would have to read over and sign, but the case was finished. The psychiatric examination would declare that she was in full possession of her faculties. Then she would be convicted and hidden away at Hinseberg. The investigation of the circumstances surrounding her mother’s death in Africa would also continue. But that had nothing to do with his own work.

The night of 4 December he slept badly. The next day he decided to look at a house just north of town. He was also going to visit a kennel in Sjöbo where they had a litter of black Labrador puppies for sale. The next day he had to go to Stockholm and speak at the police academy. Why he had given in when Chief Holgersson asked him again, he didn't know. Now he lay awake wondering what the hell he was going to say.

On that restless night, he thought mostly about Baiba. Several times he got up and stood at the kitchen window, staring at the streetlight swaying on its wire.

Just after he had come back from Rome, at the end of September, they had decided that she would come to Ystad soon – no later than November. They would have a serious discussion about whether she should move to Sweden. But her visit had been postponed, first once, then again. Each time there were excellent reasons for why she couldn't come, not yet. Wallander believed her, of course, but he couldn't quell his feeling of uncertainty. Was it still there, invisible, between them? A rift he hadn't seen? If so, why hadn't he seen it? Because he didn't want to?

Now she was really going to come. They were supposed to meet in Stockholm on 8 December. He would go straight from the police academy to Arlanda to meet her. Linda would join them in the evening and they would all head south to Skåne the following day. How long she would stay, he didn't know, but this time they would have a serious discussion about the future, not just about the next time they could meet.

The night turned into a long vigil. The weather had turned warmer and the meteorologists were predicting snow. Wallander wandered like a lost soul between his bed and the kitchen window. Now and then he sat down at the kitchen table and made a few notes, in a futile attempt to find a starting point for the lecture he was going to give in Stockholm. All the time he couldn't stop thinking about Yvonne Ander and her story. She was constantly on his mind, and occasionally she even blocked out thoughts of Baiba.

The person he thought very little about was his father. He was already far away. At times Wallander had trouble recalling all the details of his lined face. He'd had to reach for a photograph and look at it so that the memory wouldn't completely slip away. During November he had visited Gertrud. The house in Löderup seemed empty, the studio cold and forbidding. Gertrud always gave the impression of being composed, but lonely.

Maybe he finally slept for a few hours towards dawn or maybe he was awake the whole time. By 7 a.m. he was already dressed. At 7.30 a.m. he drove his car, which sputtered suspiciously, to the police station. It was a particularly quiet morning. Martinsson had a cold; Svedberg had gone to Malmö on an assignment. The hall was deserted. He sat down in his office and read through the transcript of his notes of his last conversation with Yvonne Ander. On his desk there was also a transcript of an interview Hansson had carried out with Tore Grundén, the man she had tried to push in front of the train at Hässleholm. His background contained the same ingredients as all the other names in her macabre death ledger. Tore Grundén had once served time for abusing a woman. Wallander could see that Hansson had made it very clear to Grundén that he had been close to being torn to shreds by the oncoming train.

Wallander noticed that there was some tacit understanding among his colleagues of what Ander had done. That this understanding existed at all surprised him. She had shot Höglund, she had attacked and killed men. Normally a team of policemen wouldn't be supportive of a woman like Yvonne Ander. It was possible to ask whether the police had a friendly attitude towards women at all, unless they were officers with the special stamina that both Ann-Britt Höglund and Lisa Holgersson possessed.

He scribbled his signature and pushed the papers aside. It was 8.45 a.m.

The day before, he had picked up the keys from the estate agent. It was a two-storey brick house in the middle of a big old garden to the north of Ystad. From the upper floor there was a view of the sea. He unlocked the door and went in. The rooms were empty. He walked around in the silence, opened the terrace door to the garden, and tried to picture himself living there.

To his surprise, it was easier than he had imagined. It was obvious that he wasn't as attached to Mariagatan as he had feared. He asked himself whether Baiba might be happy there. She had talked about her own longing to get away from Riga – to the countryside, but not too far away, not too isolated.

It didn't take him long to make up his mind that morning. He would buy the house if Baiba liked it. The price was also low enough that he could manage to get the necessary loans.

Just after 10 a.m. he left the house. He promised to give the estate agent a definite answer within the week. After looking at the house, he went on to look for a dog. The kennel was located along the road to Höör, right outside of Sjöbo. Dogs barked from various cages when he turned into the courtyard. The owner was a young woman who, much to his surprise, spoke with a strong Göteborg accent.

"I'd like to look at a black Labrador," Wallander said.

She showed them to him. The puppies were still too small to leave their mother.

"Do you have children?" she asked.

"None that still live at home unfortunately," he replied. "Do you have to have children to buy a puppy?"

"Not at all. But this breed of dog is better with children than almost any other."

Wallander explained that he might buy a house outside of Ystad. If he decided to do that, he also wanted to have a dog. One depended on the other.

"I'll hold one of the puppies for you. Take your time, but not too long. I always have buyers for Labradors."

Wallander promised to let her know within the week, just as he had promised the estate agent. He was shocked at the price she mentioned. Could a puppy really cost that much? But he knew that he would buy the dog if the house purchase went through.

He left the kennel at midday. When he came out onto the main road, he suddenly didn't know where he was going. Was he on his way anywhere at all? He wasn't going to see Yvonne Ander. For the time being they had no more to say to each other. They would meet again, but not now. Per Åkeson might ask him to expand on some of the details but he doubted it. They had more than enough evidence to convict her.

The truth was that he had nowhere to go. No-one really needed him. Without being fully aware of what he was doing, he headed towards Vollsjö and stopped outside Hansgården. Yvonne Ander owned the house, and would presumably continue to do so during all the years she would spend in prison. She had no close relatives, only her deceased mother. Whether she even had any friends was questionable. Katarina Taxell had been dependent on her, had received her support, just like the other women. But friends? Wallander shuddered at the thought. Yvonne Ander didn't have a single person who was close to her. She stepped out of a vacuum and she killed people.

Wallander got out of his car. The house emanated desolation. When he walked around it, he noticed a window stood slightly open. That wasn't good. Someone could easily break in. Wallander found a wooden bench and put it under the window, climbed inside and looked around. The window had been left open out of carelessness. He walked through the rooms, and looked at the baking oven with distaste. There was the invisible boundary. Beyond it he would never be able to understand her.

Now the investigation really was over. They had drawn a final line through the macabre list, interpreted the murderer's language, and found the solution. That was why he felt superfluous. He was no longer needed. When he returned from Stockholm he would go back to the investigation of car smuggling to the former Eastern bloc countries. Not until then would he truly feel real to himself again.

A phone rang in the silence. Only on the second ring did he realise that it was ringing in his jacket pocket. He took it out. It was Per Åkeson.

"Am I interrupting anything?" he asked. "Where are you?"

Wallander didn't want to tell him where he was.

"I'm sitting in my car," he said. "But I'm parked."

"I assume you haven't heard the news," Åkeson said. "There's not going to be a trial."

Wallander didn't understand. The thought had never

occurred to him, although it should have. He should have been prepared.

"Yvonne Ander committed suicide," Åkeson said. "Sometime last night. She was found dead early this morning."

Wallander held his breath. There was still something resisting, threatening to burst.

"She seems to have had access to pills. She shouldn't have had them. At least not so many that she could take her own life. Spiteful people are going to ask whether you were the one who gave them to her."

Wallander could hear that this was not a veiled question, but he answered it anyway.

"I didn't help her."

"The whole thing had a feeling of serenity about it. Everything was in perfect order. She seems to have made up her mind and carried it out. She died in her sleep. It's easy to understand, of course."

"Is it?" Wallander asked.

"She left a letter. With your name on it. I have it here on the desk in front of me."

"I'll be there in half an hour," he said.

He stood where he was, with the silent phone in his hand, and tried to gauge what he was really feeling. Emptiness, maybe a vague hint of injustice.

He checked that the window was closed properly and then left the house through the front door.

It was a clear December day. Winter was lurking somewhere nearby.

Wallander went into Per Åkeson's office. The letter was lying in the middle of the desk.

He took it with him and went down to the harbour. He

walked out to the sea rescue service's red shed and sat down on the bench. The letter was short.

Somewhere in Africa there is a man who killed my mother. Who is looking for him?

That was all.

Who is looking for him?

She had signed the letter with her full name. In the upper right-hand corner she had written the date and time.

5 December, 1994, 2.44 a.m.

The next-to-last entry in her timetable, he thought. She wouldn't write the last one herself, the doctor would do that, when he put down the time of her death. Then there would be nothing more. The timetable would be closed, her life concluded.

Her departure was formulated as a question or accusation. Or maybe both.

Who is looking for him?

He tore the letter into strips and tossed them into the water. He remembered that once, several years ago, he had torn up a letter that he had decided against sending to Baiba. He had tossed that one into the water too. There was a great difference. He would see Baiba again, and very soon.

He watched the pieces of paper float away over the water. Then he left the harbour and went to the hospital to visit Ann-Britt.

Something was over at last. The autumn in Skåne was moving towards winter.